BOOK 4

★ PEACEKEEPER
★
★ OF SOL

DRIFTER'S
FOLLY

BOOK 4

★ PEACEKEEPERS ★
OF SOL

DRIFTER'S FOLLY

GLYNN STEWART

FAOLAN'S PEN
PUBLISHING
faolanspen.com

This edition published in 2021 by:

Faolan's Pen Publishing Inc.

22 King St. S, Suite 300

Waterloo, Ontario

N2J 1N8 Canada

ISBN-13: 978-1-989674-16-1 (print)

A record of this book is available from Library and Archives Canada.

Printed in the United States of America

1 2 3 4 5 6 7 8 9 10

First edition

First printing: June 2021

Illustration by Sam Leung

Faolan's Pen Publishing logo is a registered trademark of Faolan's Pen Publishing Inc.

Read more books from Glynn Stewart at faolanspen.com

CHAPTER ONE

TEN YEARS OF PEACETIME MILITARY SERVICE. SEVENTEEN LONG years of bloody interstellar conflict. Three years of the chaotic mess that was "peacekeeping" after the fall of a galactic empire.

After all of that, Commodore Henry Wong of the United Planets had been reasonably sure he'd seen just about everything the galaxy could show him. That, of course, meant it was time for the universe to show him how wrong he was.

"Please tell me we have the cycle of that thing locked in," the tall Chinese-American officer asked his staff as he watched a pulsar rotate on the main screen. *Paladin*'s builders had chosen to keep holograms off the main working spaces of the warship as a stability concern.

"We will have more than enough warning to adjust our course if it starts swinging toward us," Georgina Eowyn told him with a soft chuckle. The sturdily built blonde officer ran his Operations department, which made her the senior person on Henry's abbreviated staff.

"And what happens if the beam actually hits one of the destroyers?" Henry asked.

He knew the answer. His three ships were the first *Cataphract-*

class destroyers the United Planets Alliance had ever commissioned, and the unique technology providing their propulsion augmented their defensive gravity shields.

"If we screw up badly enough that the electromagnetic radiation beam of a pulsar is pointed at one of our ships, that ship will be vaporized instantly," Eowyn confirmed. "But that seems unlikely. We *are* following a trail, after all."

Henry nodded his acknowledgement and returned his focus to the main screen. Over five hundred starships had made their transit through this system at some time in the past, which suggested it was *reasonably* safe for him to bring three ships through.

Destroyer Squadron Twenty-Seven was badly understrength, with only three of the new *Cataphracts* instead of the six ships Henry *should* have, but older ships couldn't keep up.

"Anything on the scanners showing where the Convoy was?" he asked.

"Not yet, but we're only just getting the Very Large Array up," Eowyn told him. "Less than ten percent of the drones are in position."

The Very Large Array was a standard tool for expanding their sensor view. Three destroyers could only see so much, but by deploying another dozen or so drones per ship, they could create a massive virtual telescope that would dramatically augment their vision.

Once it was all set up, Henry Wong and his people would be able to track where the Blue Stripe Green Stripe Orange Stripe Drifter Convoy had gone—and hopefully get one step closer to bringing to justice the people who'd betrayed a peace conference.

PALADIN, *Cataphract* and *Maharatha* were something new in the galaxy, so far as Henry knew. The United Planets Alliance had developed gravity shields before they'd ever met the Kenmiri Empire that had dominated their arm of the Milky Way, but even their ships had been propelled by the age-old solution of firing high-energy particles out one end.

Gravitic technology allowed the UPA, the Kenmiri, and the various races that had rebelled against the Kenmiri to accelerate at rates that should have liquefied their crews, but the fundamental Newtonian nature of propulsion had been fixed.

Until now. Now Henry's three ships slipped through the outer void of the pulsar system designated Ra-206 without so much as a flare of exhaust. Carefully controlled and manipulated gravity wells allowed the destroyers to "fall" toward their destination at up to three kilometers per second squared.

The gravitational maneuvering system rendered Henry's command the most maneuverable warships in space, which gave him *some* confidence as he watched the pulsar rotate again, its unimaginably powerful beams of radiation slicing through space like immense blades.

"We've got the trail on scanners," Eowyn reported. "It took us longer than I'd like, but the background radiation here is wonky."

"Is that a technical term, Commander?" Henry asked drily.

"Very much so, Commodore," she confirmed. "Trail is on screen."

He nodded and turned to the tactical display. The Drifter Convoy they were chasing consisted of hundreds of starships carrying millions of people, a nomadic interstellar nation with a powerful self-defense fleet and mobile industrial nodes.

It was *hard* to conceal the passing of a flotilla of that scale, but his prey had done a good job. It was taking longer to chase them down than he'd hoped, and he was running up against hard deadlines from the laws of physics.

The particulate trail of a fusion drive was only detectable for so long, after all.

But it hadn't dissipated yet. A red line, marked with the three letters *BGO*, crossed the tactical display.

"I assume we don't know where they skipped out yet," he said.

Part of the problem with following BGO was that it was impossible to estimate where someone would come out of a skip line. They knew which *star system* a skip line directed toward, but that still left a zone roughly a light-day long and a light-hour across in which their target could have emerged.

"Not yet," Eowyn confirmed. "We'll need to follow the trail for a bit."

"As expected." Henry studied the display for a moment more, then tapped a sequence of commands on the arm of his seat. His other staff officer, Commander Chan Rong, was supposed to handle his coms.

They were off-duty at the moment, however, and the tiny flag bridge squeezed into a spare corner of the small warship didn't have much space for excess personnel. Henry's entire staff was only eleven people—he was perfectly capable of handling his own in-squadron coms.

"Captains," he addressed the three officers his commands connected him to. "I presume you all have been updated on what we're seeing of the Convoy's trail?"

"Yes, ser," his Lieutenant Colonels chorused. All three of them were too young, in the considered opinion of Henry's five decades, but that was life.

He knew Okafor Ihejirika, *Paladin*'s CO, of old. The big Black African officer had served as Tactical officer on Henry's last command, the battlecruiser *Raven*.

Captain Aoife Palmer—*Captain* was a title instead of a rank in the UPSF, given to the commander of a starship along with the white collar on each of the three officers' uniform turtleneck—was a native of Sandoval in the Procyon System. A tall and sparsely built redheaded woman, she seemed competent enough so far.

Captain Nina Teunissen was a native of the Eridani colonies founded by the Russian Novaya Imperiya. Squat and dark-haired with hawk-like features, she commanded *Maharatha* with a strict regimen Henry wasn't sure he agreed with—but it seemed to work for her crew.

He'd only been in command of DesRon Twenty-Seven for a month. Even his destroyer captains were unknowns to him still. There was a lot of work before them to get the ships up to where he wanted them, even without the brand-new ships and brand-new engines.

"We'll set our course to follow the Convoy's with an offset of sixty thousand kilometers to preserve the trail," Henry ordered. "We're scanning for the end of the line, people. You know the drill."

They'd been in deep space following BGO for two weeks now. They knew where the Convoy had *been* when the deal had been negotiated for them to provide support for the peace negotiations with the Kozun.

It wasn't exactly a surprise that the Convoy had made a run for it after their betrayal of those negotiations had been revealed. Henry's command couldn't actually *fight* the Convoy—three of their Guardian capital ships had been enough to wreck his battlecruiser, after all—but once he found them, there were other forces in play to deal with the Drifters.

"One thing to note, ser," Palmer said. "I'm comparing our position to the maps that the Kozun gave us. They didn't include this pulsar as a skip point, but if we're where I think we are, we're almost in Eerdish space."

"I know," Henry agreed. The Kozun Hierarchy had been allies once, members of the great Vesheron rebel alliance that had overthrown the Kenmiri Empire. Then they'd been enemies, warlords trying to force other worlds into compliance with starvation and violence.

Now the Drifters' betrayal made the Kozun allies again—and the Kozun were at war with an alliance of the Eerdish and the Enteni homeworlds.

"What do we do if they fled into Eerdish space?" Palmer asked.

"We break off the pursuit," Henry told her bluntly. "The Eerdish and the Enteni are potential allies, even if they're fighting the Kozun right now. In the long term, we're more likely to get along with them than with the Hierarchy.

"*They* didn't start conquering other planets, after all."

The Kenmiri had structured their empire in complex systems of specialized worlds that limited the possibility of resistance, but the racial homeworlds had been allowed to continue in semi-autonomy.

When the Kenmiri had withdrawn, those worlds with their more-balanced economies had emerged as central powers among the specialized worlds that could either feed themselves *or* produce modern technology.

The Kozun had conquered another homeworld and several of the clusters of farming and industrial worlds before they'd overstretched. They'd fought the UPA over one of those clusters, and then they'd sued for peace.

"So, we lose the trail if they went into neutral space?" Ihejirika asked.

"Exactly," Henry confirmed. "My orders are clear: we will not risk conflict with the Kozun's enemies. Ambassador Todorovich, at my last communication, was attempting to convince the Kozun to accept our mediation in that conflict, but so long as we are allies with the Kozun, we are to avoid Eerdish or Enteni space."

"They may have anticipated that, ser," Palmer suggested.

"I suspect the Drifters have," Henry admitted. "In which case the next step of our pursuit becomes political."

In which case it became his girlfriend's problem—because almost five years after his divorce from his husband, Henry Wong was no longer single. And his girlfriend was Ambassador Sylvia Todorovich, the woman responsible for ending the war between the La-Tar Cluster and the Kozun Hierarchy.

CHAPTER TWO

"WELL, GOOD NEWS IS THAT I THINK WE'VE FOUND THE SKIP line and it *doesn't* head into Eerdish space," Eowyn declared at a virtual conference later that day.

With all of the staff and captains linked in by their internal networks, the conference room was entirely virtual. Henry himself was sitting in his office with a cup of coffee in front of him, but the image of the grandiose fake conference room filled his vision.

"Why does that not make me feel better?" Palmer asked.

"Because nobody sane uses a pulsar as a skip point," the Operations officer told *Cataphract*'s Captain. "In theory, the mass is large enough that it can shave days off a trip, but in practice, it ends up being extremely variable."

Henry waved Palmer to silence before the Lieutenant Colonel could reply to that.

"Basically, if you do it right, you can skip almost half again as far using a pulsar as an anchor point than a red giant," he told his subordinate. "But if you get it wrong, your choices are fall short or push past the twenty-four-hour line."

The Icosaspace Traversal System—or "skip drive"—didn't create a particularly significant twenty-dimensional vector on its own. Bouncing along the line of gravity between two stars, however, it could cross light-years in hours.

The bigger the stars at either end of the skip line, the farther you traveled. But it was an unpleasant experience, and every known species in the galaxy limited their ships to twenty-four hours in skip.

"The BGO Convoy appear to have skipped to a system the Kozun have labeled as Nohtoin," Eowyn continued. "That's almost forty light-years away, a frankly *insane* skip. It took them twenty-three hours and put them on the far side of Eerdish space."

"So, when they entered the space of the Eerdish-Enteni Alliance, they were coming from the opposite direction of the war," Ihejirika rumbled. "Makes sense."

"We're going to duplicate the skip," Henry said calmly, then waited for the furor to die down.

Once his officers were quiet again, he smiled at them.

"*We* can hit the skip line at a higher three-dimensional velocity than the Convoy could," he noted. "The gravity shields protect us from some of the dangers involved in pushing the skip—*and* we have the data from the Drifters' skip to refine our own calculations.

"It's not perfectly safe, no, but the Drifters took the entire *Convoy* through it," he pointed out. "They don't risk their civilian ships, people. They thought it was safe enough, so I feel it's safe enough for us to follow."

He gestured to Eowyn.

"Is there anything else about Nohtoin we need to consider before we get moving?" he asked. He knew most of what the woman was briefing everyone on, but there was still a degree of showmanship to all of this.

"Nohtoin is an uninhabited system, but it *was* a Kenmiri paramilitary logistics facility before the Fall," Eowyn told them. "The UPSF never visited the system, but we have reports from other Vesheron actions in the system.

"So far as we know, it was completely abandoned when the

Kenmiri withdrew, and what data we have managed to acquire on the region suggests the facility has been destroyed—either by the Kenmiri in their withdrawal or by salvagers since."

"Nonetheless, the debris may well provide supplies and hiding places for the Drifters," Henry warned his team. "While all evidence suggests that the Drifters will have moved on from Nohtoin as rapidly as they have left every other system we've followed them into, Nohtoin represents an opportunity for them to leave scouts or listening stations we will have difficulty detecting.

"We keep our eyes open, people. The Drifters suspect they're being chased, but I'd rather they not learn that with certainty—and I would be absolutely *delighted*, Captains, to have Drifter prisoners to interrogate."

While the UPA and their allies were *reasonably* sure they knew what the Blue Stripe Green Stripe Orange Stripe Convoy's leadership had been thinking, he'd still love to ask them.

"We will proceed to the Nohtoin skip line at standard accel," Henry ordered. "We will hold position until our Navigation departments are as certain as they can be of their calculations, then we will make the skip."

He smiled thinly.

"Remember, everyone. The Drifters likely went directly from Nohtoin to Eerdish space. We're almost certainly coming back this way."

"WE HAVE to initiate the skip at exactly the right moment in the pulsar's rotation."

Lieutenant Fulvia Charmchi looked nervous to be briefing the squadron Commodore. There wasn't much Henry could do to reassure the dark-skinned young woman, so he simply gestured for *Paladin*'s navigator to proceed.

This meeting was in Captain Ihejirika's office and was just the three of them—giving the young Lieutenant the best opportunity she was ever going to have to screw up in front of superiors in a safe environment.

Assuming, of course, she considered being alone with a Lieutenant Colonel and a Commodore the *safe environment* her Captain had intended for it to be.

"It's a vector-addition problem," Charmchi said slowly after a moment. "The pulsar's radiation beam has an icosaspatial aspect to it as well, which impacts our velocity when we skip. If we time it correctly, it's a huge boost."

"And if we get it wrong, it slows us down," Ihejirika concluded. "So, how narrow is the window?"

"Three milliseconds," the navigator told them.

Henry swallowed.

"Is it as bad coming to the pulsar?" he asked.

"No, that's a more standard mass-to-mass calculation," she said, a little bit more confident. "But when we're this close to the source neutron star..." She spread her hands. "We're lucky in that Ra-Two-Oh-Six is a relatively low-frequency pulsar with an eleven-millisecond cycle."

"So, there are three milliseconds of that cycle in which we can make the skip?" Henry asked, to confirm his understanding.

"Yes, ser. We'll sequence the computers to the sensors and rig up everything as best as we can, but it's a very tight window. There can be no human intervention once the program is triggered."

"How short do we fall if we get it wrong?" Henry said quietly. "If we jump in the *other* eight milliseconds of the cycle?"

"From three light-months to twelve light-years, depending on how far we miss the window," Charmchi admitted. "I'm not certain of the exact range, but in almost all cases, we are..."

"Fucked," Ihejirika finished for her. "We have six months of supplies aboard and can *maybe* recycle food and water to stretch that to a year. Even with the GMS, we *maybe* have enough delta-v to get to Nohtoin in a year."

"Let's not make any mistakes, then," Henry replied. "The Drifters took hundreds of ships and millions of civilians through this skip line. So long as we get it *right*, we're fine."

"We're working on refining the program, sers," Charmchi said. "Current expected error is two-point-two milliseconds."

Henry wasn't even looking at Ihejirika and he knew the younger man had just swallowed hard. *Henry*, on the other hand, smiled at the young navigator.

"And what does Navigation think is an acceptable expected error?" he asked quietly.

"A tenth of that, sers," she replied. "If we cannot refine the program to under a quarter-millisecond timing error, I cannot responsibly recommend that the squadron make the skip."

Henry was still smiling as the young Persian woman faced him, her shoulders suddenly square and her spine straight. She was still intimidated and nervous, but she was solid on that point. That was *her* responsibility.

"Good," Henry told her. "I look forward to confirmation that we're there, Lieutenant, but I have no intention of overruling our navigators' collective judgment today.

"How long until we reach the skip line?"

THE THREE DESTROYERS were in position along the skip line, their formation a rough arrow with *Paladin* at the tip.

Henry was once again on the tiny flag deck aboard his flagship, considering the large screen that was the only thing that really *made* the room a flag deck.

"All ships are in position," Eowyn confirmed. "Standing by word from the Navigation departments."

"All vessels are to skip independently," Henry said quietly. "We'll arrive at much the same time in the end, I suspect."

"Understood."

The Captains were also linked in via internal network coms, the computers in their heads sustaining a digital coms channel that would fail the moment any of them entered the skip line.

"All Nav departments confirm their programs are within acceptable parameters," Eowyn said. "Your orders, Commodore?"

"All ships will skip when ready," Henry ordered.

He brought up a virtual window through his internal network, projecting a feed of Paladin's bridge in the air in front of him. Ihejirika held down his central chair with an air of calm that Henry suspected was copied from him.

Charmchi was watching a series of readouts on her screen, then looked back at her CO.

"Skip in ten seconds," she reported. "Program is initiating with countdown."

An alarm rang through the ship, followed by Charmchi's words.

This skip had been hours in preparation. Everyone should be ready for it, with loose objects secured and so forth.

But there was only so much bracing that could be done, and Henry suspected that this one would be worse than normal.

He was right.

His stomach fell left. His brain fell right. The universe kicked him in the nuts from nineteen different directions, most of which his brain couldn't process, and then smacked him in the face from a dozen more as he winced from that.

A skip impulse only lasted seconds, but it always felt longer.

Henry exhaled a long, pained breath and looked around at his staff. Eowyn had her eyes closed, breathing slowly and carefully. Chan was doing much the same, but their eyes were open and focused on their screens.

"No external coms," Chan finally reported. "Internal coms are good."

"Thank you." Henry reactivated his link to the bridge. "Captain Ihejirika?"

"All signs show successful insertion, ser," Ihejirika told him. "Secondary impulse generation in eight hours. Everything should be quiet until then."

"I hope so," Henry muttered. There wasn't *anything* in space that could affect a ship in skip transit, not that he knew about. "I'm going to close down here for the night," he continued to his flag captain.

"Let me know if anything comes up."

CHAPTER THREE

The battlecruiser *Panther* was a deadly weapon in Henry's hands, slicing through the Kenmiri dreadnoughts like they weren't even there. The flow of time was wrong—wrong enough for Henry to pull himself back from the old dream as his ship closed with the Kenmorad evacuation transport.

"She's the last one, ser," his old executive officer proclaimed as *Panther* closed with their target. "If we kill that ship, *we* commit genocide. *We* end a species."

Neither Henry nor Emil Tyson had known that then. Operation Golden Lancelot had been structured so that none of the officers involved knew that *their* attack on a Kenmorad breeding sect was one of dozens.

Henry watched his dream-self give the orders that had doomed a species. The Kenmiri were made up of biologically separate castes— and only the Kenmorad could breed. Without the Kenmorad, the Kenmiri—and their galaxy-spanning empire of ten thousand stars— were doomed to a slow death over a century.

The actual battle had lasted almost half an hour and seen the deaths of half a dozen Vesheron escorts watching *Panther*'s back, but his nightmare blew through all of that in moments. A single gravity-driver round pierced the Kenmorad evac ship amidships, detonating with a force no real warhead could match.

"That's it, then," a grotesque goblin that no longer resembled *anyone* who'd been there, declared. "The Kenmorad are no more. The Kenmiri will die. We are victorious!"

Blood drenched dream-Henry's hands, but the scene was already shifting as Henry tried to regain control of his dreams.

He failed and was suddenly in a place he'd only ever seen on video feeds: the main plaza of La-Tar's capital city. He was standing on a wooden platform, watching as a hundred people of a dozen races were marched up in front of a Kozun firing squad.

Many of the people were of the Ashall races, people like the Kozun and Eerdish who could pass for human at a distance. About a tenth were Enteni, the clearly inhuman aliens who looked like walking Venus flytraps.

"Give the order," a voice barked in Henry's ear. He turned to see his old friend Kalad standing next to him, glaring at him. Like all Kozun, she looked human enough—except that she only had hair on the back half of her head, with armor plating protecting her forehead.

"What?" he asked helplessly.

"These people die by your order," Kalad said calmly. "So, give it."

"No," he snapped. "I won't."

"Why not?" she asked. "You aggravated us, left the innocents to die. Then you let their killers get away. So, *give the order.*"

His body moved without his permission, his hand rising and dropping in a gesture that sometimes seemed universal.

Energy weapons crackled in the night, innocents screaming and falling as another Kozun mass execution marred the once-beautiful park.

Henry tried to pull himself away and found himself somewhere else, aboard a Kozun warship. Kalad was still there, but there was a meter-long spear of metal embedded in her stomach.

"You did this," she accused him. "You organized it all. A trap—

and then you abandoned us. My daughter will never know her mother. *Because of you.*"

Somehow, that was the final straw and Henry managed to yank enough control of his dreams to jerk awake, sweating in the dark as he cursed.

His internal network pinged a warning across his vision.

Trauma nightmares detected. Repetition at level of concern. Recommend immediate appointment with ship's doctor.

"Fuck. That."

The curse word hung in the air as Henry shook himself. He'd spent four months on psychiatric leave after Golden Lancelot had ended, only to demand that the United Planets Alliance do *something* for the worlds the Kenmiri had abandoned.

That had put him on La-Tar, facing down a Kozun invasion—and now, here, in an unsteady alliance *with* the Kozun, the very people who had carried out mass executions to try to hang on to control of La-Tar.

"The *Drifters* killed you, Kalad," he whispered. "We couldn't have done anything."

His ship had been half-wrecked by the Drifters' ambush, and he'd fled into hiding while Kalad's ships had been overrun. His old friend had died to their betrayal.

His internal network was right. He needed to set up more counseling appointments—but there was one thing Commodore Henry Wong was definitely *not* doing.

He was not stepping back and turning the fight against the Drifters over to someone else. This was *personal* now.

CHAPTER FOUR

"Skip emergence in sixty seconds."

Charmchi's voice echoed through *Paladin*'s entire hundred-and-fifty-meter-long hull, the PA system warning every member of the crew that reality was about to normalize.

Henry didn't find the *exit* warning as necessary as the entry warning. There was no "kick" from the impulse generators when they left twenty-dimensional space. They just fell back into normal space, like a skipped stone sinking beneath the surface of a river.

The question today was whether they'd be entering regular space in the right place. Henry was reasonably confident, but accidents *did* happen.

"Captain Ihejirika, status," he asked *Paladin*'s CO.

"We are at battle stations and standing by," Ihejirika replied. "Lasers are charged, and missile launchers are clear. *Paladin* is ready for combat, ser."

Henry took a moment to miss the gravity driver that served as a battlecruiser's main gun. Since the size of a battlecruiser was currently set entirely by the size of the grav-driver, there was no way the smaller destroyer could carry the gun.

He still felt the absence of a main gun firing a smart projectile at seven percent of the speed of light—and the battlecruiser's small but effective fighter wing, for that matter. *Paladin* had just as many missile launchers and heavy lasers as *Raven* had carried, but she lacked the fighters and the main gun.

Her antimissile defenses were weaker, but her gravity shields were just as powerful. That was new for the *Cataphract*-class ships, a side effect of using the same projectors for the shield as the GMS.

"Emergence in ten seconds," Charmchi reported.

Henry exhaled a quiet sigh, linking his internal network into the combat systems and checking the tactical plot in front of him. Right now, the screen was empty—but Eowyn would fix that the moment they emerged.

"Emergence."

It was like someone had lifted a weight off his shoulders that he hadn't seen. A dizziness he'd ceased to notice disappeared, as did a small headache in his left temple. Everything came slightly more clearly into focus as reality returned to the regular three dimensions humans could handle.

"Welcome to the Nohtoin System," Eowyn said drily. "I'm pulling *Paladin*'s scans into the squadron tactical net... We have *Cataphract* linking in."

Several seconds passed and Henry looked at the screen with growing concern. They had made it to the target system, but if he'd lost a destroyer along the way, that was going to be a *big* problem...

"We have *Maharatha*," Eowyn reported as the third destroyer flashed into existence, the inverted canoe shape of her hull seeming to fall into existence out of nowhere. "Linking with all Tactical departments and pulling together initial reports."

Henry tried to conceal his sigh of relief. There were four hundred people aboard each of his destroyers. If he'd killed four hundred people by taking a risky skip, he'd never have forgiven himself.

From a couple of the looks his staff sent his way, he wasn't as successful as he'd have liked. The flag deck aboard *Paladin* was far too small for his taste, and he turned his focus back to the main display.

Nohtoin's geography matched the files they had from other sources. The star was an A-type small blue giant, orbited by three gas giants, all smaller than Sol's Jupiter. There were no rocky planetary bodies, though all three planets had enough rings and moons to make up for the lack.

"Nohtoin B was host to the Kenmiri fueling base," Eowyn reminded him. "Standard skip lines used in this system are here, here and here."

The skip line from the pulsar had brought them out closer to Nohtoin C. B, on the other hand, had an orbit that kept it reasonably close to at least one of the useful skip lines at least ninety percent of the time.

"Are we picking up anything useful at B?" Henry asked.

"Nothing from this distance," Eowyn admitted. "The entire place is dead as a graveyard."

Henry nodded his acknowledgement as he looked over the tactical plot.

"And the Convoy?" he asked.

"We have a trail heading to B," his Operations officer told him. "Potentially, they refueled there. What data we have suggests that B has a higher hydrogen-helium ratio than C or A."

Which would also explain why the Kenmiri had put their base there.

"Chan, orders to the squadron," Henry told his coms officer. "We'll set our course for B and investigate. Maintain one-half KPS-squared. Let's not give away any secrets until we're sure we're not being watched."

This was the first place he'd *expected* to be watched since they'd started the pursuit, which made it time to be careful. Point-five KPS^2 was the standard acceleration of the rest of the United Planets Space Force, slower than both the Kenmiri and their former Vesheron allies.

The *Cataphract*s could pull *two* kilometers per second without any difficulty, but that was a surprise Henry was hoping to keep under wraps. Even without expected observers, he'd kept the squadron to a maximum of one KPS^2 so far.

"Let's see if we spook anyone," he murmured. "If *I* were the Convoy, I'd have left a scout—but a scout isn't much use if she doesn't report."

CROSSING star systems was never a fast process. With most sensible people limiting their skips to twelve hours, most starships spent longer crossing star systems than they ever did in skip. The flight to Nohtoin B was estimated at just over a day, which sent Henry back to bed.

He was awoken by an emergency alert that hammered into his internal network, the implanted computer waking him far more effectively than any audio alarm ever could and, thankfully, with much less disorientation.

"Wong," he answered the alert crisply. "Report."

"Ser, we have a contact at Nohtoin B," Lieutenant Commander Medb Bach's voice said in his skull. The Procyon-born officer was *Paladin*'s Tactical officer—and probably should have gone through Commander Eowyn to wake Henry.

On the other hand...

"Details?" Henry asked.

"Estimate one hundred and fifty thousand tons," the Tactical officer reported crisply. "She's burning for the skip line for the Osonal System at one-point-two KPS."

Henry blinked a map of the region into existence in front of him. Osonal was in Eerdish space, which confirmed their suspicion of where the Convoy had gone after refueling.

With the current geometry, though...the scout was quite distant from the Osonal skip line. At point-five KPS^2, his ships could never catch her—the scout's captain had chosen a balance between getting out safely and getting as much information on Henry's ships as possible.

But.

"Are Eowyn or Chan up?" he asked the Tactical officer.

"No, ser," Bach said. "That's why I contacted you."

"Wake them up," Henry ordered. "And pass the orders for all ships to enter pursuit course...at full acceleration."

BY THE TIME Henry made it to the flag deck, the geometry of what was going to happen was already clear. At two KPS^2, his destroyers were radiating a *lot* of energy. The lack of engine exhaust was more than made up for by the heat created by the gravity wells themselves.

All three of his ships were covered in feather-like heat radiator vanes, easily replaced if damaged, and maintaining full acceleration required them to be functioning almost perfectly.

There was no way the scout ship didn't know they were pursuing, but the smaller ship didn't change its course.

"Confirm my math, Commander," Henry told Eowyn, a mental command flipping her his calculations.

"I make it that we will bring her to laser range at least half a million kilometers short of the skip line and have at least a full minute to engage before the earliest she can skip," he continued.

They'd be in missile range for several minutes before that, especially at the closing velocity they'd be coming in at, but there was a chance the scout ship could evade or destroy missiles. It wasn't a *good* chance, not with three UPSF destroyers closing with her, but it was a chance.

"I have the same," Eowyn told him after a few seconds. "Missile range in seventy minutes."

Henry nodded, considering.

"Assuming they're capable of one-point-five KPS-squared, how quickly would they need to increase acceleration to evade laser engagement?" he asked quietly.

"If they can increase their acceleration to one-point-five anytime in the next thirty minutes, they'll be able to evade a laser engagement," Eowyn replied. "They can no longer evade missile engagement."

Henry's ships had thirty-six missile launchers. A full salvo would probably be overkill, but Henry wasn't inclined to let the Drifters know he was coming.

"All ships have prepped launchers?" he asked.

"Yes, ser."

"Good." He eyed the tactical plot. The scout had to have *some* trick in mind, he presumed. But Henry had the advantage in numbers —and each of his destroyers outmassed the scout ship six to one.

"Chan, record for transmission," he ordered. "Let's see if we can talk them down."

The Chinese officer flashed him a thumbs-up after a few moments. Henry faced the recorder and sorted his face into a cold mask.

"Unidentified vessel, this is Commodore Henry Wong of the United Planets Space Force Peacekeeper Initiative," he told them in Kem, the Kenmiri trade language. "I have reason to believe you are fleeing to advise potential hostile forces of my presence here.

"If you do not cease acceleration and communicate, I will have no choice but to fire on your vessel. You cannot evade my ships. Surrender."

He paused, then glanced at Chan.

"Send it."

"Sent. Do you expect a response?" Chan asked.

"Fifty-fifty," Henry admitted to them. "They can do the math on the acceleration we've revealed as easily as we can—and the *other* math on whether I can let them go after seeing it."

He shook his head.

"If they're an Eerdish ship, they'd have already warned us off," he noted. "So, they're either Drifters or they're somebody *else* with hostile intent. Either way, I'd *expect* them to surrender."

"But you don't," Eowyn said softly, picking up on his tone.

"If they were going to surrender, they'd already be talking," Henry said. "Like I said, they can do the math."

"THIRTY MINUTES TO MISSILE RANGE," Eowyn reported. "They are continuing on course."

"No response to our surrender demand," Chan said.

"Not unexpected." Henry turned to his all-Captains channel. "Captains? Any thoughts?"

"She's got to be planning *something*," Palmer said. "Or she'd have either surrendered or turned to fight."

"Agreed. Make sure all of your helms are standing by for rapid course shifts," Henry ordered. "I expect to see a significant increase in acceleration and adjustment in vector, but…"

He shook his head.

"Ser?" Ihejirika asked.

"If she *could* burn faster, she would be doing it by now," he told them. "Everything she can do at this point is just wriggling on the hook. I'm half-expecting a single salvo for the honor of the flag and then a surrender."

"That's not very Drifter," Teunissen said quietly. "I've worked with them. That would be out of character."

"So have I, and I agree," Henry said. "But Drifters are also known to push the odds if they think they have a trick that can pull it out. So—"

"Vector change!" Eowyn snapped. "Target has adjusted her vector by seventy degrees in the ecliptic and 'up' forty-five degrees. Acceleration is up to one-point-seven KPS-squared."

"And there we go," Henry concluded. "Captains, adjust your courses and prepare your missiles. I don't think she's getting away."

He started running data through his personal network, trying to find the answer. It appeared quickly enough, and he hissed through his teeth in shock.

"Ser?" Eowyn asked. "They're still not going to evade us. Their vector is still going to take them into the skip line, but we'll have missile range for long enough to put at least two salvos into them.

"But why didn't they push this hard sooner? If they'd gone to one-point-seven straight away, we'd never have caught them."

"Look at the exhaust spectrograph, Commander," Henry told her. "Titanium. Iron. Carbon."

"She's burning out her thrust nozzles," the Ops officer realized.

"Exactly. And her Captain knows it. They can keep that up for maybe an hour—and then that ship is *scrap*."

"What do we do, ser?" Eowyn asked.

"How long is the ballistic course if we fire on her now?" he asked.

"Over a minute," she admitted.

"Good enough." Henry tapped a command. "Captain Ihejirika?"

"Ser?" *Paladin*'s CO asked, realizing they had a private channel.

"I want a warning shot across our friend's bow. I don't want to hit her. I don't even want to get close, really. But let's make the damn point."

"Yes, ser. It's on its way."

A single weapon blazed away from the destroyer's stubby "wings." Accelerating at ten KPS^2, it accelerated across space for five minutes until it ran out of fuel.

After that, it took seventy-eight seconds to reach its closest approach to the target, where it calmly detonated in a five-hundred-megaton explosion. A simple warhead was probably the least threatening weapon in DesRon Twenty-Seven's arsenal, but the point was made.

With a gesture to Chan, Henry focused on the camera again.

"Unidentified vessel, I can *see* you wrecking your engines," he told them. "You have fifteen minutes to cease acceleration and prepare to be boarded. If you do not, the next missiles won't miss."

HENRY WASN'T SURPRISED by the lack of response this time. He was looking forward to having a conversation with the scout's captain about what the *hell* the sentient was thinking—if the idiot survived.

"All ships standing by to fire," Eowyn reported. "Range in ninety seconds and counting."

He nodded in silence. He'd given all the orders he could. There was no way they could reliably disable the ship, much as he would like to.

Seconds ticked away as the range plummeted. Five minutes after they passed the line, that scout would cease to exist.

"Vector change!" Eowyn snapped. "Target is now accelerating *toward* us. Range is dropping—*hostile has fired.*"

Ten light-seconds of delay was enough for that to work. The scout had flipped and entered her range of DesRon Twenty-Seven before anyone had realized it.

"I have eighteen missiles incoming," Eowyn continued. "All ships have fired, three-six in space."

Henry grimaced. For the scout to have that many missile launchers, the little ship had no lasers and probably almost no ammunition for the launchers themselves.

They'd still get whatever salvos they had off. Five minutes was nothing in the time frame of crossing star systems—and an eternity in the time frame of a battle.

"Do we launch a second salvo, ser?" Ihejirika asked from *Paladin*'s bridge.

"Negative," Henry ordered. "Focus on defending your ships, Captains. We're a long way from home. Let's not waste ammo."

Two more salvos blasted clear of the scout over the following hundred-odd seconds, and then nothing.

"Three-missile launchers," Henry concluded. "That's a Vesheron trick. A *pirate* trick."

He'd worked alongside enough Vesheron ships in the war to recognize it. Since the rebel factions had limited supplies of ships and weapons alike, they'd often been forced to fall back on stolen ships with boxed weapon installations.

Those installations were easy to add to an existing ship, allowed for large salvos...and ran out of ammunition *very* quickly.

They'd still put over fifty missiles in space, all targeted on *Paladin*.

"Coordinated defense net online," Eowyn reported. "Antimissile lasers engaging."

"Scan for resonance warheads," Henry ordered—and then paused as his tactical display flickered and updated. "What the hell?"

Cataphract had just fallen out of formation, her acceleration dropping to zero as she charged her shields to defensive levels.

"*Cataphract* has lost acceleration; GMS has failed," Palmer snapped. "Shields are at forty percent expected power; acceleration is at *zero*."

"Maneuvering *Paladin* in front of her," Ihejirika reported. "They're aimed at us; let's make sure the missiles don't see *Cataphract*."

Henry closed his eyes in frustration. His ships were still half-experimental, and that experiment had just failed...at the worst possible time.

"I have to shut down reactor cores to manage thermal production," Palmer reported. "Sensors are heat-blinded."

"Understood. Focus on your ship, Captain Palmer," Henry ordered. "Ihejirika, Teunissen. Stop those missiles."

As lasers flashed across space and the missile salvos closed with his ships, Henry realized he'd forgotten his question.

"Eowyn," he asked quietly. "Do we still have time to scan for resonance warheads?"

The gravitic-resonance weapons, designed by the Drifters, were one of the few systems that seriously threatened a gravity-shielded starship. Any weapon *could*, in theory, pass through the gravity shear zone around Henry's ships.

The resonance warheads could *destroy* that shear zone, leaving his ships vulnerable to weapons they'd normally shrug off.

"No time, ser," she admitted. "I..."

"Was distracted by *Cataphract*," Henry finished. "Same as me."

The first salvo plunged in on *Paladin*, the smart weapons dodging and weaving as two ships' antimissile lasers did their best to take down the incoming fire. It was almost enough—close enough that Henry could be certain that adding *Cataphract*'s defenses would have kept any missiles from hitting his ships.

With *Cataphract* crippled and falling behind, three missiles dove toward *Paladin* and detonated, converting their entire mass into massive shotgun blasts of superheated plasma.

"No blowthrough," he heard Bach report from the bridge. "All plasma diverted. We're fine."

In theory, the odds of any given plasma conversion warhead or plasma cannon burning through a UPSF gravity field were low...but probability played no favorites and Henry had seen destroyers lost to a single missile.

"Multiple hits on the target," Eowyn reported. "Her engines are down and she is leaking atmosphere. I'm still detecting power signatures, but she is crippled."

"Understood," Henry replied. "Inform Lieutenant Commander Ngu—"

The explosion that lit up the screen cut off his instruction to prepare for boarding. He didn't even need to ask Eowyn to confirm what he was looking at.

If nothing else, the suicide charge looked *exactly* like the five-hundred-megaton warhead they'd used for their own warning shot.

"Target has self-destructed," Eowyn reported uselessly.

"Understood," Henry said grimly. "All ships, reverse acceleration and fall back on *Cataphract*. Maintain defensive perimeter and take down those missiles.

"Not much point in closing the range now."

The suicide charge would have vaporized the entire ship. No one would have installed one that didn't—the UPSF certainly didn't!

The only problem was that he'd never met a *Drifter* ship with a suicide charge installed.

CHAPTER FIVE

THERE WERE NO KOZUN WARSHIPS IN THE LA-TAR SYSTEM. THE Cluster's government—born with surprising rapidity out of an emergency defensive alliance—was willing to accept that they shared an enemy with the Kozun Hierarchy.

They were not, to Ambassador Sylvia Todorovich's strong approval, willing to permit armed Kozun vessels back in a star system that had far too recently been under the Hierarchy's boot.

Even so, the view from the flag deck of UPSV *Scorpius* was full of ships. If nothing else, there was the *rest* of the *Crichton*-class carrier's battle group: two battlecruisers and seven destroyers.

Beyond that, though, La-Tar local space was full of civilian shipping—and *that* was a heart-warming sight to Sylvia. When she and Henry Wong had arrived in the region, the Kozun had been holding on to the limited shipping available to the agriworld, leaving the four industrial worlds depending on her to starve.

Now she could pick out dozens of glittering dots that she knew were freighters, hauling food out to the rest of the Cluster and bringing technology back. The specializations of the five worlds would fade over time, but for now, their economies and livelihoods were utterly interlinked.

Local warships stood guard over those freighters; watchdogs all too aware of how close to devastation all of them had come at Kozun hands.

The La-Tar ships, crewed by a mix of half a dozen races, were all built to the standard of the old Kenmiri escorts. The Cluster had not yet had the time or resources to design their own warships, but two of the industrial worlds had shipyards with the patterns for the lighter Kenmiri ships.

"There she is," Rear Admiral Cheung Jian Chin said softly, gesturing to one of the local warships.

"Admiral?" Sylvia asked. She was a guest on Cheung's flag deck, but she didn't pretend to fully understand the tactical display she stood in front of. She was *passingly* literate in military iconography, but she couldn't pick out details beyond "big ship, little ship, friendly ship, enemy ship."

"That's *Vengeance*," Cheung said quietly, the squat Chinese Admiral making a gesture that zoomed in on the ship. "The locals have built a lot of Kenmiri escorts at this point—almost three dozen, counting the ones the Kozun destroyed when they first came to La-Tar—but *Vengeance* is their first gunship.

"Which also makes her the first time they've built a heavy plasma cannon, which is a stepping-stone to Kenmiri-style capital ships we didn't expect them to manage," he admitted. "They've laid down keels for laser-armed cruisers, but that *Vengeance* even exists tells me that our friends are going to be valuable allies in the future."

Sylvia chuckled.

"If unneeded this time, correct?" she asked.

"That's a discussion for politicians and Admiral Rex," Cheung told her. "I command the *Scorpius* group, but our future alliances are more a question of the Peacekeeper Initiative—which makes them your problem and Commodore Wong's problem."

The sharply built blonde ambassador shook her head at the older man.

"And today's crisis?"

"That discussion is for you and Admiral Rex," Cheung repeated calmly. "He is slated to command this new fleet, after all."

"Speaking of which?" Sylvia asked.

"Any minute now," Cheung replied. "*Aeryn* should be arriving shortly." He shrugged. "At last report, *Chiana* was still loading boxed fighters from Base Fallout. She'll be another two weeks."

"How many fighters are you all *bringing*?" Sylvia asked.

Cheung grinned, the schoolboy-esque expression out of place on his old face.

"A *Crichton*-class carrier is the base for one hundred twenty starfighters," he told her. "We have another forty boxed in storage. *Chiana* isn't coming out to La-Tar with *any* complete fighters on her decks.

"If the reports I have are correct, we'll be swapping all of our starfighters for the new Lancers once she arrives. The battlecruisers too," he added thoughtfully. "That will cut our reserves to the bone and most of our backups will be thruster fighters, but we'll have a first-line strike of three hundred and sixty SF-One-Thirty GMS starfighters."

Sylvia looked back at the screen. The La-Tar Cluster had a handful of converted freighter carriers, but their fighters were crude and inferior, even compared to the SF-122 Dragoon "thruster fighters" *Scorpius* currently carried.

The Dragoons had gravity shields and the local fighters didn't.

"I presume we're not going to be handing our old fighters over to the locals," she murmured. "Someone would have told me if we were breaking *that* particular stricture."

The UPA would supply the locals with anything *but* gravity shields and gravity maneuvering systems. Every ex-Vesheron power, including the UPA, used basically identical missiles, lasers, and thrusters.

Only the UPSF had gravity shields—in the Ra Sector, anyway. There had been another El-Vesheron power—external allies like the UPA—who'd possessed them, but they were a *long* way away.

The destruction of the subspace-communication network had cut everyone off from each other and shrunk the galaxy. Once, UPSF starships had struck at the far side of the Kenmiri Empire. Now, they were still fumbling in the dark in much of the Ra Sector, right next door.

"We have a Cherenkov pulse," one of Cheung's officers reported crisply. "Multiple skip signatures along the Tano line. Timing is correct for Carrier Group *Aeryn*, sers."

"And Admiral Rex is exactly on time," Cheung said after a pause to check a network clock. "Confirm signatures and ID codes as they come in, Commander."

"One *Crichton*-class carrier, a *Corvid*-class and a *Jaguar*-class battlecruiser, eight destroyers," the officer reported. "Destroyers are all *Significance*-class."

"As expected," Cheung confirmed. He looked at Sylvia. "Command is sending us the best," he told her. "Between the Initiative and our fleet, I think we're going to have every *Significance*- and *Cataphract*-class destroyer in the UPSF."

"There's not much demand back home, I would hope," Sylvia said.

"No," he agreed. "Plus, well..." He sighed. "They're decommissioning the *Tyrannosaurs* pretty quickly. Funding is getting tight."

Sylvia nodded wordlessly. The war had been over for three years. Even the current situation was officially classified as a "security deployment," though at least one with a specific budget provided by the Assembly.

The UPSF had seen their budget slashed by almost fifty percent. The only salvation was that the Peacekeeper Initiative, despite falling under UPSF command, had an entirely separate budget—and Sylvia had fought *hard* for that.

The Initiative's budget had stayed relatively steady, but it wasn't enough to absorb major fleets. It was set up to pay for the operations costs of two battlecruisers and twelve destroyers, plus a support infrastructure.

"Admiral Rex will almost certainly want to meet with you, Ambassador," Cheung told her. "This is your war, after all."

"I thought it was only a security deployment?" Sylvia asked drily.

"We're on the front lines, Ambassador," the Admiral said. "There can be no *euphemisms* here. We are here to fight the Drifters. That's a war, so far as I'm concerned."

SYLVIA'S CHIEF OF STAFF, Felix Leitz, was waiting for her when she returned to the shuttle deck. He was a heavyset man with short black hair and a neatly groomed beard—and, these days, a perpetually frustrated set to his eyes.

"If we're transferring to *Aeryn,* why did we even come aboard *Scorpius?*" he asked her, falling in by her side.

"Because we owed Admiral Cheung and Commodore Barrie that much," Sylvia replied. "Military officers are people, Felix, and I *know* you have people skills."

Leitz snorted, gesturing for her to slow up as the figure of *Scorpius*'s Captain approached. Commodore Peter Barrie was a sparsely built, athletic man, slightly more gray than his ex-husband, with the white turtleneck collar of a starship Captain.

"Military officers are fine," he conceded. "I just don't like *warships.*"

That was a telling admission, one that Sylvia would have to investigate later. For now, she acknowledged Barrie with a firm nod and handshake as the Commodore intercepted them.

"My apologies for not making time for you sooner, Ambassador, Em Leitz," he told them. "My work is rarely slow."

Commodore Peter Barrie was the captain of a fleet carrier, one of the most powerful capital ships in existence and one carrying a crew of almost five thousand—and also her boyfriend's ex-husband. Sylvia doubted he even knew what *slow* looked like anymore.

"I appreciate you making the time at all, Captain," she told him. "I know how badly command of even a battlecruiser consumes an officer's time." She gestured around the flight deck, busily swarming with UPSF FighterDiv personnel checking on the starfighters.

"I can't begin to imagine how much work a carrier takes."

Barrie chuckled.

"I have a good team, but yes," he told her. "We'll be attending the meeting aboard *Aeryn* virtually, so I wouldn't have a chance to greet you there. One does hope that the locals have provided acceptable lodgings."

Sylvia arched an eyebrow.

"La-Tar had quarters for visiting Kenmorad that have been repurposed to serve as diplomatic embassies," she replied. "They're... almost disgustingly comfortable. I do wonder if they took the cushions out of the one they lent the Kozun, though."

"I would have," Barrie muttered. "This alliance...itches, Ambassador."

"Many alliances do," she warned. "We cannot only talk with the people we like, Captain Barrie."

"I understand. But the thought of fighting alongside the Kozun again, like nothing ever happened..."

"Would you rather not have their warships?"

"No, I'll take Kozun escorts over no escorts," he conceded. "But after the last few years, the only people I think my hands would be twitchier about would be the Kenmiri themselves."

"Believe me, Commodore, if I ever get the Kenmiri to work with us on something, that will be the *crown jewel* of my career," Sylvia said.

"Even above arranging the failure of the Drifter's treachery and negotiating a peace treaty while trapped in a lifepod?" Barrie asked with a chuckle.

"That one will probably always be up there, but I don't think anyone really gets how much the Kenmiri really, *specifically*, hate humanity these days. Golden Lancelot was us, after all."

That sent a visible chill rippling across Barrie's face, and she winced. Even to Sylvia, Golden Lancelot and the slow genocide humanity had inflicted on their enemy was a sore spot, but it was still distant to her.

Over half of all serving UPSF captains and above had been involved in the operation: lied to and ordered to commit genocide. It wasn't a sore spot for the UPSF. It was still a weeping open wound.

"You need to get going," Barrie said after a moment. "Pass on my regards to Henry when you see him next, will you?"

"Always," Sylvia promised. The two men's marriage had self-destructed on the altar of the war, but there was still enough warmth there for her to feel it was worth preserving.

Someday, they might even manage to be friends again. If Sylvia pulled *that* off, it would rank up with the lifepod negotiations, at least in her own mind.

CHAPTER SIX

Sylvia's shuttle gently tucked itself to the deck on *Aeryn* with a final jet of thrusters. The ship's artificial gravity field held the spacecraft in place as she and Leitz headed down the ramp onto the deck.

Safety barriers retracted to reveal a gathered assembly of dozens of officers and spacers. There was a podium with its back to them, with clear seats for them—and an eager GroundDiv officer seemed to appear out of nowhere.

"If you'll come with me, Ambassador, we're about to start the ceremony," the young Lieutenant told her, his expression cheerful and his words quick.

"Lead on, Lieutenant Eaton," Sylvia said with a chuckle, pulling his name from her internal network. No one had warned her that there would be a ceremony—she was there for a briefing—but she was used to adapting to things like this.

Lieutenant Eaton led her and Leitz to chairs next to the podium, where a lectern waited in empty silence—presumably for Admiral Cody Rex. Sylvia would have words for the Admiral later about not warning her, but for now she'd play along with the theatrics.

There were at least five hundred people formed up in neat rows. A glance at their uniforms marked the split between SpaceDiv, FighterDiv, and GroundDiv personnel—and unless Sylvia missed her guess, the assembly was *exactly* ten percent of each division's crew aboard *Aeryn.*

A moment after she and Leitz took their seats, the traditional electronic bugle of a flag officer coming aboard rang out, and Rex emerged from a hatch onto the deck, approaching the podium alone.

Cody Rex was a tall, clean-shaven man with sharp features and a high-and-tight flat-top haircut, gone gray with age. He wore the same black jacket over turtlenecked shipsuit as everyone else, but his collar bore three silver stars on the left side. The only other decoration he wore was a pair of silver pilot's wings.

He traded a nod with Sylvia as he stepped up to the lectern and spread out a piece of archaic parchment.

"Thank you, everyone," he told them. "With two carrier groups in position here in the La-Tar System, I have formal orders to activate Twelfth Fleet. Attention, please!"

He made a show of flattening the parchment.

"To: Admiral Cody Rex. From: Admiral Lee Saren, United Planets Space Force Command, Base Halo, Sol.

"Upon receipt of these orders, you are to proceed to the La-Tar System aboard the carrier **UPSV** *Aeryn.* There, upon assemblage of sufficient forces as per your judgment, you are to activate and assume command of the United Planets Alliance Twelfth Fleet, flying your flag from *Aeryn* or another vessel as you see fit. You are charged to carry the duties and responsibilities of Admiral and commander of Twelfth Fleet to the highest and best standards and traditions of the United Planets Space Force.

"We charge you with the memory of those who came before and the fate of those yet to come.

"Signed: Admiral Lee Saren. Space Division. United Planets Space Force."

Rex folded the parchment and placed it inside his jacket, surveying the assembly.

"I hereby activate the Twelfth Fleet of the United Planets Space Force," he said formally. He let a beat hang in the air before continuing.

"There has never been a Twelfth Fleet before," he told them. "We are a new fleet assembled for a new mission, of a type the UPA has not fought before. For a new mission, UPSF Command felt we required a new formation.

"There are details of the mission that will remain confidential for now, but the situation is very straightforward. The Peacekeeper Initiative attempted to negotiate a peaceful settlement between the La-Tar Cluster and the Kozun Hierarchy.

"The peace summit was betrayed and attacked by warships of the Blue Stripe Green Stripe Orange Stripe Drifter Convoy—warships asked to act as neutral guarantors to the peace summit.

"It is the task of Twelfth Fleet to neutralize the military threat of the Blue Stripe Green Stripe Orange Stripe Drifter Convoy by whatever means necessary, to secure the safety of our allies in the La-Tar Cluster, and to secure a greater peace in the Ra Sector.

"The Drifters were our allies. Other Convoys may still be, but Blue Stripe Green Stripe Orange Stripe have proven themselves our enemies."

Rex smiled thinly, clearly visible to his audience.

"The Drifters will learn that it is folly to challenge the United Planets Alliance!"

IT TOOK LONGER to dismantle the assembly and get into the planned briefing than Sylvia liked, which meant she didn't have a chance to yank on Admiral Rex's ears for surprising her with the ceremony.

Instead, she and Leitz joined him and Commodore Usman

Angus in a conference room as dozens of people virtually linked in from the other ships of the newly activated fleet.

The last arrival in the room was the black-haired and -skinned Colonel in command of *Aeryn*'s starfighter group. Opeyemi Botha crisply saluted the Admiral in apology before taking her seat.

"One more moment, please," Rex told everyone. "Take a seat, take a breath. We're in no rush yet."

He was seated on the edge of his own chair, facing a recorder sending his three-dimensional image to every ship in his fleet.

"We are still waiting on Carrier Group *Chiana* before our preferred operational start date," he told everyone. "Depending on what information we get from the Initiative, it may be necessary for us to move sooner, but currently there is only one point of concern in the Ra Sector."

He gestured to Sylvia.

"If Ambassador Todorovich could summarize that for me? I presume you have more updated information on the situation with the Hierarchy and the homeworlds?"

Sylvia added another item to the list of things Rex should have warned her about before doing, leveling a sharp gaze on the Admiral as she marshaled her thoughts.

"The Kozun Hierarchy has been extremely successful in their campaign of conquest," she said bluntly. "They also overextended themselves quite badly, which was part of why they were prepared to negotiate with La-Tar."

She shook her head.

"The other part was that we were standing behind La-Tar with a very large club," she noted. "The problem is that between us and the Drifters, the Hierarchy no longer has a deployable capital-ship strength.

"Commodore Wong wrecked one of their dreadnoughts at the Great Gathering and took out one of their new cruisers here in La-Tar," she reminded everyone.

The Great Gathering had been the attempt by the various

Vesheron groups, including the external El-Vesheron allies like the UPA, to lay the groundwork for a post-Kenmiri galactic order. Unfortunately, the instantaneous subspace coms they'd all relied on had turned out to be a Kenmiri product—relying on a section of subspace artificially stabilized by systems concealed somewhere in the heart of the Kenmiri Empire.

Systems the Kenmiri had turned off at the worst time they could find. The loss of communications had turned the Great Gathering from a conference on the future into a multi-way melee, one that Wong had barely extracted Sylvia and her people from.

"The Drifters wiped out the last three Kozun cruisers at the peace conference," Sylvia said. "They have another four under construction, but they won't be ready for months. Their sole remaining dreadnought, *Mal Toranis*, is covering the Kozun homeworld.

"This limits Hierarchy forces to Kenmiri-style escorts and gunships and a scattering of new corvettes," she concluded. Her audience knew what those names meant better than she did, she hoped.

"Nonetheless, the Hierarchy controls the Kozun homeworld, the Tak homeworld, the Sana homeworld, and three full dependency clusters like La-Tar," she noted. "In the long run, if they can hang on to all of that, they will be the dominant player in the Ra Sector.

"It's in our interests to either dismantle or ally with the Hierarchy," she told the military officers. "For now, we are allied with them, thanks to the Drifters' treachery, and have secured the independence of the La-Tar Cluster. At the same time as they sued for peace with us, they made separate treaties with two former Kenmiri colonies and a fifth dependency cluster.

"That leaves them with two remaining conflicts: first, against the Drifters, in alliance with us and the La-Tar Cluster," she continued. Everyone knew that one. "That conflict is currently quiet, as the Drifters are running dark.

"Without knowing what their plan is, we cannot simply leave the Drifters be," she admitted. She *wanted* to, in some ways, but she agreed with the military assessment that the threat needed to be explicitly ended.

"That leaves us with one ongoing crisis in the Ra Sector that we are aware of," she said. "There may be others. Our communications through the Cluster are still limited."

Their communications consisted of a series of semi-jokingly named "post stations." Small space stations with crews of fifty or so, the prefab structures maintained a continuous link of automated skip-capable drones that carried messages back to UPA space.

Well, to the larger station in La-Tar. The exact location of the United Planets Alliance wasn't well known in the former Kenmiri stars...and the UPA wanted to keep it that way.

"We do now have a communications link with the Kozun home-world, so we are aware of the war with the Enteni and the Eerdish," she said. "Those two homeworlds have formed a defensive alliance, combined with a dependency cluster between them, and have claimed some twenty-five stars.

"They don't have the industrial strength to stand against the Hierarchy forever, not once the Kozun get up to speed, but they have the ships and firepower to frustrate Mal Dakis so far."

She raised a hand before anyone asked any questions.

"The decision has already been made that the UPA will *not* take a side in that war," she noted. "So far as we are concerned, both the Eerdish-Enteni Alliance and the Kozun Hierarchy are friends. And frankly? While we haven't yet restored contact with the Alliance's worlds, we suspect we're going to like them better than we do the Hierarchy!"

And they already *had* an alliance with the Hierarchy.

Nodding his thanks to her, Rex brought the focus of the virtual conference back to her.

"The conflict between the Kozun and the Eerdish-Enteni Alliance is of concern to us," he reminded his officers. "It is unlikely to spill over onto us, but what information we have received from Initiative scouting efforts suggests that our target is fully aware of the conflict and is heading into E..." Rex snorted. "E-Two space," he concluded, shortening the name of the alliance.

"The Drifters wish to use our desire to make peace all around against us. We need to be careful. We also need to be careful not to draw the United Planets Alliance into unnecessary conflict.

"For the moment, we will remain in La-Tar space while the Peacekeeper Initiative's ships and communications network attempt to locate our target. A third carrier group is on their way, with a full load of the new GMS fighters for all of our carriers and cruisers."

He spread his hands.

"We will make good use of this time," he told them firmly. "We will run through exercises and we will use our simulators to train our pilots on the new fighters."

"Ser, should we be planning for joint exercises with the Cluster forces?" Cheung asked, *Scorpius*'s Rear Admiral clearly studying something outside the virtual conference—probably a map of the system.

"Yes, but on a limited basis," Rex replied. "We want to give the locals a hand up, but we don't want to risk revealing too many of our secrets while working with them." He smiled thinly. "The Cluster are friends, not family."

He turned his head, studying each of the twenty-odd officers commanding his ships and starfighter wings, wearing that same thin smile.

"We have a mission, officers," he told them. "That mission is the destruction of a clear and present military threat to the UPA. We have been given more than enough resources to complete that mission, regardless of who in the Ra Sector tries to stop us.

"We will complete our mission. You will be receiving training packages on a task group and squadron level that my staff and I have been working on since we left Sol, to work up your ships for the tactics enabled by the new Lancers.

"We will update as more information becomes available. Thank you, everyone. Dismissed!"

CHAPTER SEVEN

"Admiral, a moment, please," Sylvia said severely as the virtual conference faded away, leaving her with the handful of officers from *Aeryn*. She glanced at the others. "In private, please."

Her chief of staff knew that tone, and Leitz was moving before she'd finished speaking. *Aeryn*'s officers took their cue from the diplomat without Rex saying a word. In under a minute, Sylvia was alone with Twelfth Fleet's commander.

"Strange," he murmured. "I was under the impression those people reported to me."

"They're smart enough to know when to be somewhere else," she told him. "If we are going to be working together, Admiral, you and I need to lay some ground rules."

He shrugged.

"I'm not a diplomat, Ambassador," he replied. "My job here is very clear. We aren't necessarily going to be 'working together.'"

Sylvia smiled thinly.

"Admiral Rex, please," she said. "I've seen your record and the officers around you seem impressed. You did not reach the highest rank the United Planets Space Force has by being innocent of politics.

"This posting, this mission, are political to their bones," she reminded him. "Diplomacy will be critical. You are operating outside of the borders of the United Planets Alliance and we no longer have the overwhelming threat of the Kenmiri Empire to sand away rough spots.

"One misstep on your part could undo two years of work by myself and the Peacekeeper Initiative. I will not permit that to happen; am I clear?"

He remained silent for a moment, leaning on the conference table as he studied her.

"I'm no bull in the china shop, Em Todorovich, but I'm also not Henry Wong and hanging on your every word," he said bluntly. "I will do my job. I'm not here to create conflict, but I am here to do that job."

"Admiral Rex, we have been in the same system for less than twelve hours," Sylvia told him coldly. "In those twelve hours, you have now surprised me with a major ceremony without prior warning, asked me to give a briefing without requesting it in advance, and now impugned the judgment and intelligence of the second-in-command of the UPA's Peacekeeper Initiative.

"If you are *not* a 'bull in a china shop,'" she quoted back at him, "you are doing a good impression of one. You and I have not worked together before—and you just took this meeting from a quiet correction to the active question of whether you retain command of Twelfth Fleet."

He straightened his spine, looming over her as he slammed his fists on the table.

"I will not be threatened by a civilian," he said flatly. "I think this meeting is over."

"If this meeting ends here, Admiral," Sylvia told him, "there will be a drone headed to Earth by the time I reach the surface of La-Tar. That drone will be directed to the Security Council under an Alpha-

One priority, advising them that the senior diplomat on the scene does not believe that you are capable of the delicacy required for this operation.

"You will be relieved by return drone. I can't see that taking more than twenty-one days. Your replacement will arrive with *Chiana* and your career will *end*."

Rex was taller and more heavily built than Sylvia, but she was far from a short woman. She faced him squarely, and she *knew* how sharp and dangerous her gray eyes looked when she was this mad.

"The *only* reason I am willing to consider continuing this meeting is because your officers respect you," she said into a deathly silence. "I spent ten years as a diplomat in Kenmiri space, and I came to respect the collective judgment of the officers and enlisted of the United Planets Space Force.

"That your subordinates trust and respect you tells me that I am missing something, Admiral Rex," she continued. "So, please, tell me what it is."

The conference room air could have been cut with a knife as she glared him down, until he finally exhaled. Nodding slowly, he hooked a chair out from the table and sat on it backward, a sudden grin splitting his face.

"I apologize for surprising you, Em Todorovich," he said softly, his tone completely different. "And I believe I may have deserved... well, all of that. I also apologize for implying that your relationship with Commodore Wong was likely to impede his judgment.

"I've *commanded* Wong. I'm not sure bleeding out from a gut wound would impede his judgment."

There was a silence, and then a coffeepot stand emerged from a cubby in the wall Sylvia hadn't noticed. The stand was powered and calmly rolled over to Rex, who poured himself a cup of black coffee.

"Coffee, Ambassador?"

"Not yet, I don't think," Sylvia said tersely. The sudden mood shift was positive, but she wasn't yet convinced that Rex wasn't going to be a problem.

He nodded calmly and swallowed at least half a cup of still-steaming coffee in one go.

"I have *not* slept enough," he said grimly. "Always a bad plan, I know, but I'm trying to do my best by these spacers. It's been three years since we deployed a real fleet this far. Everyone is rusty, and no one is sure how many of the old rules apply or don't apply.

"I *should* have warned you in advance about both the briefing and the command ceremony," he conceded. "I won't tell you that I assumed you'd expect both. I might have if I thought about it, but I didn't even think about it."

He shrugged.

"My staff is as rusty as anyone else. We *will* do better," he promised. "I'm also not prepared to let you throw them under the bus, and I get protective of my people. The responsibility was mine, but I'd prefer it if you *didn't* end my career over it, Em Todorovich."

"Ya schitayu," Sylvia told him in Russian. *I'm thinking.*

"Fair," he conceded, clearly following her words. Whether that was understanding Russian on his own or through a translator in his internal network, she wasn't sure. Rex *wasn't* Russian. He was from the American Alpha Centauri colonies.

"This situation out here is messy, Ambassador," he said. "But *my* role is extremely simple and extremely clear: I'm to find and neutralize the BGO Convoy. Preferably *without* actually wrecking the Convoy, given that it's mostly unarmed ships carrying civilians."

He sighed.

"That's going to be a mess all on its own, but the problem, Em Ambassador, is that I am specifically tasked to avoid getting involved in *any* of the Peacekeeper Initiative's affairs.

"I'm not authorized to intervene in local situations. Hell, I'm barely supposed to talk to the locals outside of coordinating support for Twelfth Fleet." He shook his head. "It's a *mess*," he repeated. "Technically, Ambassador, I'm not supposed to be working with you. Simply in the same region as you."

"That is a terrible idea," Sylvia noted.

"I agree, but those are my orders," he told her. "We're to lean on La-Tar for logistics and support units, but otherwise, I am not to get involved in *anything*."

"I'd appreciate it if you at least try not to make my job harder," she said.

"I have no intention of doing so, though as we have seen, I'm not perfect," Rex said drily. "I'm reliant on the Initiative to find the enemy, but I have no authority over Wong's people. Entirely different chain of command.

"The Initiative works with you. I'm just sort of...here, Ambassador. An attack dog waiting to be unleashed."

"I'm not a fan of that structure," Sylvia repeated. "I may have to send a drone after all."

Not one requesting Rex's relief—his honest apology had bought him that much—but potentially asking UPSF Command just what the hell they were thinking.

"I don't think you'll convince anyone to change it, Ambassador," Rex told her. "They want to send a message that our ambassadors are untouchable, but they do not want to get involved in a war.

"The Convoy will be dealt with." He shrugged. "And then I go home. I don't like it, Em Todorovich, but it's where we are."

"I'll take that coffee," Sylvia finally said. "I don't suppose you have anything to put in it? From the sounds of it, we both need a drink."

CHAPTER EIGHT

THE BLOCK OF LUXURIOUS MANSIONS BUILT FOR LA-TAR'S RARE Kenmorad visitors occupied a tall hill overlooking the capital city. Bulldozers had turned the hilltop into a flat plateau with an artificial ridge and moat at the edge. More landscaping and careful gardening had followed to allow the four homes to retain spectacular views while being near-invisible from anywhere but the hill itself.

Those mansions now served as the diplomatic quarter for La-Tar City, with Cluster soldiers in pale gray uniforms checking IDs as vehicles approached the entrances. The security *inside* the perimeter was subtler but still ever-present.

Even so, the guards outside the Kozun Embassy were Cluster troops. The visible pair were Sana, with pale skin and tusks at the corner of their mouths. They saluted as Sylvia exited the groundcar that delivered her.

"The Embassy has been advised of your arrival, Ambassador Todorovich," the soldier greeted her in Kem.

The Kenmiri had ruled ten thousand stars, with over a thousand inhabited planets and ninety species. With seven different El-

Vesheron powers added to the mix, the Vesheron rebels had faced an immense language barrier.

Any resistance to using the language of their enemy had been long gone by the time the United Planets Alliance had joined the Vesheron. The Kenmiri trade language, Kem, had been the lingua franca of the Vesheron factions—and now it was the language of interstellar trade and diplomacy among the Kenmiri's former subjects.

Even for fluent speakers, it was a simpler and more formal language than English. The soldier speaking was obviously *not* a fluent speaker, but she was clear and understandable.

A necessity for an embassy guard, Sylvia supposed.

"Thank you, soldiers," she told the two troopers. "Usual rules?"

"You, one aide, one bodyguard," the same woman replied. "The spikeheads are still being paranoid."

The other soldier made a hissing sound, twisted by their tusks into something truly odd-sounding to Sylvia's ears.

"My apologies," the first guard corrected herself. "The *Hierarchy* remains somewhat concerned about potential retaliation for the actions of rogue soldiers during their presence on La-Tar."

Sana didn't roll their eyes the ways humans did. The various Ashall species shared many microexpressions, entirely unconscious muscle reactions to stress and other emotions, but only a handful of more-conscious expressions would be shared between any two cultures.

Sylvia still had no doubts about the amount of sarcasm included in the description of the reasoning behind the Kozun's security protocols.

"It's nothing new," she told the guards, gesturing Leitz and a Marine out of the car behind her. "We know the drill."

INSIDE THE PERIMETER of the mansion itself, security was provided by Kozun Hierarchy commandos in black dress uniforms. None of the personnel assigned to the embassy had served on La-Tar during the occupation, Sylvia knew, but she suspected the uniforms alone would trigger PTSD in a good chunk of the planet's population.

Envoy San Taval, on the other hand, would have a hard time intimidating anyone. The Hierarchy representative to the La-Tar Cluster—no one had yet graced him with the title of "Ambassador"—used a wheelchair as he was missing both legs just above the knee—and he *radiated* plush softness as his powered chair rolled him into the drawing room to meet Sylvia.

Like all Kozun, he only had hair on the back of his head. Where most of his people kept it in a ponytail or braid that ended up looking like a Manchurian queue, San Taval kept his black hair cropped close. The only decoration he wore was silver tips on the spike parts of his forehead armor plates. Otherwise, he wore a plain black tunic that was probably easier to put on than more-formal wear.

He gestured for Sylvia and her escorts to sit, ignoring the pair of armed guards who accompanied him into the plushly decorated room. The furniture was thickly upholstered, and hand-carved bookshelves lined the walls.

Those shelves had almost certainly held *something* at one point, but they were empty now—a reminder that the embassy had been taken from the Kenmiri and had only been lent to the Kozun in the last two weeks.

The old decorations were gone and the Hierarchy hadn't had a chance to bring in new ones yet. The alliance was still tentative—which told Sylvia Todorovich that San Taval was almost certainly more dangerous than he appeared.

"Welcome to my humble home, Ambassador Todorovich," Taval greeted her. "May I offer you and your companions something to drink? Water? Liquor? Another stimulant? I believe we have Terran coffee on hand."

That would have taken some doing, Sylvia knew. Most species had a stimulant that served much the same role as coffee—indeed, she knew people who made a hobby of trying all of the ones that were safe for Ashall and humans.

"Water will be fine," she told him. "Has your staff had any problems settling in, Envoy?"

Taval spread his hands wide.

"Less than I expected, considering the travails of our occupation of La-Tar," he noted. "Most people who would regard us as friends are no longer in power. Such is the way of things."

Sylvia concealed her surprise.

"I did not believe the Hierarchy was officially calling their time here an occupation," she said.

"We are not," Taval said bluntly. "But in these meetings, I find that clarity is the most important thing."

He hadn't said anything, but a servant emerged from one of the doors with a tray of glasses and a jug of water. The Kozun woman laid the tray on a Kenmiri-made wooden table and filled the glasses.

Taval took the first glass himself, sipping from it before Sylvia or her people even received theirs. All poured from the same jug, which meant he was making a point.

"Have you had a chance to consider our proposals?" Sylvia asked after taking a small sip herself. If he was going to make an effort to show himself as trustworthy, Sylvia would make a show of trusting him.

And she also wasn't going to trust him for a moment. There was no way Mal Dakis, the First Voice of the Kozun and the unquestioned secular and religious leader of the Kozun Hierarchy, had sent someone to La-Tar who was as apparently blunt as San Taval was pretending to be.

San Taval fluttered his hand in the air.

"I have reviewed them," he conceded. "Of course, my communications home are quite limited, and some of your proposals are outside my scope."

Sylvia waited.

"We will, of course, be contributing vessels to your Twelfth Fleet," Taval continued. "The proposal that we position our ships in the Satra System to avoid offending the Cluster's sensibilities is... offensive but acceptable. We accept that our allies are potentially overly sensitive to the presence of Hierarchy warships in their systems."

Even in Satra—a red giant system a single skip from La-Tar—Sylvia knew the Cluster would be watching the Hierarchy like a hawk. They had a permanent scout presence in most of the key skip nodes around their worlds—systems the Hierarchy had formally acknowledged their ownership of.

Several of those systems would be key trade routes if the Ra Sector ever managed to fully get a new order into place. The Hierarchy's concession of them had been far from meaningless, if cheap in immediate costs.

"But you don't know what vessels yet?" Sylvia asked.

"As of the last courier, it had not yet been decided," Taval told her. "We, of course, do not have as regular a communications cycle as you do."

The Peacekeeper Initiative had *declined* to put a permanent postal station in Kozun space—and Sylvia wasn't signing off on giving drones to the Hierarchy just yet. They'd develop their own courier drones soon enough, but they *hadn't* earned humanity's trust enough to get the UPA's.

The small five-crew courier ships they were using were a decent alternative, at least.

"But you have some idea?" Sylvia prodded.

"I am not privy to the military discussions of the Hierarchy's commanders," Taval said genially. "You will know when I do, Ambassador Todorovich."

Somehow, she doubted every word of that.

"I will rely on that, then," she conceded. "And our other proposals, Envoy?"

"I have no authority to engage in the particulars of those proposals," Taval told her. "Trade, military cooperation, technology exchange...these are all outside the scope of my authority. I am solely here to coordinate our promised alliance against the Drifters."

He even managed to tell her that with a straight face, though his control of his microexpressions wasn't what he thought it was. He had more authority than he was pretending, but his *job* was to draw out the expectations and timelines on everything.

San Taval's job was to never say no...or yes, for that matter. Sylvia suspected he was *very* good at it.

"I see, Envoy," she said calmly. "It is a shame that the Hierarchy has limited your authority so. It almost renders your presence here a waste of resources."

She caught him by surprise, and he choked down a chuckle at *her* bluntness.

"We work within the limitations we must," he finally told her. "The Voices control most of our foreign policy directly. This worked better in the age of instantaneous communication, but habits do not change easily."

"The Hierarchy only had instantaneous communications as a nation for, what, a year?" Sylvia asked.

"Habits are formed more easily than lost," he said with a chuckle. "I am sure you understand."

"Perhaps," she allowed. "I must still poke on one last proposal before we decide this meeting has been a complete waste of both our time."

"Ambassador, meeting with you is never a waste of my time," San Taval told her. "The relationship between our nations is fragile and frayed. It is one of my first duties to rebuild that connection between Terran and Kozun."

"That is promising to hear," Sylvia said. The whole conversation was a fascinating dance. She wondered how many people had underestimated San Taval and ended up in deep trouble in the past—his presence there suggested that many of Mal Dakis's opponents had underestimated him.

"And leads to the final question," she continued. "We understand that the Hierarchy is attempting to extricate itself from its extensive collection of wars. As with the La-Tar Cluster, we are prepared to act as neutral mediators in those conflicts."

"I did forward that offer on to the Voices," San Taval said. "And I did receive a response, Ambassador. As I believe you are aware, we have in fact succeeded in ending most of those wars on reasonable terms."

The Initiative and the UPA were now in contact with most of the people the Kozun had been fighting. From Taval's tone, the Kozun were well aware of that.

"My understanding is that you still have several *major* conflicts remaining," Sylvia told him.

"You mean the war with the Enteni and the Eerdish home-worlds," he replied. "Their alliance has proven problematic for us, yes. However, based on our peace with the La-Tar, we do not believe we can *afford* your mediation."

Sylvia held his gaze for several long moments. The peace with the La-Tar Cluster had been bought by the Hierarchy admitting their crimes, conceding multiple contested uninhabited systems, and paying a significant indemnity.

The UPA did not, as a rule, recognize the transfer of sovereignty by conquest. They had a *tentative* agreement in place to recognize the Hierarchy's control of its conquered worlds so long as a number of criteria around internal autonomy were met within a year.

Apparently, the Kozun weren't enthused with being forced to concede everything they'd won in a second war. But that meant they were assuming they were going to get to keep it anyway...

"That is, of course, the Hierarchy's choice," she told him. "A risky one. The Hierarchy, like the UPA, faces the threat of the Drifters now."

"We believe we can find an appropriate balance," Taval told her. "We may change our minds on bringing in Terran mediation, but for the moment, we intend to press the conflict against the Enteni and Eerdish until we find a satisfactory conclusion."

Sylvia nodded gravely, her face showing none of her thoughts as she considered what that meant.

"We understand," she told him. "The offer, of course, will remain open. So long as we are on friendly terms with the Hierarchy, it is in our interests to keep the Hierarchy from wrecking themselves."

SYLVIA WAITED until they were back in the—heavily secured by her Marines—car before saying anything. She didn't trust the Kozun not to be eavesdropping on even the encrypted radios their internal networks could use to communicate.

"That mu'dak," she finally snapped when it was just her, Leitz and the bodyguard.

"Em?" Leitz said carefully. "He seemed decent."

"Oh, he did, didn't he?" she observed. "His job, Leitz, is to make us feel nice and comfortable while the Hierarchy slides a knife into our back—and he is very, *very* good at it."

"What do you mean?"

"We're getting two ships for Twelfth Fleet," Sylvia told him. "*Vessels*, plural, but barely. They're focused on that *appropriate balance*. Now that they've wrapped up all but one of their wars, the Hierarchy is going to dump fighting the Drifters on us while they press their war against the E-Two."

Leitz was silent for a moment, considering everything that had been discussed.

"And he's going to stretch out everything as long as he can before he says anything specific, isn't he?" her chief of staff finally said.

"Exactly," Sylvia agreed. "The Kozun were always risky allies to take on. We *knew* that, but we also didn't want to fight them, and the Drifters attacked us all.

"The truth is they don't *have* any useful capital ships left, so unless they're sending us entire *squadrons* of escorts and gunships, they can't really contribute to Twelfth Fleet's firepower and they *know* it," she admitted. "So, they'll send a token force, because they know it won't matter, and focus their real strength on winning the war we want them to stop fighting."

"And we can't stop them fighting it unless they let us," Leitz concluded. "And he sits there and smiles and makes us trust him, I take it?"

"He will blame every thing that looks out of line or remotely untrustworthy on his superiors," Sylvia said. "But I bet you five credits that he already knows *exactly* what they're planning to send to Twelfth Fleet."

Leitz nodded. The trip to their own embassy was almost over, and he glanced out at the La-Tar Cluster guards outside the car as they slowed.

"Do we rely on the Cluster, then?" he asked.

"We rely on the three carrier groups the Security Council decided to commit," she said. "Because the Cluster has to watch the Kozun, which means they can only spare a handful of ships.

"We knew we were only getting a nominal commitment from the Cluster," she continued. "We figured they'd end up matching the Kozun contingent, because Kozun ships with us weren't ships that could threaten them.

"But if the Kozun only send a handful of escorts—or, cutting *vessels* as narrowly as they can, two corvettes? That's all the Cluster can risk sending, too."

"Then it's a good thing we got three carrier groups, I guess," Leitz said grimly. "I wish we could resolve this without a fight, Em Ambassador."

The car slid to a final halt inside their compound, and Sylvia's face fell back into her normal calm mask.

"We can't," she told her chief of staff. "We *need* the galaxy to know that our ambassadors cannot be touched. The BGO tried to kill me. Even if *I* am prepared to let that go—and I could be convinced—the UPA *can't*.

"Or our entire plan out here comes down in flames."

CHAPTER NINE

THREE DESTROYERS HUNG IN EMPTY SPACE IN THE NOHTOIN System, their images the backdrop to everything Henry Wong thought or did. Right now, a wallscreen behind him was showing the ships in formation above Nohtoin's star.

"Where are we at?" he asked his people, looking around the conference room. His actual *staff* was only two people, Eowyn and Chan, which brought Ihejirika in as an extra set of eyes and brains.

It was still a small group—one that fit in the breakout conference room attached to the flag officer's office. It had the wallscreen and the holoprojectors for their work and shared an automated drink system with the office itself.

Four coffees sat on the small black table as Henry stood in front of his team and looked back at them.

"The Drifters clearly did not think that skipping through a pulsar was enough to cover their tracks," Eowyn told them. "They spent at least two days laying false trails all over this system, and sorting out truth from deception took a while."

A holographic map of the Nohtoin System appeared above the table.

"We are now ninety percent certain the Convoy skipped here." One of the skip lines to Eerdish space flashed. "That would take them to the Otradis System, which is a red giant that acts as a central transfer point for much of the area the Eerdish now claim."

"Which makes following them one step too far, per our orders," Henry said grimly. "I have no intention of risking a diplomatic incident with the Eerdish. We were hoping the Drifters would try and avoid Eerdish and Enteni space."

"If Otradis is as important as that, there's probably a sentry post there," he noted. "So, the Drifters made direct contact with the Eerdish. That could be a problem."

"They'll be spinning some kind of story about us," Ihejirika agreed grimly. "And given that the Eerdish and Enteni are at war with the Kozun..."

"Us working with the Kozun looks bad," Henry agreed. "The plan was always to make diplomatic contact with them in short order, but it looks like that will need to be accelerated."

He shook his head.

"Ihejirika, I'll want the Navigation teams to set up the fastest course back to La-Tar," he told his flag captain. "We'll be coming back here—or at least to Eerdish space—soon enough, so let's keep an eye on anything that might be of use. For example, nailing down that pulsar's skip sequence."

"Yes, ser," Ihejirika confirmed.

"Should we leave someone here?" Chan asked. The communications officer's role in the meeting was mostly to act as a glorified secretary, but Henry was perfectly willing to consider their input as well.

"If we had a full squadron, I'd consider it," Henry replied. "With only three ships—and with the *Cataphracts* being a higher concentration of classified tech than anything else I know!—we'll pull everyone back to La-Tar.

"Like I said, we'll be back quickly enough."

His mental network flicked a command to the hologram, narrowing it in on an icon near his ships. That icon marked where the hostile corvette had self-destructed—there wasn't even enough left to make a debris cloud.

"Eowyn, Ihejirika, what did our teams pull out on our friend?" he asked.

"Not much," Henry's operation officer admitted. She took control of the hologram, bringing up a diagram of the scout ship they'd fought. "They did a damn good job of vaporizing themselves, which leaves us with battlefield scans only.

"That's enough for us to draw some conclusions but not enough for me to say anything with certainty."

"Fair," Henry conceded. "What do we know?"

Eowyn nodded and highlighted sections of the diagram.

"As we assessed at the time, she was armed with twelve box launchers with three-shot ready magazines," she reminded them. "Minimal laser armament, only half a dozen defensive lasers.

"She *isn't*, I have to note, a retrofit of any kind," Eowyn said. "Our scans are pretty clear that the box launchers were integrated into her hull. She was designed for a short, high-intensity engagement.

"We've never seen anything like her, to be honest," the Ops officer concluded. "What's interesting is that her engines and styling... Well."

She zoomed the hologram in a bit and wiped away the datacodes and highlights, allowing the other officers in the room to study the sleek lines of the scout ship and the baroque detailing concealed around them.

"She's Kenmiri," Henry concluded. "Artisan-built, too, not just built to Kenmiri designs."

"So are half the ships the Kozun are still flying," Ihejirika pointed out. "And every dreadnought I'm aware of."

"So, she's not a custom job by the Drifters," Henry concluded. "They picked her up from the Kenmiri at some point."

"That's my guess as well," Eowyn confirmed. "As Captain Ihejirika points out, there's a significant number of ex-Kenmiri ships around the galaxy. The only odd part to me is that we haven't seen this class of ship in Kenmiri hands before.

"They had a pretty standard set of both military and civilian ships. They *had* special-purpose units, but we'd never seen their scouts."

"Turns out the Drifters had," Ihejirika noted. "Shame they didn't tell anyone."

Henry chuckled at that.

"We are only beginning to scrape the surface, I suspect, of what the Drifters didn't tell everyone," he noted. The Drifter Convoys had been tolerated by the Kenmiri, acting as semi-illicit merchant convoys providing luxuries and special services across the Empire.

They'd also provided logistical and technological support for the Vesheron rebellions, while remaining officially on the Empire's side. While the Drifters were regarded as part of the Vesheron, Henry was starting to suspect that the *Vesheron* might have been as used and deceived as the Kenmiri in some ways.

"So, they have a class of Kenmiri ship we're not used to that would normally be harder for us to detect and track," he noted. "We saw them from farther away and we caught up with them more easily than they were expecting."

"I can live with that."

"They still know we're looking for them," Ihejirika noted. "They just don't know how close we are."

"And I don't think all of their games are directed at us, ser," Eowyn said.

Henry made a go-ahead gesture as she paused.

The Ops officer returned the hologram to its zoomed-out view of the Nohtoin System and highlighted the routes the Blue Stripe Green Stripe Orange Stripe Convoy had taken around the system.

"Like I said at the start, we're ninety percent sure the main Convoy went here," she gestured at the Otradis skip line. "But we're about seventy percent sure they split off at least two other detachments, ser, that skipped either here or here."

Two other skip lines flashed.

"Those skip lines aren't on the maps we have from the Kozun and the Vesheron," Eowyn told them. "My assessment of their alignment puts them as skipping to stars on the perimeter of Eerdish space.

"Systems where whoever is there can keep in touch with the main Convoy...while not being seen by the Eerdish."

"Interesting," Henry murmured. "Any guesses, Commander?"

The room was silent.

"There may be portions of the Convoy that they don't trust the Eerdish with," Eowyn finally guessed. "The agricultural ships, for example, are critical to their medium- and long-term survival."

"But they also might be hiding something from the Eerdish," Henry noted. "Military ships or...something else."

"I can't see them splitting off defenses when moving into even neutral territory," Ihejirika noted. "Everything the Drifters do is to defend the Convoy. If they're moving the main body of the Convoy through a location where the Eerdish will know where they are... they'd keep all the big guns there to watch their own backs."

"Let's keep that in the back of our minds," Henry agreed. "You're sure that we're seeing a detachment of the Drifters and not another group of ships at a different time?"

"Absolutely, ser," Eowyn told him. "We might be misreading something on how many ships detached and went where, but they were definitely with the rest of the Convoy first."

"Maybe IntelDiv will have some idea once we drop that in their laps," Henry said. "I eyeball it at eight days back to La-Tar for us and five for the drones—using the pulsar. Twice that if we take the long way. Navigation will work up better numbers, of course."

If any of his officers couldn't at least do the napkin math to get the right number of days, he'd be shocked—and disappointed. From the nods around the room, though, at least his key staff could.

"La-Tar is almost starting to feel like home," Ihejirika mused. "At least as much as Zion and Base Fallout, anyway."

"Not quite there for me," Eowyn said. "But you and Commodore Wong have spent far longer out here."

"And if we're very lucky, someday soon we'll go back to swanning around making contact and negotiating trade treaties," Henry told them all. "The Peacekeeper Initiative was never intended to fight a war, after all."

But the price of peace was eternal vigilance—and humanity owed the wreckage of the Kenmiri Empire *something*.

CHAPTER TEN

LA-TAR WAS DEFINITELY STARTING TO FEEL LIKE HOME TO Henry, but he was also willing to admit—at least in the privacy of his own head—that was as much due to *who* he knew was there as anything about the planet or the locals.

It was still always a small shock to return to the system. Every time he came back to La-Tar, things had changed, with the locals throwing every resource they could think of into levering themselves onto their own feet.

The number of freighters in La-Tar orbit was always growing, and a new transshipment station had opened since they'd left on their scouting run. There were now six of the orbital platforms, smaller and more dispersed than the Kenmiri platform they'd replaced...but since the Kenmiri had destroyed the original platform on their way out, dispersal seemed worth it.

Over a dozen small warships, locally built escorts based on Kenmiri designs, hovered protectively over the agriworld as well. Henry knew that industrial nodes were opening in La-Tar's asteroid belts, reducing the central planet's dependency on the factory worlds for technology, but the former industrial planets were a long way from growing their own food.

The Kenmiri slave worlds had been *designed* to fall apart without the Empire. For that, if nothing else, Henry Wong would never forgive the Kenmiri.

"Ser, we've established radio contact with Twelfth Fleet," Chan told him, their voice amused. "Admiral Rex politely *requests* that you visit him aboard *Aeryn* at your convenience."

"It's actually a request, Commander Chan," Henry pointed out with a chuckle. "Admiral Rex is astronomically senior to me, yes, but he's *not* in my chain of command. I report to Admiral Hamilton...and *only* to Admiral Hamilton.

"Get us links with the other Peacekeeper Initiative ships in the system," he ordered. "I'll meet with the Admiral as soon as we're in orbit—you're not *wrong* on the Admiral's priority, after all—but it's more important that we touch base with the people I'm in charge of."

"Yes, ser," Chan reported. "It looks like we've got two destroyers in system, plus the postal station and the ground compound."

"Check in with everyone; make sure there's nothing that needs me," Henry told them. "Shouldn't be, but we've been gone for weeks. Things change."

The courier-drone cycle meant that his news from La-Tar was reasonably up to date, but things could change on *no* notice in his experience.

Henry was responsible for all Peacekeeper Initiative operations around the La-Tar Cluster. That was, including his DesRon Twenty-Seven, eight destroyers, a dozen small stations with courier drones, and a ground facility on La-Tar that supported the UPA Diplomatic Corps embassy.

He was the second-ranked officer of the Initiative, which gave him blanket authority over *all* deployed Initiative ships. Admiral Sonia Hamilton had yet to move forward from the central Initiative base in the Zion System, on the edge of the UPA, which left him acting as her field commander. That hadn't changed since he was commanding one of the Initiative's battlecruisers. Then he'd "just" been the senior Colonel.

All of which made his relationship with Admiral Rex...complex. It would take some careful dancing to show proper respect to a dramatically senior officer while making sure Rex didn't attempt to order around the Peacekeeper ships.

Henry was hunting down the Drifter Convoy for both of them—but the Initiative had a far broader mission out there than Twelfth Fleet did.

✦ ✦ ✦

"THANK YOU FOR JOINING ME, COMMODORE," Admiral Rex greeted Henry as the boarding ceremony began to dissolve. "I appreciate the Peacekeeper Initiative's assistance in Twelfth Fleet's mission out here."

"Your mission is aligned with ours," Henry said calmly. "Shall we speak in private?"

"Of course; my office is waiting," Rex told him. "You know your way around a *Crichton*-class?"

"Enough to find the Admiral's office and not much more," Henry admitted with a thin smile. "*Panther* escorted *D'Argo* on one mission, but I've never actually served on one of them. My time in FighterDiv was aboard *Lancelot*-class ships."

The premier fleet carrier of the UPSF when the Kenmiri had arrived, none of the *Lancelots* had survived the war. Of the pilots serving on them when the first invasion had begun, only twenty-six had survived the so-called Red Wing Campaign.

All of them had painted the center of their pilot's wings red to mark the sacrifice of their fellow pilots—and immediately transferred out of the forward-combat starfighter groups. Henry and Peter Barrie had been the only survivors from their carrier.

Only eleven were left and only four were still in uniform. Half of the people who'd wear red-centered pilot's wings were currently in the La-Tar System.

"Those were good ships," Rex said grimly. His glance at the single insignia on Henry's uniform jacket showed his thoughts had gone the same place as Henry's. "I conned a destroyer at Procyon, Commodore Wong. I'm still breathing because of pilots with that damned red dot."

"Not many of us left who were there at the beginning, ser," Henry said quietly. The war had lasted seventeen years. Outside of the flag ranks and a handful of senior Colonels and noncoms, most of the people who'd started the war were retired, medically discharged, or dead.

"Some of us have to be, though," Rex told him. "Some of the younger crew and officers...they never served in combat in their own space. It shows, too often, in my opinion."

They reached the door of the Admiral's office, which slid open to a command from Rex's internal network.

"That's what Twelfth Fleet is about," Rex said as he gestured Henry in. "Your Peacekeeper Initiative is about helping the people out here. *My* job, Commodore, is to make sure we never again see enemy warships in the United Planets."

IT TOOK the office system a minute or so to produce coffee for both flag officers, time Henry took to subtly inspect Admiral Rex's office. The space was designed on much the same principles as his office aboard *Paladin*, except for being four times the size.

Fleet carriers had a lot more space to spare than destroyers, after all.

The desk and automatic drink equipment were the same, as were the wallscreen and the powered bulkhead that would open to reveal the breakout meeting room. One wall was covered with a bookshelf split into unitized display cases, each of which held a detailed model of a ship.

Henry recognized several of them, including *Aeryn* herself, and realized that the models were of each ship that Rex had commanded or flown his flag from. The top left box, however, was for the first portion of Admiral Rex's career and held...

Henry had to swallow an outright laugh. The top corner, celebrating Rex's early days as a *GroundDiv* officer before becoming a GroundDiv assault transport XO and then a destroyer skipper, held three highly detailed five-centimeter-tall figurines of UPSF power armor—and roughly a dozen simplistic green plastic army men.

Rex laid the coffees on the desk and grinned broadly.

"I see you spotted the army men," he noted. "They were a gift from my last platoon sergeant when I accepted the posting on *Bernadette*. He said I'd always have backup this way. They're something of a good luck charm now."

"They appear to be doing their job well," Henry observed. To his knowledge, Rex had never lost a ship in combat.

"That they are," Rex agreed. He took a sip of his coffee. "I know you don't report to me, Commodore, but I was hoping you'd be able to give me a report on what you ran into chasing the Drifters rather than making me wait for the formal papers."

"I can do that," Henry said. He'd expected as much. "It wasn't a particularly fruitful expedition in a lot of ways. The Drifters were avoiding anywhere we know to be inhabited, and trying every trick in the book to lose us."

"Which they failed at," Rex noted. "That's impressive, Commodore."

"The *Cataphract*s have an improved sensor suite over even the *Significance*s, ser," Henry pointed out. "I don't think the Drifters expected us to have the resolution or patience that we did. We held their trail until they hit Eerdish space, as per the standing orders regarding the Eerdish-Enteni Alliance."

"Starting to call them the E-Two around here," Rex said. "But that makes sense. The Drifters guessed we'd tread lightly around the E-Two, though?"

"Not really guessing," Henry said. "They know us. Better than anyone, I think. We relied on Drifter support through the entire war. Research, tech, fuel, munitions—all of it came from Drifter Convoys for a lot of our operations.

"We didn't work much with Blue Stripe Green Stripe Orange Stripe, but they were all of a one when we had subspace coms." He shrugged. "I think the loss of the subspace network hurt them more than anyone else."

"So, they have a detailed psych profile on the UPA, you figure," Rex said.

"Basically. They *knew* we wouldn't risk an incident with the E-Two," Henry said. "In hindsight, we should have figured they'd use that against us and gone out with a diplomatic contingent."

He shrugged.

"By the time I hit La-Tar again, we knew we were too damn far behind them to waste more time," he admitted. "Hindsight is twenty-twenty, but I think if I'd stopped to pick up a Cluster diplomatic team, I might have lost the trail entirely."

"Not my place to judge your choices, Commodore," Rex noted. "That's on Admiral Hamilton—and God help you."

Henry chuckled.

"The Admiral and I go a long way back," he said. "It won't be the first strip of skin she's torn off me if she decides I was wrong."

He doubted it would go that far. It was a question of judgment, always, and he'd made a call. It had made sense at the time, and he knew that would be enough for Hamilton.

"What may be relevant to Twelfth Fleet is that we ran into something interesting," Henry told Rex. He transferred the files on the Drifter scout ship from his internal network to the Admiral's network.

"The Drifters seem to have at least one Kenmiri ship of a style that's not in our files," he said. "I'd almost say she was built as a commerce raider, except the pre-Fall Kenmiri would never have needed one of those.

"She makes a good sentinel and scout, as we saw, though they underestimated both the speed and the sensor range of my *Cataphracts*. We ran her down and disabled her, but her crew self-destructed her before we could capture her."

A hologram of the ship appeared above Rex's desk and the Admiral studied it in silence for a few moments.

"Self-destructing is outside of normal Drifter protocols," he noted.

"They've been known to do it," Henry countered. "During the war, I saw it happen at least once when they were determined to make sure the Kenmiri didn't connect them back to their Convoy.

"They needed to make sure the Kenmiri thought they were neutral."

"While they were stabbing the Empire in the back," Rex said quietly. "Golden Lancelot would have been *impossible* without the Drifters. They were the only people who saw enough of what was going on to realize what we were doing.

"The rest of the Vesheron were like us field officers: they knew the part they were involved in. But the Drifters...they knew we were committing genocide. And they made it possible."

"Against people who thought they were reliable allies."

"It's a bit damning when you look at it that way, isn't it?" Henry asked. He shook his head. "It's easy to accept treachery when it's against something as clearly monstrous as the Kenmiri Empire was to us, but then I have to worry about what they're doing *now*."

"We'll know more when this is over, one way or another," Rex promised. "My orders are to neutralize the BGO Convoy as a threat by whatever means necessary. This *ends* with GroundDiv troopers on BGO ships, Commodore—because while God knows I will *not* be involved in another genocide, I also trust these people as far as I can throw this carrier!"

"I can't argue that point, ser," Henry agreed. "What does our next step look like?"

"The plan hasn't changed, Commodore. We need to locate the Convoy and then we take Twelfth Fleet against them." Rex shook his head grimly. "The assessments I've seen of the E-Two tell me that Twelfth Fleet can take them—and Ambassador Todorovich's reports suggest that if it comes to that, the Kozun will gladly work with us."

"That is not the plan," Henry said. Starting a war with the Eerdish-Enteni Alliance—the E-Two—would be directly counter to the Peacekeeper Initiative's goals.

"No, it's not," Rex agreed. "But if it comes down to it, Commodore Wong, my orders are clear. The betrayal of a diplomatic summit and the attack on our ambassador *must* be punished. We *want* to be friends with the E-Two.

"But if they refuse to allow us to pursue the people who attacked *Raven* and Ambassador Todorovich into their space, they will be brushed aside with whatever force is necessary."

CHAPTER ELEVEN

THE PEACEKEEPER INITIATIVE COMPOUND ON LA-TAR WAS A fortified camp roughly thirty kilometers outside the city limits of La-Tar. When Henry and Commander Alex Thompson had selected the location, there had been exactly two criteria: firstly, to put it far enough away that they weren't imposing on the sovereignty of their ally—and secondly, to make *very* certain that the city of five million souls was under the protective umbrella of the surface-to-space missile batteries that guarded the Compound.

The prefabricated defensive installations still loomed over the rest of the compound. Adding to the *loom* factor was one of the Kozun Guardian platforms that the locals had captured and loaned to the Initiative. The surface-to-space laser on the platform had proven capable of burning through even the gravity shield of a UPSF battle-cruiser that dared to enter planetary orbit.

Henry had *vivid* memories of that particular experience. He was delighted to see one of the big mobile guns on his side.

The area between the two sets of surface-to-space weaponry was filled with a walled compound. The walls were nanocrete, prepro-grammed forms assembled from local materials and compressed to withstand nukes. There were no weapons visible on the walls or the corner towers, but Henry knew they were there.

The UPSF Ground Division was still only lightly supplied with energy weapons. While most of the former Kenmiri slave worlds could manufacture energy sidearms and rifles, humanity was barely able to get their energy weapons down to man-portable sizes.

Still, the antiaircraft cannon that tracked the approach of Henry's shuttle were energy weapons, pulsed lasers that would shred the atmospheric craft's armor in seconds, and the guards that met him on the surface were equipped with plasma carbines.

Drifter-manufactured plasma carbines. Bought, in fact, from the BGO Convoy before the summit they'd betrayed.

Henry hoped the guns had been inspected *very* closely before being issued. Shoving that aside, however, he returned the soldiers' salutes and gave Lieutenant Colonel Alex Thompson a firm handshake.

"Welcome to the La-Tar Peacekeeper Initiative Compound," Thompson told him. The big blond trooper could have stepped out of a recruiting poster. He was also directly involved in saving Sylvia Todorovich's life after the Drifters had destroyed the ship they'd both been aboard.

Henry had a lot of warm feelings for the man who'd commanded his GroundDiv contingent aboard *Raven*.

"That's a mouthful," he noted. "It came together pretty quickly in the end, I see."

"GroundDiv can throw together a forward logistics depot in under twelve hours," Thompson pointed out as he gestured for Henry to follow him. "Minimal fortified fire base in three. You gave us a *week*, ser."

Henry chuckled as he looked around. Prefabricated buildings were set up in neat rows, subdivided into streets and blocks by a clear grid pattern. There were even *street signs*.

"I'm guessing the troopers don't call it the La-Tar Peacekeeper Initiative Compound?" he asked.

"L-Pick," Thompson said instantly. "The locals are lucky the troops *like* them. No one has come up with anything scatological for La-Tar or the Cluster itself yet. Not that I've heard, anyway."

"I'm hoping this will be a boring deployment," Henry said. "And they have lots of time to change that."

"So far, the Cluster seems to have all of their planets well in hand," the GroundDiv officer told him. "We were asked to provide some drones to round up the last stragglers of the Kozun special ops on Tano so we could send the buggers home. That's...it."

"Quiet. I like quiet," Henry replied. "If only the SpaceDiv side was looking that way."

"Rumor has it the Kozun are playing games with their promise to reinforce Twelfth Fleet," Thompson said. "Any truth to that?"

"Nothing that anyone has included in formal reports," Henry said. "I'll probably get an earful from Em Todorovich in our meetings later if that is the case, though."

It probably was. His first independent command had been supporting the Kozun Vesheron as they fought for their homeworld's freedom. He *knew* the Kozun—and he knew Mal Dakis, their leader.

The only Kozun he would have trusted without question was dead. The Drifters were going to pay for that...but even with that, he wasn't going to trust Mal Dakis or Mal Dakis's government further than he could throw their planet.

"My people are running security at the embassy, so we've had a few brushes with the Kozun embassy security," Thompson said after a moment. "They're on their best behavior, but those commandos still think they own the place."

"Any problems?"

"Nothing that made it to my ears, so it's been dealt with by my Chiefs and theirs." Thompson grunted. "Whatever they call their Chiefs, anyway."

"We need to be on our best behavior with them, too," Henry noted. "Consider it a project, Colonel."

"I already do," his subordinate replied. "Sooner or later, we get everyone talking to each other and having dance parties, right?"

"Something like that," Henry chuckled.

"As for the other project, everything's ready," Thompson told him.

"Oh?"

"You have a car and driver waiting for you," the GroundDiv officer said. "The driver has the locations of three top-tier florists in her GPS, and I already made a reservation with the best restaurant in town."

He coughed delicately.

"My officers and I tested it out a few days ago; they live up to their reputation," he noted. "They understand the security parameters and were decent at coordinating with our detail. Once you're done with your meetings, we'll try and keep security quiet."

Henry nodded and sighed.

"That's the best you can do, I know," he said. "Arranging a date in these circumstances takes effort and help. Which I appreciate tremendously. Thank you, Alex."

"You and the Ambassador are good for each other, ser," Thompson replied as they reached the armored car waiting for Henry. "I'm glad to see you both happy."

With one final salute, Henry was on his way into the city.

CHAPTER TWELVE

If Henry had entertained any doubts about the mix of respect and affection that the assorted UPSF personnel assigned to him held him in, their near-unanimous support and assistance with his dating Ambassador Sylvia Todorovich would have laid them to rest.

The driver, a GroundDiv Petty Officer Second Class, not only had the location of a florist included in the car's route to the embassy, she'd also looked up flower color meanings both locally and in Russian culture.

With the able assistance of both PO Hailie De Angelis and the local florist—who Henry was certain had undercharged him for the flowers—he'd assembled a bouquet of thirteen deep red local flowers.

La-Tar apparently had quite the tradition of flower-gifting, as detailed as any he'd encountered on Earth, and the florist had insisted on layering the red roses with a local white wildflower that set off the crimson gloriously.

Henry wasn't even sure that Sylvia Todorovich *liked* flowers. It had been an instinctive thought on his part—one that had been reinforced when De Angelis had spent the drive to the flower shop filling him in on Russian traditions and rules around flower-gifting.

As the car pulled into the embassy, he reflected that even if she *didn't* like flowers, it was still hard to go wrong with a gift. He was surprised, though, by how nervous he felt. He'd taken a single battle-cruiser into the teeth of a Kenmiri dreadnought squadron with more calm than he felt facing his girlfriend after several weeks apart.

On the other hand, he'd *faced* those dreadnoughts. So, he took a deep breath and left the car, concealing the bouquet behind his back as he approached the main house.

The door swung open before he even reached it, a GroundDiv trooper stepping swiftly aside to allow Sylvia Todorovich to step outside with almost undignified haste. She looked every bit as sharp and severe as she usually did, in a crisply tailored suit with her platinum-blond hair tied back in an austere bun.

When he met her gaze, however, he knew that every scrap of nervousness had been completely unnecessary.

"Em Todorovich," he greeted her, bowing slightly.

"Henry, if you try to be formal with *me*, I am going to insist on kissing you in front of fifty of your soldiers and my people," Sylvia told him. "Pick your poison."

He laughed, his features splitting in a broader smile than he was used to, and then produced the bouquet as they stepped within reach of each other.

"As you insist, Sylvia," he murmured. "For you."

For a few seconds, even her sharp-edged features softened as she smiled brilliantly.

"Really?" she asked, an entirely out-of-character near-gasp. Then she shook herself and held out a hand for the flowers.

Henry passed them over and Sylvia buried her face in them, taking in the scent. The smile remained when she looked back up, though she'd regained some composure for public consumption.

"Thirteen red roses," she murmured. "Or as close as you get on La-Tar. How very Russkiy of you."

"I got as far as *flowers* on my own," he admitted. "The rest was everyone around us making sure we did it *right*."

Sylvia chuckled at that.

"Speaking of doing it right, we do have work," she conceded. "With me?"

Nodding, he followed Sylvia—still holding the flowers to her heart—into the embassy house.

It was much what he expected of a building built for the Kenmorad. The doors were designed for beings that were three meters tall on average. The furniture was heavily stuffed and easily able to swallow humans whole. The walls were covered in gold-fili-gree murals of Kenmiri stories.

The Artisan Caste of the Kenmiri would never create something plain when something ornate would do—and they saved their best efforts for their parents. A single queen and consort pairing could produce ten thousand Kenmiri larvae a year, which would develop into Drones, Artisans, or Warriors based on the hormones applied during gestation.

Birthing *Kenmorad* had been a far more demanding process, actually requiring that a specifically treated larva be implanted into the third Kenmorad sex, the Mora. Any Kenmorad triad was seen as parents by any and *all* Kenmiri they encountered.

A world like La-Tar may well have never seen a single triad, let alone a full breeding sect. But the mansions had been built to house and protect them.

The irony of using those mansions to house the allies that had doomed the Kenmiri Empire was not, Henry suspected, lost on the locals.

"In here," Sylvia instructed as they reached a door in the long central corridor.

Henry followed her into what looked like a conference room—but he didn't have a chance to take in much of the space before Sylvia had her arms around him and he suddenly had *far* better things to pay attention to.

They came up for air after a moment, and Sylvia carefully checked that they hadn't damaged the flowers.

"I'll have to find a vase for these," she murmured. "I imagine we have some somewhere in the building. Though I suppose the Kenmorad might not have gone in for those."

"The Kenmorad generally did not go for living decoration, no," Felix Leitz said in a perfectly calm tone from the other side of the table. "If we have any vases, they're going to be ridiculously overdecorated."

He paused.

"I'll send someone into the city for something and we'll make it work until then," the chief of staff concluded.

Henry stepped slightly back from Sylvia and saw that Leitz was the only person in the room, standing next to a locally made table and chairs lacking in any adornment. The Kenmiri-style furniture wouldn't have fit any Ashall or Enteni meeting, he supposed.

Leitz was poking at a trio of datapads on the desk, presumably the briefing files for this meeting. While Henry would have made the trip to see Sylvia regardless, there was actual work they needed to discuss as well—there was a vast gap between getting summary reports on what was going on diplomatically and getting Sylvia's direct personal assessment.

"We're scheduled for about two hours for this meeting," Leitz told them after a moment—probably giving someone the instructions to find a vase via his internal network—"and after that, you're both free for the local evening. I made sure of it," he noted drily.

"My people have made reservations and security arrangements at a local restaurant," Henry told Sylvia quietly. "If you will permit me to take you to dinner after we are done work?"

"I think I'll permit that," she said with a smile. "First, sadly, I'm not sure two hours is going to be enough for us to go over everything. Shall we get started?"

BY THAT POINT, the Peacekeeper Initiative had regained contact with the three homeworlds in the Kozun cluster, the Beren homeworld and—counting La-Tar and the three under Kozun control—seven of the Ra Sector slave-world clusters.

They had five postal stations in the La-Tar Cluster, one at Beren and currently four in the other dependency clusters. Ten space stations maintaining relatively consistent communication with twenty-one inhabited worlds—and they let the Kozun courier service maintain communication with the Hierarchy and its eighteen inhabited worlds.

"Our problem remains more the uncontacted systems than anything else," Sylvia finally told him after spending thirty minutes going over their basic status with each of the contacted worlds. "The Sindic, Orta and Vash Clusters aren't politically unified the way the La-Tar Cluster is, but they are at least feeding all of the worlds and talking to us.

"Eventually, we'll want post stations at all fifteen worlds in those clusters," she observed. "For the moment, we have four. We're starting to run out of resources to assemble a sector-wide communication network."

"In the long run, we'll want to either privatize that or bring the locals in on it," Henry told her. "We want to keep control of the skip drones for now, but that requires *us* to put people on every inhabited planet we want contact with—and that's *sixty-five worlds* in the Ra Sector alone."

"My inclination is to help fund a private corporation to take up a post-office role in the region," she agreed. "That's something we'll need to get on quickly, but for now, I've sent in the requests for more UPSF communications personnel to be assigned to the Initiative."

"Is there anyone I should be making sure my people head toward *other* than E-Two space?" he asked. "We need to make contact with them now, there's no way around that, but there are other planets out there still."

"Your people got a bit distracted by a war," Sylvia said drily. "You're at, what, half the sector?"

"Around there," he confirmed. The catalogs were up to about Ra-258 for system names, though they'd never *use* the number for an inhabited system. "And we're in contact with thirty-nine worlds and aware of the status of twelve more through the Kozun."

The Kozun had given them information on the E-Two Alliance—the Enteni and Eerdish homeworlds and an allied slave-world cluster—and the Trast Cluster, who had managed a defensive alliance against the Hierarchy if not a political union yet.

"Which I trust as far as I can throw this house," Sylvia observed.

"The Kozun or their data?" Henry asked. "I agree with you on both, to be fair."

"Felix?" She gestured to her chief of staff.

"We haven't yet had any chance to validate information on the Trast or the E-Two Alliance that the Kozun provided us," Leitz said grimly. "We *have* been able to compare their information on Beren and the Sindic Cluster versus what the locals have to say."

"How badly are they lying?" Henry asked bluntly. He'd fought alongside the Kozun for years. He *wanted* to trust them—or, at least, specific individual Kozun—but the Hierarchy had not demonstrated a general trustworthiness.

"The Sindic Cluster is relatively close to La-Tar, as a region of five hundred stars and several hundred thousand cubic light-years goes," Leitz noted. "Kozun information on the Sindic Cluster mostly aligns with what the locals have told us. Both sides claim the other lost more ships in the conflict than that side reports, but that's normal.

"Hierarchy forces landed on Zotr but failed to take it," Leitz continued. "The Hierarchy says they made a strategic decision and withdrew with light losses. The *Zotrians* say they basically wiped out the invasion force, forcing the Hierarchy to retreat with empty transports."

"The Zotrians and Sindics have asked us to assist in arranging a repatriation agreement for seventy-eight *thousand* Kozun ground troops," Sylvia noted drily as Henry considered Leitz's words.

"That does suggest that the Zotrians' version is more correct, doesn't it?" he murmured. "Have we had that discussion with them yet?"

"Not in detail," Sylvia admitted. "San Taval has not been as available for discussions as I would like—and far from as cooperative as I'd like."

Henry grimaced. He'd read the names in her briefings and looked up his old mission reports.

"I haven't met San Taval," he admitted. "I did know his sister, but she died storming the prison camp he was held in. A common-enough story then."

Going through the mission reports had been a grim reminder. Over seventy percent of the Kozun fighters, operatives and ship handlers he'd met during his tour with them had died before his tour was over. Maybe a *quarter* had lived to see their homeworld liberated —and he didn't want to check to see how many had died in Mal Dakis's wars of conquest.

"You knew him by reputation, then?" Sylvia asked.

He shook his head.

"*Panther* provided fire support for those rescue ops as one of the last things we did with the Kozun," he told her. "Those prison camps provided Mal Dakis the numbers to actually invade Kozun."

For all of his concerns about the post-Fall Hierarchy, he had to admit that Mal Dakis had achieved the almost-unequaled feat of freeing his homeworld *while the Kenmiri Empire existed*. Henry's battlecruiser had been whisked away to other duties within hours of that victory, but he'd been there for it.

"San Shora specifically chose to lead the assault on the camp her brother was in, but that's all I know about him," he said. "There's a few mission reports from other officers who've interacted with him since, but I assume you've read those."

"I have," Sylvia admitted. "He lost his legs in the assault on

Kozun and ended up serving as a key part of Mal Dakis's transition administration, earning the First Voice's trust. Now he's here, where his job is to *waste my fucking time*."

Henry saw her inhale sharply after the curse and hesitated. That was out of character for her.

"He's spinning things out, I take it?" he asked.

"I am reasonably sure San Taval knows the answers to most of our questions and has the authority to negotiate on the rest," Sylvia said. "He is under orders to hold out as long as he can on any point. They haven't even committed to what they're providing Twelfth Fleet beyond *ships*."

"So, two corvettes?" Henry guessed. From Leitz's concealed snort, that had been the diplomatic staff's guess as well.

"We're hoping for better, but Taval's job is to obfuscate and cover while his government attempts to finish the one war they have left," Sylvia told him. "I don't blame him for doing what he's been told to do, but it makes him irritating to interact with.

"The Kozun, so far as I can tell, believe they can defeat the E-Two Alliance, seizing another seven worlds, two of them *homeworlds*, before finally stopping to digest their conquests," she concluded.

"We've advised them of the terms we'll accept their conquests under," Henry pointed out. "Is there any sign that they're planning on meeting them?"

"Again, San Taval is equivocating," Sylvia said with a sigh. "We have some data."

"The La-Tar Cluster government has infiltrated agents into the Roaf Cluster," Leitz told Henry. "That's helped by the fact that there is a significant Kozun population on the former slave worlds."

Henry nodded. There were seven species homeworlds in the Ra Sector. The fifty-five slave worlds had been set up with massive drafts of workers from those planets—which was why the homeworlds had been allowed to operate with some degree of internal autonomy.

So long as they were willing to hand over ten million people every few years. It wasn't a deal Henry would have taken—but he also knew the Kenmiri hadn't given those races any choice.

"What intelligence the Cluster has provided us suggests that the Kozun *are* actually planning on meeting our terms," Leitz said. "They certainly seem to be implementing administrative structures that would allow for a moderate level of local autonomy, at least on par with the homeworlds under Kenmiri rule."

"That's a low bar," Henry observed.

"Frankly, it's the bar I was hoping for," Sylvia admitted. "Nobody out here knows what a democratic government looks like, Henry. Even most of the La-Tar Cluster basically just swapped out Kenmiri administrators for locals and used the same infrastructures."

"Arbiter Ran's role is still more of a mediator than a ruler," Leitz pointed out. "He's determined to come up with *some* kind of popular mandate for his replacement. We're helping."

Casto Ran had been the Lord Nominated of the Skex System, a Tak tradition where an individual was given dictatorial powers for a specified length of time—with assassins infiltrated into their body-guards to make sure the term limit was respected, one way or another!

Now he was the Arbiter of the La-Tar Cluster and determined to create something that would survive his term in that role.

"I trust Ran further than some of *our* people," Henry admitted. "But he can only commit so much firepower to Twelfth Fleet."

"We're honestly expecting Ran to match whatever the Kozun give us," Sylvia admitted. "So, the dance with San Taval is frustrating—but we're still weeks away from *Chiana*'s arrival with Twelfth Fleet's new fighters."

"And Twelfth Fleet can't deploy until we know where the BGO Convoy went," Henry said. "And that means we need to know what's going on with the E-Two Alliance—which means our next steps are a political question, not a military one.

"Not even a Peacekeeper Initiative one."

That was the meat of the meeting. The briefings and explanations back and forth brought the two of them up to speed on what the other was thinking, but the real task in front of them was the Eerdish-Enteni Alliance.

"The Kozun would be *delighted* if we were to move against them militarily," Sylvia noted. "Admiral Rex seems...a tad too ready to embrace that option, in my opinion."

"Admiral Rex has been a UPSF officer since I was two years old," Henry murmured. "When your entire life is spent working with a hammer, everything looks like a nail. He's flexible enough, I believe, but if we're depending on *his* diplomacy, his words will be backed by fleet carriers."

"And that is a very particular type of diplomacy, isn't it?" Sylvia said. "I do not believe, Henry, that conflict with the Eerdish-Enteni Alliance is necessary or desired. Quite the opposite—I think that they represent a critically important potential ally and counterweight to the Kozun Hierarchy.

"We've already basically agreed to leave the Hierarchy in place," she reminded him. "That means that Mal Dakis and his people are going to be the preeminent power of the Ra Sector for the foreseeable future.

"We'll try to bend the arc of their development toward what we regard as a moral world, but that will be easier to do if they *can't* just overrun everyone who irritates them."

"The more active powers there are in the Ra Sector, the more the Kozun are limited, and the better off I think we'll all be," Henry agreed. "Plus, based on our encounters here, I *like* the Enteni. Crazy meat-eating plants that they are."

La-Tar's planetary government had ended up being led by an Enteni, Adamant Will—and Adamant Will's child, Rising Principle, had accompanied Henry and Sylvia to negotiate the alliance that had liberated La-Tar from the Kozun.

They were also the only non-Ashall aliens native to the Ra Sector. Some of the slave worlds would have other non-Ashall people on them—the Kenmiri hadn't always limited the colonist drafts to nearby worlds—but *most* of the Ra Sector's people were Ashall. The Seeded Races.

Folks who could pass for human in a dark alley.

"Me too," Sylvia told him. "Which I think actually gives us our answer, doesn't it?"

"Oh?"

"The La-Tar Cluster has both Eerdish and Enteni diplomats and officers," she noted. "I suggest we organize a meeting with Adamant Will and Casto Ran and arrange to borrow some.

"We assemble a diplomatic contingent of our own people and the Cluster's people, and then we go pay the E-Two Alliance's leaders a visit. Rather than chasing the Drifters in via that pulsar, we just knock on the front door and go say hello to their leadership."

"That does reduce our chances of confusing people or surprising them," Henry admitted. "My inclination is to bring that diplomatic contingent and still chase the Drifters in, though. Then we're in 'hot pursuit' and have a clear objective."

"The problem is that everything *they* know about what's going on comes from the Kozun," she pointed out. "And they're at war with the Kozun."

"So, they're going to see us as an enemy," Henry guessed. "And if we don't come through, lights shining and asking to be taken to their leader..."

"They might shoot first and feel bad later," Sylvia said. "I'd like to borrow you and DesRon Twenty-Seven. That way, if we do get permission to hunt, we'll have the hulls and ships on hand.

"Plus, your *Cataphract*s are nice and...awe-inspiring."

"New, shiny and more advanced than anything they'll have seen before," Henry agreed. "You and I and a bunch of La-Tar diplomats? Why does this sound familiar?"

"Because we've done it before," she told him. "*Twice.* I'm starting to feel like we're imposing on the Cluster's goodwill."

"From what Casto Ran has told me, we'd need to do a *lot* more than borrow a few dozen diplomats to actually impose on that account," Henry said. "They may have saved themselves in the end, but we *did* help. A little."

"Hopefully, they'll be willing to help us help *everyone*," Sylvia said. "I'd very much like to end the damn war between the Kozun and the E-Two, Henry, and having coms with both sides is definitely the first step to that."

"No," he countered quietly, considering the situation with a sad smile. "The first step is talking to the E-Two without getting shot. Let's go with your plan."

"All right. If that decision is made..." She smiled brightly. "I believe I was promised a date, Commodore?"

"I do believe you were," he agreed, letting her smile infect him. "Felix, do we have that vase yet?"

CHAPTER THIRTEEN

THEIR SECURITY TEAMS WERE TRYING TO BE COVERT, BUT Henry had spent too long coordinating with GroundDiv protection details to miss the presence of the troopers around them. Their car was armored and protected, a slow beast that wound its way through the city unimpeded.

The car that preceded them didn't *look* like it was unusual, but Henry recognized the special communications-and-sensor array in the back seat. There were two more—that he saw—in the traffic around them that were also part of their convoy.

Still, that was security being subtle, and they reached their destination without difficulty. The restaurant was tucked away in a warehouse district and had clearly once been concealed from Kenmiri oversight.

Now a large sign had been hung on the front of the building proclaiming it THE FIRST KITCHEN in Kem, and staff in long formal tunics were organizing a crowd of waiting guests. De Angelis pulled the car into a space that was waiting for them, and one of the uniformed staff was waiting to open the door.

"After you, Sylvia," Henry told her with a smile.

"Em Todorovich, Em Wong, your table is ready," the staffer told them in Kem as they stepped out into La-Tar City's evening sun. "This way, please?"

Henry restrained himself from correcting the address—the long-tunicked Eerdish knew who he was, but tonight they were both theoretically civilians. Just lovers on a date.

A date that was currently keeping at least twenty security troopers busy. He shook his head at that and offered Sylvia his arm.

"What is it?" she murmured, stepping into his side.

"Just recognizing the sacrifices made to give us a relatively normal night," he told her. "Better to realize it's happening and appreciate it than take it for granted."

"Agreed."

Their guide led them past the waiting line and into the restaurant. Henry heard desultory complaints in at least four languages from the crowd—and while he didn't hear the Kem part clearly or understand the other three tongues, he could guess at the content.

"Why do they get to go in?"

"Because they have a reservation," the bouncers would reply, soothing ruffled feathers while still not giving a centimeter.

Inside, the First Kitchen looked like exactly what it was: a warehouse space that had been converted into a restaurant. Faced with the limitations of their space and the original need to hide operations from the Kenmiri, the renovators had leaned in to it.

The ceiling was at least six meters above them, with clear, exposed rafters. The tables were utilitarian, with seats that could be easily swapped out for species with different geometry. Light fixtures hung from the rafters above each table, providing islands of soft, brighter light in an overall dim illumination.

Henry didn't get much of a look at the main floor of the restaurant, as their server led them toward a section at the back where multiple entire platforms, each presumably holding a table and a set of chairs, were elevated above the main floor for privacy and security.

Their guide tapped a command on a concealed wrist-mounted

computer, and a stairway folded down from the most isolated platform. He then stepped aside and gestured for them to go up the stairs.

"This is your table, Em Todorovich, Em Wong," he told them.

Sylvia led the way up the narrow stairs, with Henry two steps behind. Despite their being both collapsible and flimsy-looking, there was no sway to the stairs as they walked up.

There were only two chairs at their table, placed close enough together that they'd be able to touch hands. Dinnerware was already waiting on the table, placed on decorative hand-woven mats that offset the utilitarian white table perfectly.

The platform itself was surrounded by a short wall of one-way glass. They could look out over the entire restaurant, but no one could see them. Henry couldn't stop himself glancing over the surrounding elevated tables to confirm his initial suspicion.

There were six elevated tables in total, the prestigious private spots in the most prestigious restaurant in the capital city of five star systems. Theirs was the highest, allowing him to get half a look into the others. Two were empty, and the "diners" in the other three were *definitely* GroundDiv security details dressed up in local clothes.

Henry chuckled and took his seat. So far, the only thing on the table to actually eat or drink was water, so he took a sip of that.

"The other private tables are our security?" Sylvia murmured.

"Got it," he confirmed.

A dark-purple-haired Sana waitress appeared at the top of the steps a moment later, her tusks gleaming in the light. It took Henry a moment to realize that the young woman's tusks had been capped with silver.

"Em Todorovich, Commodore Wong," she greeted them in smoothly fluent Kem. "I am Lotansa, and I will be handling your meal and needs tonight."

She produced a green glass bottle from behind her back and placed it on the table.

"We have sourced a bottle of Terran Merlot for you this evening," she told them. "I have a listing of our other beverages if that is unsatis-factory?"

"No, that is fine," Henry said after a glance at Sylvia. He suspected that the chefs at the First Kitchen had done everything they could to curate a complete experience for them—both he and Sylvia were important to the people of La-Tar.

Saving people from slavery tended to do that.

"We also have a set menu specifically created for the two of you," Lotansa said a moment later, confirming Henry's suspicion. "Our chefs have studied Terran cuisine and taste profiles and, ah, experimented on several of the officers from your embassy."

"I will inform Lieutenant Colonel Thompson that his efforts are appreciated," Sylvia said with a smirk. "We would be delighted to have the set menu, Em Lotansa. And the Merlot."

She shared a glance with Henry.

"Who is paying for this?"

"Arrangements were already made with the Initiative Compound," Lotansa told them. "My aunt, General Kansa, was barely too late in her attempt to cover the costs."

"I see," Sylvia said carefully.

"Everyone at the First Kitchen is determined to make this experience as perfect as we possibly can, Em Todorovich," Lotansa told her. "If there is anything I or any member of the staff can do, you have only to ask."

"I think we are going to be fine," Henry said. "You appear to have a plan, Em Lotansa. Carry on."

The young woman—apparently the niece of an officer Henry knew from another of the Cluster's worlds—bowed and poured the wine before leaving down the stairs. The steps weren't visible from where he was sitting, but he *heard* them retract to underneath the platform.

He toasted Sylvia.

"We appear to have made an impression, my love," he told her in English.

"That we have," she agreed, smiling as she clinked glasses with him and took a sip of the wine. "You know, most people hold off on that word."

"Love?" Henry asked. He snorted. "It takes me a year to get to know someone enough to decide they're attractive. I think I can justify rushing the first steps of the relationship."

"I'm not complaining," Sylvia said. "Just observing...my love."

He smiled and took his own first sip of the wine. Then he paused, blinking at the bottle.

"This is terrible, isn't it?" he whispered to his girlfriend.

"Oh, yes," she agreed brightly. "I don't know where they got it, but the bottle *might* be ten credits in a store on Procyon. Someone *robbed* the First Kitchen when they sold them this."

Henry considered the bottle.

"Want to bet the food is matched to the taste of the wine?" he asked.

"No bet," Sylvia told him. "On the other hand, that gives the Kitchen's chefs a chance to redeem the wine."

"And the wine a chance to destroy everything they make," he observed. "I wasn't expecting dinner to be quite so much of an adventure."

"Henry, you took me to a restaurant on an alien planet with alien cooks. Dinner was *always* going to be an adventure." Sylvia's smile barely managed to soften her severe features, but it definitely managed to soften Henry's heart.

"We'll be fine."

CHAPTER FOURTEEN

SYLVIA TODOROVICH WAS FEELING QUITE PLEASED WITH herself—and Henry Wong, for that matter—the following morning. It had been a *very* good night, even if she now had to face the realities of her actual job.

Arbiter Casto Ran ran the still-under-construction administration of the La-Tar Cluster from a newly built office building on the outskirts of La-Tar City, closer to the spaceport than anything else.

He met Sylvia and her Commodore in the main lobby, smiling broadly as their three security details met and intermeshed around them.

Ran was a tall Tak, an Ashall with pale red skin and white head tentacles instead of hair. He wore a plain black uniform with no insignia and bowed slightly as Sylvia approached.

"Ambassador Todorovich, Commodore Wong, it is always good to see you both," the Cluster's interim head of state greeted them in Kem.

"And to see you, Arbiter," Sylvia replied. "I appreciate you making the time for us on such short notice."

She'd freely left it to Leitz to organize the meeting while she and Wong had their date night. After being separated for a month, she was willing to lean on her subordinates to get her lover to herself.

"There are few people who have done as much for the Cluster as you two have," Ran told them. "Come. I doubt this is purely a social visit."

"Is Rising Principle here?" Henry asked. "This will involve your diplomats as much as anyone else."

"They are on their way," Ran said. "Their parent needed them for business of the planetary government this morning. They will join us shortly.

"Please, come."

CASTO RAN'S office was on the third floor from the top of the tower, putting him barely twenty stories above the ground. It wasn't even a corner office, providing three interior walls that Ran's people had covered with military-style displays allowing the Arbiter to track all of the reports about the Cluster he led.

Casto Ran had been a Vesheron not-quite-pirate during the era of the Empire. He'd ended up in the Skex System when the Empire had fallen and had put his three ships at the disposal of the local rebels as they took control of the industrial world.

They'd swiftly turned around and made him their leader. Everything that had followed suggested that had been one of the better ideas Henry had seen in his lifetime.

"Rising Principle will be a bit longer than I had hoped," he admitted, stepping past his large-but-utilitarian desk to stand by the window. "I will continue to keep myself out of the current issues until they ask for my help.

"The Cluster government will not survive long if we start interfering and micromanaging."

"But you know what is going on?" Sylvia asked, amused.

"Of course," he agreed. "I cannot mediate their conflicts if I have to trust their information, can I?"

Sylvia's impression was that Ran had friends and operatives layered throughout all five of the system governments of the Cluster. He was inevitably best informed about La-Tar, but she suspected only communication delays kept him less informed than the local governments on the other worlds.

"Have you guessed what we need?" she said. She figured Ran had more than enough information to put together the situation.

"I am not certain," the Arbiter told them. "But the desire to include our diplomatic corps, such as it is, combined with the ongoing presence of Twelfth Fleet and the return of Commodore Wong's squadron... There are clear signs, I believe.

"You have most likely determined that the Drifters have entered the stars claimed by the Eerdish-Enteni Alliance and would like to borrow Enteni and Eerdish diplomats to help smooth your way.

"Am I correct?"

"Yes," Sylvia confirmed with a swift glance at Henry. "We suspect, given our alliance with the Kozun, that the Enteni and Eerdish may well regard us as potential hostiles. Entering their space without being extremely careful and diplomatic could easily result in a conflict none of us want.

"The assistance of diplomats from the La-Tar Cluster as both heralds and cultural advisors could smooth over troubled waters and clear the way for a joint approach to the threat."

Ran nodded jerkily, turning to look out the window at the city around them.

"It is hard, as someone born on a factory world and who led a factory world, not to hold grudges against the homeworlds," he said softly. "I understand, intellectually, that their seemingly privileged position was simply a more delicate form of slavery, with still-brutal controls and horrific costs.

"But they can at least breathe their own air. Build their own ships. No slave world could do both. The homeworlds possessed the industries and resources to survive even as the Kenmiri left the slave worlds to die.

"And the only homeworld ships we saw in the La-Tar Clusters were those of the Kozun, demanding submission," he concluded. "Seven homeworlds in the Ra Sector, and none, it seems, reached out to help the worlds around them."

"Your own species never had a chance to," Sylvia reminded him. "The Kozun overran Tak before the subspace coms even failed. And the others looked to save their own people."

Ran waved a red hand dismissively.

"You do not need to excuse the failings of the homeworlds or my own cousins to me, Ambassador Todorovich," he told them. "I understand the burdens they faced. It is always too easy, as a leader, to look solely to those you are responsible for. They are your first duty, after all.

"And yet it is when we stand together that we achieve great things. Skex alone could not have liberated La-Tar from the Kozun. None of the Vesheron alone could have overthrown the Kenmiri."

The silence that followed Ran's words was broken by the door to his office opening again. A single figure stepped through, looking like nothing so much as a mobile black Venus flytrap. The massive, fanged maw was open, revealing the eyestalks inside that allowed Rising Principle to see them all.

"I apologize," the Enteni told them. "The delay is-was greater than were our anticipations."

"These things happen," Sylvia said. "We were discussing our needs with Arbiter Ran."

Rising Principle took a seat on the specialized stools designed for their people.

"I am-will prepare to help," they told the others.

"We need a diplomatic contingent from the Cluster to accompany us into Eerdish space, to assist in negotiations with the Eerdish-Enteni Alliance around the pursuit of the Blue Stripe Green Stripe Orange Stripe Convoy," Sylvia laid out swiftly.

"This will provide both us and the La-Tar Cluster with an opportunity to establish long-term friendly relations with the Enteni and Eerdish homeworlds and hopefully clear the way for Twelfth Fleet to pursue the Drifters who betrayed us all."

"There are no systems in the Ra Sector I would not be delighted to have mutual trade and communication with," Arbiter Ran noted. "The more friends we make, the fewer wars our children may have to fight."

"That is-was our duty, yes," Rising Principle agreed. "The Enteni homeworld is-was quite some distance, the far side of the Eerdish world and the Makata Cluster. You can-will traverse to the Eerdish homeworld most easily of the worlds that is-are members of their alliance.

"Your problem is-will be that they will see you as Kozun infiltrators. Even with my-our diplomats, you risk conflict before any words are-can be exchanged."

"That is a risk we cannot avoid," Henry said grimly. "We can minimize it by heading directly to the Eerdish homeworld and transmitting on entry into each system. If we can make contact before the shooting starts, I would hope that between Ambassador Todorovich and your people, we can avoid a fight."

"It is-was possible," Rising Principle agreed. "I believe an Eerdish diplomat is-are your best choice. I have-has a recommendation."

"We would be content with anyone you send with us," Sylvia told them. "We would prefer a team, preferably with both Eerdish and Enteni members."

She wasn't expecting to get Rising Principle themselves. While they were theoretically a Standard of the Council of Supply that ran La-Tar itself, their main role was as the leader of the entire Cluster's nascent diplomatic corps.

"Agree-agreed," Rising Principle said. "We can-will send a team of twelve, including support and some security. The lead diplomat is-will be Yonca, but you know-knew her security chief and lover-partner, Trosh."

Sylvia smiled at the memory.

"I owe Trosh my life," she reminded the others. "He was with us aboard *Carpenter*, as your security chief then, Rising Principle."

"Trosh is-was very good at his job," the Enteni agreed. "Yonca is-was equally good at hers. You will be well aided."

Sylvia glanced at Henry. His tiny, almost-invisible shrug deferred the decision to her.

"I will meet with Yonca before deciding," she told them, "but I do not expect problems. Together, we will help build a better future for this region. I promise."

That was what all of this mess was about, after all. They'd knocked down an exploitative enslaving galactic empire. Now they were trying to help build *something* in its place!

CHAPTER FIFTEEN

Sylvia ended up meeting Yonca at the spaceport the next morning. Henry had already returned to *Paladin*, a decision that would have disappointed her more if she wasn't supposed to follow him within a few hours.

Exactly three minutes before the scheduled time, there was a calmly confident knock on the door of her borrowed office. There were enough GroundDiv troops following Sylvia around everywhere for her to be confident it could only be Yonca—if nothing else, Felix Leitz was also outside.

"Come in," she instructed in Kem.

The woman who entered at her command did not look alien to Sylvia. At all. Yonca was about a hundred and sixty centimeters tall, plump where Sylvia was skinny, and had a pitch-black skin tone that could have as easily come from Nigeria as Eerdish.

Looking for signs that Yonca wasn't human allowed Sylvia to pick out a slight green edge to the darkness of her skin, but the Eerdish could have passed for human to anyone who didn't know what an Eerdish was.

"Envoy Yonca," Sylvia greeted the woman, rising from her chair and bowing slightly. The bow was a Kenmiri tradition but, like the Kem trade language, it served as a handy universal tool for interacting with very different cultures.

"Ambassador Todorovich," Yonca replied, bowing in turn. "I thank you for seeing me. Rising Principle briefed me on what you are hoping to achieve."

The room was empty except for two chairs, and Sylvia gestured Yonca to the empty one.

"Are you familiar with the Eerdish homeworld?" she asked, still speaking in the Kem they shared.

"Not personally," Yonca said. "My parents were from one of the last drafts from Eerdish, however. They raised me in as much of our true culture as they could. Not something the Kenmiri made easy."

"Not as I understand it, no," Sylvia murmured. "You were raised here? On La-Tar?"

"Yes," the other woman confirmed. "I can tell you exactly which crops on this planet can feed which species most efficiently, and which fertilizers each of them needs."

She snorted and shook her head.

"I was raised to be a farmer, but I ended up being the one negotiating between farming communities," she told Sylvia. "When one of the communities came up short on their drafts, the Kenmiri were brutal. We made sure that no one ever did by the time I was an adult, but that meant a continual trading of favors."

The woman's lips twisted. It was a more neutral expression in Eerdish culture than most Terran ones, but her eyes and microexpressions told everything to Sylvia. There was some *old* bitterness there.

"One thing led to another, and by the time the Empire fell, I was coordinating guerilla logistics across a continent," Yonca continued. "That turned into a mediator role for the Council of Supply and then, well"—she gestured around them—"a trade-negotiator role for first La-Tar and then the whole Cluster.

"I hope we can open additional pathways for our goods with my parents' homeworld," she noted. "But I understand that is a secondary goal at best."

"An important one," Sylvia said. "The UPA wants to open communication networks and trade routes ourselves, but we face the obstacle that the Eerdish almost certainly think we are the enemy."

"Entirely likely," Yonca confirmed. "The alliance with the Kozun will be the only thing they are certain of about both the UPA and the La-Tar Cluster. However, the UPA is more likely to have doors opened for them than the Cluster is. A combined approach will benefit us both, but you do not truly need us."

That was an odd negotiating tactic, and Sylvia smiled thinly as she leaned back and studied the Eerdish woman.

"How do you think you will benefit us, then?" she asked.

"The Terrans are known by reputation to the Eerdish from before the Fall," Yonca told her. "They know you as El-Vesheron and they know you fought the Kenmiri. I presume Terran ships probably fought alongside Eerdish ships at times. You are a known entity but not a close friend.

"Those past sacrifices and alliances will buy you time to speak, and it is possible that you will say the right things and keep the doors open," she continued. "The La-Tar Cluster, on the other hand, is a complete unknown to them. They know of our worlds at best as a former Kozun target and at worst as a current Kozun ally—potentially even a Kozun dependency, if the news they get is slanted enough.

"They are far enough away that our prior conflict with the Kozun will open no doors, given our current defensive agreements. But, unlike you, I know Eerdish and Enteni culture and understand the structures and etiquette they are using.

"I know how to sell what we have on offer well enough to keep the doors open so we can negotiate an agreement," Yonca concluded. "They will not listen to me if I show up on a Cluster ship—but I know what to say and you do not.

"Working together benefits us both, above and beyond our shared alliances and objectives."

Sylvia was silent for a moment.

"And what do you think our best-case scenario here is?" she asked.

"We want permission for your Twelfth Fleet to pursue the Drifters who destroyed *Carpenter* and killed several of my friends," Yonca said flatly. "And you probably want to be able to negotiate a peace between the Kozun and the Eerdish, though that will take cooperation from both sides.

"I want that peace as well, and I also want to open trade routes to allow us to sell the assorted products of the Cluster for the things we still cannot produce."

She spread her hands.

"Our objectives are aligned with each other, Ambassador Todorovich," she noted. "And, in truth, I think our objectives are well aligned with the Eerdish-Enteni Alliance's needs. We just need to convince them of that."

"I agree," Sylvia told her. "Is your team ready, Envoy Yonca?"

The Eerdish grinned.

"They have packed their things and are waiting to be called to the spaceport," she told Sylvia.

"Then call them," Sylvia instructed. "Our shuttle is waiting, and the sooner Commodore Wong's ships are under way, the better."

CHAPTER SIXTEEN

HENRY MADE A POINT OF PULLING EVERYONE TOGETHER INTO A virtual conference as they headed toward the Satra skip line. All three ship captains, both of his staff officers, as well as Sylvia and the Eerdish diplomat from the locals.

Most of the members of the meeting were in a single room on *Paladin*, though they'd split the diplomatic contingent over all three ships. None of the *Cataphract*-class ships had a lot of spare space.

Yonca was aboard *Maharatha* and linked in with Lieutenant Colonel Teunissen. Lieutenant Colonel Palmer was linked in alone from *Cataphract*. Henry, Sylvia, Ihejirika, Eowyn and Chan were all aboard *Paladin*.

Yonca was wearing a bulky headset linked to *Maharatha*'s computers and providing her a real-time translation of the English conversation.

"Thank you all for making the time for this," Henry told them. "We're about two hours out from the Satra skip line, which will put us out of contact for an extended period. Nature of the game, but I wanted to lay out some of the situation before us."

He gestured the astrographic chart of the region into the air between them all. The La-Tar Cluster was marked in bright blue. The Kozun Hierarchy, somewhat more vaguely defined, was marked in dark blue. The distinction between *those* two shades wasn't something Henry would explain to Yonca—because it meant that the UPA regarded the Cluster as a *reliable* ally and the Hierarchy as an *unreliable* ally.

Most of the other stars in the region were flagged in various gradations of yellow—neutrals, with the shades selected solely to distinguish between them. The largest of those entities was the subject of their mission, the Eerdish-Enteni Alliance.

"The Ra Sector, people," he told them. "We are here, at La-Tar."

The star was already highlighted and there was a blinking icon marking DesRon Twenty-Seven's location. There were more icons there, marking Twelfth Fleet, individual Peacekeeper Initiative destroyers and Cluster formations.

"The last known location of the BGO Convoy was *here*, the Nohtoin System," he continued. That system flashed. "That system is eight days away if we use the pulsar, *here*, to cut four days off our travel time."

"That definitely has advantages," Palmer observed. "The E-Two should have much lighter defenses on the far side of their territory from the Kozun. We can follow the Drifters' trail and avoid colliding with their defenders."

Henry had already assured Sylvia they weren't going to go that way, but Palmer also had a point. And...part of him was worried. He'd agreed with Sylvia's point, but now he was wondering if he'd agreed to it because it was the right plan...or because it was *Sylvia's* plan.

"That's one option," he agreed carefully. "Let's look at them all before we charge in like bulls in a china shop."

Several star systems flashed green around the limits of the yellow blob marking the E-Two.

"Our most direct approach is *here*," he noted. "Ra-Ninety-Two. It's on a minimum-time course from La-Tar to Eerdish itself. It is not on the front of their war with the Kozun, but it is a red giant I would expect them to have garrisoned.

"Our sneakiest approach is the one that Captain Palmer has indicated," he continued. "We use the same pulsar the Drifters did and enter E-Two space from the opposite direction of the Kozun Hierarchy. That will likely allow us a material amount of time to locate the Drifters before we encounter the E-Two."

"And dramatically increases our likelihood of a firefight with a potential ally," Sylvia said sharply.

Henry carefully didn't look at her. He was turning the options over in his head and he still figured Ra-92 was their best choice. But the thought that he might have gone along with Sylvia's plan just because it was hers left him unsure—and the best answer to *that*, he figured, was to get buy-in from all of his officers.

"Those are the two obvious options," he noted. "Both have pros and cons. Does anyone have alternatives to suggest?"

"Two, I think," Eowyn noted after a moment's thought. "Neither is a *good* idea, I don't think, but I'll throw them out there."

Henry nodded and passed control of the map to her internal network.

"First, we can use our mission as a way to...*influence* Kozun operations," his Operations officer noted. "The last thing they want to do is get Twelfth Fleet pointed at *them*, so they're going to walk on eggshells around us.

"If we transit through *here*, we're coming through the front line between the Kozun and the E-Two," she said, highlighting a star system. "It's only two days longer than going through Ra-Ninety-Two, but if we're successful in making contact, we will likely force the Kozun to suspend operations for several days at least."

"That seems like a fraught plan," Ihejirika pointed out. "We'd be flying *into* prepared defenses in a war zone. That's a good way to get shot."

"It definitely has its disadvantages," Eowyn agreed. "Frankly, I think it's a terrible idea, but the chance to force a temporary suspension of combat ops might be worth it."

"That's worth a lot," Henry allowed. "I'm not sure it's worth risking this squadron, though. Your other thought, Commander?"

Eowyn glanced at Yonca's image, then shrugged.

"If we limit ourselves to the same acceleration ranges as a *Significance*-class destroyer, we have almost no visible heat emissions," she said. "We know they're going to be garrisoning Ra-Ninety-Two. But if we skip in through *here* and *here*, we'll avoid their main forces."

The two systems she highlighted were uninhabited red dwarfs. It would take an extra three days to follow the route versus Ra-92—a system that *definitely* had an Eerdish name Henry's people didn't know—but those systems would have limited military presences, mostly scouts to bring in the nodal fleet from Ra-92.

"Using our GMS at low energy, we have a decent chance of slipping through those systems undetected," Eowyn continued. "We then skip from Ra-Two-Fifty-Two directly to the Eerdish System and present our diplomatic papers."

"We avoid their main defenses, but we still go say hi right away."

That was probably a better plan than trying to make contact via the front line of the E-Two's war with the Hierarchy! It still involved sneaking around in the dark, and Henry was inclined toward only doing that if the Drifters were in play.

"There are a lot of risks baked into sneaking around a neutral nation we want to see us as friends," Sylvia said coldly. "Either sneaking in through Nohtoin or via uninhabited systems both have the same risk: if we are not open about our presence and clearly friendly from the beginning, we risk losing the very friendship and peace this entire mission is about.

"While I accept that there may be military reasons to try something different, this frankly *isn't* a military mission until we have negotiated freedom of passage."

"Step carefully," Yonca suggested, the Eerdish speaking for the first time. The translator was only one-way, so she spoke in Kem.

"These people were not all Vesheron. Many were simply slaves of the Kenmiri and surviving from day to day. With the Kozun attack on their systems, *that* is the image they hold of the Vesheron.

"The old alliance we want to use to open doors is one they see as a source of their current threat. They have been betrayed by Vesheron before. The name may still have positive memories, but if we even appear to be a threat..."

"We throw away our easiest chance at a peaceful resolution and new ally," Captain Teunissen said, returning to English. "I have to agree with Envoy Yonca, Commodore. Anything short of full transparency and visibility risks our mission more than it helps anyone."

"I also agree," Ihejirika said. "Charging in like we know all the answers and everyone else must adapt to our actions is rude at best, dangerous at worst. Our mission is to ask permission. We should do that first, before anything else."

Eowyn chuckled.

"Both of my ideas were terrible," she admitted. "But we were already considering a terrible one with trying to sneak in via the pulsar. We've got to talk to them, people."

A military command wasn't a democracy, but it made Henry much more comfortable with his own decision that his people were on his side. He held up a hand before anyone else spoke up.

"I think that's my decision made, then," he told them. "We will proceed to Ra-Ninety-Two and make contact with the E-Two defensive fleet there. This is, as Ambassador Todorovich noted, a diplomatic mission first.

"Only once we have permission to hunt in the E-Two Alliance's space will we hunt."

He smiled thinly.

"Of course, we will keep our sensors *very* sharp as we head in," he told them. "Who knows what we might find?"

CHAPTER SEVENTEEN

SYLVIA DIDN'T EVEN BOTHER TO KNOCK BEFORE ENTERING Henry's office, riding a storm cloud of anger that surprised her as she barged in. Wordlessly, she crossed to her boyfriend's desk, pulled a chair clear and took a seat.

To her surprise, he didn't object, eyeing her levelly across the desk for a few seconds before sighing.

"I believe I owe you an apology," he told her. "We had previously discussed the strategy we were going to take, and I appeared to have changed my mind."

That cut some of Sylvia's steam out, but she still glared at him.

"If you were going to play sounding board with your people to get them on board, you could at least have warned me," she told him. "I didn't come into that meeting prepared to argue for that position, Henry. I thought it was made."

There were a dozen ways to get to the decision point they were now at, but she'd expected her *partner* to tell her if they were playing Socratic games.

"I thought you trusted my judgment," she admitted after a moment, getting to the heart of her annoyance.

"The question, Sylvia, was never *your* judgment," Henry said, his tone soft. "My fear was around *my* judgment. Whether I had accepted your plan because it was the best plan. Or whether I had accepted it because it was *your* plan.

"I was not certain, so I decided to use my officers as a sounding board to check my judgment." He shrugged. "Unfortunately, this wasn't a planned decision," he admitted. "More a weakness of the moment. I should have warned you somehow, Sylvia.

"Having everyone raise options and knock them down to one is a useful method of acquiring buy-in from my subordinates, but if that was my *plan,* I should have included you in that.

"I did not."

He spread his hands.

"I am sorry," he concluded. "Not everything I do can be shaped by our relationship, but in this case, I allowed my fears around my emotions to undermine our *professional* partnership."

Sylvia was still glaring, but it had lost some of the heat.

"At least you recognize when you fuck up," she said, her tone still chilly but not as sharp as before. She sighed. "Us being an *us* can't get in the way of our work, Henry. If it risks your ability to take my advice and handle diplomatic matters that way..."

"I trusted your advice beyond life itself *before* I realized I loved you," he said quietly. "The confusion is mine, Sylvia. I..." he sighed. "I wish I could promise it won't happen again, but I am human.

"More, I am a military officer and part of my responsibility to my people is to occasionally question my judgment in private to make certain that I am making the right calls."

"Believe me, Henry, I can bloody well question your judgment enough for both of us," Sylvia snapped. "This one was dumb."

"Yes. But the end result is that we have full buy-in to your plan from the officers accompanying us," he pointed out with a ghost of a smile. "Had I thought everything through in advance, this might well have been my plan anyway.

"But had I thought things through, I would have brought you in on that plan."

"That would have been wise," Sylvia said. She glared at him for a moment more, then sighed and waved a finger at him. "Don't do it again, Henry. Can you manage that?"

"I promise to *tell* you what I'm planning in meetings where I need you to play along," he said. "Good enough?"

"It'll have to be," she conceded, shaking her head.

"I don't know if it will help make up for that, but my steward is putting together a dinner for us in the Captain's mess," Henry noted. "And unlike the First Kitchen, *he* knows what wine he's picking!"

CHAPTER EIGHTEEN

"Ser...I think we're being watched."

Henry turned in his chair to look at Eowyn as she spoke quietly.

"What do you mean, Commander?" he asked. "I assume you don't mean our Cluster friends."

They were still in the Satra System, where a trio of Tano-built escorts stood sensor watch. Henry's three destroyers were on their way to the skip line to the Avas System, the first of five skips through neutral and E-Two territory that would bring them to Eerdish.

"When you checked this place out for the Cluster, you saw ghost contacts, right?" Eowyn asked. "I read the report."

"We found the source, though," Henry pointed out. He'd swept the system with *Raven* and a group of Cluster escorts. "A Kozun corvette hidden in an ice rock."

"Except that a bunch of your ghosts were over here, weren't they?" Eowyn tapped a gas giant. "And I just got another ghost there."

"Show me," Henry ordered.

She brought it up on the main display, marking all of the information they have.

"The heat signature is minimal," he noted. "It could just be a heat reflection off a high-metal-content rock."

"It could, yeah," his Ops officer confirmed. "It matches up to a few of the ghosts the locals reported as well, but the full sweep with escorts didn't find anything."

Henry nodded and exhaled slowly.

"Whatever it is, if it's been here for months, it's not a problem for today's mission," he pointed out. "Keep an eye on it and fire off a data packet to the local ships when we hit the skip line. If the Kozun are still playing games, we want to confirm that. Admiral Rex has some sensor shuttles and probes he can use to open up anything that's hiding here."

The descendant of AWACS aircraft, those shuttles were designed to provide targeting assistance to fighter strikes. The six of them could read a newspaper over your shoulder from the other side of a star system, though, so Henry figured they could find a hiding Kozun ship.

"Keep your eyes open, though," he ordered. "That's the kind of thing we want to be looking for." He grinned. "Once we're in E-Two space, past Avas and Ra-One-Sixty-Six."

AVAS, though, only raised more questions. Avas was an M-type red dwarf, never inhabited but named by *someone* whose records were in the UPSF's navigation databases. Those databases weren't so helpful as to name the sources of the names they included.

"Okay, so that's three different locations throwing off wonky sensor signatures," Eowyn concluded after they'd been in system for two hours. "Nothing that looks like a starship, so I'm *guessing* unofficial rogue colony."

"But one of those would have ships of some kind," Henry pointed out. "And we'd *see* those ships, because they'd be completely visible."

"Not if they were hiding from the Kenmiri," Eowyn said. "On the other hand..."

She shook her head.

"What?" he asked.

"We have some of the best sensors the UPSF has," she reminded him. "Better resolution, range, frequency breadth, the works. The estimates I've seen say that we have better sensors aboard these ships than the Kenmiri *ever* had. '

"And all I'm getting are ghosts and anomalies," she noted. "The Tactical officers aren't doing any better. They've all noticed the pattern, but it's nothing we could flag as a threat. Nothing that's definitely a ship, nothing that's even definitely a *space station.*"

Henry nodded slowly, looking at the details of a couple of the anomalies.

"The system flags when we have more than a certain number of anomalous sub-detection signatures, right?" he asked.

"Yeah, that's what pinged us in Satra. And then again here, and I started going into the sub-detection threshold scans. I mean." She waved her hands helplessly. "There's still false positives in this mess," she told him. "All three of my ghost groups could be entirely false positives, for that matter.

"Sunlight on ice and sunlight on iron do a lot of screwing around at these frequencies and energy levels. That's why we *have* a detection threshold built into the software."

"But you don't think it is," Henry said grimly. "This is neutral space, Commander. The La-Tar Cluster doesn't claim Avas. The E-Two don't claim Avas. It's an uninhabited mess that is only a useful pass-through between La-Tar and Eerdish. If Ra-Ninety-Two and Satra were *three light-years* closer, no one would ever come here."

"And because it's a bunch of backwater stars that takes ten days to travel through with nothing of value or interest, there hasn't really been much contact through here."

"Ten days for *us,*" Henry pointed out. "We're pushing four times most ships' cruise acceleration, Commander. Over twenty days for anyone else, with some long and painful skips."

"So, if I were hiding, say, a logistics depot for a stealth scouting program..." Eowyn trailed off. "There's a lot of people those ghosts could belong to."

"Or they could just be ghosts," Henry said grimly. "The fact that we can't definitively call them *anything* is enough for me to want to leave them be for now.

"But as with Satra, let's flag them and record everything," he ordered. "I agree with you, Commander. We're being watched. In Satra, I'm pretty sure they're Kozun. Here, I'm less certain. If nothing else, what I'm seeing here suggests some pretty effective stealth tech."

"I don't believe in stealth in space, ser," Eowyn said dryly. "So, these people *offend* me."

"*If* we're looking at some kind of stealth ship, Commander, what are they doing?" he asked.

She sighed, looking back at the data.

"I'd say they cut their engines as soon as they detected us, except our ghost numbers never dropped in a way that would line up with that. So, either they weren't accelerating to begin with, or they don't think that we can pick them up at this range."

"Your closest ghosts are two light-minutes away," Henry pointed out. "That could be a reasonable assumption against most people if they have stealth tech."

"Yeah." Eowyn glared at the display. "*If* my largest ghost is a Kozun corvette with engines online and some kind of stealth system, she's sinking or redirecting over ninety-eight percent of her heat output. *Redirecting* would assume that they knew where we were, so that's probably out."

"Heat-sinking would also imply they figured somebody was here," Henry observed.

"Depends on how they do it," she replied. "If they discharge their heat sinks at each of their destinations and keep most of their flights short, it's...theoretically possible that they could be sinking all of their heat for their entire flight. Every flight."

"Could we do it?" Henry asked.

She laughed.

"Not a chance in hell," she told him. "You command the stealthiest ships the UPA has ever built, but that's only in comparison. At this range, running at point-five KPS-squared? We'd be underneath most people's detection thresholds...but we'd be more visible than this."

"What about optical examination?" Henry asked.

"I had Bach and her team take a stab at that," Eowyn admitted.

Henry nodded—that made sense, and he had faith in *Paladin's* Tactical team.

"And?"

"Nothing. So, either *I'm* crazy or they've got optical camo on the hull. *That* we can do, before you ask," she told him, "but it's pointless because the heat signature gives you away and, well, for us the gravshield and drive both screw up any visual on us."

"Keep watching," Henry ordered again. "I don't want to detour, but I want to know as much as we can. Someone is out there, Commander, and they're hiding in a way we didn't think they could."

"That is always going to make me nervous."

"Me too, ser."

Henry studied the screens grimly, double-checking the distance.

"And Commander?"

"Yes, ser?"

"If any of those ghosts start heading our way, let me know *immediately*," he ordered. "I don't care what I'm doing. Emergency-ping my network. Am I clear?"

"Yes, ser."

CHAPTER NINETEEN

"Ser, can I show you something?"

With the current level of not-quite-alert, Henry had left the door to his office open. He was still surprised to see Chan sticking their head in.

The Chinese officer was broad-shouldered and heavyset, with their head shaved and subtle makeup to soften their features. Right now, they looked...intrigued.

"Probably," Henry said with a chuckle. "Unless Eowyn's ghosts decide to charge us, it's going to be a quiet trip."

"That's what I wanted to talk to you about," Chan told him. "Do you have a few minutes to walk with me?"

Henry was curious now. That didn't sound normal. With a wave and a thought, he shut down his network's link to his office systems and rose.

"Certainly, Commander," he said. "Lead the way."

Chan waited for Henry to join them, and then set off to the exit from the bridge.

"You know that the first-wave *Cataphracts* still have subspace transceivers, right?" the communications officer asked.

"I recall that coming up, yes," Henry conceded. "They're nonfunctional, but taking them out would be a pain and they don't take up that much space. As I understand, current construction is being done without them."

"Exactly. But *Paladin* has one, and Lieutenant Commander Jackson and I have been experimenting," Chan explained as they walked. "How much of the theory behind it all do you follow, ser?"

Henry snorted. Mehitabel Jackson was *Paladin*'s coms officer—and, along with Chan, one of about five people on the destroyer who actually understood the theory of their late FTL coms.

"I know what it did, Commander, and I know the Kenmiri shut it down," he noted. "I *think* subspace was a three-dimensional space offset from our own?"

"Basically," Chan said. "Subspace is a stable set of three spatial dimensions, except that as we normally track dimensions, they're dimensions seven through nine.

"That level of stability was recognized early in the twenty-second century, but the level of noise in them rendered them useless for anything," the coms officer continued. "Then, shortly after the Unification War, we found three sets of stable frequencies in subspace.

"A lot of math and hair-pulling went into the theory explaining how they existed, because we had no reason to believe they were artificial." Chan sighed. "Now, of course, we know that what we were looking at was a stabilizing carrier signal transmitted from Kenmiri space."

"But we didn't know that then, so we just started using it?" Henry guessed.

"Basically. Now we're researching the crap out of how that stabilization was done and we've realized that, well, it's easier to stabilize a subspace frequency across an entire galaxy than to localize it."

"Hence us accessing the Kenmiri frequencies."

"Exactly."

Chan opened the door to the subspace transceiver facility. There was no one inside, but the systems continued to hum along. They weren't any *use*, but they ran along.

"How does this impact us?" Henry asked.

"Couple of ways," Chan told him. "R-Div has every ship with an operating transceiver running it twenty-four-seven and reporting everything that pings back to them. The data is critical, according to some of the researchers I've interacted with, to learning how subspace looks *without* a stabilizing carrier frequency—which should help us *create* such a frequency."

"I seem to recall something along those lines in the standing orders," Henry said. That kind of order was outside of a Captain or squadron commander's authority and didn't really impact him. They didn't get remembered unless they came up, even with a computer network in his head. R-Div—the UPSF's Research Division—had a wide authority to order low-impact data collection like that.

"On top of that, Mehitabel and I have been poking at the receivers to see if we can find any sensible patterns in the mess," Chan told him. "So, we've been experimenting with the hardware and running pattern-recognition AI through the noise that we're recording for R-Div."

Henry stared at the humming displays around him as Chan's words sank in, then he turned to face his officer directly.

"You found a pattern in subspace?" he demanded. That could be...huge.

"Yes, ser," Chan confirmed. They crossed to one of the consoles and tapped a few commands.

An image appeared in the air between Henry and Chan, projected to their internal networks. It was...nonsensical to Henry, a three-dimensional display of lines and colors.

"What am I looking at?" he asked.

"This is a representation of our current passive receipts of subspace activity in the Avas System," Chan told him. "Notice anything?"

"Not really," Henry admitted. "An incoherent mess."

"Don't worry; that's all I see in this, too," Chan said. "Right now, there's nothing out there. This is subspace's normal, natural state." They shrugged. "Given the variant sizes and not-exact-correlation between our regular three dimensions and the three in subspace, that cube covers about fourteen light-years of space."

"Okay," Henry said. "So, what now?"

"What I'm about to show you is a thirty-six-second clip that our pattern AI picked out," Chan told him. "Watch carefully."

Henry registered the moment the time stamp changed, but the starting point was still just as chaotic as the original video. Then, after five seconds, he saw what the AI had picked out.

A sudden flat disk of solid signal, a pulse that crossed the entire meter-wide cube and stayed that way for ten seconds. Fifteen. Twenty.

Then it was gone, and only chaos remained.

"While I coded that to augment the visibility of the pulse for you, if any of our coms people had been watching the data when that happened, we'd have picked it out," Chan observed. "The AI wasn't necessary. That was *obvious*."

"What was it?" Henry asked.

"That, Commodore, was a time-and-distance-constrained subspace carrier signal," the coms officer said quietly. "Someone stabilized the thirty-two-point-six-six-megahertz frequency of subspace for twenty-two seconds. More than long enough for a compressed data burst."

"When?" Henry said quietly. He could guess, but there was no time stamp on the recording.

"About five minutes after the farthest of Eowyn's ghosts would have picked up the lightspeed signal of our arrival."

"So, we *are* being watched," Henry noted. He pulled up the map of the system in the air as well and looked at their position.

They'd been in Avas for eighteen hours now and were still ten hours from the skip line to Ra-166. That said, they'd only been increasing the distance from Eowyn's ghosts, who had positioned themselves clear of the most likely transit routes through the system.

Going to investigate would add at least two days to their trip—ignoring whatever time actually investigating or dealing with the ghosts would take.

"Who do you think they are?" Henry asked.

"First instinct is Kenmiri, but we're a long damn way from the Remnant here," Chan said. "It might be the Drifters—there's a lot they didn't tell anyone. They might have more information on the subspace coms than they told us."

"It's definitely not the Kozun," Henry said, as much to himself as Chan. "If they had subspace coms, they'd be playing very different games. But there are others out there..."

"We won't know unless we can ID a source," Chan said. "So far, all I can really tell you is that the source was somewhere in Avas. It could have been any of the groups of ghosts Commander Eowyn picked up—or those could even be just sensor anomalies and the transmission was from somewhere else."

"It's not worth turning back, then, especially if we don't know who it is," Henry decided. "Record *everything*, Commander."

"Of course, ser. We already are."

"Then do two more things for me," the Commodore ordered. "First, Avas is now blacklisted in our drone computers. It'll add time to their return flights to the La-Tar postal station, but we *know* Avas is home to an unknown.

"I'm not picking fights without more data, but we are also not sending our mail right through their gunsights."

"Will do, ser," Chan confirmed. "And the other?"

"Get the same receiver modifications and software running on the other two ships," Henry said calmly. "See if you can rig up a triangulation program as well. We definitely can't locate a source with *one* data point, but with *three*... With three, I hope we can.

"And if you can give me a definite source for a subspace transmission, I *will* risk a fight to go say hello."

CHAPTER TWENTY

"You look like the proverbial cat that ate the canary... except I think your canary was poisonous," Sylvia observed to Henry at dinner. The counter was ticking down to the Ra-166 skip, but no one in the squadron was expecting trouble until they made the skip *after* that.

Ra-197 was the first system they'd enter that was claimed by the E-Two, and even that was an uninhabited star they'd claimed for security purposes.

She still figured that Henry was looking particularly pleased with himself, though there was an edge of tension to it all. It might just, she reflected, be that he was probably getting laid tonight—but that hadn't been unusual on this trip.

Both of them had been single for a while before finding each other, after all.

"I probably do," he conceded, his grin settling a bit as he took a sip of water. "We've found some...interesting things in Avas. I don't think they're relevant for our mission to Eerdish, except potentially as negotiating points with the E-Two."

"All right, you've piqued my curiosity," Sylvia noted. "Talk, Commodore."

"And if it's classified and I can't?" he teased.

"If it was classified and you couldn't talk, you wouldn't have mentioned it," she told him. "So talk."

Henry grinned wider, and then his face settled back into his usual professional mask as he considered work.

"Avas is being used as a central base for somebody," he told her. "We don't know who, because their tech is notably ahead of ours in several concerning ways. That's the poisonous part of this canary, love."

"There aren't many people out there with tech ahead of ours," Sylvia noted. That was concerning.

"I know," he allowed. "So, the fact that they're *here* is concerning...but we now *know* they're here and know we can, at least to some extent, detect them. Which is definitely worth something."

"That's fair. Do we try to talk to them?" she asked. Powerful neighbors felt like someone they should try to talk to.

"Right now, I'm betting that they think we didn't see them," Henry said. "They carried on with their activities, assuming their stealth tech covered them." He shook his head, a thoughtful look on his face.

"If they think we missed them, I want them to keep thinking that for now," he continued. "We'll arrange a meeting at a better time for us, I think. You'll get to talk to them sooner or later, my love. Powerful neighbors who hide are scary."

"Yes," Sylvia said drily. "That doesn't seem quite worth the canary expression, Henry."

"They have a working subspace com and we've learned how to detect it," Henry told her. "Which means we are now going to know if these people are around and calling home. They aren't going to be sneaking around our space or La-Tar space anymore, and I have to suspect that they were.

"And because *we* know we can hear them and they don't know we can, we may have a few surprises in store for them."

"Now, *that* explains the canary-eating," Sylvia said. "Do we even know who they are?"

"No," he admitted. "I'm guessing Drifters right now. Or potentially somebody we don't even know—neither the stealth nor subspace com tech lines up with anyone we've met."

"So, trouble," Sylvia murmured.

"Or potential allies," he said. "I mean, I'm *expecting* trouble, but I plan on unleashing you on them." He raised his water glass. "I have faith in your ability to make friends with people I haven't shot."

Sylvia had spent enough nights with Henry by now to know about his nightmares. Internal network control and therapy were holding him together, but her lover was an injured man. Like an amputee with an artificial leg, he could still function and lead, but the injury persisted.

"Don't joke about things like that," she said gently. "We're out here to minimize the shooting."

"That's why we're walking right up to the Eerdish and knocking on the front door," he agreed. "No, I have faith in our mission, Sylvia. These strangers are a concern, but I have faith in our ability to deal with them—one way or another."

"And the Avas System is far enough from everyone not to be a threat," Sylvia observed.

"Exactly. If they were in La-Tar space or Eerdish space, I'd be considering different options," he admitted. "But out here? Out here, I'm going to record everything I can and let them think they fooled us."

CHAPTER TWENTY-ONE

The Eerdish had made certain anyone entering the Ra-197 System knew they claimed it.

"The beacons are positioned at six cardinal points around the star," Chan reported five minutes after they'd skipped into the system. "The message is pretty simple: the Moti System is property of the Eerdish. Settlement, exploitation or violence is forbidden.

"Then, basically, 'If you are friends, proceed to Seppen and speak with us,'" Chan concluded. "From the directions included, Seppen is Ra-92."

"So, the instructions are to do what we planned on," Henry replied. That was always helpful. It hopefully meant that the E-Two forces in Ra-92—Seppen—would be willing to talk before they opened fire.

"Is there anything else here?" he asked, glancing over at Eowyn.

"Red dwarf system. M-one-type star, point-five solar masses," she reeled off. "Four small planets, none habitable or even of much interest to anyone. One gas giant, a potential target for refueling infrastructure but currently unexploited.

"There's an asteroid belt between the planets and the gas giant which, combined with the gas giant rings and Trojans, makes for a decent target for resource extraction." She shrugged. "There are better systems for just about any purpose out there, but this one *is* only a nine-hour skip from Seppen."

"So, less than three days' travel from Eerdish itself," Henry said. "Not convenient, not inconvenient. Worth claiming...like they did."

Any star system contained a near-infinite quantity of resources. Eventually, the easily extractable ones were used up, though—at which point it might become economical to extract readily available resources from another star system for shipment.

"Really, the only value of this system is that it's only a nine-hour skip from Ra-Ninety—Seppen," Eowyn told him.

UPSF doctrine was to use local names for stars once they were known. Henry and his people were already attempting to make the change for Moti and Seppen, but it would be imperfect for a while yet.

"I'm surprised there isn't a picket or something here," Ihejirika said from the bridge, *Paladin*'s Captain looking at something on his own screens. "Other than the beacons, the system is dead."

"If the Eerdish were at peace, they might keep a ship here," Henry suggested. "But they're not. We don't know what their ship strength is, but they've been fighting the Kozun for over a year, and this system isn't on any likely approach vector from the Hierarchy.

"So, they concentrate their forces in Seppen and count on that to stop any approach through Moti," he concluded. "We'll likely see a significant defensive force at Seppen, but they can't spare ships for picketing a star no one really cares about."

"We proceed as planned?" Eowyn asked.

Henry nodded.

"All ships make your course for the Seppen skip line at one-point-five KPS-squared," he ordered. "I don't see anything here to worry about."

⁂

SOMETHING in the back of Henry's mind had him keeping his ships' acceleration down. It was probably pointless—his squadron had spent enough of their trip moving at two KPS^2 that if they *were* being watched, that person knew what they could do.

The empty system had the hairs on the back of his neck standing up, though, especially after everything they'd bounced off of in Avas. The Ra-166 System they'd visited in between had been truly empty, but Henry's paranoia had been sharpened by the ghosts and subspace signals in Avas.

"Ser?" Chan said suddenly—and everything snapped into clarity.

"Commander."

"We have a signal," the coms officer told him quietly. "Subspace carrier signal is live and holding. We can't identify transmissions any more than we could on the old stabilized frequencies, but..."

"It's gone," Chan concluded. "Sixteen seconds."

Henry nodded, studying the map of the star system on his main display. His three ships were the only green icons in that massive expanse of void and rocks. Six yellow icons for the Eerdish beacons.

And someone else was out there.

"Definitely in Moti?" he asked.

"Yes, ser," Chan confirmed. "It's a much lower-strength wave than the original stabilization frequency. I can't be certain, but I'd say we're looking at a range of maybe two hundred light-years—but that's assuming the person you're transmitting to knows what to look for.

"We won't pick this up at more than maybe one or two light-years."

"Same frequencies as in Avas?" Henry asked.

Chan checked.

"Not quite, ser," they said. "We may be able to narrow down the ranges they're using, but I don't think we'll ever be able to detect these pulses at long range. Same-system detection is the best I can offer."

"That can be worked with," Henry told them. "*If* we locate the bugger."

"Pulling in the last data from *Cataphract* and *Maharatha* now," Chan reported. "Jackson is running in her numbers..."

Chan trailed off, their focus entirely on their console for several seconds.

Then a new icon appeared on the main screen, a flashing orange icon in the gas giant's rings.

"Source is on one of Moti-Five's moons," Chan reported crisply. "I don't have names for the gas giant or its moons, but it's the second-largest planetoid in orbit of the gas giant."

"Thank you, Commander Chan," Henry said loudly. "Now get me a senior officer's virtual conference. Get Ambassador Todorovich in as well.

"The situation has just changed dramatically."

IT SOMETIMES FELT like Henry's military career was one percent acquiring new traumas, fifty percent paperwork and waiting, and forty-nine percent meetings.

Today suggested that it was going to potentially be both the last and the first.

His Captains linked into his office virtually over the course of about two minutes. Eowyn and Ihejirika were holding down the watches on *Paladin*'s flag deck and bridge respectively, but Chan had joined Henry in his office.

"What is this about, ser?" Palmer asked.

"Just one moment, Captain," Henry said, checking his network. "We need one more person for this."

Before Palmer or Teunissen could ask who, the door to Henry's office slid open and Sylvia Todorovich entered.

"Take a seat, Ambassador," Henry suggested. There were enough chairs in his office for everyone to be physically present, even if less than half of them were.

"Officers, Ambassador, we have a problem and an opportunity," he told them once Sylvia had seated herself—and leveled a questioning gaze on him.

"You were all briefed on the discovery in the Avas System," he continued. "We know there was someone present with stealth ships we couldn't quite localize—and we also know that someone is in possession of a new iteration of the subspace communicator.

"We set up each of your ships' subspace communicators to duplicate the work that Commander Chan and Lieutenant Commander Jackson had done to *Paladin*'s systems," he reminded them. "Today, that work has paid off in spades.

"We have not detected anything in the Moti System. There are no stealth ships, no colonies, nothing here except for the Eerdish's beacons.

"And ten minutes ago, Commander Chan detected a subspace-com transmission," Henry finished. "Thanks to the updates to everyone's systems, we have isolated the source of the transmission to Moti-Five-Six."

He gestured and a map of the system appeared amidst them all, rapidly zooming in.

"Moti-Five is a midsized helium-heavy gas giant," he noted. "She has eleven moons that we've detected today—she may have more, but we don't have the Eerdish's files on her.

"The sixth moon is the second-largest, approximately five thousand kilometers in diameter, making her comparable to Ganymede in Sol.

"Commander Eowyn, have you had any luck?" he finally asked.

"We have," she told him. "While we have not yet detected any electromagnetic signals, the surface installation does not appear to have been heavily disguised against optical analysis.

"May I?"

He surrendered control of the shared display to her. The hologram zoomed in the moon, then on its south pole. It *kept* zooming until the surface of the moon became their horizontal, and they were looking at a projection of a crater.

"At first glance, there isn't much here," Eowyn noted before anyone said anything. "But look more closely, here and here and here."

Highlights appeared along sharp edges that were definitely *not* natural. Once the first few structures had been highlighted, Henry could easily pick out the rest.

Because he could recognize the design.

"Everyone in this room knows what that is," Sylvia said into the silence. "We've been dancing around it since Avas, trying to pretend that we're looking at Drifters or an unknown player. But there's only one power out there that is able to develop a stealth system unlike anything we've ever seen, that is intimately familiar with the nature of the subspace coms, *and* has a reason to keep an eye on what we're doing in the Ra Sector.

"*That*, people, is a Kenmiri deep-space-surveillance outpost."

HENRY'S OFFICE was silent for at least a minute while all seven of the people physically and virtually present processed Sylvia's words.

Then he sighed and nodded.

"All right, people. We all agree with Ambassador Todorovich's conclusion, yes?" he asked.

He looked at each of his people in turn, holding their gazes until they finally nodded.

"Then we're under Initiative Protocol Twenty-Seven now," he told them. "For those of you don't remember Protocol Twenty-Seven, it is fundamentally a recognition that we never actually *ended* the war with the Kenmiri."

Sylvia grimaced as the officers looked concerned.

"They unilaterally withdrew from the outer provinces," she reminded everyone. "The Vesheron didn't feel that we had the resources to go after them at that concentration of force and wrote off eight provinces and four thousand stars as lost for the next hundred years or so."

"A hundred years being all the Kenmiri have left," Palmer murmured.

"Exactly," Henry told them. "There were plans for rebuilding the economies and industry of the outer sectors and using them to build fleets and armies to liberate the inner provinces by force. That was part of what the Great Gathering was about.

"But the Kenmiri found the right tool to wreck *that* and we turned on each other," he said. "Which left the Remnant untouched —but Protocol Twenty-Seven was written with the understanding the Kenmiri may well not regard the war as over.

"Under Protocol Twenty-Seven, we are required to divert from our mission to engage any Kenmiri presence we judge ourselves capable of engaging," he told them. "For the moment, I have no intention of returning to the Avas System. That will likely be a task for one of Admiral Rex's carrier groups before they go home.

"However, we are in the space of a potential ally and have discovered a surveillance outpost watching their stars. I do not expect a single surveillance outpost to have the firepower or ground forces to withstand this squadron—and presenting evidence of Kenmiri spying can only help when we're trying to make friends."

"We are assuming that the Eerdish don't know they're here," Sylvia pointed out. "They may have their own discussions and schemes going on."

"If neutralizing a Kenmiri outpost hurts us with the Eerdish, we may not want to be allies with them in the first place," Henry said. "In which case there are other means of dealing with the Drifters hiding in their space."

From the momentary microexpressions that leaked through Sylvia's mask, he wasn't the first person to point that out. He'd seen the assessments of the level of force needed to deal with the E-Two Alliance.

Twelfth Fleet was, they hoped, over-gunned for the Drifters.

Admiral Rex had more than enough firepower to overrun the Kozun Hierarchy—and the E-Two had only held their own against a *portion* of the Hierarchy's forces.

"Regardless of whether the Eerdish want us to take out their secret nosy neighbor, I wrote Protocol Twenty-Seven to be as nondiscretionary as possible," Henry told them with a small smile. It was occasionally worthwhile to remind both his people and himself that *he'd* done a large part of the work of setting up the Peacekeeper Initiative—including writing at least the first draft of the entirety of the Protocols.

"That was to remove a certain degree of hesitancy on the part of field officers assigned to what are, fundamentally, non-war missions," he continued. "Protocol Twenty-Seven exists because we are still, by any rational standard, at war with the Kenmiri Empire.

"And that makes that surveillance outpost a strategic military target." Henry glanced around, making sure no one looked concerned by his conclusions.

Even *Sylvia*, however, was nodding along. Diplomat or not, his partner's career had been forged in the fires of the war against the Kenmiri. Her job had been finding allies against the Empire, not making peace.

"We have no means of preventing them from detecting us or from advising their friends about our attack," Henry reminded them all. "So, there isn't much point in playing games here. All ships will set their course for Moti-Five.

"We'll see how the Kenmiri respond to our approach quite quickly, I expect."

CHAPTER TWENTY-TWO

HENRY WAS BACK ON THE FLAG DECK BY THE TIME THE ORDERS were actually all passed, with Sylvia dropping into an observer's seat near his but out of the way.

All three ships turned on a dime, jumping to their maximum acceleration of two KPS^2 and pushing for the still-distant gas giant. Still over three light-minutes away, it would take them three hours to reach the gas giant's orbitals.

"Turnover in ninety-two minutes," Eowyn reported. "All scanners are live. We're too far away to get anything useful with active scanners, but if they bring a ship online or something similar, we'll see it."

"Standard Kenmiri protocol for a facility like that is a mix of surface and orbital weapons emplacements," Henry said calmly. "Minimum of four laser platforms in orbit and twenty missile launchers in each place.

"Depending on what they're doing for concealment, they may have restricted themselves to concealed orbital weapons platforms. Automated systems on minimum standby wouldn't show up at any serious distance."

He eyed the display.

"They'll start booting them up as soon as they're sure we're coming for them," he concluded. "We won't have any data on surface weapons until they fire at us or we're *very* close, but we'll detect the orbital platforms at a light-minute once they power them up."

Eowyn was quiet for a moment.

"You've done this before," she noted.

"As a battlecruiser Tactical officer, a destroyer XO, a destroyer captain and a battlecruiser commander," Henry confirmed. "The Kenmiri's eyes were always on our target list—and the difference between a surveillance outpost and a forward logistics base is negligible."

He shook his head grimly.

"Chan. I want a conference with the GroundDiv Lieutenant Commanders in one hour," he told the coms officer. "I assume *they've* done this before as well, but I want to be certain.

"We are *not* going to screw this up, people."

THE VIRTUAL CONFERENCE with the three GroundDiv officers was much less formal than the meetings with Henry's SpaceDiv officers. Each of his three GroundDiv Lieutenant Commanders was responsible for a destroyer's company of GroundDiv troopers, three thirty-trooper platoons and a ten-trooper command squad.

In total, Henry had three hundred GroundDiv troopers, a short battalion equal to the force Commander Thompson had led aboard *Raven*. However, unlike the battlecruiser's short battalion, DesRon Twenty-Seven didn't have an O-4 Commander in charge of everything.

Lieutenant Commander Quang Nguyen, aboard *Paladin*, was the senior of the three officers, which put him in command of Lieutenant Commanders Omar Jian and Karina Vargas, of *Cataphract* and *Maharatha,* respectively, for combined operations.

The three officers represented the usual standard of third-millennium UPA ethnic mutts to Henry's eyes. Quang Nguyen was a Beijing-born Vietnamese man, both less and more Chinese than Henry Wong himself, depending on your view. Omar Jiang, on the other hand, was a Chinese-Arab mix similar to Henry's own Chinese-American—and Karina Vargas was a classic Euro-mutt from Sandoval in the Procyon System.

All three were already wearing their body armor with their hair tied back in nets ready for their helmets. While the conferencing software wasn't giving Henry much of a background view, he had enough to tell that all three were standing on the edge of the shuttle bays where their people would be prepping.

"All right, people," he greeted them. "According to my files, you've all made assault drops on Kenmiri facilities, but only as platoon commanders. Correct?"

"Yes, ser," Nguyen confirmed. "Vargas dropped on La-Tar as one of Thompson's platoon commanders as well, ser."

Henry eyed the dark-skinned woman. He barely remembered her, but his network confirmed that part of her record. She was an old *Raven* hand, but she'd been a junior enough GroundDiv officer that he hadn't interacted with her much.

"The Kenmiri will be a different story from the Kozun," he warned Vargas. "Your troops are all equipped with energy weapons?"

"Yes, ser. All of the platoons were reequipped when they were assigned to DesRon Twenty-Seven, ser," Nguyen said swiftly. The two junior Commanders were clearly content to let him take the lead. "Long arms were all manufactured in the UPSF facilities on Mars, ser, so no worries about Drifter tricks."

The UPA wasn't quite up to manufacturing energy sidearms yet, and Terran-made rifles were still inferior to Kenmiri weapons in several ways. Henry would almost have preferred if his platoons had the weapons they'd bought from the Drifters—but he understood why *GroundDiv* preferred Terran-made guns.

"What is your plan, Lieutenant Commanders?" he asked. "I don't want to micromanage, but I *have* commanded these strikes before and, well, you haven't. I may have useful suggestions."

There was a long pause, and while Henry couldn't quite tell in the conferencing software, he suspected his three officers were sharing a look.

"I'd appreciate your input, ser," Nguyen finally admitted. "But as the GroundDiv CO, the plan remains my call."

"Yes. It does," Henry agreed firmly. "Believe me, Commander Nguyen, if I feel it's necessary to overrule your attack plan, you will have *far* larger problems than SpaceDiv-GroundDiv interforce conflict. Understood?"

Henry was reasonably sure that both Vargas and Jiang had to stifle chuckles in response to that. Nguyen, for his part, took the implied rebuke with a calm nod and gestured an image of the crater and Kenmiri installation into view.

"We haven't confirmed the entrances or the connecting tunnels between the structures," Nguyen pointed out. "But if they're following the standard layout, there will be six entrances at these locations."

Six icons flashed red on the map.

"There will also be antipersonnel weaponry concealed around each entrance and likely at other points around the facility," he noted. "Most likely, I suspect that the crater ridge *here* will either have bunker positions or automated ranged weaponry.

"I'd *like* to open with EMP bombardment to disable automated weaponry, but I am presuming we want to capture as much of the facility's data stores as intact as possible," he said.

"Unfortunately, yes," Henry agreed. He used his network to measure the distance between the crater ridge and the main installation. "On the other hand, that ridge is fifteen hundred meters away from the main target. Easy range for computer-controlled weaponry, you're right—but far enough away that the destroyers can hit it with kinetics without risking damaging the primary target.

"If they're dug in there, I can dig them out for you."

"That would help," Nguyen conceded. "I didn't want to assume orbital fire support, so my plan called to neutralize those positions with fire from our assault shuttles as we came in."

"I expect us to have neutralized spaceborne resistance by the time we reach orbit," Henry told the GroundDiv officers. "Even if we have to pursue a runaway, I can plan to leave at least one destroyer in place to provide fire support."

"Honestly, the ridge is the only place I'm worried about where we could use it," the GroundDiv CO replied. "I'm *hoping* to identify any antiaircraft weaponry from a distance, but that is likely to be inside the facility and require precision attack from the shuttles."

"There are targets that we will be taking out from a distance, regardless of the risk to everything else," Henry warned. "We're expecting ground-based missile launchers. The moon is atmosphereless, so there may even be lasers.

"All of those will be destroyed before you're deployed."

"Understood." Nguyen paused for a moment, clearly recalculating. "We'll have to adjust on the fly for that, but opening with a kinetic bombardment of the ridge clears the path.

"We'll bring the shuttles in low from the north...*this* north." An icon flashed on the crater ridge. Technically, *every* direction from the polar base was north or near enough. "We'll use the crater as cover from their antiaircraft weaponry while the kinetics clear the ridge itself.

"We'll deploy *here*, in the bombardment zone, and neutralize whatever is still intact while the shuttles sweep the compound and destroy any weapons they can detect. Once the shuttle pass is complete, we'll make our assault down the crater, targeting all three of the entrances on that side of the compound.

"Once inside, we're hoping that it's a standard layout. If it's not, we'll improvise, but the goal is to get to and secure the power plant and the datacores. The power plant could be overloaded to destroy the entire facility and we want the datacores intact."

Henry looked at the map and nodded.

"It sounds like a plan, Lieutenant Commanders," he told them. "How long?"

"Assuming everything goes to plan, we'll be in the facility within ten minutes of touchdown," Nguyen confirmed. "After that..." He shook his head. "Without data on what the internal layout looks like, anything I'd say for securing the facility itself would be a guess and not even an educated one.

"A minimum of three hours. Potentially more. If the Kenmiri have set the tunnels up for defense and have significant numbers of Warriors..."

"Understood." Henry appreciated that Nguyen wasn't trying to claim a miracle strike that would overrun the facility with ease. The younger officer might be trying to cover his ass for later, but Henry would prefer honest uncertainty over overconfidence.

"You'll deploy once we've secured the space about Moti-Five," he told them. "I expect that to be relatively quick. Unless this base is far more heavily defended than others of its type, they have no chance against DesRon Twenty-Seven."

CHAPTER TWENTY-THREE

"Subspace pulse," Chan reported. "It looks like they've seen us and are letting everybody know they're burnt."

"Sucks to be them," Henry said coldly. He might have nightmares about killing off the Kenmorad—but he *also* had nightmares about the people he'd pulled out of Kenmiri work camps. His sympathy for anyone on the Kenmiri side that wanted to restart the war was limited.

"Range will be one light-minute in ten minutes," Eowyn reported. "I'm expecting to be able to start picking out orbital weapons soon."

"Good," Henry replied. "Weapons status on the squadron?"

He had access to all of the information, both in his internal network and on the displays around him, but the Book wanted double confirmation—and he agreed with the Book. The last thing he wanted was to discover he was missing a missile launcher at the wrong moment.

"All ships report green on both lasers and all twelve missile launchers," Eowyn told him. "All magazines at hundred percent. The squadron is ready to engage the enemy."

They were still a long way away from that. Their maneuvering would bring them to zero velocity in a high orbit of Moti-V-6 in roughly seventy minutes. They'd be decelerating into orbit the entire way now, but that was why the destroyers had the same lasers as *Raven*: spinal weapons that could fire forward or backward.

Henry suspected that they would find that the GMS didn't need to be aligned with the structure of the ship in the long run, but for the moment, the gravity well had a fixed position. First, they needed the drive system to *work*. Later, they'd discover what extra tricks it made possible.

"Contact," Eowyn suddenly reported. "Multiple contacts around Moti-Five-Six. I have active fusion cores; I have active scanners... Warbook is analyzing."

Henry waited. He was reasonably certain he knew what he was looking at, but it was always possible he'd been wrong.

"Warbook and CIC cannot confirm the platform class," Eowyn said quietly. The "warbook" was a database of all known ship classes combined with a smart pattern-matching algorithm. *Paladin*'s combat information center would be taking a human eye to the same process because the algorithms had problems making intuitive leaps.

"What do we know?" Henry asked calmly.

"CIC makes the likelihood that contacts are Kenmiri eighty-five percent, ser," the Ops officer said. "Fusion-core emission patterns are correct, though power levels are different from expected. We may have a more solid idea as we get closer and they bring sensors online, but CIC believes we are looking at an entirely new platform design. Still almost certainly a Kenmiri prefab."

"As expected," he concluded. "Are we dialed in for weapons fire?"

"We are. Platforms are not in range yet, though."

"I know," Henry agreed. "Are they evading?"

There was a pause.

"Not as of a minute ago," Eowyn confirmed.

Henry leaned back in his chair. Automated platforms, but the people issuing them orders weren't used to only having computers. That made sense.

"All ships are to engage with extreme-range laser fire until they start maneuvering," he ordered. "Let's see if we can make them jump."

Even if they connected, his lasers weren't going to do much at a full light-minute. They were set with focal points of around a million kilometers. This was well beyond their useful range.

But if the platforms weren't evading, he could *hit* them. It wouldn't hurt as much as it would at a closer range, but they'd feel it.

"We could also engage with missiles in ballistic mode," Eowyn suggested.

"Those will be seen coming, and whoever is responsible for those platforms will realize they need to *tell* them to evade," Henry replied. "We'll save those for when we're in their active range."

The lasers opened fire a moment later. At this range, it was almost two minutes from firing to getting the report of the impact.

"Six shots, five hits," Eowyn reported. "All targets intact, but I'm seeing some fluctuation in the emissions. Second salvo...four hits, targets are now evading. Other shots will— Whoa!"

Henry had seen it too. One of the platforms had taken three of the nine hits—every shot from *Cataphract*, if he judged correctly— and even at this range, that was apparently too much. The fusion-core containment had failed and now the weapons platform gone.

"How many left?" he asked.

"Eleven," Eowyn told him. "They're big, ser. As big as the staffed weapons platforms we've seen in Kenmiri space, but they were cold and dark before we started toward the base. They have to be automated."

"I imagine the Kenmiri are working hard on upgrading their automation," Henry pointed out. "Their Drone population is dropping precipitously with every year. Given another decade, the

Warriors and Artisans will be all that's left, and that means they're going to be running short on hands."

The short-lived Drones had a life expectancy of barely ten years —and made up ninety-five percent of the Kenmiri population. Most of the extant larvae would have died with their Kenmorad parents, but there might have been hatchings up to six months after the deaths of the breeding sects.

Henry sighed. The whole situation was a nightmare and there shouldn't have been Kenmiri there. One way or another, the outpost had to cease to be a threat...but they *probably* owed the crew a chance of some kind.

"Chan, get a directional transmission set up, standard protocols for transmitting to the Kenmiri," he ordered. That meant a *lot* of cyber-security, air-gapped computers and a transmission in clear.

"Ser?" they asked.

"We killed their entire species, though it may be taking a while to stick," Henry pointed out. "Let's see if we can manage to talk this lot into laying down their weapons.

"Do you really think that'll work, ser?" Chan asked.

"No," Henry conceded. "But I feel like we have to try."

"All right. You're live on your command."

He nodded and faced the recorder, activating it with a mental command.

"Kenmiri surveillance outpost," he said in Kem. "I am Commodore Henry Wong of the United Planets Space Force. You are outgunned and outmatched. I can destroy your facility from here if I wish.

"If you surrender, I will see you repatriated to the Kenmiri Remnant. If you fight me, I will turn the *survivors* over to the local government to decide what to do with you.

"This is the best offer you will get. I suggest you consider it."

⁂

HENRY only really held out hope for a few minutes—and it was a tiny thing, flickering more out of a need for it to exist more than any realistic belief.

"No response," Chan reported.

"Weapons range in less than five minutes, ser," Eowyn reported. She hesitated, glancing at the coms officer. "Any change to the plan?"

"Negative," Henry said swiftly. "We will proceed as previously ordered. No changes."

He leaned back in his seat, watching as targeting carets appeared around the weapons platforms they'd picked out. Eleven stations, each big enough to have a crew of forty or more—except that they showed no signs of being inhabited.

And it wouldn't have changed the plan if they were. If the Kenmiri were in the outer sectors, they'd violated the implicit agreement that had ended the war—their insistence on stealth and hidden bases showed they understood that.

"Targets assigned," Eowyn said into her microphone. "Confirm assignments."

The carets on the main display flashed green as each destroyer's Tactical department confirmed they'd received their targets. They'd start one at a time, working their way through the list in a logical order—unless Henry Wong told them to do something differently.

And at this point, Henry literally had *nothing* to do unless he saw a reason to change the firing pattern.

"Range in thirty seconds," Eowyn chanted. "Flight time, five minutes. Watching for outbound fire. They've upgraded their coms and stealth... They may have upgraded their missiles."

One of the minor oddities of the war, caused by the fact that the Vesheron and Drifters had started their arsenals with stolen Kenmiri missiles, was that everyone had used basically the same missiles. With a few minutes of flight data, Henry's people could identify UPA-built versus Drifter-built versus Kozun-built missiles, but the overall performance envelope was fundamentally identical.

But after three years, that might have changed.

"Missiles away," the Ops officer reported. Seconds ticked away. "Missile launches detected on orbital platforms. Estimate two hundred twenty missiles inbound, repeat, two two zero missiles inbound."

"Make certain we ID the resonance missiles," Henry ordered. "Intel still puts the odds at sixty-plus percent that the Drifters got them from the Kenmiri."

"Scanning," Eowyn confirmed. More seconds ticked by as the missiles hurtled toward each other at a combined twenty KPS^2.

"Ser, I do not detect any resonance missiles," she said formally. "All missiles show radiation signatures consistent with Kenmiri fusion-conversion warheads."

"Interesting," Henry said calmly. He glanced at the individual screens on the arm of his chair, showing the commanders of his destroyers. "Captains. Fight your ships."

That was the last trick he'd been watching for. If anything *else* happened, well...they'd improvise.

His three ships adjusted formation as the missiles closed. Now they formed an equal-sided vertical triangle, with five thousand kilometers between each ship and her sisters. Close enough to cover each other with antimissile lasers, far enough that the missiles had to pick an individual target.

"Laser range will be sixty seconds after first missile impact," Eowyn told him. "Orbit...some fifteen minutes after that."

Henry nodded. There wasn't much chance the Kenmiri platforms would still be around when his destroyers made orbit. It was *possible* they'd get lucky and damage one of his ships—but their best chance was at close laser range. And they weren't going to get that chance.

"Scans confirm the platforms have raised energy screens," one of Eowyn's people reported. "We accounted for that in the targeting plan, no adjustments. Impact in sixty seconds."

"Defensive systems online, antimissile lasers engaging," Eowyn added. "Destroyer Tactical teams have control; we are flagging targets for assist."

There was no way Henry's three ships could shoot down over two hundred missiles. A proper battlecruiser group, with a *Corvid*-class ship and half a dozen destroyers, might have been able to. DesRon Twenty-Seven was doing well, Henry noted, but his estimate was that they'd still have over a hundred and fifty missiles hit the ships.

So long as the gravity shields were up, his people could handle that.

ONLY THE AFTER-ACTION report would tell Henry how many missiles of that first salvo made it through the squadron's antimissile fire. They detonated in a tidal wave of fire that washed over his ships like a storm breaking, and he held his breath.

He knew this drill, but that didn't make that wash of flame any less intimidating.

"Report," he ordered.

"Minor blowthrough on *Cataphract*'s shield," Eowyn said after a moment. "No damage."

The gravity shield created a shear zone a handful of centimeters wide where gravity went from nothing to thousands of gravities and then back to nothing. They could open gunports in it to fire their own weapons and adjust their scanners for the shear factor, but any incoming weapon or plasma burst had to hit that shear zone and stay intact and on target.

The odds were very much in the shielded ship's favor.

"And our fire?" Henry asked.

"Target one is destroyed. Two and three are showing signs of damage but remain intact," his Ops officer told him. "Second salvo is adjusting automatically. Laser range in forty seconds, second-wave impact in ten."

Their own antimissile fire was already blazing out, tearing gaping holes in the incoming second salvo. There would be multiple full-strength salvos to weather still, fired before the loss of the first defensive platforms.

More plasma fire washed over Henry's ships and he grimaced.

"Still no resonance warheads?" he asked.

"None," Eowyn confirmed. "Their ECM has improved; we're not getting as many as I'd like. No blowthroughs that time, though."

"Trouble tracking their missiles?" Henry said.

His Ops officer chuckled.

"No, because our counter-ECM has improved more than their ECM," she noted. "But against their wartime missiles, we'd be scoring ninety percent kills-per-shot. We're actually around eighty, it looks like."

"And them?"

"Target two and three are destroyed; four is leaking hydrogen fuel and has ceased firing missiles. Five through eleven..."

Eowyn shrugged.

"Laser range in five," she concluded.

Henry barely had time to nod and breathe before they crossed the line where his computers calculated they could reliably hit evading targets—roughly seven hundred thousand kilometers.

"Laser strikes on the gravity shields," Eowyn reported. "Multiple strikes on all ships, multiple complete misses... No blowthroughs so far."

Each of the remaining eight platforms had two lasers, very similar to the armament of Henry's three destroyers. Their energy shields were far less resilient than his people's gravity shields, though, and the focused beams of three destroyers obliterated target four in a single salvo.

Five through eight died a few moments later as the lasers shattered shields in time for missiles to detonate, converting their mass into enormous shotgun blasts of plasma that vaporized huge chunks of the space stations.

Sixty seconds after they reached laser range, still over ten minutes from slowing into orbit of Moti-V-6, there was nothing left in orbit of the moon but drifting debris.

"*Maharatha* took a glancing blow from one of the lasers," Eowyn reported. "Captain Teunissen reports that they're mostly looking at lost heat radiators, and she has teams on their way to replace them."

"Watch for ground installations," Henry ordered. "We've eliminated the defenders we can see, but let's not take any extra chances. Especially if Teunissen is putting people on her hull."

It was a measured risk. Unlike older ships, the *Cataphracts* actually had enough power to run everything at once—even on *Raven*, Henry had had to balance capacitors to feed his lasers and shields simultaneously—but they paid for that by having almost *no* excess heat-radiation capability at full power.

With *Maharatha* at full battle readiness, she *needed* every heat radiator she could get—but they were also the first thing she was going to lose to glancing blows.

"Orbit in ten minutes," Eowyn reported as the clock ticked down. "Is Commander Nguyen clear to deploy?"

"Not yet," Henry ordered. "Full active sweep of the target site, please, Commander. We're guessing where the weapons systems are and that there are no antispace systems.

"Let's stop guessing. I want to be able to read the base commander's name tag."

So far as he knew, the Kenmiri didn't *use* name tags. Certainly, the UPSF didn't—why, when every citizen of the UPA had an internal network installed at age six? Henry's network would give him the name of every person he encountered, though cultural tradition still required introductions.

"Understood. Scanning the target site."

Henry kept himself impassive, his face a mask as the distance continued to evaporate. He was all too aware of Sylvia's presence behind him, conscious of the fact that an error there would kill her as well as him and his people.

That had bothered him a bit when she'd "just" been a civilian advisor. Now that bothered him quite a bit...but Henry was also confident in his ability to do his job.

"We are picking up multiple installations outside the crater," Eowyn told him. "I'm guessing they're linked by cable, as first analysis suggests that they're communication and sensor-relay platforms.

"Nothing looks big enough to be an antispace laser or missile platform."

"And in the crater?" Henry asked.

"They've activated some kind of jamming field that is diffusing both EM and infrared signatures, ser," Eowyn admitted. "I suspect there are *definitely* antispace weapons in the main facility that they are attempting to conceal."

"Adjust course to position us over the northern pole," Henry ordered. "Set kinetics to drop at one hundred thousand kilometers to bombard the entire circumference of the crater rim to support Commander Nguyen's approach."

He considered the display for a few more seconds.

"If they're holding on to those weapons, they've wasted them," he concluded. "We'll be out of their arc of fire momentarily, and Nguyen's plan renders them pointless."

"It's down to GroundDiv then, ser?"

"It is." Henry paused, then nodded firmly. "Once we're in that polar position, Commander Nguyen is cleared to deploy. Time the kinetic strikes with his approach."

"Yes, ser."

CHAPTER TWENTY-FOUR

"You're secure to bring the ships around to this side of the planet now, ser," Nguyen reported. The visual attached to the call was of what the GroundDiv officer was seeing: currently, the inside of an underground tunnel with a twisting abstract mural along its walls.

"Shuttles took out two of the lasers and we are in control of the third," the GroundDiv officer continued. "It looks like they had most of their Warriors dug in on the ridge. We found the remnants of some pretty complex defensive structures there—they probably had an underground link to the main complex, but the kinetics didn't leave them in a state to be worth looking for."

A distinctive and memorable crackle echoed in the background of Nguyen's channel and Henry buried a shiver. He'd been trapped on the ground for one memorable disaster during the war. He knew his place: on the decks of a warship!

One of his therapists had pointed out that that was a trauma reaction...and then laughed and said it was the right call anyway. Just because an impulse was reinforced by trauma didn't make it *wrong*.

"We have control of the power plant, which doesn't appear to have been large enough to wreck the facility if overloaded," the GroundDiv officer told them. "We're having less luck with the datacores. It looks like they've got one last squad of fully armored Warriors and they are holding that part of the complex.

"We have not encountered any Artisans," Nguyen observed. "Currently eyeballing the Kenmiri at about a hundred, maybe a hundred and twenty hands all in. Eighty-plus are Drones, the rest Warriors. This is unquestionably a military installation."

"Any prisoners, Commander?" Henry asked.

"A handful, all wounded," his subordinate replied. "We've medevacked them back to the shuttles, but my medics say they'll make it. Seven, I think?"

Henry nodded grimly. He wasn't going to order Nguyen to risk lives to take prisoners, and Kenmiri Drones and Warriors weren't known to surrender. Artisans had been known to order Drones and Warriors under their authority to lay down arms—and their subordinates would usually obey—but without the often-wiser Worker Caste, the Kenmiri would fight to the death.

"Is there any support we can provide from up here?" Henry asked. "Once we're in position, we should be able to do penetrating scans of the site and provide intelligence."

"That's what I was hoping for, Commodore," Nguyen admitted. "Tell me where they are, and I can finish this in short order. They have the advantage of interior position guarding the computer cores."

Henry couldn't see the man shrug, but the movement of the helmet camera suggested the gesture.

"Pull them back," Nguyen suddenly snapped, the words addressed at one of his subordinates. "We are not charging into the teeth of a multiblaster if we have *any* alternative."

He turned his attention back to the call.

"Intel would be handy," he reiterated. "I don't think we're getting the computers intact, ser. On the other hand..."

"Commander?" Henry prompted.

"We are in possession of a chunk of the complex that definitely includes what I recognize as a major subspace-com installation...and a lot of gear I do *not* recognize but appears to be intact."

"If that's the subspace stabilizer, Commander, you may have just earned yourself that second steel bar," Henry said calmly. "Taking that intact will more than outweigh losing the computer cores."

Even if the Kenmiri had wiped the operating software of the subspace communicator, the hardware would give the UPA's scientists everything they needed to duplicate the tech. That would *definitely* be enough for Henry to recommend promotions all around for Nguyen's people.

"We'll be in position above the site in two minutes," Henry said after a glance at the main display. "We should be feeding you live tactical data within sixty seconds of that."

"Understood. I'll hold all my people in position until then," Nguyen replied. "If the bugs decide to rush *me* in that time, I'm not going to argue!"

✦✦

"I DON'T SUPPOSE there's much point in us going down there, is there?" Sylvia asked as *Paladin*'s scanners showed Nguyen's final assault.

With three destroyers using penetrating radar and high-resolution infrared scans at barely ten thousand kilometers of altitude, there was no hiding from the GroundDiv troops. That had allowed Nguyen to find an entrance they hadn't identified before—and then to both launch a feint and *know* that the Warriors had fallen for it.

"The prisoners will be brought up here," Henry replied. "We've already arranged a team that's going to go down and *very carefully* dismantle the subspace communicator."

He shook his head.

"I would *very* much like to not give that to the Eerdish," he told her. "The prisoners are theirs unless they don't want them, and I'll use the fact that this place *existed* as a lever, but I'd prefer to keep the communicator."

"They do have a legitimate claim to it," Sylvia said. "This is their space."

"I know, and that's why my techs are going to take every possible scan of the communicator as we bring it aboard, but R-Div is going to be *very* upset if we don't deliver it."

"I know," his partner agreed. "We'll do what we can. We're not exactly going to be starting on the best foot with the Eerdish, though. The presence of the Kenmiri in their space should help, you're right, but us unilaterally deciding to deal with them might not."

"And here I was hoping dealing with the old enemy would gain us brownie points," Henry replied. He exhaled and shook his head as several icons on the display suddenly flickered and changed color—from red to yellow.

There was a cascade from there, and in a few seconds, there were no red dots left.

"Huh," he said. "That's it...but that's different."

"Henry?"

"The Warriors laid down their arms," he told Sylvia. "They've surrendered—but the *Warriors* started it. There's no Artisans on the base, just Warriors and Drones.

"And neither of those usually surrenders."

"That's a good sign, isn't it?" she asked.

"Yeah," Henry agreed. A stab of the usual guilt took him in the gut, but he pushed it down. "I suppose they're as aware of their species' doom as anyone else. That's got to change how suicidal you're willing to be."

"I'd assume." Sylvia looked over his shoulder at the display. "Can we transport that many prisoners?"

"Looks like thirty or so to me," he noted. "We can handle that. I imagine we'll be lucky to get name, rank and serial number out of them, but we'll see what they say before we turn them over to the Eerdish."

"And if the Eerdish don't want them?"

"Then we haul them back to La-Tar and impose on the locals there," Henry suggested. "I suppose, in the worst case, we can even take them all the way back to UPA space. We've...never had to worry about handling Kenmiri prisoners before."

There was a long silence.

"I was under the impression that we *did* take them," Sylvia said slowly.

"Oh, we did," he confirmed. "And once they were interrogated, we loaded them into an escape pod and dropped them off in the nearest Kenmiri star system. No point keeping POWs when the enemy's resources are as immense as the Empire's were."

He shivered.

"And we didn't trust the Vesheron with them," he admitted. "Sending them home in escape pods was a reliable way to repatriate. Handing them over to our allies...not so much."

"And now you want to hand them over to the Eerdish?" Sylvia asked.

"I don't feel we have a choice—though you are the diplomat and can tell me I'm wrong," he noted. "But that said...I also feel that the post-Fall *government* is less likely to torture them to death for amusement than the wartime revolutionaries were."

CHAPTER TWENTY-FIVE

It was a relief to finally see the Seppen System.

They'd ended up spending six whole days in Moti, packing up everything of value they could find in the Kenmiri surveillance outpost. Neither the base computers nor the Kenmiri prisoners had been forthcoming about anything, but the facility itself was useful.

And a dark sign of things to come, Henry knew. Protocol Twenty-Seven had been written with the understanding that the Kenmiri might *not* regard the war as over the same way their former enemies did. If they were secretly spying on their old stars, it suggested they might still be planning on reclaiming them.

Henry wasn't sure what the dying race would *do* with those stars, but the Remnant could still cause a lot of bloodshed and horror if they chose to.

Hopefully, the Eerdish and their Enteni allies saw things the same way.

"Hold position at the skip line," he ordered as the three ships' networks resynced. "Omnidirectional transmission, please, Chan."

"You're on," his coms officer told him.

"Eerdish, Enteni and allied forces in the Seppen System," Henry said in Kem. "This is Commodore Henry Wong of the United Planets Space Force. We are here on a diplomatic mission to make contact with the Eerdish-Enteni Alliance, hopefully to gain permission to pursue hostiles into your space."

He paused.

"I understand that you are at war with the Kozun Hierarchy and that word has likely reached you of our own alliance with them. While further details will need to be formally discussed in person, I must assure you that our treaty with the Hierarchy is purely defensive and does not extend to any involvement in your conflict with them.

"My ships will remain at the Moti-Seppen skip line until granted permission to enter farther into the system," he promised. "Our passage through Moti resulted in a discovery that I believe will be of critical strategic import to the Eerdish and their allies, and I intend to provide that information and proof of our claims freely once we have established a secure channel.

"It is in all of our interests that I do so," he finished.

He cut off the recording and nodded to Chan to send it.

"What are we seeing, Eowyn?" he asked, switching back to English with long-practiced ease.

"Geography is about what we expected," she told him. "The UPSF has been to Ra-Ninety-Two before. One massive red giant star and a single super-Jovian gas giant planet. Some scattered asteroids, but pretty much nothing of importance outside of the Leppen planetary system."

Leppen was the super-Jovian gas giant, Henry's internal network calmly informed him. Its planetary system had several rings and moons, a solid source of raw materials and supplies.

"The Kenmiri maintained a logistics base in Leppen's rings, using the gas giant for fuel. We're still reading active signatures from there, so it looks like the Eerdish either have it back online or built their own."

"I'm assuming there's a nodal defense force around here somewhere?" Henry asked. Looking at the map, he noted that Leppen was currently close to the Eerdish skip line. It would be reasonably so for about forty years of a hundred-and-fifty-year orbit, he realized as the screens and his network updated with the data on the system.

"We're still processing data to that level of resolution," Eowyn admitted. "There are definitely *ships* at Leppen and at what appear to be at least two more positions elsewhere in the system. The other spots are... There we go."

"Commander?" Henry asked.

"They're engaged in training exercises, ser," she told him. "That's my guess, at least. I see two five-ship battle groups positioned about a light-minute apart several light-minutes from Leppen. And...yep. Fighter wings in the space between them."

"Building up their fleet to stand off the Kozun," Henry murmured. "Makes sense. I'm not going to poke *too* hard at our hopefully-friends, but what have they got?"

"Feeding the visual to the main screen now," Eowyn told him. "It's limited, but I'll update the data as we process it."

New images appeared on the display, and Henry gave a mental command to zoom in on the closer of the two training groups. As Commander Eowyn had said, each of them was five ships.

Two of the ships were what he'd expected. Standard half-megaton Kenmiri-design escorts, though it was likely they were post-war builds. The design had a lot of weaknesses, but it also had significantly more firepower per ton than Henry's own destroyers.

Two of the ships were bigger, roughly the same size as his own nine-hundred-thousand-ton destroyers. They were simple ships, straightforward triangular prisms of metal with clear protrusions for heat radiators and weapons systems.

The fifth ship was fascinating, though. It was the same triangular prism as the larger escorts but almost three times the size—with a familiar style of large hatch at the end Henry was studying it from.

"That's a carrier," Henry murmured.

"CIC confirms," Eowyn replied. "I was focusing on the fighters, but we've got some scans and metrics on all three classes."

"Lay them out," he ordered.

"Escorts are standard Kenmiri. The destroyers are obviously not. Estimate one hundred eighty meters in length, thirty-meters on each side. Slightly less dense than us, just over one megaton based off their thrust signatures.

"Carrier is three hundred meters long, forty meters on a side. Three million tons. Based off what's in space between the two groups, carries ninety starfighters."

"That's less than a *Crichton*, but on three-quarters of the mass, it's not bad," Henry said. "On the other hand, even if they're TIEs... well, the Kozun are still going to get a shock."

"The Kozun can fight these guys, but with their cruisers out of the game, they're going to need more of a numbers edge than they think," Eowyn concluded. "Wait..."

"Commander?" Henry prodded.

"Oh, you are *not* clever enough," she murmured.

"Commander Eowyn?" Henry said again.

"I think they believe we're too far to see the fighters," she told him. "Our wartime scanners wouldn't have had the resolution. They hesitated once they saw us, then started pulling the fighters back to the carriers...but they didn't hide the trump card, at least, fast enough."

"And what's the trump card?" Henry asked, looking back at the screen—and then realized it himself as the data fed onto the main display. A new icon appeared next to the E-Two starfighters; an icon he'd never seen on anything smaller than the Kozun's cruisers.

"That's not possible," he said grimly. "The Kenmiri never mounted energy screens on anything smaller than a dreadnought for a reason."

Only their automated weapons platforms had managed to fit the systems in—at the price of having no space for a crew.

"It looks like the E-Two broke that miniaturization problem, ser," his Ops officer told them. "Because we are definitely picking up the signature of an energy screen on half of those fighters—with probables on a good chunk of the rest."

"How powerful?" Henry asked. The screens mounted on a Kenmiri dreadnought—or the Kozun cruisers—could stand off multiple heavy laser hits or conversion-warhead plasma blasts. "If they can put a shield on a starfighter..."

"Then they're at least on those new-build destroyers and quite possibly retrofitted into the escorts, depending on how much shielding they want," Eowyn confirmed. "It's not possible to get a perfect assessment at this range, but the signatures *suggest* a one-and-done deal. The shield will take *a* hit—and might well not be able to regenerate from it.

"But that's a massive increase in survivability versus *anybody* else's starfighters," she said. "Add energy screens to those destroyers and escorts..."

She shook her head.

"The Kozun are fucked," Henry said grimly. "Those carriers, even the destroyers, look like they're unarmored hulls. Just giant sheets of steel welded together to protect their systems. The interiors can't be that simple, but I'd guess they've shaved off every complexity they can to get something big, powerful and cheap."

"If there's two carrier groups here in Seppen...either that's all of them, exercising in one place, or the E-Two have at least twice that," Eowyn guessed. "That does change the situation, doesn't it, ser?"

"It doesn't change our mission," Henry replied. "Twelfth Fleet still outmatches those carriers—though it does add some extra impetus to Ambassador Todorovich's desire to make peace between the Kozun and the E-Two. That said..." He considered. "Make sure all of the Tactical teams know the data on those shields is classified," he ordered.

Both the UPA and Henry, personally, would be perfectly fine with the Kozun needing to sue for peace after getting their asses handed to them. He still remembered the gallows his GroundDiv troopers had photographed and then burnt on La-Tar.

"Looks like everybody has seen us and received our message," Eowyn reported. "The training groups are heading back to Leppen at one KPS-squared."

"All right," Henry murmured. "Chan, do we have a response yet?"

"Not yet. How long do we wait, ser?"

"At least twenty-four hours," he told them. "And even then... we're not starting a fight here, people. We're looking for friends, not new enemies."

IT TOOK over thirty minutes for the locals to make any response, by which point the training ships hadn't even made it one percent of the way back to the Leppen fleet base. The base and the carrier groups were both about five light-minutes from DesRon 27.

Henry figured whoever was transmitting from the fleet base had also contacted the commanders of the carrier groups before making the call.

"Message is definitely from the base at Leppen," Chan told him. "Basic Vesheron encryption, so not exactly a secure channel."

"Understood. Put them on screen."

A ten-minute back-and-forth was going to make this a long conversation, but that was life in an age without subspace coms. The dismantled transmitter aboard Henry's ships was the first thing to give him hope for instant communications since the Great Gathering.

The image that appeared on the screen was of an Eerdish man with skin so pale green as to be translucent, even the veins on his face visible in a disturbing mask. He wore a stark-white tunic with three blood-red stripes painted on the right breast.

"Commodore Wong, I am Defender-Lord Deetell of the Eerdish

Security Forces," he said in slow Kem. "Your presence here is a surprise and not a welcome one.

"We are aware of your alliance with our enemies, and the presence of armed vessels of your United Planets Alliance in our systems is undesirable." He paused, looking down—potentially confirming his translation.

"However, we recognize the critical contributions of your forces to our current liberty from the Kenmiri, and I appreciate your willingness to remain at a safe distance. Since this distance will make communication difficult, I am prepared to permit *one* of your vessels to approach the Leppen Security Facility.

"This vessel will keep all active sensors and weapons disabled and follow all directions from Leppen Security Facility control. Any deviation from these instructions will result in the immediate destruction of your ship."

The message ended, freezing on Deetell's vein-marked green face.

"Do we have any data on what the Eerdish are using for a rank structure?" Henry asked. "Is *Defender-Lord* an Admiral? A Commodore? Is he the system commander or..."

"Based on the people we have interacted with, I think *Defender-Lord* would be about O-nine, ser," Eowyn told him. "He's the system commander. Scans from here suggest the LSF has another twelve ships—four of them destroyers, the rest escorts—plus at least some fighter hangars on the facility itself."

"So, once we're close enough, he can almost certainly follow through on his threat," Henry concluded. "He's asking us to offer up one of our ships as a hostage. Which, frankly, seems entirely reasonable."

"We're going to take him up on that, ser?" Eowyn asked.

"My inclination is yes, but I'm going to talk to the Ambassador first," Henry replied. "I'll be in my office. Let me know if we have any further updates from our soon-to-be friends."

※

SYLVIA ACCEPTED his call the moment he pinged her.

"I presume Chan forwarded you Deetell's message?" he asked. He hadn't ordered it—if he'd *needed* to tell his communications officer to forward the communications to the on-board diplomat, he'd need to have a conversation with them.

"They did," Sylvia confirmed. "They're not exactly being welcoming."

"We are formally allied to people they're fighting, and now have a pile of sensor data on their new fleet that they'd *really* like us not to give the Kozun," Henry pointed out. "They can't catch us, but they don't know that."

Henry had no doubt that his *Cataphracts* could out-accelerate everything in the system except *maybe* the Eerdish's new fighters— and those couldn't follow his ships through a skip line.

"They have every reason to be suspicious, but I'm hesitant to give them this much leeway to start with," Sylvia told him. "If they get the idea that we're going to be *that* accommodating..."

"On the other hand, they will also know that I have two ships they can't catch that now know everything about their new fleet," Henry noted. "That's a hell of a weight we're holding over them."

His partner blinked.

"What am I missing, Henry?" she asked. "I see that they've built big new ships, but everything I've seen says the Kozun have outbuilt them in tonnage and numbers."

"Their ships have shields," Henry said simply. "Not gravity shields, but they've miniaturized a Kenmiri-style energy screen down far enough to fit it on a *fighter*. For the first time since we met the Empire, we're looking at someone else's starfighters my people can't call TIEs."

TIE, drawn from an old series of movies, was the shorthand nickname for an unshielded starfighter. UPSF starfighters had gravity shields of their own, making them incredibly hard to kill. TIEs, on the other hand, tended to disappear the moment they were even *close* to a real weapon.

"With shielded destroyers and starfighters, they can go toe-to-toe with everything the Kozun have and win," he explained. "Same firepower but twice the survivability, at least? The Hierarchy has already lost this war and they don't know it yet.

"And I'm not going to *tell* them. That's your decision."

Sylvia snorted.

"But we have that intelligence on all three ships, so if they turn on us...the Kozun will know what they're in for and prepare countermeasures," she concluded.

"Exactly. Though I'm not sure what countermeasures the Kozun *could* prepare," Henry admitted. "We have answers for energy screens—and our grav-shields are just straight-up better overall. I'm not sure what the Kozun would do."

Though Henry had to wonder about the power draw and size of the new energy projectors. A Kenmiri escort had twice as many launchers and lasers as one of his destroyers, despite being barely three-quarters of the size. The power and volume demands of the grav-shield generators were a good chunk of the difference.

"I'd still prefer to negotiate more...fair terms for our approach," Sylvia noted.

"That is your prerogative as the ambassador," Henry told her. "I'm your escort. I can tell you that I'm comfortable taking you in under these terms, but I can't speak to the diplomatic aspect of the situation."

"And that recognition of the difference in our spheres is why we worked well together even *before* we became an item," she said with a chuckle. "I assume Chan is ready to send a message back if I record one?"

"They are," Henry confirmed.

"Then I will make a call."

CHAPTER TWENTY-SIX

THE ONLY REAL CONCESSION THAT SYLVIA MANAGED TO negotiate out of the Defender-Lord was that *Paladin* was allowed to approach with her gravity shields and antimissile defenses up and her laser capacitors charged.

Sylvia was well aware that *Paladin* literally couldn't *move* with her gravity shield down—and that the shield would prevent the Eerdish ships from checking the status of the destroyer's weapons. Still, getting Defender-Lord Deetell to formally concede those points set the right tone for the discussions.

She was entirely willing to work with the E-Two, but she had her own objectives and wasn't going to let the UPA get walked over in these discussions. The Eerdish definitely seemed to be "feeling their oats," to use a delightfully European expression, but her quick and dirty briefing from Henry suggested they might be putting up something of a façade, too.

Eight escorts, twelve destroyers and two pocket carriers made for an impressive fleet—but it also easily represented fifty percent of the Eerdish homeworld's building capacity over the last three years. The

E-Two Alliance also had the Enteni homeworld and the Makata Cluster, but the fleet at Seppen was a major portion of their strength.

Deetell would likely be torn between suggesting the carrier groups were a *larger* portion of their strength than they were—to have the UPA pass on an underestimate of their strength to the Kozun—or the opposite. It depended on his people's plans.

For the moment, Sylvia checked the flags in her office and settled herself behind the desk. The blue flag of the United Planets Alliance with its sharp half-circle of eight gold stars was directly behind her, flanked on the right by the flag of the UPSF—the same curved V on a stylized rocket—and on the left by *Paladin*'s own commissioning seal —a gleaming silver helmet.

"Chan, link me through to the Defender-Lord, please," she told the squadron coms officer. Henry's holographic image appeared at her right hand, an image of his own office with its matching UPA flag. He'd let her run this meeting, but he needed to be present.

They'd always had a good working relationship. That respect was part of why she'd fallen for him in the first place, after all.

After a few seconds, the wall in front of her disappeared behind a holographic representation of an office that had *clearly* been designed by a Kenmiri Artisan. A baroque gold mural covered the wall behind Deetell. A black curtain covered it, but under the lights of the office, the material clearly wasn't as opaque as expected.

The Eerdish himself sat behind an opulent dark wood desk, with similar detailed abstract carvings across its surface covered in industrial-strength plastic to protect them.

"Commodore Wong, Ambassador Todorovich," he greeted them calmly. His Kem was slow and hesitant, and Sylvia suspected he had a datapad out of the camera view providing text translations.

She'd seen the eye-movement patterns before.

"I understand that is now a secure channel, yes?" the Defender-Lord stated.

"It is," Sylvia confirmed. "Your communications staff has been quite helpful."

They were using a modification of an old Vesheron encryption protocol, not a standard encryption for either of them, but hopefully, one no one would be able to quickly break either.

"My instructions," Deetell said slowly, "forbid me from permitting foreign vessels any deeper into our space. Your ships are arguably enemy vessels, making that forbid double.

"What is it that you desire?"

"Firstly, we need to do the Eerdish a small favor," Sylvia said with a smile. "Commodore Wong, if you would brief the Defender-Lord on what we found in the Moti System."

"The Moti System is ours," Deetell countered.

"Yes," Henry agreed. "That is why we feel that you should know what we found."

There was a long pause.

"Proceed, Commodore," Deetell finally allowed.

"Were you aware there was a Kenmiri listening post in your space?" Silvia's boyfriend asked.

There was a second pause—this one very clearly Deetell confirming that he had understood the Kem words correctly.

"We were not," he finally said. "That is impossible."

"I have seventeen Kenmiri prisoners aboard *Paladin* that I would like to render into Eerdish custody," Henry said. "We captured them in your space, and I feel that their fate should be yours to decide."

"A listening post?" Deetell confirmed.

"Indeed. We detected their communications and attempted to make contact," Henry told him. "They opened fire on us; we returned fire and stormed the facility. They successfully wiped their computers and the prisoners have been noncommunicative, but I can provide you with scan data and similar information to confirm this report."

"The presence of Kenmiri in our space is completely unacceptable," Deetell said. "I... I am not certain that my superiors will appreciate you engaging them without discussing it with us, but their elimination can only be of benefit to my people."

"And mine," Henry said. "As I said in my initial message, I believed that it was of critical strategic importance to both our peoples that you know about this. The presence of Kenmiri listening posts in the outer sectors is a threat I did not expect to encounter on this mission."

"We... We will take custody of those prisoners and that data," Deetell agreed. "I will need to review this information before I make any decisions based on it."

Henry had *not*, Sylvia noticed, mentioned the subspace communicator. That hot potato was being left in her court.

Which was fair.

"The discovery of the Kenmiri outpost, while a potential future threat, is secondary to our mission here," she finally said.

"So I understand," Deetell replied. "I understand your mission is not about contacting my people."

"We wish to open diplomatic channels with both the Eerdish and your Enteni allies," Sylvia told him. "We have a diplomatic contingent aboard our other ships from the La-Tar Cluster, and we will want to involve them in any further discussions.

"For this initial...door-opening discussion, I felt it was best we keep it to the UPA and you."

"I do not have the authority to permit you to enter the Eerdish System or the Makata Cluster," Deetell told them. "If you have sufficient need to discuss with my superiors, I will forward a message and my government will make that decision.

"My mission is the security of the Seppen System."

"That is understandable," Sylvia said. "But there are time constraints on our mission, Defender-Lord. We are in pursuit of the people who betrayed our peace conference with the Kozun and murdered hundreds of UPA, La-Tar Cluster and Kozun Hierarchy personnel under sign of truce."

There was another long silence, then Deetell swallowed—a disturbingly visible movement, given his pale green skin.

"You mean the Drifters," he said flatly.

"The Blue Stripe Green Stripe Orange Stripe Convoy betrayed our trust and the sacred oaths they swore," Sylvia said calmly. "The United Planets Alliance cannot allow that to stand.

"We *will* pursue them, no matter where they flee. We would far prefer to do so with the cooperation and assistance of the Eerdish-Enteni Alliance...but we will do so either way."

From Deetell's expression, he understood *exactly* what she was saying.

"THAT WENT BETTER than I was afraid of," Sylvia admitted later, after Deetell had left the channel to make arrangements to receive the prisoners.

"Agreed." Henry shook his head, his gaze seeming concerned.

"You're worried," she told him.

"I don't want to fight these people, Sylvia," he admitted. "I will, if I have to, but is it really worth starting another war to avenge the Drifters' betrayal?"

"I don't know," Sylvia confessed. "*Policy* says that we need people to think our ambassadors and envoys are untouchable, that they can't harm our people without fear of drastic consequences. There's a logic to that."

She agreed with the logic. She didn't necessarily *like* it, but she hadn't much liked talking rebel cells into active revolutions that she'd known were going to get most of them killed, either.

"The Convoy has already fled. They're terrified of us. Maybe that's enough." Henry sighed. "Or maybe it isn't. Who knows what they're planning where we can't see? I think..."

He trailed off and Sylvia smiled sadly as she recognized what he was thinking.

"The presence of the Kenmiri is making you nervous," she guessed. "That's a war that's supposed to be over, but if they're here..."

"I'm also reminded of just how far my superiors are prepared to go," Henry said quietly. "I don't expect Admiral Rex to engage in an atrocity—our orders explicitly countermand one, in fact—but that we *did* once..."

"You won't let that happen again," Sylvia told him firmly. She probably knew as much about Operation Golden Lancelot as anyone outside the UPSF—she'd been fully briefed in preparation for her role at the Great Gathering—and one of the things that had stuck out to her was how compartmentalized it had been.

No one carrying out the actual attacks had realized they were engaged in a campaign of genocide. Each individual attack had been told it was a demonstration strike, an attempt to bring the Empire to the negotiating table by proving that the Kenmorad were not invulnerable. A modern equivalent of the Doolittle Raid on Tokyo during the wars of the mid-Twentieth Century.

The people who'd organized and planned it all had left the execution to others, others who didn't know the full plan. They'd compartmentalized the knowledge so no one would hesitate.

"I won't," Henry agreed grimly. "It shouldn't be necessary, either. But the thought terrifies me."

He sighed.

"A courier just left the fleet base," he told her. "Heading for Eerdish at full thrust. It appears the Defender-Lord has decided we are above his pay grade."

"He'll take the prisoners, and someone else will decide if we get to Eerdish," Sylvia agreed. "I'll use the communicator to open the door to the skip line if I have to, Henry, but I don't think that will be necessary."

"I'd really like to keep that," he said with what she suspected was a forced smile. "Scans and images will only help R-Div so much."

"Given a choice between keeping the subspace communicator and having an alliance with the Eerdish and the Enteni against the Drifters—and potentially the Kenmiri!—I'm giving them the communicator, Henry," Sylvia told him firmly.

He sighed and nodded.

"That is...a political question, I suppose," he conceded. "And that makes it your call. My people are still scanning and photographing as we speak. If we *can* learn anything just from that, we will."

"Does anyone on DesRon Twenty-Seven actually know anything about subspace coms?" Sylvia asked.

"Of course," he said. "That's how we detected the Kenmiri in the first place. Do they know enough to work out what this thing does?" He snorted and shook his head. "I don't think any human—any *non-Kenmiri*, for that matter—knows that much yet.

"But we will learn."

CHAPTER TWENTY-SEVEN

HENRY STOOD IN *PALADIN*'S CRAMPED SHUTTLE BAY, WATCHING grimly as the Kenmiri prisoners filed onto the waiting shuttle. The Eerdish spacecraft was only mildly different from the Terran space-craft that belonged there, and could have been on any ship he'd seen for two decades.

The Vesheron and the successor states they'd become still relied heavily on ex-Kenmiri hardware and designs. It would be a long time before any of the ex-Vesheron powers had shuttles that weren't identical.

His focus couldn't stay on the shuttle forever, though, and his gaze inevitably drifted to his prisoners. They all looked like Earth ants scaled up to a larger size, with heavy chitin carapaces that could resist light projectile fire.

Henry knew that, unlike ants, the Kenmiri had something similar to a skeleton inside their chitinous skin, supporting their height and weight. The comparison was still inevitable to humans as the bipedal creatures with their three-part bodies walked across the deck.

The lead four Kenmiri were Warriors, towering two and a quarter meters tall with dull black carapaces and sharp edges to the chitinous armor on their upper arms. Their eyes were multifaceted gems, tracking every movement around them—and Henry's people had double-manacled every Warrior.

There would be no risks with the Kenmiri military caste.

The other dozen prisoners were smaller, barely a hundred and forty centimeters tall with carapaces colored in delicate patterns of blue and green. The Drones' eyes were less capable than the Warriors', but their gazes still swept the shuttle bay.

They were awake and aware and paying attention. Part of him had expected the Kenmiri prisoners to be subdued and lackadaisical, a direct manifestation of their dying race.

The difference was probably a solid metaphor for his errors about the Kenmiri Remnant itself.

Eerdish troopers in full body armor and face-concealing helmets stepped off the shuttle, energy rifles at parade rest as they took over control of the chain line from Henry's GroundDiv troopers. There were quiet conversations, likely in Kem, that Henry couldn't hear.

He had to watch. He had to make certain that the Kenmiri were off his ship. His sanity couldn't permit anything less.

To his surprise, however, one of the helmeted Eerdish stepped away from the line of prisoners at the direction of the GroundDiv squad leader and walked in his direction.

Focusing to the moment, Henry smoothed his emotions from his face and stepped forward to greet the alien.

"I am Commodore Wong," he told them. "How may I assist?"

There was an audible gust of air as the Eerdish disconnected their helmet, the atmosphere seals releasing as she took it off. A tightly-wound crown braid kept the Eerdish woman's thick black hair under her helmet and she saluted crisply, UPSF-style, with the helmet under her arm.

"I am Shield-Bearer Cochall," she greeted him in Kem, tapping the single blue stripe painted on her armor. "On behalf of the War-Shields of the Gathered Tribes, I wanted to offer our thanks for the capture of these Kenmiri.

"Politics between the Gathered Tribes and the United Planets Alliance may prevent proper recognition of your actions, but know that the War-Shields understand and appreciate what you have done for us.

"Thank you, Commodore Wong."

"You are most welcome," he told her. "The Kenmiri are our shared enemy. I could not leave a knife at my neighbor's door."

"Some would," Cochall told him grimly. "Some would."

She turned back as the last of the Kenmiri Drones vanished aboard her shuttle.

"You will hear from the Defender-Lord soon, I believe," she promised. "Again, thank you, Commodore Wong.

"It is good to know that the ideals that brought us together as Vesheron are not yet *entirely* dead."

"NEW TRANSMISSION from the Leppen Security Facility, ser," Chan reported as Henry returned to the flag deck. "Video data packet flagged for you and the Ambassador."

"But you have a guess what it is," Henry said drily. That much was clear from their tone.

"A courier just skipped back in from Eerdish," they replied. "Timing is about right for them to have traded a single set of messages back and forth from the planet to the courier we saw leave yesterday —and for Defender-Lord Deetell to have reviewed it before sending *this* message."

That fast a turnaround was probably good news, though Henry had been unpleasantly surprised before.

"You've forwarded it to the Ambassador?" he asked.

"Of course."

"I'll take it in my office," Henry told Chan. "I'll update everyone once I know what our green friend has to say."

His office was only a few steps away, and he didn't bother to sit in either the flag deck or the office before activating the message. It was a bit odd that it was a recording, given that they were close enough for a live conversation—that had been the point in bringing *Paladin* closer, after all.

Deetell's image appeared above his desk as Henry stood, arms crossed, facing the projector.

"Commodore Wong, Ambassador Todorovich," he greeted them formally in Kem. "I have been asked to relay the formal invitation of the Sovereign of Sovereigns of the Gathered Tribes for you to attend Them on Eerdish.

"While the word of honor of the United Planets Space Force still carries some weight here, They have laid specific requirements for your entry into the Eerdish System," Deetell continued. "You will be permitted to skip one vessel into Eerdish until further negotiations have been completed.

"All of your diplomatic personnel must arrive on that vessel. No more than four representatives and four bodyguards will be permitted to leave your ship at any time. You will not exceed acceleration of point-three KPS-squared, and you will be under the escort of the Eerdish Security Forces at all times.

"An exact course has been attached to this message. Deviation from that course will result in the destruction of your ship," Deetell told them, his voice still formal and calm.

"You may exchange personnel with your other two vessels, but you are expected to commence the assigned course within five hours.

"This is the Will of the Sovereign of Sovereigns, and the law of the stars that honor Their Name."

The recording ended and Henry snorted. So, the point of the recording had been to stop him or Sylvia from interrupting or arguing with the formal pronouncement. He had some idea of both the level of authority the Sovereign of Sovereigns held...and of the *image* of the Sovereign's authority the leaders of the Gathered Tribes chose to present.

He gave a mental command as he grabbed a coffee from the

machine and took a seat. A few seconds later, he had a channel to Sylvia.

"You saw the Defender-Lord's message?" he asked.

"I did," she confirmed. "Seems a bit...much for my understanding of the Sovereign's authority."

"Mine too, but you know that better than I do," he agreed cheerfully. "Talking up their figurehead?"

"That's my guess as well," she said. "Can we transfer the La-Tar contingent in the time they gave us?"

"Easily," Henry told her. "They chose their time window carefully. If we take the full five hours, we'll be in Eerdish orbit in about thirty-three hours. Faster if we, say, take *Paladin* back to the other ships at full GMS speed.

"I don't see a *military* reason to rush," he concluded drily. "But if you feel we need to make a good impression, I'm prepared to entertain reasons to expose more of our ships' ability."

"I see no diplomatic reason to rush for the Eerdish," Sylvia replied with a dry chuckle. "Certainly not enough of one to expose the full capabilities of your ship's gravity engines. Thirty-three hours sounds like plenty of time for us to prepare for the negotiations and your people to get an eyeful of Eerdish."

"We will definitely have our eyes open," Henry agreed. Hopeful allies or not, the Eerdish were a power in the Ra Sector—which meant they were a power within operational distance of the United Planets Alliance.

The more the UPA knew about them, the better.

CHAPTER TWENTY-EIGHT

No UPSF ship had ever entered the Eerdish home system before today. The Kenmiri had treated the homeworlds with a specifically careful touch during their reign. The key component was that non-Kenmiri only ever *left* the homeworlds.

Massive drafts of millions of colonists and janissaries left their home systems aboard massive transports. No one came back. The only ships allowed to enter the homeworlds' space were Kenmiri.

Henry had spent time on the Kozun homeworld both before and after its liberation and knew that restriction had often been broken in practice and the homeworld populations knew far more about the rest of the Empire than they'd been supposed to.

On the other hand, the homeworld governments were still, at least on the surface, self-run. They were collaborationist structures that answered to Kenmiri Governors, often more concerned with the preservation of their own privileges than protecting their people, but they'd been made up of locals.

With at least the esthetic of self-government, combined with access to their local space, a dribble of Kenmiri technology uplift and properly diversified economies, the homeworld populations had lived almost-normal lives under the Empire.

And when the Empire fell, they'd had the industry and government structures to survive, build fleets and reach out to the stars around them. Some of them had already quietly been doing so during the Empire, their resources underwriting the most powerful of the Vesheron factions.

Others had served the Kenmiri well and were now free to hopefully serve their people well.

Henry's faith was...limited.

Despite the politics and concerns, Eerdish was so like Sol as to actually trigger a moment of homesickness. Eight worlds, half rocky balls in the inner system, half smaller gas giants in the outer system—and with an asteroid belt dividing the two types of planets.

The star—Henry assumed it had a name other than *Eerdish*, but he didn't know it—was the same G2 type as Sol and the orbits were even similar. The inner two worlds were heat-scorched balls of rock, but the third world was in the liquid-water zone. Warm compared to Earth, Eerdish's burning skies were likely the cause of its people's usually dark coloration.

The fourth world was also warmer than Mars and arguably habitable. Their scans didn't show much habitation *there*, but the Kenmiri would hardly have encouraged in-system colonization—and Henry didn't know how much space travel the Eerdish had had when the Kenmiri had arrived.

"Our escort has arrived and matched courses," Ihejirika told him, *Paladin*'s commander sounding slightly worried.

"Some concern, Captain?" Henry asked, eyeing the icon of the ship sitting barely ten thousand kilometers from *Paladin*'s starboard wing. "You've never had a dreadnought sit on you before, have you?"

"I don't think I've ever been this close to a dreadnought, ser, and that includes the ones standing watch over the Great Gathering," his former Tactical officer told him. "Did they warn us that we'd have a dreadnought watching us?"

"Not in so many words, no," Henry said. "I was expecting a carrier group, to be honest."

The ship escorting *Paladin* had probably been assigned to Eerdish before the Fall. That it was still there suggested that the Kenmiri hadn't left Eerdish as smoothly as they'd likely hoped—the ship was on the small side for a dreadnought, at a "mere" six megatons, but the Kenmiri hadn't voluntarily left *any* dreadnoughts behind.

Paladin's shields were as powerful as a *Corvid*-class battlecruiser's, a side effect of the more powerful gravity projectors required for her GMS. Even at ten thousand kilometers, Henry would have backed the destroyer against almost any threat in the galaxy.

Against even a small dreadnought? The odds weren't in her favor. Six superheavy plasma cannon, eighteen lasers, thirty missile launchers... *Paladin* might manage to escape before those guns achieved enough blowthroughs to obliterate her.

Might.

"ETA to Eerdish orbit?" Henry asked.

"Just over four hours, ser," Ihejirika said. "Are the diplomats getting antsy?"

"If they are, Ambassador Todorovich hasn't passed it on," Henry said. Managing the diplomats had eaten up all of Sylvia's time since bringing the La-Tar contingent on board. He hadn't actually *seen* his lover since Yonca and Swaying Reed, her Enteni junior diplomat, had reported aboard.

"They know the laws of physics limit us," he continued. "They have some patience. And we, Captain, are keeping our eyes *very* open."

"Every passive sensor we have is feeding to CIC and the flag deck," Ihejirika confirmed. "Bach hasn't pointed anything of immediate threat to me yet."

"No, but it's a fascinating sight, isn't it?" Henry murmured.

Eerdish might have a similar planetary layout to Sol, but her industry paled in comparison to humanity's home system. Still, it was almost on par with, say, Keid, the younger of the European Union's two major colonies. There were a handful of Kenmiri heavy industry nodes in orbit of the homeworld itself, the same style as the Empire had installed over their own colonies, but most of the stations were home-built.

The homeworlds hadn't been allowed skip drives, but in-system travel was fine. The asteroid belt mining operations were clearly extensive, feeding raw material back to the refineries and factories that orbited Eerdish.

Unlike the factory worlds, the homeworlds kept their industry in orbit—where it belonged, according to most people. Gravity wells made for some advantages, but they hardly offset the pollution and devastation caused by massed modern industries.

On the factory worlds, the rapid degradation of the air and ability to grow crops was part of the point. Some of them had never even *had* a breathable atmosphere—though most had. It made the initial setup easier.

The part of all of the industry that *Henry* was most interested in, though, orbited the fourth planet—the not-quite-uninhabitable world the Kenmiri had to have actively banned the Eerdish from living on.

The industry there was clearly new, but rows of building slips now orbited the planet, gleaming with fresh steel as another dozen destroyers and three more carriers were coming together—and two even larger construction yards took shape behind them.

"If these are the resources of a homeworld, no wonder the Kozun have been such a pain," Ihejirika said quietly. "They had Kozun free what, a year before the Fall?"

"Thirteen months," Henry agreed. "So, look at everything the Eerdish have done here and add a third more time. Plus, they've conquered two more homeworlds along the way. Until they ran into us and an alliance of *multiple* homeworlds, I think they were starting to think nothing could stop them."

"I guess there still are the old Kenmiri colonies," *Paladin*'s Captain murmured. "Do we know what's going on there?"

"No," Henry admitted. "Truthfully? Because the E-Two are between them and both us and the Kozun. There are three true Kenmiri colonies in the Ra Sector, and we haven't communicated with them since the subspace coms went down. The Kozun have fought them and talked to them, but they haven't told *us* much of anything."

Though that told Henry one thing: the Kozun had *lost* when they'd fought the ex-Kenmiri colonies. The systems couldn't be doing too badly.

"I'm guessing they're on the list."

"When we get to them," Henry agreed. "Making peaceful contact with the Eerdish and the Enteni is key to that. So, Captain?"

"Ser?"

"I know we like to throw our weight around and remind everyone that we fly our own course, et cetera, et cetera," Henry said quietly. "But if the Eerdish ask you to do something over the next few days... just do it. We're not sure of the protocol here, and if we get it wrong, we're going to be in real trouble."

The dreadnought was a problem for *Paladin*. War with the Eerdish...well, that would kill a lot of people from a lot of places.

Henry didn't want to be responsible for that.

CHAPTER TWENTY-NINE

COORDINATING EIGHT PEOPLE OF THREE SPECIES ONTO A shuttle was harder than it had any right to be, in Sylvia Todorovich's considered opinion. She'd done it enough times that it was hardly new to her, but it was still...frustrating.

Finally, she got herself, Henry Wong, their two UPSF GroundDiv bodyguards, Yonca, Trosh—Yonca's lover, bodyguard, and chief of staff—Swaying Reed and Burning Skies—the Enteni diplomat and their Enteni bodyguard—settled into the tiny spacecraft.

"We're all good to go," Henry said into thin air. Presumably, his internal network passed the words to the shuttle's pilot, allowing Sylvia to knock one final task off her list.

The shuttle's engines flickered to life, lifting them gently off *Paladin*'s deck.

"Does this shuttle have one of your gravity drives?" Yonca asked in Kem.

"No," Henry replied. "It actually does not even have gravity plating. Sacrifices were made to equip shuttles of this class with a defensive gravity shield. She is designed to accelerate at one gravity the majority of the time, providing an equivalent downward thrust."

"Please remain seated for the trip," Sylvia added. "We will be approximately fifty-five minutes."

She was half-expecting someone to ask where the bathroom was, but her diplomatic contingent simply nodded and settled into their seats. Fitting the mobile Venus flytraps of the Enteni into proper safety gear had taken some arranging by *Paladin*'s crew—but at least they'd known it was coming!

The non-Terran members of the delegation drew tablets from their gear. The humans had their internal networks to review files on.

Sylvia quickly realized just how sparse the files she had on the Eerdish homeworld were. Henry's analysts had a decent assessment of the Eerdish's likely industrial and combat strength, plus the system's defenses, but that didn't tell her what she needed to know about the people she had to deal with.

"Envoy Yonca," she finally said. "Would you be able to brief us on the Council of Tribes and the Sovereign of Sovereigns? Just what are we getting into here?"

The Eerdish nodded slowly, focusing on her tablet as she clearly pulled up notes to review.

"Remember that while I am Eerdish, I have not set foot on my homeworld before," she told them. "Everything I know is from my parents, and my parents were part of a labor draft for La-Tar fifty-six years ago.

"Things may have changed in that time or during the Fall."

Having laid out her preconditions, Yonca nodded firmly and checked her notes one last time.

"The Eerdish population is divided into tribes. My parents did not know the exact number, and it does not appear to be in the files we have access to. The tribes are each led by a Chieftain, whose method of selection varies from tribe to tribe.

"Each group of tribes selects a Sovereign. This was once the ruler of those tribes and regions but under the Kenmiri was their representative to the global government, the Council of Tribes. When my parents left, there were one hundred and twenty Sovereigns.

"From their own number, the Sovereigns selected the Sovereign of Sovereigns, the theoretically absolute ruler of the Eerdish." She lifted a hand in a one-handed shrug. "Of course, even laying aside that the Sovereign of Sovereigns was answerable to the Kenmiri Governor, it was generally accepted that the Council of Tribes held the real power.

"While the form and esthetic of absolute power on the part of the Sovereign of Sovereigns was upheld, they could make no decisions on their own and that 'absolute power' was actually held by the Council of Tribes, each member of which was subject to recall by their Chieftains."

Who were, Sylvia presumed, subject to recall by their own tribes. Tiered representative democracy—at least in theory.

"The etiquette and rules around interacting with the Sovereign and Council require that we cannot meet with the Sovereign of Sovereigns alone," Yonca told them. "We will always meet with the full Council, but we are required to ignore the other Sovereigns. They are supposedly irrelevant servants and only the Sovereign of Sovereigns is worth our speaking with."

"But it is-was the Council that can-will decide our fate," Swaying Reed concluded, their translator having the usual struggles with Enteni tenses. "By popular vote, yes-yes?"

"Exactly," Yonca agreed. "But when meeting with them, we must act and speak as if we are dealing with the absolute ruler of the Eerdish in the person of the Sovereign of Sovereigns. Of course, the Sovereign of Sovereigns will not speak Kem and will speak through an interpreter. We must also ignore the interpreter."

"I have done worse," Sylvia said drily. "What else?"

"The Sovereign of Sovereigns is..." Yonca paused, clearly considering how to phrase something in Kem. "An entity without dimension."

"I do not understand," Sylvia admitted after a moment.

"They have no tribe, no clan, no family, no gender," Yonca said simply. "They are addressed as the gestalt of all Eerdish. To imply they are male or female, or of a tribe—even the tribe of their birth—is a grave insult.

"They *are* the people of Eerdish. All of them...and none of them. They have no dimensions of their own."

The explanation actually made sense to Sylvia—but she was used to twisting her mind around different cultures. She glanced over at Henry and sent him a mental question.

"*I've put in our files that the Sovereign is nonbinary,*" his mental voice replied in her head. "*That should suffice to avoid most problems.*"

Sylvia nodded and smiled. It wasn't like they were going to try to add different names other than the one they were given. Pronouns were their most likely mistake.

And she refused to blow up an interstellar negotiation because she couldn't use the singular *they* in Kem.

CHAPTER THIRTY

Hazalosh—the name meant "Place of Tent Gathering," according to Sylvia's translation software—had clearly once been a fortified mesa, a neutral meeting ground for a nomadic people in the center of an immense rolling plain.

The Eerdish had not, so far as Sylvia knew, been primarily nomadic for centuries before the Kenmiri had invaded. But Hazalosh remained the center of their culture and their government.

That, of course, meant that it was far more than a place to pitch tents. There was a ceremonial field of tents visible from the shuttle. Sylvia counted a hundred and twenty, which she guessed meant that all of the Sovereigns were present.

The rest of the mesa was crammed with structures, squat rounded buildings twenty meters in height at most. Some were clearly much older than others, with the majority of the structures made of a baked brick that would have been familiar to any denizen of Earth's Middle East.

At the north end of the mesa, like a tumor of steel, gold and guns, rose the baroque edifice of a Kenmiri Governor's residence. At the south end of the mesa rose a smaller but still-palatial structure of stone and brick.

The mesa was about a kilometer in diameter, elevated about a hundred meters above the plain. Other than the Kenmiri palace, everything on the mesa itself was either ancient or built to an ancient style.

The city *around* the mesa had been built with no concern for matching those aesthetics. The towers had bricks built up around their bases and were more rounded than most Terran structures, but they were the same steel-reinforced concrete of skyscrapers the galaxy over. Several towers rose to the same height as the mesa—Sylvia even saw one with a skybridge linked to the ancient fortifications on the mesa's edge.

Even with the skyscrapers, Hazalosh spread for dozens of kilometers in every direction. There had to be a hundred million people living in the megalopolis, making this *single city* rival the population of some of the Kenmiri slave worlds.

"Sers, we are being directed to the Kenmiri Governor's mansion," the pilot reported—speaking in Kem out of consideration for their passengers. "Is that expected? The antiair defenses are active and tracking us."

"There is unlikely to be a shuttle pad at the Palace of Palaces," Yonca pointed out. "I expect either the Sovereign and Council have taken over the Kenmiri Governor's mansion, or we will be transported to the Palace of Palaces to meet with them.

"Either way, I suspect that the old Governor's mansion has the only shuttle landing site on the mesa."

"Take us in, Lieutenant," Henry ordered calmly from next to Sylvia. "We don't want to be rude."

SYLVIA WAS unsurprised that there were vehicles waiting for them —low-slung and open-topped electric groundcars of a style she hadn't seen before. The local style, she supposed, safe enough for dry plains where rain could be seen coming for days.

The real surprises came when they entered the Palace of Palaces. Sylvia was familiar with the Eerdish *people,* but she'd never truly encountered their *culture.* Most of the citizens of the slave worlds adopted a generic mishmash of cultural wear and grooming, a mix that didn't suggest any threat to their overlords.

The guards wore armor carved from what she suspected *was* jade —or the local equivalent to the semiprecious stone, anyway. Finger-length scales of dark green rock were linked into modern body armor, shifting with surprising quiet as the guards moved and carried their equally modern energy rifles.

They led Sylvia and her companions along jade-tiled floors that had clearly been polished within the last twelve hours. None of the guards spoke, making the entire process an eerie journey. The silence was broken by the soft sound of chimes hidden away throughout the palace, a delicately beautiful background chorus.

The grand hall of the Palace of Palaces was roughly what she'd expected in terms of shape. She'd seen enough audience chambers over the years to know the type. This one resembled a high school gymnasium in many ways, with neat rows of benches on stepped rows on either side of the room, creating a long passageway to the immense dais at the other end.

The dais and its throne had been carved from a single immense piece of flawless pale green jade. Collectors and gem enthusiasts alike on Earth would have fallen over themselves to spend billions to own the thing. It was literally priceless, and even in its simplistic styling Sylvia guessed that the Eerdish would kill to keep it from moving a single centimeter.

The occupant of the throne—and the occupants of the stone benches lining the walls of the grand hall—was *not* simplistically styled. The profusion of colors and complex hairstyles that filled the stone benches along the sides of the hall were a kaleidoscope that could easily draw the untrained eye.

Sylvia's eye was *not* untrained. Her focus was on the dais ahead of her as she walked along the grand hall. Her network told her that the bodyguards had paused at the entrance, leaving only the diplomatic contingent to approach the being in the jade throne.

There were two Eerdish soldiers flanking the throne, wearing the same jade armor as the guards outside. Sylvia presumed there were others concealed behind the walls—she'd be stunned if there weren't individual concealed soldiers with weapons trained on each member of her party.

A third Eerdish, with a shaven head and wearing a plain white robe that Sylvia suspected had specific ritual meaning, stood at the Sovereign of Sovereigns' right hand. That, she guessed, was the interpreter.

Not irrelevant, but the etiquette required her to ignore the white-clad man as much as she ignored the guards and lesser Sovereigns. Her attention, from what Yonca had said, needed to be focused entirely on the occupant of the jade throne at the focal point of the room.

It was almost impossible to identify the actual appearance of the Sovereign of Sovereigns beneath their ceremonial garb. Their hair had been grown long and twisted through a ceremonial crown of gilded animal antlers, rising almost fifty centimeters from their head. Flowing robes, a mix of silver cloth and more jade scales, spread out across the throne and concealed the Sovereign's figure entirely, and heavy makeup turned their face into a mask.

Without rising, the Sovereign spoke in the staccato syllables of the Eerdish language. A moment later, the interpreter repeated their words in Kem.

"Representatives of the United Planets Alliance and the La-Tar Cluster, you are greeted and welcome in the Palace of Palaces and before the eyes of the Sovereign of Sovereigns."

Yonca stepped up beside Sylvia and made a small gesture, bringing the entire party to a halt five meters from the dais. She spoke in Kem.

"We are grateful for the Sovereign of Sovereigns' welcome," the Eerdish told them. "We know that your fleets guard your worlds against great threats and that permitting us to come here is a sign of great faith."

The Sovereign leaned forward—Sylvia noted that they did *not* need their interpreter to render Kem into Eerdish for them—and spoke again, waiting for the interpreter to catch up and then continuing slowly.

"Eskala, the Sovereign of Sovereigns, says that they are aware of your actions against our shared enemies in the Moti System," the interpreter said. He paused for a moment, listening to his Sovereign, then continued. "It is this action, combined with the blood we have shed together with the United Planets Alliance, that has permitted your presence here.

"We know both La-Tar and the United Planets Alliance are now allied with the Kozun."

Yonca and Sylvia had agreed on a series of gestures for the Eerdish diplomat to use to let Sylvia know when she should speak. Both of them knew Sylvia was in charge of this mission, but Yonca knew the local rules.

This time, she was passing the response to Sylvia.

"Sovereign of Sovereigns Eskala," Sylvia addressed the Eerdish leader. "Our alliance with the Kozun Hierarchy is strictly limited. We are no enemies of the Eerdish or your allies. We hope, in time, to build trade and permanent connections between our people."

She hesitated, then mentally shrugged and continued.

"We of the United Planets Alliance are, in fact, prepared to act as mediators between you and the Kozun," she offered. "While the Kozun have not yet agreed to any discussion, we would be willing to carry an offer of peace back to them."

"But this is not why you are here," Eskala said through their interpreter. "You speak of trade *in time*. You speak of being *prepared*. These are not why you are here. What brings you to the Sovereign of Sovereigns?"

Sylvia let Yonca field that one. She suspected that this was the most sensitive part of the discussion.

"We are here, Sovereign of Sovereigns, on a matter of justice and honor," Yonca told their audience. "Until short months ago, the La-Tar Cluster was at war with the Kozun Hierarchy, as you remain now.

"The United Planets Alliance had committed to assist us, and fought alongside us, against the Kozun. They aided us in liberating La-Tar from the Hierarchy's soldiers and in forming our new government.

"But we are not yet strong and we wished to make peace with the Kozun," Yonca admitted. "The Terrans were prepared to defend us until we could stand on our own, but we did not wish to ask that of them.

"Therefore, we and the United Planets Alliance reached out to the Kozun and arranged a peace summit. A discussion between three states to bring an end to our conflict before more innocents died."

Yonca paused, letting that sink into her crowd. She was *good*, Sylvia reflected.

"And at that peace summit, warships of the Blue Stripe Green Stripe Orange Stripe Drifter Convoy betrayed our faith," she told them. "They attacked the meeting ship belonging to my people and destroyed it. They destroyed the entire Kozun contingent and heavily damaged the United Planets Alliance detachment.

"We survived and learned of their treachery due to the intervention of additional Terran ships—and the skill of Commodore Henry Wong, commander of the surviving United Planets Alliance ship, and his crew."

She gestured to Henry, who somehow managed to stand even straighter.

"This is concerning," the Sovereign replied, the interpreter waiting for them to finish speaking before repeating. "But how is this the business of the Gathered Tribes of the Eerdish?"

"Our ships pursued the Convoy across the Ra Sector," Sylvia

said. "Commodore Wong himself followed them to the Nohtoin System, where they entered the space claimed by the alliance of the Gathered Tribes of the Eerdish and the Highest Principals of the Enteni.

"We seek the permission of the Sovereign of Sovereigns to pursue these murderers into your stars and bring them to the justice their actions demand."

Sylvia's attention, as she'd been instructed, was focused on Eskala. She could still hear the reaction of the Council behind and around her. Shuffling and whispered words in a language she didn't understand rippled down the hall.

"It is not the nature or desire of the Gathered Tribes to break the oaths of hospitality or agreements made in good faith," the Sovereign's interpreter said swiftly, barely keeping ahead of Eskala's rapid-fire staccato speech.

"The Drifters may have entered our space, but they are not allies with our enemies. Promises and agreements were made. You speak of treachery, but is the ally of our foe a trusted source on the deeds of our friends?

"You speak of honor, but *our* honor must also be satisfied."

Yonca tried to gesture for Sylvia to remain silent, but Sylvia ignored her, intentionally stepping forward and pushing the distance she was allowed to approach the Sovereign of Sovereigns.

"We will provide any proof that the Sovereign of Sovereigns desires," she told him. "We are not and have never been your enemies. We were not and had never been the *Drifters'* enemies. The same treachery that betrayed us lurks at your back—and it is not honorable to leave a knife at our neighbor's door."

The ripple of conversation was sharper now—and Sylvia was absolutely certain the Council of Tribes had a way to issue instructions to the Sovereign of Sovereigns. Eskala was silent for long enough that they were *definitely* receiving some kind of communication that Sylvia couldn't hear or see.

"The Sovereign of Sovereigns will consider your words," they finally said. "A recess is called, until the sun rises again above the mesa. You will be shown to quarters and fed. By the honor of the Gathered Tribes, you are safe here.

"This audience is over."

CHAPTER THIRTY-ONE

A WHITE-ROBED EERDISH WOMAN WITH A SHAVEN HEAD MET them just outside the hallway, another collection of eerily silent jade-armored guards with her.

"If you follow me, please, I will show you to the quarters the Sovereign of Sovereigns has requested for you," the woman told them, speaking slow but understandable Kem.

"Of course," Sylvia replied. "Do you have a name?"

The woman gave a half-bow.

"I am a Servant of the Palace," she said firmly, the capitals clear. "My name is forgotten while I wear the robe."

That was... Well, that was far from the weirdest thing Sylvia had dealt with for palace servants. She fell in behind the Servant with the rest of the contingent and mentally linked her network to Henry.

"The Drifters are still in their space, most likely," she told him silently.

"So I gathered. Does this change anything?" he asked.

"Not yet. I need to learn more, but I don't get the impression the staff will be cooperative."

"What interesting people."

The internal network communication didn't carry much in terms of emotion or thought processes, but Sylvia knew her lover well enough to know that he wasn't even being sarcastic. Eerdish culture was strange to them, but she also suspected that much of what they were seeing in the Palace of Palaces was ceremony and show.

The Sovereign of Sovereigns, after all, was very clearly *not* a supreme ruler.

The Servant stopped in front of a set of stone doors at least four meters tall. She produced a small bell from inside her robe and rang it. The doors instantly slid open, retreating into the walls on smooth bearings.

"In here, please," the Servant instructed. "This is the Suite of the Morning Sun Garden. It has bedrooms for each of you. I will show you."

Sylvia followed, obedient for now, as the white-robed woman gave them a quick and efficient tour. There was no kitchen, but otherwise the Suite had every amenity they could want, from a formal dining room to comfortable beds—even if the beds were set into recesses in the floor.

More chimes rang gently throughout the space, a slightly different but still beautiful background music to everything in the brick-built palace.

"A meal will be brought with the falling sun," the Servant told them. "If you have any needs, ring the bell by the doors and I or another Servant of the Palace will attend."

She gave the same strange half-bow and retreated out of the Suite with the jade-armored guards, the heavy stone doors sliding shut behind her.

Sylvia looked at the doors, then glanced over to meet Henry's gaze.

"Those doors don't appear to have controls from this side," he said drily. "Are we guests or prisoners?"

"Can you communicate with *Paladin?*" she asked.

"Relaying via the shuttle," he told her. "I've advised the pilot and crew to wait for us. The locals have offered them food and lodging as well." He grimaced. "The pilot declined, since the shuttle has comfortable-enough spaces and rations for them. I hope that wasn't a major error."

"It should not be," Yonca said in Kem, the Eerdish diplomat rejoining them in front of the door. Her understanding of English was clearly getting better. "Some paranoia on our part is both expected and tolerated. That we have been put up like this, while intimidating, is also a guarantee of our safety.

"The Council cannot permit anyone under the Sovereigns' protection to be harmed without a grand trial and gesture."

"Are we being kept for such a trial?" Henry asked, switching to Kem.

"Not likely. Most likely, the Council of Tribes is having a long discussion over whether they believe us or the Drifters," Sylvia told them all. "Who knows what the Convoy has told them. We have the data records from *Raven* to prove the Drifters' treachery—and even information from the Kozun's scans and analysis of their missiles to prove that the Drifters managed to fire their weapons remotely."

"It's going to be an interesting morning," her lover said grimly. "My network makes it three hours to sundown, eleven to sunrise."

"We will be taken before the Sovereign of Sovereigns exactly at sunrise, from what was said," Yonca told them. "The Sovereign of Sovereigns is theoretically bound to tell the truth, though they will conceal and deflect around things they do not wish to reveal."

"Hence saying the Drifters *may* have come here," Sylvia agreed. "We will need to watch what Eskala says closely."

"We have the proof of the Drifters' treachery, and I do not think the Council of Tribes will take the Drifters' actions lightly," Yonca said. "*Honor* and *honesty* are words to conjure with here, even if practicality has a weight all its own."

"We shall see at sunrise, I suppose," Henry said grimly. "But I warn you, we can't break our way out of here. Not with five energy pistols against the guards of an entire palace."

Sylvia concealed a mental chuckle as she traded looks with him. From the eyebrow he arched at her, Henry knew as well as she did that everything they said was being recorded.

As Yonca said, *practicality had a weight all its own.*

CHAPTER THIRTY-TWO

Several Servants came for them in the morning, different Eerdish though all in the same white robes and with the same shaven heads. More green-armored guards accompanied them as well, the escort enough larger than the prior day that it took Sylvia several minutes to realize they weren't heading back to the grand hall.

"*We're going somewhere different,*" she messaged Henry.

"*I noticed. Neither you nor Yonca seemed concerned, so I was choosing not to be,*" he replied. "*Should I be?*"

Sylvia had to think about that for a moment. They were still, so far as she knew, under the protection of the Council of Tribes. Wherever they were going, it was probably going to be safe.

"*I don't think so. I'm just not sure what we're getting into, and that concerns me.*"

She was entertained to see Henry shift ever so slightly closer to her, as if to reassure or protect her, whichever was needed.

Not that the energy pistol he wore on his hip—the reconfigured sidearm of a Kenmorad consort, taken as a prize of war long ago—would help protect them against a dozen jade-armored soldiers with energy rifles.

Eventually, they were taken down a set of steps that curved in a wide spiral, descending into the bedrock of the mesa. The stairs were broad and well lit, but it rapidly became clear that they were underground.

Finally, they were led out into a surprisingly small square room with several rows of descending benches carved into it, like an inverted stepped pyramid. There wasn't enough space for the entire Council of Tribes to be there.

The Sovereign of Sovereigns was seated in a simpler chair than their grand jade throne in the grand hall, though this seat was carved from a single piece of granite that was still attached to the ground beneath them. Everything else in the room might move, but the Sovereign of Sovereigns was rooted to the ground.

Their hair was done up in a meter-wide golden fan today, glittering in the mix of electric lights and literal torches that lit the room. Today, the robes were jade over deep blood-red fabric that took Sylvia several seconds to realize *was* silk.

For silk to have made it to Eerdish from Earth, it must have gone through at least a dozen middlemen. There was likely no more expensive garment on the entire *planet*.

The dozen Sovereigns of the Council of Tribes who surrounded Eskala were dressed only slightly less flamboyantly than their figurehead—though Sylvia realized there were no white-robed interpreters today.

The Eerdish weren't alone, either. A contingent of five Enteni had been set up at the Sovereign of Sovereigns' left hand, the dark-skinned flytrap-like aliens holding their mouths wide open to show their tentacled eyes as they watched Sylvia's people advance.

To the Sovereign of Sovereigns' *right*, however, was the delegation that Sylvia had half-expected—and half-wondered if they would exist. Wrapped in enshrouding black robes with only face masks visible, six Drifters also waited for Sylvia's arrival.

There would be a grand trial and spectacle before any guest of the Council of Tribes could be allowed to come to harm. The question, Sylvia now knew, was *which* set of guests was going to be found at fault today.

The Sovereigns in this room would be the Eerdish's true leaders. The Enteni ambassador would be an observer. If Sylvia wished to turn memories of a broken alliance into a future pact, she needed to not only convince those Eerdish leaders that the Drifters had betrayed the UPA and the La-Tar...but that they were going to betray the *Eerdish*.

And that was the job the United Planets Alliance had sent Sylvia Todorovich to do.

"AMBASSADOR SYLVIA TODOROVICH, be known to Ambassador Blue-Stripe-Third-Green," Eskala said calmly in perfect Kem. It was hard to tell through the makeup and ceremonial garb, but Sylvia suspected that the Sovereign of Sovereigns was smiling at Sylvia's surprise.

"There are times that ceremony and tradition must give way to the practicalities of power," the Eerdish man sitting to Eskala's right said. He wore a tight-fitted black bodysuit, either a spacesuit or intentionally intended to look like one, which had been covered in a whirling pattern of hand-inlaid gold leaf.

"We"—the man gestured to the Eerdish in the room—"represent the leading Sovereigns of the Council of Tribes. Between ourselves and the Sovereign of Sovereigns, we are capable of making decisions for the full Gathered Tribes of the Eerdish.

"In a private meeting such as this, the forms of ceremony must be laid aside for the simple words of truth and power."

Sylvia doubted that the truth of the smaller meeting space and less-formal meeting was *quite* so simple, but at the very least, Eskala wasn't speaking through an interpreter there.

There were, in fact, no Servants of the Palace in the room at all. Only the leadership of the Eerdish and the diplomatic contingents.

The fact that Sylvia's people's bodyguards had been permitted into the room with them told her that there were still defenses present but the Eerdish Sovereigns were unattended.

"Ambassador Todorovich, also be known to Ambassador Passionate Iron," Eskala continued after their companion had finished speaking. They indicated the Enteni sitting in front of their delegation, a redder-toned Enteni unlike any Sylvia had seen before.

"Ambassador Blue-Stripe-Third-Green, Ambassador Passionate Iron," Sylvia greeted the other two diplomats with a small half-bow. "I expected the presence of the Enteni, given the Gathered Tribes alliance with the Highest Principals. I must admit to surprise at the presence of Ambassador Blue-Stripe-Third-Green, however."

"You wished to spin your lies without those who bear the truth to answer, did you?" the Drifter asked calmly. Their Face Mask was exactly what the name they used described: the top two-thirds were white, the bottom third was green, and a diagonal blue stripe crossed from the top right to the bottom left.

"I am fully prepared to provide, as promised, the full details of the events in the Lon System," Sylvia told the Eerdish Sovereigns. "If the Drifter Ambassador wishes to provide their people's version of events, that is more than welcome.

"I do not desire to deceive the Sovereign of Sovereigns or the Council of Tribes. Our *war*"—she stressed the word carefully, watching the heavily robed Drifter contingent out of the corner of her eye—"is with the people who betrayed a peace summit and murdered our spacers.

"The people who, in fact, destroyed the ship *I* was on to negotiate with the Kozun Third Voice," Sylvia continued calmly. "I only survived thanks to the ingenuity and foresight of our La-Tar allies—whose protection of the Third Voice brought peace between their worlds and the Kozun Hierarchy."

No one here needed to know that the Third Voice, Oran Aval, was the mate of the *First* Voice, Mal Dakis—and had been pregnant with his child at the time. The Drifters had very nearly killed the heir presumptive to the Kozun Hierarchy before she'd been born.

Mal Dakis was ruthless and pragmatic enough to delegate his vengeance to the UPSF and Twelfth Fleet—but Sylvia suspected that was only because he knew there was no real point in his reinforcing Admiral Rex. If there had been any chance in Dakis's mind that the Drifters might escape...there'd have been a lot fewer games being played by the Kozun.

"In truth, we Drifters do not know all that passed in the Lon System," Blue-Stripe-Third-Green told the Eerdish. "Our ships were ambushed and our people murdered by the United Planets Space Force."

"Then perhaps I can illuminate all of the events of that fateful day," Sylvia offered. "Indeed, you may be able to offer some explanation as to why your people betrayed us and our attempts to bring peace to the Ra Sector."

"We were not the ones with an entire fleet standing by, were we, Ambassador Todorovich?" the Drifter asked sharply.

"A necessary precaution, as it turned out," Sylvia replied calmly. "Or Commodore Wong here would now be dead and your people's treachery concealed from the galaxy."

"Enough," the unnamed Eerdish Sovereign who'd spoken before snapped. "You are never going to convince each other to change your positions. The question today is which of you the Council of Tribes will believe.

"The Drifters came to us in their normal patterns, offering trade and information as they always have," he noted. "We do not know Blue Stripe Green Stripe Orange Stripe of old, but we have dealt with the Drifters before. The usual promises of hospitality and trust were exchanged.

"You, Ambassador Todorovich, come to us in strange ways," he continued. "Allies to our enemies who claim to not be our foes, you speak of treachery by those whom we have offered sacred hospitality."

The Sovereign of Sovereigns held up a hand, wrapped in gloves of the same red silk as their robes.

"Were you anyone else, Ambassador Todorovich, we would have denied you entrance to this star system," Eskala told them. "But you bring diplomats from the stolen children of our people, and we would learn their fates and work with them.

"And we are not blind to the acts of the United Planets Space Force. Was it not Commodore Wong himself who struck the final blow and cast down the last of the Kenmorad? To the UPSF we owe our newborn liberty.

"We would poorly repay the sacrifices made on our behalf if we were to ignore you."

Sylvia didn't even need to look at Henry to know that wouldn't sit well with him. *Raven* had been the farthest-flung force of Golden Lancelot. They'd been less than an hour later than the rest of the attacks, but it was suspected that the Kenmorad breeding sect that had tried to escape him had known they were the last.

Henry certainly hadn't known that when he'd killed them—but that was a tiny shield against the realization you'd *personally* ended a species.

"I do not ask any of this lightly," Sylvia told the Sovereigns. "I understand the weight of what I am requesting, but our duty and honor leave us no choice. Blue Stripe Green Stripe Orange Stripe's actions cannot go unanswered.

"If they are innocent, Sovereigns of the Gathered Tribes, why are they running?"

"Enough, Ambassadors," Eskala said softly. "Torus, provide Ambassador Todorovich with the control pad for the holographic projector.

"Show us your evidence, Ambassador. This argument leads us nowhere that we could not predict."

Torus was apparently the Sovereign who'd been speaking. He produced a standard Kenmiri datapad and handed it to Sylvia.

"I presume, Ambassador, that you have your evidence with you?" he asked.

"Of course," Sylvia confirmed. Everything she'd needed had been loaded onto a standard Kenmiri datachip, which she slotted into the control pad. It took her a second to make sure she was looking at the correct controls—she would normally have left this part to Leitz, but bringing Henry and the La-Tar diplomats had been more important than bringing an aide.

Bringing Henry had now been fully worth it, she judged. Her boyfriend might not *like* the reputation he had in the former Kenmiri Empire, but he'd already paid for it and Sylvia would damn well use it.

"You are all capable of reading standard Vesheron tactical iconography, I presume?" Sylvia asked. Standard Vesheron iconography was, of course, also standard *Kenmiri* iconography—and noticeably different from the data presentation used by the UPA or the other external powers that had helped the Vesheron.

No one admitted they couldn't, and Sylvia filled the center of the inverted-pyramid meeting room with a holographic display of the Lon System. Three Kozun cruisers, three Drifter Guardians—capital ships built to defend the Convoys against Kenmiri dreadnoughts—a La-Tar escort, a UPSF destroyer, and the battlecruiser *Raven*. Henry's old command.

"Now, certain aspects of what you are about to see are confusing," Sylvia warned. "It was not a straightforward sequence of events, and I will provide evidence to support certain statements once I have played the recording.

"Before I begin, however, I would like you to consider one question: who sold the Kozun their missiles?"

She received several questioning looks, but she ignored them as she started the recording.

Sylvia had watched this recording several times, but it was still painful. All nine ships seemed to be calm, waiting for the result of the negotiations taking place aboard the escort *Carpenter*—and then the three Kozun cruisers fired.

They only fired their missiles, but that was enough. Dozens of weapons launched at close range, swarming over *Carpenter*, the UPSF destroyer, and *Raven*.

Only *Raven* survived, almost instantly flipping in space to accelerate away from the chaos. If the Kozun had *planned* this, the Terran battlecruiser would have died in the following moments, as she remained well inside the range of their plasma cannon.

Instead, the next ships to fire, almost a minute later—about six seconds, in this accelerated recording—were the Drifters. Plasma fire hammered into the Kozun cruisers' energy screens—and, at least initially, the Kozun didn't fire back.

Instead, they ran. One of their ships was almost *dead* before they started firing back at the Drifters, and even then, many of their turrets —turrets sold by the Drifters—were nonfunctional.

While the Guardians pursued the Kozun, their fighters blasted out after *Raven*. A daring strike by *Raven*'s tiny handful of fighters drove them off, buying the ship time to hide.

The recording froze after the death of the last Kozun ship—to a pre-laid minefield—and Sylvia cleared her throat.

"I can continue the recording at a faster time acceleration, but the Guardians' search for *Raven* took almost an entire day before Carrier Group *Scorpius* arrived to relieve them," she noted. "None of the Guardians attempted to surrender, and they destroyed several planetoids where then-Captain Wong had rigged up decoys to look like *Raven* was hiding."

The meeting room was quiet now, the Eerdish looking up at the frozen recording silently. Finally, Blue-Stripe-Third-Green broke the silence.

"I do not see the treachery you claim from my people in this recording," they pronounced. "Clearly, the Kozun fired on the diplomatic ships—and your people reacted by firing on mine when we attempted to assist!"

"Certainly, if the Kozun had continued firing after that first salvo, I would have believed that," Sylvia said quietly. "While I now *know* that Star Voice Kalad had no such orders, I do believe that she would have obeyed orders to destroy the summit, including her own diplomat."

Knowing what she did about Oran Aval and Mal Dakis, Sylvia knew there was no chance such an order would have ever been given —but Kalad *would* have obeyed it.

"But she would have carried out such an attack with far more competence than that," she continued. "A single missile salvo, then no follow-up fire for several minutes? While the Drifters fired on them? Does that strike you as a clever plan for destroying a peace summit, Sovereigns?"

She tapped a command, and the hologram zoomed in on the minefield that had destroyed the last Kozun ship.

"I am not familiar with the design of these mines," she noted. "They're not a Kenmiri design, though they appear quite standard-ized. I don't suppose any of you are familiar with them?"

"They are a Drifter export product," Torus pointed out, his tone grim. Sylvia had apparently guessed correctly that that particular Sovereign was military or former military—the spacesuit was a dead giveaway.

"One that the Kozun have purchased in quantities as large as you have, Sovereign," Blue-Stripe-Third-Green pointed out.

"The Drifter Ambassador's point is fair," Sylvia said. "On the other hand, would Kozun mines have fired on a *Kozun* ship? And Commodore Wong...does the UPSF have any significant quantity of those mines?"

"The UPSF does not have *any* space mines, Ambassador," Henry said formally. "We have generally judged that the variability in skip-line emergence renders them useless unless you know your enemy's exact target. We could fabricate some, but the design in our fabrica-tors is actually *Kenmiri*, not Drifter."

"All of that is secondary, however," Sylvia said, her tone

pristinely calm as she looked at Blue-Stripe-Third-Green's mask and brought up a second set of data. "We had the opportunity, after the Battle of the Lon System, to dismantle several missiles sold to us, the Kozun, and the La-Tar Cluster by Blue Stripe Green Stripe Orange Stripe."

The schematics of the missiles glowed brightly in the air, sliding apart and lighting up with new icons that marked who had owned each set of missiles.

"All of the missiles contained software and hardware capable of initiating an emergency-jettison cycle from *any* standard missile launcher," she told her audience. "I am not certain, given the explanation I was provided, that any sanely designed missile launcher would retain these missiles once the process was initiated.

"Once so jettisoned, the missile would acquire a target based on a profile downloaded to it and activate exactly as if it had been normally launched—but this entire process could be activated remotely via a coded signal."

That had the attention of the Eerdish and Enteni contingents.

"Reviewing the sensor records from the Lon System, we confirmed that such a signal was sent from the Drifter Guardians shortly before the Kozun appeared to fire on the UPA contingent," Sylvia concluded. "The failure after that of the plasma turrets mounted on the cruisers that had been provided by the Drifters tells a similar story.

"The Kozun purchased much of the hardware and ammunition for their initial military buildup from Blue Stripe Green Stripe Orange Stripe," she told the Eerdish, her gaze focused on Torus. "And the Drifters made very sure *they* held the triggers.

"I suggest, Sovereigns, that we take a recess while you provide this data to the Eerdish Security Forces and they review *your* Drifter-purchased missiles," Sylvia concluded.

"This is preposterous," Blue-Stripe-Third-Green spluttered. "Why would we sell tainted hardware to our allies?"

"I see no reason," Eskala said, sounding like they agreed with the

Drifters. "Which means, of course, that such a review would turn up no such traps in the missiles and systems we purchased from your Convoy, would it?

"Sovereigns, I believe a review of the munitions and so forth acquired from the Blue Stripe Green Stripe Orange Stripe Convoy would be wise. Does anyone disagree?"

"You already had-will reviewed them when you took them into service, I would-will hope," Passionate Iron observed, the Enteni's translated voice flat.

"A sample of a specific modification could perhaps permit us to find something we missed before," Torus said calmly. "I believe it would be in everyone's interest for us to check our systems. If there are no such traps, then the Drifters have dealt fairly with us and we must consider the evidence presented to us by other metrics.

"But if the Drifters have betrayed us as well..."

The Sovereign trailed off, glancing at his fellows.

"I believe that a recess to review the evidence and allow our forces to examine the Terrans' data is in order," he suggested. "I second the Sovereign of Sovereigns' call."

What followed looked like nothing so much as a twelve-player game of rock-paper-scissors to Sylvia. Each of the ten Sovereigns who hadn't made a statement made a three-beat hand gesture.

She didn't know what the gesture of three fingers splayed out in the air meant, but it was a clearly unanimous choice.

Eskala made a sweeping hand gesture.

"Servants of the Palace will see the ambassadors back to their suites," they told them. "We require that the Drifter and UPA contingents remain in their suites until our investigation is complete.

"You will hear from our Servants when you are summoned once more."

And if nothing else, the fact that the *Drifters* now appeared to also be under house arrest told Sylvia she was winning.

CHAPTER THIRTY-THREE

A FULL DAY PASSED IN "QUIET CONTEMPLATION"—MOSTLY pacing around in circles, since there was a limit to what they could talk about aloud and Sylvia wasn't sure how far they could trust even their network-to-network coms. Those radios were extremely low-power and heavily encrypted, but nothing was unbreakable.

In a diplomatic suite, she didn't even feel that she could get away with dragging Henry to bed. That left her and everyone else just...waiting.

"Sunset," Henry murmured. He'd been the least noticeably bothered of her people, but she knew that was simply long practice at hiding his stress. Even the *Enteni* were more obviously stressed than he was, to Sylvia's eyes.

But she also knew him. She followed his gesture and looked up from the small courtyard in the center of the Suite of the Morning Sun Garden. Dawn looked prettier from the garden—hence the suite's name, she presumed—but the sunset lit up the red brick of the Palace of Palaces and the rest of the mesa's building in glorious colors.

It was sufficiently epic a view that she missed the sound of the doors opening until they *thunk*ed into place and footsteps echoed through the suite.

"We have visitors," she told Henry, rising from the bench and turning toward the entrance. The door was still open behind the visitor, with two jade-armored guards and two white-robed Servants waiting in the open entrance.

Ahead of them, delicately stepping into the sunken garden, was Torus. The black-shipsuited Eerdish was almost blending into his faux uniform in the mixed lighting as he approached them, but his eyes were calm and his jaw was set.

"Is the recess over, Sovereign Torus?" Sylvia asked politely.

"Not officially," he said calmly. "May I sit?"

"These are your people's benches," Henry said drily beside her. "We are your...guests."

"You would never have been prevented from leaving," Torus said, taking a careful seat on the stone bench. "We would always have gladly transported you to your shuttle, though it would have done your cause a great disservice."

"So we waited patiently," the Commodore agreed. "If the recess is not over, Sovereign..."

"The Drifters left, didn't they?" Sylvia asked.

There was a long pause, then Torus laced his hands together and rolled them to splay, palm-outward, toward them. He chuckled along with the gesture.

"More than our hardware was corrupted by the Drifters, it seems," he said calmly. "A software worm was introduced into our orbital scanners. I do not know when. Combined with an authorization for launch that their shuttle should not have received, the Drifter embassy has now left Hazalosh."

"You did find the trigger devices, then," Sylvia guessed.

"We did," Torus confirmed. "Our own missile production is such that we will not be significantly impeded by discarding the Drifter weapons, but it is unfortunate and awkward. The plasma cannon we had purchased from them have not yet been installed, which renders their additions there even less harmful.

"But that is a matter of timing and luck," he noted. "While I do not expect that we would have come to conflict with the Drifters without your visit, we would have been at a dangerous disadvantage without your warning."

"You are welcome," Sylvia said. "We provided that information for our own reasons, but I am pleased that our honesty has served you as well."

"Will the Drifter Ambassador be captured?" Henry asked, his tone eager.

"Unfortunately, no," Torus replied. "Their ship is faster than most of our warships and appears to be equipped with stealth technology we have not encountered before. We know which skip line they are heading for, but...that is insufficient to catch them."

"Damn. Our ships are faster," Henry offered. "We can help."

"Not yet," the Sovereign said. "There will be another meeting of the Close Council at sunrise. You will be invited once again. There, you will be permitted to make your case for what you wish from us.

"Until we have a specific agreement and plan, we have no intention of allowing your ships to run wild in our territory," Torus noted. "We now believe your warnings about the Drifters and we *will* permit you to pursue, but this will not be an open account, Commodore Wong."

"We are willing to abide by restrictions set by the Gathered Tribes, I believe," Sylvia promised. That was...partially a lie. So long as the restrictions were *reasonable*, they'd live with them. To a point.

Sooner or later, though, Twelfth Fleet was going to go after the BGO Convoy. The Eerdish would either allow that or be pushed out of the way.

"I expect we will come to a reasonable agreement," Torus said. She suspected he figured *exactly* where the UPA stood. "While I cannot *guarantee* that the Close Council will allow your pursuit of the Drifters through our territory, I also cannot see any reason we would deny you now.

"But a balance must be struck between our sovereignty and the Kozun threat to our stars and allies and your mission, Ambassador Todorovich," he warned. "Eskala and I believe that balance can be found, but we do not control the Close Council, let alone the full Council of Tribes."

He inclined his head.

"You needed to be updated on the state of affairs," he told them. "We will speak again in the morning, when the Close Council gathers once more to deal with this problem you have created for us."

Torus rose with the same calm elegance that he had seated himself with.

"The Servants will shortly bring your meal," he promised. "Please, feel free to ask of them for anything you need. You are not, I remind you, prisoners here—though I will admit that you are more honored guests this eve than you were this morn."

MORNING BROUGHT them all back to the underground chamber with its descending benches. Once again, the Sovereign of Sovereigns was seated before Sylvia and her people entered the room. They were joined by the Enteni ambassador but not, for reasons obvious after Torus's evening visit, the Drifters.

"Welcome again to the private chamber of the Close Council," Eskala greeted them. "Torus advised you last night of our initial learnings around the Drifters' treachery. The night has brought more news, but the fundamentals of the matter are unchanged."

"How may the UPSF assist the Gathered Tribes and Highest Principals?" Sylvia asked.

"The Drifters have not acted against us, though the traps they laid through the arms they sold us suggest a preparation for such," one of the other Sovereigns said. "We have no need to act against them so long as they do not attack our people."

"But the protection they were granted by our sacred hospitality is now lifted," Eskala countered firmly. "We are prepared to consider permitting you to act against them. So speak, Ambassador Todorovich, of what the United Planets Alliance would have from us."

Sylvia glanced at Yonca, who gestured for her to answer the question. That much was obvious, she supposed.

"The UPSF has assembled a strike force capable of neutralizing the defenders of the BGO Convoy," she admitted. "The destroyers under Commodore Henry Wong's command are scouts, seconded from our normal peacekeeping forces in this region.

"We pursued the Drifters to the Nohtoin System but did not violate your space. Now we request permission for Commodore Wong's ships to follow Ambassador Blue-Stripe-Third-Green back to the Convoy and locate them.

"Once the Convoy is located, we request free passage for Twelfth Fleet to proceed through your space to engage the Drifters and neutralize their threat."

The *plan* was to seize control of the Convoy until they were certain they knew *why* the Drifters had attacked them—and hence could make sure it didn't happen again. The destruction of the Convoy wasn't anyone's plan.

In theory, at least, the Convoy's threat could be neutralized without killing their civilians.

"We do not require the Eerdish-Enteni Alliance's assistance in dealing with the Drifters," she noted. "And we will formally commit to share no sensor data from our mission with the Kozun Hierarchy.

"Beyond this particular mission, we hope to negotiate peaceful trade agreements for ourselves and to open doors for the La-Tar Cluster to negotiate trade agreements of their own," she noted. "We are certainly prepared to act as intermediaries between you and the Kozun as well, though we understand that peace negotiations require two willing parties."

Eskala traded glances with their fellow Sovereigns, then leaned forward to hold Sylvia's gaze.

"We are prepared to authorize passage for Commodore Wong's three destroyers," they said. "We will provide a Sovereign Writ to draw on Eerdish Security Force logistics for fuel and supplies, if needed, and to grant free passage through our stars.

"In exchange, we will require full copies of your sensor data from your trip through our stars and everything you learn of the Drifters," the Sovereign of Sovereigns concluded. "Once you have located the Convoy, *then* we can discuss whether the Gathered Tribes and our allies are prepared to permit you to bring a *fleet* into our stars."

Passionate Iron leaned forward and fluttered a limb as Eskala paused.

"We can-will also provide free passage to the stars-we-claim of the Highest Principals," they noted. "Our Alliance stands as one in this."

"It is appreciated," Sylvia said with a small bow of her head. "We are prepared to negotiate passage for the fleet at a later date, but locating the Convoy is critical. We are willing to provide that sensor data in exchange."

She knew that Henry might reduce the resolution and integrity of that data to give away less of the *Cataphracts'* abilities, but they could certainly pass over the data.

As for negotiating Twelfth Fleet's passage, it was possible the Drifters would be well beyond the space of the E-Two Alliance before the Terrans could catch them. At that point, the negotiation would truly just be for *passage*—which would be cheaper than permission to wage war in Eerdish space.

"Then it is agreed," Eskala said firmly. They waved a hand around the room. "As for trade agreements and peaceful communications, these are discussions that will take more time than I expect Commodore Wong wishes to spend here.

"We are prepared to open those discussions with yourself and the La-Tar representatives, if you will remain here?"

"I must remain with Commodore Wong's squadron," Sylvia admitted. She hadn't honestly expected the Eerdish to want to commence trade negotiations immediately—that implied that *they* might be shorter on trade partners than she'd suspected.

Even if she had to go, though, there were options.

"I can, however, leave another empowered representative of the United Planets Alliance here with Envoys Yonca and Swaying Reed," she said. "Envoy Felix Leitz would be able to speak on behalf of both myself and our government for those discussions while Commodore Wong and I search for the Drifters."

There was always the hope that she could talk the Drifters down from the precipice they'd walked themselves out onto. Sylvia wasn't sure what they could *do* to convince the UPA that they weren't a threat now, but the possibility existed, so a diplomat had to be attached to the scout mission.

"This is acceptable," Eskala told her. "Please, Ambassadors, Envoys, Commodore. We have an agreement for now. Dine with me?"

For the first time in the hidden chamber, white-robed Servants emerged. Each carried a plate of food and Sylvia concealed a smile.

She doubted that most people, even diplomatic representatives, were invited to eat breakfast with the Sovereign of Sovereigns. They'd apparently made quite the impression there.

CHAPTER THIRTY-FOUR

HENRY WAS BARELY ABLE TO CONCEAL HIS RELIEF WHEN HE finally stepped back onto the metal decks of his flagship. Potentially hostile planets were always stressful—and he was discovering he wasn't a large fan of spending time locked with Sylvia in close quarters and *not* being able to take advantage of that fact.

She was a step behind him exiting the shuttle, but the two of them had been the only passengers on the shuttle. Their bodyguards were remaining on the surface to augment the security detail going down with Felix Leitz.

A permanent embassy was allowed significantly more aides and security personnel than a representative of a potential enemy, it turned out.

Captain Ihejirika and Commander Eowyn were waiting for them as Henry and Sylvia cleared the safety barriers around the shuttle landing zone, both saluting Henry crisply as he approached.

Henry returned the salutes.

"Welcome back aboard *Paladin*, ser," the destroyer's massive Captain told him. "It's good to see you and the Ambassador well."

"We were never in danger, as it turned out," Henry replied with a chuckle. "Ambassador Todorovich had the entire situation well in hand."

"It helped that apparently the Drifters couldn't keep themselves from screwing with *all* of the missiles they sold," Sylvia said drily. "There's a lot of potential here, but that'll be on Felix. For us... I don't suppose you got a good look at the Drifter ship when they ran?"

Henry chuckled again.

"The Ambassador is asking my questions before I can," he told his team. "Update us as we walk? You may as well fill her in, too."

"Yes, ser," Ihejirika confirmed, falling into step with Henry. Both of his subordinates quickly realized Henry was heading to his flag-deck office.

He was feeling out of the loop and that meant getting back to work.

"We had a front-row seat to the worm knocking out Eerdish Security Forces' sensors," Eowyn said quietly. "I've never seen anything quite like it. So far as the ESF could see, that ship just *wasn't there*."

"It was that obvious, was it?" Henry asked.

"She flew about fifty kilometers in front of *Hazalosh*'s bow on her way out," the Ops officer said grimly. "Whoever was in charge *knew* the locals couldn't see her—and figured *we* weren't going to open fire without Eerdish permission."

"Honestly, we didn't put together what we were looking at until the ship was well on its way," Ihejirika grumbled. "I thought the ESF was doing some kind of exercise. It was an odd-looking little ship, even smaller than that raider corvette the Drifters used in Nohtoin."

"The Eerdish said it had other stealth systems as well?" Henry said.

"Once we realized what was going on, we watched her the entire way to the skip line," Eowyn replied. "Or we tried to, anyway. She vanished about a light-minute from the planet."

"Vanished, Commander?" Henry asked. He traded a swift salute with a working party as the four officers dodged around an open panel where the team was working on some of *Paladin*'s electricals.

"Like in Avas, ser," she told him. "Stealth systems. They started running a mirroring program on their hull and sinking their heat. We knew where she was, so we could keep a decent probability cone on her, but..."

Eowyn shook her head.

"If we hadn't been watching her, I don't think we'd have seen her at that one light-minute. I can see, mostly, how their system is working. But I'll be damned if I think we have the tech to replicate it."

"Is it less or more visible than GMS at half a KPS-squared?" Henry asked. He'd been pleasantly surprised by how sneaky his ships were at low accelerations.

"Less," she warned. "Not a lot less, but less—and they were burning faster than that. We know which skip line they took, but even with our scanners, they were hard to follow."

"Are we going to be able to follow their trail on the other end?" he said.

"Maybe," Eowyn warned. "Maybe not. We may need to rely on the locals having picked them up as they pass."

"Then that's what we'll do, if necessary," he agreed. "Blue-Stripe-Third-Green is a fresher lead than the trail in Nohtoin, so let's follow him home. When is the rest of the squadron due to arrive?"

"*Cataphract* and *Maharatha* have confirmed receipt of orders by return drone," Eowyn said. "They'll be entering the skip line around now and arriving in Eerdish in nine hours."

"We'll want to run the numbers on whether it's more efficient to rendezvous and then follow the Drifters or have them head to the skip line independently," Henry ordered. "Or have you already done that?"

"My team has been working on it," Eowyn confirmed as they reached the flag deck. She blinked as she received a message. "And they're done. Good timing."

"And?"

"We'll save about four hours if we all head directly to the Sohn System skip line when the rest of the squadron enters Eerdish," she told him.

"Get the orders drafted," Henry replied. "Captain?"

"I'll have my navigators working on a course," Ihejirika replied. "*Paladin* is ready to deploy in all respects. The locals have provided us with fuel and food to restock our supplies. We're scanning it all right now, but I'm not expecting any trouble."

"Wise," Sylvia murmured as they reached Henry's office. "Trust but verify. These people are now tentatively friends, but let's not forget they're at war with our explicit allies."

"The Kozun are going to regret that," Ihejirika replied. "If the Enteni are running the same gear as the ESF, the Hierarchy has no idea what they're walking into."

"I didn't ask who developed their new energy screens," Sylvia said. "It is on Felix's plate to see if we can buy a few. I know R-Div would *love* to have an energy screen they could layer inside the gravity shield."

Henry had sent his coffee order on ahead and took several cups from the machine as the others took seats around his desk. Passing them around, he smiled thinly.

"All right, people. To new friends here...and a giant pile of work." He toasted with the coffee cup. "What else do the Ambassador and I need to catch up on?"

LATER, Henry and Sylvia finally found some alone time in his quarters. After catching up on time without privacy, the pair lay in his bed, with soft music playing in the background.

"I definitely missed privacy," Sylvia purred at him, her head resting on his shoulder. "Though I worry about scandalizing your crew."

Henry chuckled and kissed the top of her head. It was a little late for *that* concern.

"If there is anyone on the crew who didn't know we were a couple when they reported aboard, their Chief made sure they knew about it *long* before they could cause an issue," he noted. "The Chiefs make the Space Force run, and, *believe me*, I'd already know if they disapproved."

In private, much of his lover's sharp mask faded. Some remained —as Henry knew, you could only wear a mask during every working hour for so long before it became your real face—but she was more open with her emotions when it was just the two of them.

"The Chief network in full play and power, huh?" she asked.

"Without noncoms, we don't have a Space Force," he told her. "That's not always clear from a civilian perspective, I don't think, but it's all too true. And, hell, I had *commissioned* subordinates suggesting I find flower shops well before I realized how I felt."

"Possibly before you even felt it," she murmured. "I did some research. It takes a while for demisexuals to open up to anyone romantically. If we hadn't been working as closely together, you probably never would have been as attracted to me."

"I know," Henry agreed, then kissed the top of her head. "The Space Force's councilors do as much as possible to make sure nobody gets out of the Academy without knowing what their sexuality is and how that works for them. Makes managing the interface of careers, relationships and sex much cleaner when everybody knows what direction their own switches flip."

"Oh so sensible," Sylvia said.

Henry sighed.

"Rules and policies like that are written in blood, Sylvia," he said quietly. "They make us study historical incidents in command training. Failures of discipline. Domestic abuse. Sexual assault. Abuse of authority.

"Knowing which way your own switches flip doesn't necessarily prevent all of these, but it's one tool in our kit. Those problems lasted a long time in militaries, longer than they ever should have. The UPSF is determined that they will *not* happen in our uniform."

He realized he'd tensed up when Sylvia lifted her head from his shoulder to look at him.

"That's a good thing," she told him. "Hierarchy always risks abuse—that's true in the diplomatic corps, too—but military hierarchies tend to be more rigid. It's...good to know that the Force I keep working with are trying their damnedest."

"We are," Henry said, exhaling a long breath. "Doesn't stop us getting in all kinds of other trouble, but we seem to have a lot of old problems beat."

He shook his head, staring up at the roof for a moment as he ran through a conscious muscle relaxation exercise.

"Do you think we're going to talk the Kozun down from fighting the E-Two?" he finally asked. "You're the diplomat."

"You know the Kozun better than I do, still," Sylvia noted. "I thought they were rolling up *all* of their wars, not concentrating their forces for one last fight."

"Right now, if they fight the E-Two, they're going to lose," Henry murmured. "We can't *tell* them that—they wouldn't believe us—but it worries me. If the Kenmiri are coming back around, I'd rather have all of our allies at full strength and on the same side."

"Short of picking a side, my love, I don't think we can stop that war," she told him, her admission sending a shiver down his spine. "Both sides know we're prepared to act as intermediaries, and that will help end it earlier than it might end otherwise, but the Kozun have picked a path and they're going to walk it until they get a bloody nose out of it."

"That's what I figure as well," he admitted. "I'm just afraid of the Kenmiri's revenge, I suppose."

The bedroom was quiet except for the music.

"Me too," Sylvia finally whispered. "They...are not inclined to half-measures."

CHAPTER THIRTY-FIVE

FIVE SKIPS AND NINE DAYS BROUGHT THEM TO THE FOURTH STAR system of their search—a star system that technically *wasn't* claimed by the Eerdish Gathered Tribes. The Zo System was claimed by Tadir, one of the industrial worlds of the Makata Cluster and a member system of the Eerdish-Enteni Alliance.

"Scanning for the trail," Eowyn reported in a tone that hovered between bored and frustrated. In the three prior systems, it had taken coordination with the local pickets to find the ambassador's trail.

In the last system, that "picket" had been a joke. The Voso System was only named because its star was visible from Eerdish. Its only *value* was that, despite being a mere red dwarf, it was conveniently positioned as a link between several systems and made a useful stopover for ships unwilling to risk full twenty-four-hour skips.

The entire picket was six unshielded starfighters supported by a damaged freighter that had been turned into a logistics depot. Fortunately for Henry and his mission, they'd *also* seeded the system with surveillance satellites.

"Ser, we have a trail," Eowyn suddenly reported, snapping upright in her seat.

"The ambassador stopped being sneaky, did they?" Henry asked, giving mental instructions to the computers to bring up the main tactical display.

"Can't speak to that, but I've got the Convoy," his Ops officer replied. "Looks like they were here for a bit and refueled at the gas giant. Still running analysis on the timeline, but they were *here.*"

"So, *they* weren't being as careful, were they?" Henry echoed himself with a cold smile. "Good. That makes chasing the ambassador much less of a problem. On the other hand..." He studied the data feeding in from the scanners.

"Do the analysis on when they left, of course," he told Eowyn. "But I suspect Chan is going to get us the actual answer. What do you make of the contacts at Zo-Four?"

Zo-IV was a super-Jovian gas giant, Zo's junior partner in an eternal dance that left the system's smaller gas giant and four rocky worlds in an eternally erratic orbit. There were multiple energy signatures in orbit of the gas giant, suggesting at *least* a permanent infrastructure to Henry.

"Looks like a fuel depot, probably with a logistics base in support," Eowyn told him after a moment. "I don't see any of the Eerdish's larger carriers, but I *am* seeing several of what I'm pretty sure are their shielded fighters, supporting a trio of escorts and what *might* be a converted freighter."

"I would be surprised if they didn't have a pile of converted escort carriers running around somewhere," Ihejirika noted, the destroyer's Captain clearly listening in from the bridge. "They had to test the hardware and concept before they started building the proper carriers."

That *any* of Henry's people were prepared to call the E-Two's ships "proper carriers" was a telling sign of respect to the Commodore. Henry couldn't think of *any* other ships he'd heard Terran personnel give that moniker.

It helped that the Kenmiri had regarded fighters as a waste of time and most of the Vesheron had treated them as an expendable stopgap to even up the missile launchers in the opening salvos. No one had seen them as *worth* building specialized ships to carry— except that the E-Two now had starfighters who were far closer to the weight of the UPSF birds than anyone else had.

They'd built the ships to carry them, and the close-range scans Henry and his people had done told them those ships were worthy of respect. Closer to the UPSF's light carriers than their fleet carriers in both size and capability, but still capable support platforms mothering effective fighter craft.

"I'm surprised we haven't seen them before," Henry said. "On the other hand, we are pretty close to the edge of the territory the E-Two is protecting. Can we tell if those ships are Tadir or Eerdish?"

"Unclear at this distance," Eowyn admitted.

"Fair enough. Chan, get coms set up with the locals," he ordered. "Pass on our authorizations from the Eerdish and Enteni and request whatever information they have on the Convoy and the ambassador.

"If the picket *is* from Tadir, we'll have Ambassador Todorovich ask for permission to operate in their space," he reflected aloud. "For now, let's get the channels of communication open and see what they can tell us about BGO."

"IT IS easy to feel the lack of the subspace coms we once had," the being on the screen told Henry and Sylvia. The Tadir officer was Beren, a pale-skinned Ashall race with orange eyes and catlike pupils. Alala was a woman holding the descriptive rank of "System Military Authority."

"Ambassador Blue-Stripe-Third-Green and their ship passed through here less than a day ago," she confirmed. "We had no basis on which to hold them, though their course was such that we might have had difficulty doing so regardless.

"That ship of theirs was fast."

"We have a lot of information on where it has *been*, Authority

Alala," Henry said with a calm chuckle. He'd limited his own people's push initially, believing they could catch up without exposing all of their secrets to the E-Two.

Even if he *hadn't*, he didn't think he'd have caught up now. The needlelike fast courier Blue-Stripe-Third-Green had fled aboard could make almost two KPS^2—it accelerated slower than his ships, but not by much!

"We also do not have permission from the Tadir government to operate in your space," Sylvia added. "We would need to make contact with you regardless."

"Blue Stripe Green Stripe Orange Stripe exited into Enteni space from here," Alala told them. "Also, I must be clear: enough of the vessels under my command are Eerdish that the Gathered Tribes' Writ will not be denied here, even if I wanted to."

She shook her head, a gesture the Beren shared with their Terran cousins. If *cousins* was the right word. None of the Ashall were quite sure what *Seeded Races* even *meant*, let alone how the various races were connected.

"The evidence included in the files you sent me is more than sufficient for my action," she noted. "My people will be spending some time going through the supplies we purchased from the Convoy itself."

"How long ago were they here?" Henry asked.

"Eighteen days," she told him. Time translation from Kem to English was automatic for Henry, to the point where he barely registered the actual Kem time unit Alala used. "They left toward the Tollal System, in Enteni territory, eighteen days ago.

"We didn't see much of the Convoy itself, just the tankers they brought in to pick up fuel and the transports that delivered the goods they paid for that fuel with," she noted. "They stayed well outside the range at which our sensors would get a clear look.

"That seemed...about what I expected from the Drifters, so I did not question it."

"It is about normal for them," Henry agreed. "Thank you, Authority Alala. You have been most helpful."

"If you require fuel or consumables, your papers from the Eerdish give you authorization to draw on my stockpiles," Alala told him. "I am also authorized to trade fuel and other items for munitions or other weapons systems."

Henry checked the fuel status of his squadron through his mental network and shook his head slightly.

"We will continue our pursuit at maximum speed, I think," he told the Beren officer. They'd made the time to swing in to the logistics base as a courtesy, but now he had a course for his enemies.

And he was itching to be about it.

THE CHANNEL from Alala closed and Henry looked over at Sylvia.

"Do you have time for a senior officers' briefing or are you booked up?" he asked, returning to English with the smooth ease of long practice.

"My schedule is surprisingly open right now," she said drily. "My job, for the moment, is to talk to civilian leaders to open doors for you. Since our work on Eerdish seems to be enough for now...I'm wherever you need me, Commodore."

The words were perfectly professional, but Henry couldn't stop his brain going somewhere extremely *non*professional from that. Sylvia caught up with that a second later and flushed.

"That *too*," she murmured. "Though that wasn't what I meant."

"I know, I know," he assured her, grinning broadly. He marshaled his self-control and pinged Chan.

"Commander, can you pull together a staff-captains-and-XOs call ASAP?" he asked.

"Is this ASAP as in *in twenty minutes on the hour* or ASAP as in *link them to my office now*?" Chan clarified quickly.

"The latter, Commander," Henry decided.

"On it," the communications officer told him. "Activating the virtual conference net now, and I will link people as I pin them down."

Half of Henry's office vanished into a holographic illusion of a conference surrounded by windows on all four sides. The impossible space was clearly positioned on top of a mountain on Earth, with snowy slopes sweeping away in every direction.

Eowyn linked in moments later, followed by Aoife Palmer and her XO. Avshalom Sandor was an Orthodox Jew, with special dispensation around his hair and headwear that made him stand out from most UPSF officers.

Nina Teunissen and Visvaldas Lemaire linked in from *Maharatha* about ten seconds later, joined by Ihejirika and Chan.

"Commander Giannino is off-duty and asleep," Ihejirika said. "She's due on *Paladin's* bridge in three hours. Should I wake her, ser?"

"No," Henry decided after a moment. Waking someone unnecessarily in the middle of their sleep cycle was not just rude, it would be counterproductive for a meeting. Aruna Giannino wouldn't be able to contribute to the meeting if she was groggy—she could review a recording later to catch up.

"All right, everyone," he greeted his officers. "Ambassador Todorovich and I have spoken with the local commander, System Military Authority Alala of the Tadir.

"Both the ambassador and the main BGO Convoy passed through here," he continued. "The Convoy left for Tollal eighteen days ago. The ambassador followed in the same direction just over one day ago.

"We have the scent of our prey again at last," Henry told them. "We're going to go after them at full acceleration. No games, no worrying about concealing our new maneuverability. We need to pin these people down."

"What about ambushes?" Eowyn asked. "If they're being this

obvious, they might have thought E-Two space was safe, but they could also be preparing a trap for us."

"There's a good chance of *something*," Henry agreed. "We'll keep our eyes open and watching for oddities ahead of us."

"And the Kenmiri?" Ihejirika asked.

"If we locate more listening posts, we will make a call based on their location," Henry told them. "If there is an E-Two force within a single skip of the post, we will send them a drone and carry on our way. The E-Two have no more interest in having the Kenmiri in their space than we would—and while we managed to not tell them about the subspace transceiver at the listening post, I'm not so wedded to keeping that secret as to not tell friends about a nearby enemy."

"And if the E-Two aren't that near?" Eowyn asked.

"Then we will follow Protocol Twenty-Seven and neutralize the outpost ourselves," he concluded. "Where we have friends who can and will deal with them, we will enable that. But we will *not* leave intact Kenmiri listening posts behind us.

"It's not our primary mission today, and if we hit enough of them that it starts to seriously slow us down, we'll reconsider," he conceded. "But we *will* deal with them."

"We lost sixteen GroundDiv troopers taking the last one," Eowyn noted quietly. "We can't sustain losses like that very often."

"And that, Commander, is why I have no intention of *landing* at the next one," Henry told her.

Against an atmosphereless target like the last listening post, his space-to-space missiles would handily bury a five-hundred-megaton warhead a hundred meters into solid rock before detonating. A dozen missiles from his command might not destroy the entire listening post...but they could be *very* sure the post wouldn't be talking to anyone.

CHAPTER THIRTY-SIX

THREE DESTROYERS FLASHED BACK INTO THREE-DIMENSIONAL space with a final twenty-dimensional kick to the stomach, and Henry grimaced. The trail said the Drifters had spent six days in Tollal, which meant they should have gained almost a week on the Convoy now.

"Scanning for trails," Eowyn reported. "I have zero energy signatures on the scope. System is dead."

"I'm not sure anyone even bothered to *claim* this place," Chan replied, their voice dry. "Most people wouldn't ever *skip* to this small a dwarf."

They'd spent twenty hours in skip to travel a bare handful of light-years. The system didn't have a name on any records—it probably hadn't even been counted in the "five hundred stars" of the Ra Sector.

Henry's records now made it Ra-261. The two hundred and sixty-first system in the Ra Sector visited by the UPSF.

"I have the Convoy's trail," Eowyn said. "It's hard to miss a few hundred starships blazing their way across a star system. Especially a place like this, where there is nothing to hide the trail."

"That's not entirely true," Henry pointed out. "It looks like they ran pretty close to the asteroid belt, such as it is."

The system's minuscule M9 primary hadn't managed to coalesce its collection of dust and space debris into actual planets. Instead, a roughly defined belt of small planetoids, the largest maybe three thousand kilometers across, hung between two and three light-minutes from the star.

"Total mass of the belt is estimated at about a quarter again that of Sol's Belt," Eowyn said after a moment. "It ends up being a bit less dense, but still. That's everything in this joke of a star system."

"Do we have a line on the Convoy's exit skip?" Henry asked. "I'm guessing they didn't stick around here for long. It's a good place to hide, but a few too many people saw them head here."

"They might have still been trusting the E-Two to keep their mouths shut and stayed here until the ambassador caught up," Sylvia suggested softly. "The surrounding systems only became neutral-to-hostile recently.

"And as you said, it's a good place to hide."

"We're tracking the burn path now," Eowyn replied. "Haven't picked up an exit skip yet, but there aren't very many options. The star is small enough to seriously limit where it's safe to skip to from here."

"We'll follow the trail," Henry ordered. "Two KPS-squared; keep an eye on that belt. There's nothing *else* to hide in in this system."

"Scanners are active and wide," the Ops officer said calmly. "No contacts so far, just the burn trail."

"Let me know the moment we've IDed their exit skip," Henry said. "Not much in this place that makes me want to stay."

HENRY JERKED awake as his internal network chimed an alarm. For once, he wasn't having a nightmare—probably because Sylvia was currently pressed against his back, her arms wrapped around his midsection.

The time wasn't right for his usual alarm, which meant one of his officers was trying to reach him. He accepted the call on "mental audio" only.

"Wong," he subvocalized as crisply as he could.

"Ser, it's Ihejirika," his flagship Captain said grimly. "I hate to wake you...but we've lost the Convoy's track."

Henry was bolt upright in a moment, slowed only by removing Sylvia's arms as gently as possible as he moved to the edge of the bed.

"How do we *lose* five hundred starships?" he demanded.

"The trail cut into the asteroid belt and then dispersed," Ihejirika told him. "It looks like they may have used plasma cannon and some fusion warheads to conceal their next steps. Ser...if the trail ends—"

"It's an ambush," Henry snapped, no longer subvocalizing. "Take all ships to battle stations. Shields to maximum grav-shear. I'll be on the flag deck in two minutes."

Sylvia was awake, her gaze meeting his as he rose.

"Are we in trouble?" she asked.

"I think we got suckered," he told her. "The question is whether they have enough of a sucker punch ready for us."

"Go," she urged. "You don't need me to fight your squadron."

"No," he agreed. He was still dressing but took a moment to press a kiss to her forehead anyway. He could spare the seconds.

It only took forty seconds to make it to the flag deck from his quarters, after all.

REACHING THE FLAG DECK, Henry realized there was one more order he should have given over the com.

"Vector the squadron away from the trail and the asteroid belt," he ordered as he took his seat, systems activating around him. "Do we have any contacts yet?"

"Negative," one of the Chiefs replied, looking gratefully toward the door as Commander Eowyn stepped in. "No artificial energy signs, nothing. Scopes remain clear."

"But the trail is gone," Henry concluded, looking over the display. "All ships at battle stations?"

"Yes, ser," Eowyn replied as she slid into her seat. "*Paladin* is green. *Cataphract* is green. *Maharatha* is...green. DesRon Twenty-Seven is at full battle stations and ready for your command, Commodore."

Henry hesitated. The distance between them and the asteroid belt was now growing by the second...but at the same time, the next clue to their enemy's location was *in* the asteroid belt.

"Eowyn, get me a full analysis of what we're looking at with the trail," he ordered. "All ships are to maintain acceleration away from the belt. Ihejirika—have your Nav team draw up a course for the squadron that brings us to a halt relative to the last location we have confirmed of the trail at long missile range."

Squadron maneuvering plans were the responsibility of Eowyn's Operations department, but the problem with running a destroyer squadron was that Henry's flagship didn't have the space for a large support staff for the Commodore.

He wanted the Ops team on the analysis, which meant he *didn't* want them drafting the course—and he had three competent Nav departments to lean on.

"On it," both officers confirmed.

Henry exhaled a breath, watching the icons on the screen.

"What were you thinking?" he murmured. "What *are* you thinking..."

"Contact!"

The shout was from the destroyer's bridge, carrying through Henry's link with Ihejirika by sheer volume.

"Multiple contacts, vampire, vampire—no, *mines*. Mines at thirty degrees by forty-five degrees, danger close!"

Henry swallowed a curse as a pox of new red icons flashed onto the display. Mines were only useful if you knew *exactly* where the enemy was going to be—but the Drifters had known he was following their trail and had guessed when he'd detect the point where they'd started concealing their path.

They'd got his vector wrong, both because he'd delayed giving the order to break off and because his sensors were better than they'd expected, but they hadn't needed to get it *that* right.

Not with bomb-pumped X-ray laser mines.

"Lasers on the shields," Eowyn snapped. "All ships evading; all ships reporting laser strikes."

The red icons rippled on his screens, vanishing in sequence as they detonated and flung devastatingly powerful beams at Henry's ships. The range was barely fifty thousand kilometers—but if it had been half that, Henry's entire command would have died.

"Report," he finally ground out.

"All ships still reporting in," Chan said. "*Maharatha* is reporting a hull strike. Damage report incoming."

"*Cataphract* and *Paladin* report zero direct hits," Eowyn continued. "*Cataphract* took a glancing blow that burnt off some heat radiators. Drones are deploying replacements."

"Direct channel from Captain Teunissen for you, ser," Chan told Henry.

"Put her through directly to my network," Henry ordered. "Eowyn, I want a full sensor-drone spread. That's an opening salvo; they did not expect it to finish us off."

An image of Lieutenant Colonel Nina Teunissen's squat visage appeared in front of Henry, projected directly to his mind by his internal network.

"We got handled rougher than I like," she said without preamble. "I'm down a missile launcher and Laser Two. My chief engineer thinks he'll have Laser Two back online, given thirty minutes, but the launcher is just *gone*, ser.

"Eleven confirmed dead so far, but I've got twenty wounded and we're still searching for ten more," she concluded. "It's bad, Commodore."

"Understood. Tell your chief he's got *ten* minutes for that laser, maybe," Henry said grimly. "I'm expecting hostile contact in short order. Shield and GMS status?"

"Hundred percent still," Teunissen replied. "I'll tell the chief, but..."

"It will take what it takes," Henry conceded. "But we're going to need that laser sooner rather than later, Captain. Tell him."

"Yes, ser."

Teunissen's image vanished, and Henry looked at the screen, searching for what he *knew* had to be there.

"Drones have them," Eowyn quietly reported in the silence of the bridge. "Six escorts and a Guardian advancing out of the asteroid belt. Probably took them this long to bring their engines up from dead cold."

"Understood." Henry swallowed a breath. "Formation Delta-Six. *Maharatha* on the point. All ships clear for action."

CHAPTER THIRTY-SEVEN

"FORMATION DELTA-SIX" WAS ONE OF MANY VARIATIONS ON A basic triangle formation—like the Greek letter it was named for, Δ. Delta-Six was ecliptic relative to the enemy, with the base of the triangle pointing toward them.

That put the third ship, *Maharatha* in this case, behind the other two and mostly protected by their gravity shields. *Maharatha* would still be able to launch missiles, but she'd have a degree of protection from enemy fire.

"Range is seven hundred thousand kilometers," Eowyn reported as the UPSF ships rearranged into formation. "Our current velocity is four hundred kilometers per second away from them; they are closing at one-point-five KPS-squared."

Henry nodded, taking in the battlespace without giving orders for the moment. Their velocity away from the asteroid belt and the Drifters put them out of missile range, and he could *keep* it that way if he chose.

But that wouldn't provide him with answers or let him investigate the Convoy's trail. A Guardian and six escorts were a hell of a weight of metal, but he had gravity shields and they didn't.

"Adjust course to take us in to meet them," he ordered quietly. "Maximum missile range."

"We'll cut accel in eighty seconds, remaining velocity ninety KPS," Eowyn told him after a few seconds. The destroyers were now "falling" toward the Drifters. "Range will be seven hundred twenty-three thousand, but with the reduced separation velocity, the missiles will have range."

"Understood." He studied the tactical plot. His destroyers didn't have quite the payload options his battlecruiser had possessed. Without the spinal gravity driver, their missiles couldn't guarantee the velocity for the hard-tipped armor-piercing rounds *Raven* had carried for her main gun.

Instead, he had conversion warheads—which used shaped fusion charges to create massive plasma shotguns in space with a terminal range of hundreds of kilometers—standard five-hundred-megaton fusion bombs and shield-penetrator missiles.

The last were intended to jump past gravity shields to deliver five-hundred-megaton warheads but also worked effectively on energy screens—like the ones the Guardian would be carrying. The escorts would be unshielded...unless the Drifters had bought the Eerdish's new shield generators.

"Sylvia," he pinged his lover. "Did we find out whether the Eerdish had sold the Drifters shield generators?"

"They dodged the question," she admitted. "Which I take to mean 'Yes, they did.' Probably only a few, though, enough that they can replicate them eventually."

"But probably not enough to reequip an escort squadron in a few days," Henry murmured, watching the seconds tick down. The first missiles in his launchers were conversion warheads. If he wanted to do something tricky, he needed to do it with his second salvo and decide before the first salvo launched.

"Eowyn, targeting and loadout orders," he said clearly, pulling his Ops officer's attention. "Designate the escorts one through six. Escort One gets the full first salvo from all three ships. All ships will then load with shield penetrators for three salvos, focused on the Guardian, then switch to conversion heads and return focus to Escort One."

They'd be holding the range at a five-minute flight time. That meant he'd get five salvos into space before the first one landed. He'd reassess salvo six after he saw the result of his first salvo—and the *Drifters'* first salvo.

"Passing the orders," Eowyn confirmed. "First salvo launching in fifteen seconds. I expect the Drifter launch simultaneously."

"Make sure nav orders are to reverse acceleration and match theirs at zero v," Henry said quietly. The Drifters had likely expected to have an acceleration advantage over his ships. They'd already learned their error as his people closed at two KPS^2, and shortly they'd see that DesRon Twenty-Seven controlled the range of this fight.

That was going to take away the Guardian's biggest influence. The modular Drifter capital ship would have multiple superheavy plasma turrets, mounting the same weapons as a Kenmiri dreadnought, but they couldn't hit his destroyers at seven hundred thousand kilometers.

Same with the lasers on both sides. Lucky hits were possible, but his gravity shields would shrug them off. This was going to be a missile duel, with the question of whether DesRon Twenty-Seven's gravity shields offset the fact that they had thirty-five launchers—and the Drifters likely had about a hundred and fifty.

"Launching," Eowyn reported, new green icons appearing on Henry's screen. Lightspeed delay meant it was several seconds before the red icons of the enemy weapons appeared. "Enemy launch detected. I'm reading an estimated one hundred fifty-five missiles. We will narrow down the numbers as they close."

"Scan for radiation signatures," Henry ordered. "We *know* the Drifters have resonance warheads, so let's identify them. There should be fewer disruptors, so target them."

The resonance warheads could set up a cascade that would

collapse their gravity shields—but the *Cataphracts* had new and updated power breaker systems to reset their shields almost immediately, and the disruptor missiles didn't have space for warheads.

In the worst case, his destroyers could take a kinetic hit to the hull. They *couldn't* take a conversion warhead's plasma blast to the hull. If it was easier to wipe out the conversion warheads, they'd risk the disruptors—but if there were more conversion warheads, they'd take down the disruptors and trust their shields to handle the plasma blasts.

"Second salvo away," Eowyn reported. "Enemy second salvo detected."

Both forces were now accelerating at one and a half KPS^2. That meant that Henry's missiles would hit before the Drifters' missiles did, but it didn't make as much difference as the base velocity could.

"Three minutes to impact," the Ops officer noted.

It was very quiet on *Paladin*'s flag bridge, the air feeling chilly on Henry's skin. He understood the logic of lowering the temperature of a ship at battle stations—if nothing else, it gave them extra thermal capacity aboard the ship if the heat radiators were damaged—but it still felt strange in the wait between battle being joined and the first blows landing.

"Drifters are maintaining course," Eowyn said. "Chan, any coms?"

"Nothing," the coms officer replied. "They're not saying a word."

"Rude of them," Henry murmured. "Defensive nets are up?"

"All ships are interlinked; Tactical officers have the ball," Eowyn reported. "We have IDed twenty disruptor warheads in the first wave. The salvo appears targeted on *Cataphract*."

Henry nodded and said nothing. He'd given his orders and now it was down to the team around him. Lasers began to flicker in the display and red icons started to vanish. *Maharatha* was adding less to the shared defense than she would have in a different formation, but that was fine.

He'd allowed for that. The odds were that his ships could take half a dozen disruptor hits before their shields went down and hundreds of conversion-warhead hits before the statistical chance of a blowthrough caught up to them.

The *Cataphract*s had sharper gravity shears than the battlecruiser he'd conned at the end of the war. If the Drifters thought his destroyers were fragile, they were going to learn an unpleasant lesson today!

"ESCORT ONE TOOK THREE HITS," Eowyn reported as their first salvo struck home. "She appears to still be fully functional."

Henry didn't say anything. His own focus was on the missiles plunging down on *Cataphract*. His three destroyers couldn't shoot down over a hundred and fifty missiles. They had managed to shoot twenty-three, which was impressive on its own.

And now the moment of truth as the remaining hundred and thirty–plus weapons crashed over the destroyers like a tidal wave, warhead after warhead exploding and sending blasts of plasma into the gravity shield.

"All disruptors were down," the Ops officer reported. "*Cataphract* is still with us."

"Chan, what's Palmer's status?" Henry asked.

"She's reporting a single minor blowthrough, no connection with the hull," Chan replied. "No damage."

"Good." That was what he'd *expected*, but it was still nerve-wracking to watch that many explosions wash over a ship under his command.

"Tighten up the formation," he ordered grimly. "Let's get close enough to *Cataphract* to try to pull some of the fire onto us. We *should* be fine under hundred-missile salvos, but probabilities wait for no one."

"Understood. Passing the orders," Chan confirmed.

"First penetrator is skipping...*now*." The shield-penetrator missile was an evolution of the skip drones that humanity now used for interstellar coms—and had used before encountering what they now knew was the Kenmiri subspace carrier signal.

The current use of skip drones for communications worried Henry. Their miniaturized skip drives were intentionally larger and cruder—and cheaper—than the ones used in the penetrator missiles, but the function was the same.

The penetrator missiles activated their skip drives as they plunged toward the Guardian's shields. For a few seconds, they were twenty-dimensional objects instead of three-dimensional objects, offset from normal space by a few meters in dimensions that the energy screens didn't enter.

Without the gravity of stars to pull them along like stones in a river, the missiles didn't travel any farther in normal space than they normally would have—but they traveled that distance in a space where energy screens and armor didn't exist.

Multiple five-hundred-megaton warheads detonated in the gap between the Guardian's shields and its fragile, built-in-pieces hull. Atmosphere and vaporized metal gusted into space, but the battleship kept coming.

"That's...interesting," Eowyn murmured.

"Commander?" Henry snapped.

"The Guardian appears to have a secondary energy shield, right on the hull," she reported. "It's nowhere near as powerful, but it helped protect the hull from the close-range explosions from the penetrators."

She shook her head.

"Our former allies seem to have picked up on our favorite tricks, ser," she warned.

Henry grimaced—but that was all he had time for before the Drifters' second salvo crashed in on *Cataphract*. *Paladin* had pulled away some of the missiles this time, with a dozen conversion warheads firing their plasma blasts uselessly into the shield of his flagship.

But two of the disruptor warheads had survived in this salvo, and they hammered into *Cataphract*'s gravity shield with their usual chaotic effect. Two resonance disruptors weren't enough to bring down the gravity shield, and Henry was already dismissing the impact, turning to check on the next offensive salvo.

And then everything went to hell.

CATAPHRACT'S drive went from running with the rest of the squadron at one and a half KPS^2 to spinning in space with her acceleration wildly spiking in a dozen different directions.

Henry watched in horror as her drive repeatedly spiked to ten times her standard thrust and spun three hundred and sixty degrees. Red damage alerts flashed up on the screen and then it all stopped.

And so did *Cataphract*'s gravity maneuvering system. Her shield was flickering, the gravity shear badly reduced, but her drive was completely offline.

"Chan, get me Palmer," Henry snapped. "Flip the delta; put *Paladin* and *Maharatha* in front of *Cataphract*. All conversion salvos to defensive mode. *We cannot let any disruptors through.*"

The conversion warheads weren't designed for that, but they could do it. Retargeted by Eowyn's orders, all but one of their in-flight salvos turned to immolate themselves against the Drifters' missiles.

"This is Palmer."

Henry exhaled in shocked relief when he heard *Cataphract*'s Captain's voice.

"Report," he snapped.

"We're fucked," she said bluntly, clearly in pain. "GMS doesn't apply thrust, so no one got spaghettified, but tidal forces and...and vector shifts... I've got a lot of injuries and I don't have damage reports.

"You may have to leave us, ser."

"Not happening, Captain," Henry snapped. "Focus on your GMS. This fight is over, but we can get out if you get your engine back."

"I'll tell Vitalik," she replied. "I don't know what else we've got, ser. A lot of structural damage. She may be a write-off."

"She'll get you home, Captain," Henry told her. "Nothing else matters."

He looked up at the tactical display as his two remaining ships spat out twenty-three more missiles—these all with the icons of standard fusion warheads. They were overkill, but they'd thin the herd heading toward Henry's ships.

"Ser, final salvo skipping," Eowyn reported, her voice forced to crispness. "Impacts on the Guardian... We have an internal hit! She's breaking up!"

Henry breathed a sigh of vindictive relief. That would buy time. Right now, his ships weren't accelerating and the Drifters were starting to close the distance.

Not quickly. Not yet—but they didn't have forever and he had to hope the enemy would hesitate now that Henry's people had just obliterated their flagship.

"Ser, I've got a blip on *Cataphract*," Eowyn reported. "Just a few gravities, but their drive is moving."

The link to Palmer chirped alive a moment later.

"Commander Utkin is a miracle-worker, ser," Palmer's pained voice told him. "We're bringing the GMS up slowly, but we think we've got her. What he's warning is if we bring it to full power, we have to give up almost the entire shield shear. We don't have the projectors for both anymore."

"And weapons?" Henry asked. He could guess the answer.

"I don't have the power for main lasers, and I've got warping in the launcher feed tubes. With all hands focused on the GMS, I don't even have defensive beams online, ser."

"Good enough," Henry told her. "Set your course for our

entrance skip line at the best accel you can pull. Rest of the squadron will match your acceleration and cover you."

"Sorry, ser," Palmer said. "I don't like running."

"I'll take a lost battle over a lost ship, Captain Palmer. Get your ass moving."

CHAPTER THIRTY-EIGHT

HENRY WASN'T SURE WHO WAS MORE SURPRISED: HIM AND HIS people at the presence of two shielded escorts and twenty shielded starfighters at the skip line when his ships emerged back into the Zo System—or the local ships at the atrociously battered state of his command.

"*Paladin*, this is Detached Authority Oka Nal," an earnest—if *far* too young-looking—Tak officer greeted Henry in the video link. "System Authority Alala sent my command forward to secure the skip line against potential problems, but..." He trailed off, his dark red head tentacles rippling in concern.

"Do you require assistance?" Oka Nal finally asked.

It was a live channel, so Henry refrained from rolling his eyes. *Cataphract* was no longer actively leaking atmosphere—but her gravity shield was barely online, revealing the *twisting* her hull had undergone when her GMS drive had gone mad.

They were lucky so few had been killed. The free-fall effect of the GMS was little protection against rapidly shifting changes of direction in gravity, and if there was anyone uninjured aboard Palmer's ship, Henry wasn't aware of it.

But the Drifters had taken the destruction of their Guardian as the salutary lesson he'd hoped and declined to continue the engagement. They'd shadowed his ships across the system, but the battle hadn't been rejoined.

That meant Henry still had three ships...but one of them was an obvious cripple.

"My ships are capable of maneuvering under their own power, Detached Authority," Henry finally told the younger officer. "I would request an escort to the Zo logistics base, if that is something your detachment can do."

"Are there...enemies pursuing you?" the Tadir System officer asked. "I will still want to make sure the skip line is secure."

Henry generously did *not* point out that the skip line was just that—a *line* that stretched from one star to the other. While there was definitely an *easiest* point along the line to emerge—hence his ships meeting Oka Nal's at all—it wasn't that large of a difference unless you approached far too close to the star.

Oka Nal had two ships and twenty starfighters to cover a useful safe emergence area roughly a light-hour across and five light-hours long—with a *less* useful emergence zone roughly a light-*day* long. There were ways to do that, but sitting at zero velocity relative to the standard emergence point wasn't one of them.

"I do not believe the Drifters have any interest in starting a fight with your alliance, Detached Authority," he said instead. "Though, in honesty, the escort would be as much for my people's nerves as anything else."

The Tak bowed his head in acknowledgement.

"One of my fighter squadrons is due to rotate in ninety-seven minutes, in any case," he noted. "If I send them back early, System Authority Alala can accelerate deployment of the replacement wing."

"I appreciate the assistance, Detached Authority," Henry said. He paused. "Would you be prepared to accept some advice from an old hand, Oka Nal?" he asked quietly.

"I am prepared to listen," the officer said carefully.

"I have some Kem-translated tactical patterns I will forward you," the Commodore told the younger Tak. "There are better ways to watch the skip line than you're using, and since we are friends if not necessarily allies...I think you can use them."

The clearly inexperienced officer bowed his head again in thanks. Like most of the successor states of the Kenmiri Empire, the Tadir System had a shortage of officers. If a system didn't have any ex-Vesheron to draw on, their best options were janissary ground-troop NCOs and freighter crews.

There were a lot of systems and militaries learning war for the first time right now. For all that Henry wished none of them had to, he had to admit it was better than the alternative.

Better a messy rebirth than life as a slave.

BY THE TIME they actually reached the base, Alala had both sent a second wing of fighters to the skip line to replace the ones escorting them and sent a third wing to join their escorts. Henry's three ships decelerated into the logistics base with twenty of the E-Two Alliance's brand-new starfighters around them.

"You know, I think I'm glad these guys are on our side," Ihejirika noted on his private link with Henry. "Those shields aren't super tough, but they'll take at least one hit from just about anything, and fighters are annoying enough *without* needing two hits.

"Looks like four missiles, same as our Lancers, and they've got the compensators for two KPS-squared. Nasty little planes. I love them when they're flying escort on my ship."

Henry chuckled. He didn't even have to force it, though exhaustion was taking its toll. He hadn't slept since he'd been awoken to find they'd lost the Convoy's trail.

"Everything's much nicer when it's on your side and not the

enemy's," he agreed. "I much prefer tactical and technological surprises when they're *mine*."

"The GMS was always going to have its hitches," his flag captain warned him. "None of us anticipated the resonance disruptors having that kind of impact on it, but..."

"I'm going to have to check the research documents," Henry said. "We've known about the damn things for long enough; someone should at least have done the math on it."

"They might have figured the shield had to be done for it to affect the drive," Ihejirika argued. "That's what *I* would have figured. That the cascade hit the GMS field without overwhelming the shield was a surprise."

"And one that basically killed a modern destroyer." Lieutenant Commander Vitalik Utkin had finished his initial survey. *Cataphract* would be able to bring her people home without too much difficulty, but the Epsilon Eridanian chief engineer was not at all certain she could be repaired.

If she could, it would require a major shipyard, probably all the way back in Sol. Nothing less than a complete rebuild was called for.

"What's *Paladin*'s status?" Henry asked Ihejirika. "And your people's morale?"

"We got our teeth kicked in and our sister ship crippled," the African Captain said flatly. "My people don't like it. They're angry and they're a bit afraid—we're not used to UPSF ships being one-hit kills for *anybody*.

"That said, *Paladin* is fully functional. Our only real issue is that magazines are down to sixty percent. If the locals can give us some new chassis and fusion bombs, we can fabricate warheads and penetrator busses, but I can't build and fuel three-thousand-KPS-delta-*v* missiles from scrap and asteroids."

"I'll see what System Authority Alala is prepared to give us," Henry said. "But since I'm also going to be begging for an escort back to La-Tar for *Cataphract*, I suspect I may be using up all of our goodwill here."

"Anything that gets us back in the field after these people, ser," Ihejirika told him. "My people have been knocked back, but we have not been knocked down, and we want to take the fight to the Drifters.

"They just keep digging...and that's a hole we're looking forward to filling up."

CHAPTER THIRTY-NINE

System Authority Alala greeted Henry with a small bow of her head when they linked the channel together.

He was alone in his office, a coffee at his left hand to try to keep him somewhat functional after almost two days awake. It was a bad habit and a terrible idea, but there'd always been *something* that needed to be done.

After this call, he'd sleep. He promised himself.

"System Authority, I thank you for the escort and the watch on the skip line," he told the Tadir officer.

"What happened to your squadron, Commodore?" she asked.

"The Drifters ambushed us and had a new weapon," Henry told her. That wasn't entirely accurate, but it was close enough to cover the reality of things. The Drifters probably hadn't expected that the disruptors would be as dangerous to the gravity maneuvering systems, either.

"We destroyed the Guardian anchoring their task force and withdrew to protect my crippled ship," he continued. "One of my ships has minor damage as well, but we should be able to repair that here if you will permit us."

"I have updated instructions from the Council of Tribes, confirming your Writ," Alala said. "I have also exchanged messages with my own superiors on Tadir. As a gesture of goodwill to the United Planets, I am authorized to provide any and all reasonable support you need, Commodore."

Henry blinked. That was a surprise. They were *hoping* to make friends and allies of the Eerdish-Enteni Alliance's member states, but no matter how well Felix Leitz was doing on Eerdish, they weren't there yet.

The E-Two appeared to want that friendship as much as the UPA did, if they were basically telling their local commanders to give him a blank check.

"We do not need much for *Paladin* and *Maharatha*," Henry admitted. "Munitions, fuel and basic materials for repairs. For *Cataphract*, however..."

"I can provide munitions and fuel, Commodore. That is easy— this is a logistics station," Alala promised. "But there are no repair slips here. Tadir, perhaps, could help your ship, but..."

"She has deep structural damage that will require drastic repairs," Henry said. "And she is Terran-built. I do not believe that there are any yards outside the United Planets Alliance that can do what *Cataphract* needs.

"But given everything I have learned since leaving La-Tar to hunt the Drifters, I do not believe that I can send a crippled ship all the way back to the UPA on her own," he said. "I do not know, System Authority Alala, if the orders you have been given stretch this far.

"But the aid I truly need is an escort to protect *Cataphract* on her return trip to La-Tar, where a UPSF fleet will be able to take over her security."

Alala closed her slitted orange eyes in thought for long seconds.

"I have one converted carrier and three escorts, Commodore," she told him. "To secure a logistics base we now fear is only a few skips from a potentially hostile Drifter fleet. Any ship I send to La-Tar will be away for weeks."

Around fifteen days each way for ships limited to a single KPS^2, Henry estimated.

"I know," he said. "I do not ask this lightly, System Authority, and I will accept if you cannot spare the ships."

He wasn't sure what he'd *do* if he couldn't get that escort. He'd probably have to run *Cataphract* back to La-Tar himself. It would take him less time than the E-Two Alliance ships, but not *that* much less.

The *Cataphracts'* superior acceleration only reduced the real-space part of the trip. The skips still took just as long.

"Give me some time, Commodore," Alala finally said. "I may command here, but not all my ships are Tadir. To detach a unit, I must consult."

"I understand," Henry said. "I appreciate you even considering it, System Authority. As I said, I know what I am asking."

"WE DON'T NEED AN ESCORT. Our engines are fine now; we can make it to La-Tar alone."

Henry just *looked* at Aoife Palmer after she said that on the virtual conference, waiting to see if she realized how much of an idiot she was being.

"Bull*shit*," Ihejirika said loudly, putting out what Henry, Eowyn and Teunissen were all thinking.

The five of them were on a virtual conference while the XOs and Chan sorted out logistics planning with Alala's people.

"You have no weapons," Henry said calmly into the silence as Palmer flushed. "No offensive weapons, anyway—and, what, a third of your defensive lasers? You're down a power plant. You're down fifty-two percent of your gravity projectors, which means you can't generate more than five hundred gravities of defensive shear even if you cut your acceleration to half a KPS-squared.

"Yes, you can fly all the way to La-Tar on your own," he agreed.

"And what happens when a stealthed Kenmiri raider decides you are far too tempting a target? Your ship represents the current pinnacle of the UPSF's warfighting technology.

"Even some of our *friends* might be tempted to say you never showed up," he concluded with a grimace. "I think the E-Two are sufficiently determined to build a relationship that asking them for an escort is safe, but there is no way in *hell*, Captain Palmer, that *Cataphract* is going home alone.

"We'll also be transferring *Maharatha*'s severely wounded and dead to you," he noted. "I'm not risking your people or Teunissen's on a point of pride. If Alala can't provide a ship to escort you home, we're taking you home."

"What happens then?" Ihejirika asked grimly. "We don't know for sure where the Convoy is, but Twelfth Fleet should be fully assembled now."

"By the time *Cataphract* makes it to La-Tar, either way, they'll have the Lancer crews trained up and they'll be ready to deploy," Henry confirmed. "If we take the entire squadron back, it will become difficult to argue against a reconnaissance in force."

"By the entire Twelfth Fleet?" Eowyn said. "That seems like it might be worth it, ser. We're never going to have the Convoy's location exactly nailed down.

"We're working on identifying possible locations now, but if we've got it down to three or four systems...maybe we should go get the Fleet."

"The problem, Commander Eowyn, is that the Eerdish and their allies are only going to give us permission to bring a three-carrier-group battle fleet into their territory if we have a definitive target," Henry reminded them all. "From a military-effectiveness perspective, there is no reason to hold Twelfth Fleet in La-Tar Cluster territory.

"From a *political* perspective, we do not want to bring those carriers into Eerdish space without explicit permission from both the Council of Tribes and the Highest Principals," he said. "And I don't necessarily believe that Admiral Rex is willing to wait for that permission.

"And while the Eerdish currently want an alliance with us, if we start barging around with capital ships without permission, they may start to reconsider their evaluation of our friendship."

Henry shook his head.

"No, people. If at all possible, we need to locate the Blue Stripe Green Stripe Orange Stripe Convoy. Once we have direct visual of where they are, *that* is enough for us to get permission for Twelfth Fleet to pass through Eerdish space."

"We know they were here in Zo not that long ago," Teunissen pointed out. "Wouldn't that be enough?"

"Every forty-eight hours or so that passes from positive confirmation of a target location increases the zone the Convoy could be in exponentially," Henry reminded them. "Once we have *seen* them, we can send skip drones and shadow the Convoy from a distance.

"Until then, I am unprepared to risk a potential alliance with the second-most powerful group in the Ra Sector. I will make that argument to Admiral Rex in person, if necessary, but our best-case scenario remains pursuing the Convoy with *Paladin* and *Maharatha*.

"Which leads to my next question," he said with a forced smile. "Captain Teunissen, how long until your ship is as repaired as possible?"

"Three days," she said instantly, with a smile that aggravated her resemblance to a bird of prey. "We're not getting that missile launcher back short of a shipyard, but we'll have the laser online and the hole in the hull patched over."

"All right," Henry said. "So, we have three days to get *Paladin* and *Maharatha* ready. By the end of that, we should know what's happening with *Cataphract* and can plan from there."

CHAPTER FORTY

HENRY HAD KNOWN HE WAS GOING TO CRASH AND CRASH HARD once he finally slept. He'd pushed far beyond what he should have to get through the meetings with Alala and his Captains, and then he'd finally retreated to his quarters.

He didn't remember even taking his boots off, let alone getting under the covers on his bed. He was surprised to wake up and find himself tucked into the bed in his underwear. His dirty uniform was gone, potentially retrieved by his steward—but that worthy wouldn't have undressed him.

At that point, his internal network informed him that someone had asked to be sent a ping when he woke up. Checking, Henry smiled and gave his implant permission to send Sylvia a notice that he was awake.

Checking the time, he realized he'd been unconscious for over sixteen hours, and a spike of panic jolted him the rest of the way out of bed.

"Sit your butt down," Sylvia told him sternly, appearing at the door to his bedroom as if by magic. "Eowyn, Ihejirika, Quaid and I have spent a *great* deal of effort keeping the wolves from your door while you slept."

Arthur Quaid was Henry's steward, the poor bastard assigned to handle the care and feeding of one of the UPSF's many damaged flag officers. Combined with his operations officer, flag captain and diplomatic counterpart, those four could definitely make sure nothing made it through to his implant or his quarters.

And Henry realized he trusted that four's collective judgment enough to know that if something had *needed* to reach him, it would have.

"Okay," he conceded, sitting back down on the bed. Sylvia smiled and waved a half-threatening, half-promising finger at him before disappearing back into his lounge.

A minute or so later, she entered his bedroom with a tray holding two coffees, two juices, a carafe of each, and a single sandwich.

"Hydrate, eat, caffeinate," she instructed, passing him the orange juice. A table unfolded from the wall for her to place the tray on—though Henry was *reasonably* sure the chair she sat down on hadn't been there when he'd fallen asleep.

"Where are we at?" he asked softly.

"I'm waiting on a response from the Tadir government," she told him. "So's Alala. I *think* she has a solution of her own, but three days was enough for her to kick the answer upstairs."

The skip from Zo to Tadir was fifteen hours, but there had been two courier ships on that skip line every time Henry had looked. So long as there was a courier on each side, a back-and-forth message was thirty hours plus an hour or so of lightspeed lag.

"Makes sense," he conceded—and then realized he'd inhaled an entire glass of orange juice. Sylvia promptly reclaimed the glass—her own was only half-empty—and passed him the sandwich.

"Thank you," he murmured.

"Partners, my love," she told him. "Convincing the Tadir government to lend you a warship is more a political problem than a military one. That makes it my job. I think I made a good case—the only real question is whether they have the ship to spare."

"Always," Henry agreed around a mouthful of sandwich. He swallowed. "We don't know nearly enough about the strength of the various successor states, even the ones we have opened channels with."

"We simply don't know nearly enough about anyone," Sylvia countered. "We know the people who were Vesheron. But everyone else?" She shook her head. "We're still learning about the Ra Sector, and they're practically right next door. We haven't even made contact with the former Kenmiri colonies yet. Our only information on them is secondhand through the Kozun—and the Kozun were *shooting* at them until recently."

The only people left on the Kenmiri colonies were the slave populations who'd run the industry and agriculture, but they had access to *better* and more-balanced industry and agriculture than anyone else.

And while Henry's intelligence on them was shaky, if there was a functioning dreadnought-sized building slip anywhere in the Ra Sector, it was at one of the three former Kenmiri worlds.

The sandwich finally done, Sylvia passed him a second glass of juice. He eyed the coffee cup past her with greedy eyes but obediently drained the glass.

"I figure we've got another day or so before we hear back from Tadir," Sylvia noted. "You are going to do a *regular* shift rotation today, okay? Or I will have Dr. Uehara give me sedatives for Quaid, am I clear?"

Henry leaned past her and took the coffee cup while intentionally overreacting to the implied threat. Lieutenant Commander Dr. Sho Uehara was *Paladin*'s ship's doctor and chief medical officer.

"That would qualify as an assault on a superior officer," he told her over the rim of the cup. "You wouldn't put poor Quaid up to that."

"Oh, so I'd have to find *other* ways to make you rest?" Sylvia said with an overly dramatic leer at his bare chest.

"Behave, Ambassador," Henry said. "I need to finish this coffee at least."

"Then drink fast, Commodore," she told him. "Because I've set everything up to give us another hour before you need to be on duty —and I don't plan to waste it."

CHAPTER FORTY-ONE

THE FIRST COURIER SHIP TO COME THROUGH FROM TADIR HAD everyone on the flag deck on edge—except that it was only twenty-four hours since the ship carrying Sylvia's message had skipped toward the nearby industrial world.

The courier ship had left six hours before their messages had arrived and only carried the standard daily mail between the logistics base and the crew's home system.

It was another twenty-four hours before a response actually arrived—hours in which Henry was careful to keep a proper sleep schedule and even made time to work out. He didn't need his partner to remind him that the two days he'd spent awake after the battle at Ra-261 had a price to pay.

He was still in his office when the courier jumped in.

"Chan, let me know if the courier transmits to us," he told his coms officer. "Or if Alala reaches out. It's likely that ship has our answer on it."

If he could manage it, he wanted to be on his way with his two combat-ready ships before another day had passed. There was an itch at the base of his neck that told him that something was wrong, and he was running out of time to locate the Drifters.

"Will do, ser," Chan replied. "Sensors show they've commenced a message download to the station, so the System Authority should know soon enough."

"Thank you." The channel was voice-only, so Henry refrained from nodding, forcing his attention back to the data in front of him.

He was looking at a "stick and ball" model of the region, showing the skip lines between the assorted systems around him in a simplistic fashion. His internal network could instantly give him the travel time along any given skip line. Crossing times for systems were harder, but he had estimates.

The Convoy had been *there*, at Zo, on a known date. They'd been at Nohtoin at a known date. They'd gone to Ra-261 from Zo, but Henry didn't know how long the main body had stayed in Ra-261 after they'd set their ambush.

He could investigate Ra-261 again. The Drifters had probably withdrawn after losing their flagship and he could investigate there now—except that the Drifters would have done everything in their power to obscure their course there.

If he could guess where they'd gone *from* Ra-261, he could cut their trail at a later point. A point where they perhaps *hadn't* been as careful. The answer was somewhere in the map, he was certain of it.

"Ser, System Authority Alala is requesting a conference with you and Ambassador Todorovich," Chan's voice cut into his thoughts. "She asked what your availability was, but you said you would want to talk to her immediately?"

"Yes," Henry confirmed, closing the map with a wave of his hand. "Todorovich should be available, but double-check with her. Then link us all in."

There was a momentary pause.

"The Ambassador is available," the coms officer confirmed, the speed suggesting they'd been talking to her at the same time. "Connecting everyone now."

Sylvia Todorovich's holographic image appeared across Henry's desk, nodding slightly to him with a small smile—a smile that vanished behind her work mask as System Authority Alala appeared as well.

"Commodore Wong, Ambassador Todorovich," the Beren greeted them in Kem's staccato syllables. "I have received news from Tadir in response to our messages, and my superiors have come up with a solution that I believe will work for us all.

"I am authorized to detach one of the Tadir Fleet escorts under my command to take *Cataphract* back to La-Tar. A squadron of six of our new-build corvettes will join me in Zo to replace her in a few days."

"That is perfect, System Authority," Henry said. "Will you need to wait until the corvettes arrive to send *Cataphract* on her way?"

"I do not believe that will be necessary," Alala replied. "I believe we are all agreed that the Drifters are unlikely to launch a major offensive against Zo or Tadir, and we are several skips from any threat from the Kozun.

"I am authorized to send the escort immediately. That should enable you to continue your mission, yes?"

"It will, yes," Henry confirmed. He glanced at Sylvia. He wasn't sure just how effusive he should be in his gratitude, but he understood just how much of a gesture sending a ship away for a full month was.

"We are grateful, System Authority," Sylvia said, smoothly taking over for him. "I will send my own thanks and regards to your government. Knowing that *Cataphract* and our wounded will be seen safely to our comrades at La-Tar is important to us.

"The UPA will not forget this service."

No formal promises, Henry noted, but a formal acknowledgement of a debt. He wasn't always comfortable with the politics and diplomacy of interacting with other nations, but he was comfortable with one thing: the United Planets Alliance honored their debts.

"We all do what we can to stand together," Alala told them. "We hope for a long friendship between our people."

"So do we," Sylvia said firmly. "Our goal is peace in the Ra Sector, System Authority. The more friends we have, the easier that will be."

Henry nodded his agreement. His chunk of the Peacekeeper Initiative might have been dragged up in this damned punitive expedition, but the Initiative was still working toward that goal.

The problem, every so often, was the choice between fighting *for* peace and enabling warlords and conquerors. That had dragged him into the war with the Kozun and now into this pursuit of the Drifters.

"I wish you luck in your mission, Commodore Wong," Alala told him. "We will see your people home safe. You have the sacred word of the Tadir Fleet."

THE SYSTEM AUTHORITY'S image vanished, and Henry sighed, looking over at Sylvia.

"Back to the hunt," he told her. "We've got work to do. I don't suppose you have any brilliant insight?"

"Not particularly," she admitted. "What do you want insight into?"

He chuckled and waved the stick and ball model back into existence. A mental command shared it with her.

"We know the Drifters were here, at the Ra-261 System," he told her. "Somewhere between six and twenty-some days ago. So, that gives me potential locations of, well..."

Some twenty systems lit up with pale red highlights.

"Of course, the Drifters do *not* enter inhabited systems, so we're only *really* looking at these." Half of the systems disappeared. "Which still leaves us with twelve systems to search for a trail. Systems in which the Drifters were likely trying at least some degree of subtlety and concealment."

A pale red line appeared on the map, tracing a route from Nohtoin to Ra-261.

"We know, roughly, the route they took to get to Ra-261," he said. "And I'm pretty sure they're not going to backtrack. They paused in a number of these systems to trade, refuel or acquire raw materials.

"You'd think they'd be running faster, knowing we're hunting them," he noted. "But they've been moving only a bit faster than their usual pace."

"They can't move much faster than their usual pace," she reminded him. "You've been aboard a Drifter Convoy, haven't you? Everything is a careful balancing act of air, food and fuel. They can only press so hard."

"I can see a logic to them trying to keep us and the Kozun fighting each other," Henry said. "But in their place, I think I'd have owned up and paid reparations or *something* immediately. If they can't run and they can't fight..."

"They might not expect mercy from us," Sylvia said quietly. "They're used to the Kenmiri, after all."

Henry nodded, staring at the map. A hazy blue highlight appeared over the Nohtoin System as Sylvia poked at it.

"Your report from Nohtoin said that they split the Convoy there," she noted. "That...didn't make sense to me. Any idea what happened there?"

"No," Henry admitted. "I'd forgot, to be honest. The main body definitely has the garden ships and the factory ships, so that's basically the Convoy. Anything else is just...detachments."

"But what would they have detached before entering Eerdish space?" she asked.

"Something they didn't want the Eerdish to see," Henry said quietly. "Though..." He was looking at the route the Drifters had taken. "Though definitely something they wanted easy access to."

"You sound like you just spotted something," she told him with a soft chuckle.

"If we assume that they're following a preplanned course and coordinated it with whoever they detached at Nohtoin..."

A purple line appeared on his model, running between gray stars —stars no one claimed and skip lines that Henry's map didn't necessarily have confirmed—as he mapped it out.

"There's a course here, one that stays outside of E-Two space but keeps that *someone* within seventy-two hours' travel of the Convoy," he said, pointing at the line. "If we assume the entire detachment can pull one-point-five KPS-squared—updated escorts or gunships, basically, no civilian ships—that's closer to sixty hours." He took a thoughtful swallow of coffee.

"If we use that as a constraint and assume they're otherwise pushing on a direct line away from UPA space, a projected course is..."

A yellow line appeared from Nohtoin, cutting through the space of the Eerdish and their allies...and almost exactly matching the course the Drifters had taken.

"They'd rendezvous with their detachment here, wouldn't they?" Sylvia asked, highlighting one of the gray stars in the same blue haze. "We don't know that system, do we?"

"It's visible from the Enteni homeworld," Henry noted. "They call it Blue First Dawn. It's apparently visible about an hour before dawn on one of their main habitable landmasses. We've got long-distance data on it but otherwise...nothing.

"No habitable worlds, no really useful skip lines. That's about all that's in the high-level Kenmiri atlases, and we don't have detailed files for that area."

The Kenmiri Empire had done detailed surveys on each of the ten thousand star systems they had claimed and subdivided into twenty provinces. So far as anyone had been able to discover, though, most of those surveys had not been kept in the provinces themselves.

So, now twelve provinces had been abandoned, and all they had for most of those six thousand stars was the high-level atlas information.

"If they're heading there, when would they get there?" Sylvia asked.

Henry checked.

"Assuming they're following my projected course and have to make their usual stops for fuel, et cetera...another five days," he said. "And if we take the GMS to full power and make a run along the shortest possible route—which will take us through both Tadir and Makata, which is why the Drifters wouldn't use it..."

A green line now marked the map, cutting a near-straight line between Zo and Blue First Dawn.

"Six days," he said quietly. "We can almost certainly be there before they leave—assuming we're right."

"You have to put your own eyes on them to be sure of that?" she asked.

"I think I need to put my own eyes on them for the E-Two to give us permission to bring *three fleet carriers* through their space," Henry replied grimly. "Twelfth Fleet could conquer the entire Alliance in a week. Their leadership is understandably nervous about it."

"But Blue First Dawn isn't in their space, so they're more likely to give Rex permission to pass through," Sylvia murmured. "As opposed to giving us permission to attack the Drifters in their space."

"Agreed." Henry smiled thinly. "It's no guarantee, but it's the best logic we've got. If you'll excuse me, Sylvia, I need to bring my team in on this.

"The sooner we're on our way, the more likely we are to find them where we want them."

CHAPTER FORTY-TWO

Both during and after the war, Sylvia Todorovich had seen a *lot* of Kenmiri factory slave worlds and their star systems. Tadir was a representative example. The Kenmiri picked the systems for having technically habitable planets, rich asteroid belts and at least one gas giant.

Tadir had been more *technically* habitable than most, and the sheer scale of the industry and pollution unleashed upon a factory slave world had put paid to that limited habitability quickly. The planet was a sickly yellow color from a distance, a toxic mess that required breathers to go outside and *still* somehow supported three hundred million people.

Another thirty million people lived in the orbital stations and the asteroid belts, an unusually high proportion for a slave system and likely responsible for the Tadir government's focus on their fleet.

"I assure the Governor that, as we promised before we entered the system, we have no intention of doing anything except passing through at maximum speed," she told the recorder point at her office desk.

"Our mission requires us to take the shortest route possible to hopefully head off a mutual threat to both the UPA and the Tadir System. While I understand that we do not have an alliance or even any treaties between our worlds, we both desire positive long-term relationships.

"I ask that you regard Destroyer Squadron Twenty-Seven as favorable neutrals at worst, friends at best," she urged the locals. "The estimate I have from our Navigation departments is that we will be exiting the system in approximately seven hours and forty-six minutes, via the Oshala skip line toward Makata.

"Both I and Commodore Wong understand that you would have preferred we request passage before entering the system, but we are up against a tight deadline."

She considered her closing carefully.

"We await further communication. Ambassador Todorovich, signing off."

Shaking her head in the privacy of her office, she gave a mental command and flipped the recording over to Chan to send to the planet.

Sylvia and Alala *had* sent a courier on ahead to request passage. She'd warned in the message on the courier that they would be only a few hours behind the ship—three, as it turned out.

That clearly had *not* been enough time for Tadir's government to make a decision, so now Sylvia was presenting them with a fait accompli. The fastest ships in the system could *maybe* make one-point-five KPS^2.

DesRon Twenty-Seven's two ships were accelerating at two KPS^2. The locals could intercept them if they chose, especially as they decelerated toward the exit skip line, but what was the point? Everyone there wanted to be friends, after all.

But the time limit that Henry and his navigators had calculated hung over the two destroyers like the Sword of Damocles. If they got to Blue First Dawn before the Drifter Convoy left, the com drones they carried could set the whole complex mechanism of permission and deployment around Twelfth Fleet into place.

But they needed a confirmed sighting and identification before they could do that. Sylvia knew that Felix Leitz was working on laying the groundwork for Twelfth Fleet's passage through E-Two space—and that *everyone* would be happier if the UPSF fleet caught up with the Drifters in unclaimed space.

The sooner they had eyes on the Convoy, the better off they were.

And until then, Sylvia Todorovich would pour oil on troubled waters. Negotiating passage after they'd already breached a system's territory was *nothing* compared to some of the things she'd arranged during the war.

Hopefully, she didn't have to try to negotiate passage after someone had started *shooting*. That would be…significantly more difficult.

THE FORMAL PERMISSION TO travel through the Tadir System finally arrived five hours later. Sylvia wasn't certain what Tadir was using for a government system, but the delay suggested they had discovered some of the delights of democracy.

"I thought we *had* permission to travel through E-Two space," Ihejirika said when Sylvia told a group conference their permission had arrived.

"We do," Sylvia told him. "Both the Eerdish and the Enteni gave us full permission to operate in their space, draw on their fueling stations, et cetera, et cetera. The Tadir gave us permission to operate in their claimed stars and draw on their fueling stations.

"Included in all of that, though, was the unspoken assumption that we would not charge into inhabited systems at full speed without prior notice," she said. "We come through a skip line and immediately go to full thrust, everyone is going to assume it's an attack.

"Sending messages as far ahead as we can helps, but theoretically, we should be waiting for an okay before we enter Makata, for example."

"Are we going to?" Teunissen asked.

"No," Henry told them all, arching an eyebrow at Sylvia. "Though as I understand, we *may* get it?"

"Tadir has the same courier setup at the Oshala skip line as they had to Zo," Sylvia noted. "I requested that they forward a message to Makata. It depends on whether there's a link from Oshala to Kitpal and from Kitpal to Makata.

"Messages travel at lightspeed inside systems, so if there are couriers in place, Makata could get our message in less than two days. If they respond immediately, we could get it when we arrive in Kitpal."

Sylvia ran the math in her head and smiled austerely.

"Most likely, unless they are *completely* unable to come to a decision, we should have permission to cross Makata before we reach the Kitpal-Makata skip line. In fifty-seven hours."

"What happens if the Makata deny us permission to enter the Makata System?" Teunissen asked.

"It's unlikely," Henry told his Captain. "Right, Ambassador?"

"Exactly. As Ihejirika pointed out, we *have* permission to go anywhere in Alliance territory. Requesting permission before we enter inhabited systems is a courtesy that's only truly required because we're blazing through at an acceleration they haven't seen before."

Even for Sylvia, watching the destroyers zip around at over two hundred gravities of acceleration was a new experience. She was getting used to it—she certainly had no *problem* with it—but after a career aboard ships that accelerated at half a KPS^2, it was definitely a bit odd.

"*If* they decline, we do have an alternative route," Henry noted. "It will add sixty-three hours, taking us through the Coro System and another unnamed red dwarf. While I think it's safe to expect that the Drifters will still be there twenty-four to forty-eight hours after our estimate of their arrival, adding sixty hours to that changes the odds drastically.

"So, let's hope the Makata are feeling cooperative. I want this done, people. The Initiative has a lot of uses for these ships that *aren't* playing scout for Twelfth Fleet."

Sylvia had to agree with that. They'd created the Initiative to *help* people, not fight a war across the breadth of the Ra Sector!

CHAPTER FORTY-THREE

The Kitpal System turned out to be where the E-Two Alliance had posted their main nodal defense force for the Makata dependency cluster. From what the UPSF people around Sylvia were saying, it sounded like the Kitpal task force actually *could* catch DesRon Twenty-Seven.

"That's four of their carrier conversions," Ihejirika reported. Sylvia wasn't sure if the flag captain knew that she was in Henry's quarters—but Henry was playing the report in audio so she could listen.

It was also limited to audio because she was currently face-first on his bed while he massaged her naked back with oil. They were now *hours* past when she'd expected to hear from the Makata government, and she was feeling the stress.

She wouldn't show it to anyone *else*, but she'd admitted it to Henry—who'd insisted on taking time to help her relax, returning the favor from when she'd brought him breakfast after his multi-day stint of wakeful watch.

"So, a hundred and twenty fighters?" Henry replied to Ihejirika, his hands still moving across her back and massaging out knots.

"About that," the Captain confirmed. "Other ships, too, but with the geometry and our acceleration, the fighters are the only thing I'm worried about. So far, they're not acting like we're doing anything outrageous, though."

"*They knew we were coming*," Sylvia silently messaged Henry.

"They did know we were coming," he echoed to Ihejirika. "If the nodal fleet isn't freaking out at us, verbally or otherwise, we probably don't have to worry too much about our passage into Makata.

"Still, I'd be more comfortable if we'd heard from them. Let me know the moment any courier ships come through from Makata."

The audio channel closed with an audible *click* and Henry sighed.

"Silence is nerve-wracking," she told him.

"And knot-inducing, it appears," he replied. She winced as his questing fingers found a key point. "We have ten and a half hours in Kitpal still before we make the skip to Makata. Those carriers aren't as far out of our weight class as I imagine they'd like to think, but they can still be a real problem.

"If only because their fighters can catch us and not much else here can."

Sylvia exhaled into the pillow as the knot he was working on suddenly released.

"You know, if I'd known you were *this* good at massages, I might have tried to bribe you into them even *before* I jumped you," she purred. "It helps."

"I was married during a war, Sylvia," Henry pointed out. "Peter and I took massage classes together on several of our shared leaves. *Everything* was stressful then."

"And now?" she asked.

He chuckled.

"*Many things* are stressful," he conceded, his fingers moving up to her neck. "But not *everything*. We'll hear from Makata, Sylvia. Soon enough, I'm sure."

"Soon enough that I'll even keep my pants on," she agreed with a dramatically mournful sigh.

"Probably, yes," he agreed with his own exaggerated patience.

SYLVIA WAS BACK in her office when the response *finally* arrived —less than four hours before they were due to hit the skip line. Chan forwarded the video to her and she started it immediately.

A dark-blue-skinned Kozun, with the armored forehead spikes of that race, appeared in front of her. He wore a baroque blue and gold robe that had *clearly* originally been made for a Kenmiri Artisan and modified to fit him.

Everything about the room around the Kozun man was similar to the robe. Converted from Kenmiri furniture and decorations, but in a way that intentionally left it clear that the conversion had been done.

"I am Kal Satirus," the man greeted her, bowing slightly over crossed hands. "I greet Commodore Henry Wong, the Destroyer, and Ambassador Sylvia Todorovich."

Sylvia was alone and allowed herself to wince as Satirus used the nickname several of the Vesheron had started for Henry. It came with being the man to kill the last Kenmorad, she supposed—but she also knew he hated it.

"I am the Secular Voice of Makata," he explained after a moment. "I speak for no god, but I speak for this world."

The Voices who led the Kozun Hierarchy were technically priests—even *prophets*, supposedly—picked by their gods. The adjacent symbolism was fascinating.

Not that Sylvia was going to have time to do comparative xenoanthropology on this trip.

"I have reviewed your message and request again and again," he told them. "At first, I must admit I was offended that you wished to pass through our glorious system without setting foot on our world and seeing what we have to offer.

"Makata is a beautiful planet, one that I am pleased to show to all outsiders," he continued. "But...I was Vesheron once. I understand the urgencies of war, and so I calmed my offense before I chose to respond to your missive.

"You have permission to pass through the Makata System," he told them. "But." He held up a delicately manicured hand. "I ask that, in turn, you both come visit our planet when you can. With neither gods nor masters, we are building a new paradise here, and I wish to show it to all who could be our friends."

Neither gods nor masters certainly sounded hopeful enough, but everything about the Secular Voice of Makata's presentation made Sylvia suspect he was one of the people who had become the unquestioned dictator of their world.

"I look forward to meeting you in person," Kal Satirus concluded, and the message ended.

Somehow, Sylvia felt vaguely oily after watching it, and she shivered.

"Not everyone on our side has to be good people," she told herself aloud.

She suspected the E-Two Alliance had their own thoughts on the Secular Voice...and she doubted it was unrelated that the Makata Cluster was determinedly staying as five separate states rather than unifying as La-Tar had done.

CHAPTER FORTY-FOUR

THE RIDEA SYSTEM—NAMED FOR AN ANCIENT TAK HERO AND forming the "eye" of one of their key constellations, as Henry understood it—was an immensely bloated red supergiant with no planets of any kind. A vast ring of debris, like a gas giant's rings on a supercharged scale, orbited the star. Some quirk of geometry had prevented it ever coalescing into planets, making the Rings of Ridea a fascinating challenge in navigation.

One that, thankfully, Henry's people didn't need to worry about. The skip line from Leba—the system after Makata—brought them into the outer system. A six-light-minute arc around the outside of the Rings would bring them to the skip line to Blue First Dawn.

Four hours. In four hours, they'd begin the final skip to see if their estimate was correct.

It was a *long* skip, though—a full twenty hours. There were longer skips, but Henry knew his navigators were twitchy about anything over eighteen hours that hadn't been previously charted by UPSF ships.

The *next* UPSF crew to make the jump to Blue First Dawn would have their data. But *Paladin* and *Maharatha* did not.

He leaned back in his chair and studied the maps and displays swirling around him. There were no new answers falling out today. If the Drifters weren't at Blue First Dawn, he had three secondary places to investigate within two skips of the unclaimed system.

Of course, if the Drifters had gone to those systems instead, he was once again running against the clock of distance and probability. Only the limited speed of a convoy of hundreds of ships had given him any chance of bringing them to bay—and part of him knew that if he missed the trail on this round of investigations, the mission was over.

He wasn't even sure that was a bad thing. He understood the logic of a punitive expedition and he knew that Rex wasn't planning atrocities against the civilian population of the Blue Stripe Green Stripe Orange Stripe Convoy, but it still felt vaguely wrong.

Still...he was confident they'd guessed right. And that meant he needed to pull the ideas and discussions everyone had been having over the six days of their high-speed run through E-Two space into an actual plan.

"Chan," he pinged his coms officer. "Get the captains, staff and Ambassador Todorovich together on a call. On the hour if everyone is available for it. ASAP after that if they're not."

WITH *CATAPHRACT* SENT BACK to La-Tar, the six of them could have fit in the breakout meeting room in Henry's office. Eowyn, Chan and Todorovich *did* join him there, with the two ship Captains linking in from Ihejirika's bridge and Teunissen's office, respectively.

"We are hopefully less than a day away from finally having eyes on the BGO Convoy," Henry told them. "I know we all have rough ideas of what we're planning on doing there, but I want to go over my plan and make sure we're all on the same page."

He looked over at Sylvia.

"First, though, Ambassador Todorovich is the only one who has seen Blue Stripe Green Stripe Orange Stripe themselves," he noted. "Ambassador, if you could remind us what you saw?"

Sylvia nodded—he'd let her know what he needed before his staff had joined them—and took mental command of the shared holographic display.

"BGO is a three-stripe Convoy," she explained as images of the Convoy from when she'd visited came onto the screen. "That means a minimum of five hundred ships and five million people. When I visited aboard *Shaka*, they had six hundred and forty-plus ships and an estimated six million people aboard."

She paused, studying the image of the immense fleet. The ships in the Convoy ranged from a handful of small couriers to the immense self-sustaining biospheres of the garden ships. Almost all of them dwarfed the hundred-and-fifty-meter length of the two *Cataphract* destroyers—just as they had dwarfed the destroyer *Shaka* that had brought her to visit the Drifters.

To challenge that armada seemed the height of arrogance—but then, that wasn't DesRon Twenty-Seven's task.

A mental command highlighted sixty of the ships in a bright red.

"*Shaka*'s crew identified sixty warships," she noted. "Fifteen were Guardians; the remainder were a mix of Kenmiri-style escorts and assorted self-built ships of equivalent or lesser size and firepower.

"Those ships were distributed around the exterior of the Convoy in defensive positions. I met with the commander of BGO's defenses, Protector-Commander Third-White-Fifth-Gold, aboard this ship."

The largest Guardian flickered on the screen.

"We have every reason to assume that all of the defensive ships carry a full complement of antigravity resonance disruptor warheads," she noted softly. "I recommend caution."

Henry knew his plan didn't qualify as cautious—though Sylvia was *right*. Survival was his highest priority once he'd found the Convoy, but only the highest. There were other priorities, and those called for at least *some* risk.

"We know they are down at least four Guardians," he reminded everyone. "Between us, the Kozun and Battle Group Scorpius, three were destroyed at the Lon System. We took out another at Ra-Two-Sixty-One.

"Eleven Guardians still represents more capital ships than the Kozun and the E-Two muster between them at this point," he said grimly. "My best-case scenario for the E-Two gives them five real carriers, and both sides have *a* dreadnought.

"Even with shields on the E-Two's fighters, destroyers and escorts, the Convoy's defensive forces are sufficient to engage and destroy every known military in the Ra Sector except the UPSF. That's why Twelfth Fleet exists."

Henry manipulated the data Sylvia had provided, focusing in on the sixty warships *Shaka* had identified.

"Twenty-two escorts. Twenty-three smaller ships—we've encountered at least one raider corvette that was probably Drifter. Fifteen Guardians—now eleven."

He shook his head.

"If they did not possess resonance missiles, I wouldn't be worried about Twelfth Fleet engaging them at all," he told his people. "As it stands, I want Twelfth Fleet to have all of the intelligence they can."

"That doesn't sound like *caution*, ser," Ihejirika pointed out.

"Because it's not," Henry agreed. "We are going to make a close-range scouting run of the BGO Convoy. Emerging into Blue First Dawn, both ships will maintain point-*three* KPS-squared until my command.

"At any significant distance, that should leave us functionally invisible." Not quite as much as the stealth ships they'd seen in the Avas System—ships he now grimly assumed were Kenmiri—but enough that he was comfortable getting way too close to the Convoy.

"Once we've located the Convoy, we will proceed toward them at point-five KPS-squared," he continued, converting the data on the Drifters into a tactical plot. "We will step down our acceleration by a tenth-KPS-squared at four light-minutes, three light-minutes, two light-minutes, and one light-minute.

"At point-one KPS-squared, my understanding is that we should be able to approach as close as five or six light-seconds before being detected—and our base velocity at that point will be significant."

"How close are you thinking about getting, ser?" Eowyn asked. She'd run a lot of the numbers for this plan for him, but she clearly hadn't anticipated *this*.

"At five light-seconds, we are outside reasonable weapons range for both us and them," Henry noted. "Their likelihood of detecting us at that point is decent, but we will have both the base velocity and the reserve acceleration to escape pursuit without being engaged.

"I want as much data on the Convoy as we can get," he concluded. "We will fire drones back to La-Tar and Eerdish the moment we have confirmed their location, but I intend to maintain both a continuous watch over the Convoy and a continuous communication with Twelfth Fleet until Admiral Rex arrives.

"And if we happen to spook the Drifters while we do so, I'm not going to worry overly much," he told them. "We're going to buzz them fast and dark and hope they don't see us—but if they *do* see us, all it's going to do is make them nervous.

"Now. I'm open to suggestions for improving and expanding the plan. Your thoughts, people?"

There was a long silence as his people looked at the maneuvering icons and notes on the tactical plot he'd created.

"Drones," Teunissen finally suggested. "Two options. First is a risk, but if we fire them early enough, they may be able to coast through the Drifter formation at even closer ranges without being detected."

"Lock down their active sensors and engines?" Eowyn asked. "The missile launchers add a thousand KPS to our own velocity, so we *should* be able to coordinate them to pass through when we do.

"It's a risk, though; you're right," she confirmed. "The drones will be more detectable and may give away our presence even if the low-energy grav drives cover the destroyers."

"Agreed. Second suggestion is to hold them in the magazines

until we're detected," Teunissen offered. "Then we drop twenty-three of them directly into the Convoy at full drive power with active scanners. It's not subtle, but it gets us a lot more data if we get detected."

Henry nodded slowly.

"I hadn't considered sending the drones in without engines," he admitted. "Good idea, Captain. I suggest we prep for both—we're already accepting a significant chance of detection and arranging for our own safety, so adding the ballistic drones isn't a major chance and may get us a lot more data.

"And then if we are detected, sending in active sensor drones will get us even more while we bolt for the outer system. I like it."

CHAPTER FORTY-FIVE

SKIPS STILL SUCKED. THERE WAS NO REAL WAY TO DESCRIBE THE sensation of being punched in twenty dimensions when the human brain only processed three. Even outside the moments of icosaspatial impulse, there was always a vague discomfort that Henry had never managed to get used to.

He'd met a few people who claimed it didn't bother them. He figured they were lying.

Sleep helped. Sex helped. Getting drunk, despite his own claims when he was younger, definitely did *not* help.

The second impulse moment passed in a blur of getting repeatedly kicked, and Henry exhaled a long sigh of pain. The privacy of his quarters allowed for that, even if he'd never show it on the bridge.

"Do you ever get used to that?" Sylvia asked, echoing his own thoughts.

He considered for a moment, then chuckled.

"No," he admitted. "Was just thinking about it. I guess you get used to *enduring* it?"

"That makes sense," she conceded. She leaned against him for a few seconds, then sighed. "Still doubting whether your judgment is clouded around my suggestions?" she asked.

Henry blinked.

He hadn't *forgotten* that he'd said that, per se, but he'd mostly moved past that fear. Sylvia...perhaps hadn't?

"Are you worried I rejected your suggestion to be cautious because of that?" he asked.

"Hard not to wonder," she admitted. "Emotions are bullshit things, aren't they? But this won't work if I'm hiding behind a mask with you, will it?"

"No, it won't," he agreed. He turned to look at her, holding her gaze with his own as he took her hands. "Your reasoning was entirely correct, Sylvia," he told her. "I agree with it and I respect your judgment.

"In this case, though, being cautious doesn't meet all of our needs," he continued. "I knew that before you ever briefed everyone on the Convoy. We *need* a better idea of what we're sending Twelfth Fleet into.

"So, caution, yes. That's why we're making the scouting run in stealth and at high speed, making allowances to make sure we don't get engaged. The close approach and the speed may not *look* cautious, Sylvia, but they actually *are*. Unless something goes very different from what I expect, they can't catch us—and if they can't catch us, they can't hurt us.

"So, no, my love, I am not mistrusting my judgment with respect to you anymore," he told her firmly. "Your judgment in this case was impeccable—but you were not aware of all of the necessary military components of the situation. That's my job, not yours—just as it was your job, not mine, to smooth the ruffled feathers of our charge through Tadir and Makata."

"Fair," she conceded, a small smile hovering around her lips as she relaxed slightly. "Apparently, I still have relationship anxieties in my old age."

"If you're old, Sylvia, I should be planning my retirement," he said drily. She was a full decade younger than he, though neither of them was *young* anymore. "And since I think I have something like three decades of active-duty service ahead of me, I'm going to take the risk of saying you aren't old."

"That's your plan, is it?" she asked. "You've already given the UPA thirty years of your life, Henry. Another thirty?"

"Thirty-four years, actually," he corrected softly. "Four years of training, thirty of active service. I figure another decade to full Admiral, at which point Hamilton will probably chain me to the big desk at the Peacekeeper Initiative for a decade.

"But...nightmares and trauma and all of that included, this is what I do, Sylvia. And I'm damn good at it. Better to be damned to hell by my own hand than sent to heaven by someone else's."

She leaned against him silently for a minute or so.

"Not much I can say," she finally admitted. "I may want you to do something safer, but that's selfish and I know it. And...it's not like I'm retiring from the diplomatic corps anytime soon, and *that* is going to be sending me into all kinds of situations, isn't it?"

"Give us thirty years, love, and we'll have the entire former Empire eating out of your hand," Henry said with a chuckle. The Ra Sector might be taking them longer to put in order than he'd hoped, but there was a definite light at the end of the tunnel—and the sheer amount of money the new trade deals were sending home was going to do positive things to the Initiative's budget in the long run.

"They didn't know what they were getting into, did they?" she asked. Her smile was a bit forced, but it was real, and he kissed her.

"I've got the warlords who won't talk to us and you've got the sensible folks who will," he told her. "How could we go wrong?"

Sylvia paused thoughtfully, then dramatically checked the time.

"Not enough of either sleep or sex," she told him with a wicked tone. "But my math says we have time enough for both still."

CHAPTER FORTY-SIX

"Contact."

Henry hadn't even realized he'd been holding his breath since they'd emerged in Blue First Dawn until Eowyn's quiet single-word report echoed through the bridge.

"Distance is just over nine light-minutes," she continued after a few seconds. "We're not getting much in terms of detail, but it's a big contact."

"Big enough?" Henry asked softly.

"Big enough," she confirmed. "If it's *not* the Drifter Convoy, it's another collection of several hundred ships that have decided to all refuel at the same gas giant."

The system geography was filling in as the contact report updated. Blue First Dawn was a blue star, a rare Be stellar type that glittered blue as it engaged in an eternal dance with an immense gas giant *just* too small to ignite on its own. A smaller gas giant roughly the size of Jupiter orbited both, and the intermingled gravity waves of the three massive objects had prevented anything else of significant size from forming.

"Where are they?" Henry asked.

"Contact is approximately one light-minute from the smaller gas giant, making a slow approach into orbit," Eowyn told him. "They're taking it easy. I estimate another six hours before they're in a close-enough orbit to commence fueling."

"They may well be planning on staying here for a bit if they think they've lost us," Chan suggested. "This system is pretty off the beaten track, though Blue First Dawn's size may make a useful relay point as we expand the contact network."

"If they want to wait here for Twelfth Fleet, that will make everyone happy," Henry replied. "We need to get close enough for a confirmed ID, I think. Bring the squadron up to point-five and set a zero-zero course based on stepping down as we get closer."

"Understood. It'll be just seven hours for us to get to five light-seconds from them," Eowyn said. "Passing maneuvering orders to both ships."

"Let's be about it, people," Henry ordered. "Let's see what the Drifters have been so desperate to hide."

MINUTES BECAME hours as the distance shrank. Half a KPS^2 shouldn't have felt slow to Henry or his people—they'd spent most of their careers with that being the maximum thrust that didn't require them to retreat to acceleration tanks—and yet...

After months aboard the *Cataphracts* with their gravity maneuvering systems, they seemed to *crawl* across the star system. Four hours had allowed them to cross almost six light-minutes in Ridea, but here, four hours barely carried them three and a half light-minutes.

It was close enough for one part of the mission.

"We have now confirmed in excess of five hundred individual signatures," Eowyn told him. "While we can't ID warships reliably at this range, we have definitely picked up several garden ships and matched their emissions to those reported by *Shaka*.

"This is *definitely* the Blue Stripe Green Stripe Orange Stripe Drifter Convoy."

Henry took a minute to confirm what she was seeing. He trusted Eowyn beyond a doubt, but when that conclusion required him to set into motion the largest offensive deployment of the UPSF since Operation Golden Lancelot, he wanted to be *certain*.

"I agree," he finally said aloud. "Chan?"

"Ser!"

"Prep...seven skip drones," he told them. "Three for La-Tar, two for Eerdish, two for Enteni. Duplicate data to them all, supporting the conclusion that we have confirmed the location of the BGO Convoy.

"Envoy Felix Leitz is to confirm passage rights for Twelfth Fleet," he continued. "The drones to the Enteni are for their information only, as we have no one there to negotiate with them.

"Leitz is to communicate directly with Admiral Rex, but the Ops plan calls for Admiral Rex to begin movement along the minimum-time course to the target system immediately. That sets a strict time limit on Leitz's work."

And a dangerous risk for failure. Rex wouldn't *stop* if Leitz hadn't confirmed authorization to pass through E-Two space. Henry was putting a lot of faith on people he couldn't say much more to.

Fortunately, he knew Felix Leitz. Sylvia's chief of staff might not like military officers—and most of Henry's people had generally returned the opinion—but Henry had a solid respect for the man's competence in his own field.

Leitz would open the path. Even if he didn't do so in time, Henry knew Rex's reputation and doubted that Twelfth Fleet's CO would make the situation worse than it needed to be. He'd brush past any E-Two ships that tried to stop him, but he'd never fire first.

And Henry figured there'd be enough questions being asked that just bulling past the Eerdish and their allies would be enough to get Twelfth Fleet through without bloodshed.

"Once all of that is loaded, launch the drones immediately," Henry ordered softly. "They shouldn't be detected at this range."

"Drones loading sensor data," Chan confirmed after a moment. "We ran a downgrade algorithm on the data for the Eerdish and Enteni. The Convoy isn't quite as clear afterward, but it should be good enough."

They paused.

"Download complete. Drones launching."

"And that's that," Henry murmured, his gaze riveted on the green icons as they flashed away. They'd hit the Ridea skip line and follow the shortest possible course to their destination—and with six KPS^2 of acceleration to play with, they'd be there a lot sooner than any of the ships.

Seven days to Eerdish. Eight to Enteni. Twelve to La-Tar—and eighteen days for Twelfth Fleet to make it to Blue First Dawn.

For the next thirty days, at least, Henry needed to shadow the Drifters without being caught. Fortunately for everyone, he really wasn't worried about *that* part.

Despite his assurances to Sylvia, he was worried about this part. By the time DesRon Twenty-Seven arrived, the Drifters would be in orbit of the gas giant. His ships would pass them at five light-seconds, traveling at over eleven thousand kilometers a second. If he wanted, he could fire missiles into the Convoy while closing and cause untold havoc.

Instead, he was going to send in drones. Today was about information. Information allowed precision—and while precision was a frail shield against atrocity, it was the only shield he could create.

And the die had been cast. Twelfth Fleet was coming.

CHAPTER FORTY-SEVEN

EVERYTHING WAS GOING ACCORDING TO PLAN, AND THAT MADE Henry nervous. His two ships were rapidly catching up with the pre-launched sensor probes, all of the distances he was tracking rapidly trending toward zero.

"Probes will make their closest approach at between fifty thousand and three hundred thousand kilometers," Eowyn reported. "All are ballistic and fully locked down. They *should* be invisible or mistaken for natural meteors."

"And us?" Henry asked.

"One million five hundred and twenty-two thousand kilometers," she told him. "In about five minutes. I don't recommend that anyone hold their breath."

"And our velocity?"

"Eleven thousand two hundred kilometers per second, and we continue to accelerate at point-one KPS-squared," Eowyn confirmed. "We are in the field of the Drifters' active scanners, but nothing we're detecting through the grav-shield suggests that we have been seen."

Their thermal signature was as low as they could make it. Despite the unconscious urge, there was no point in staying still and quiet aboard the ship—with multiple *fusion reactors* running, at however low a level, anything a human could do was irrelevant.

The gravity shield and the gravity maneuvering system smeared that thermal signature across hundreds of kilometers—thousands, at this velocity. What would have been noticeable as a single point source was a minor background anomaly when spread over a hundred thousand cubic kilometers.

Hopefully.

"The data is solid?" Henry asked.

"As a rock," Eowyn confirmed. "We probably don't need to close to five light-seconds, though…"

He waited. His subordinate knew better than to leave him hanging—though her questioning tone drew his attention to the data they were gathering. His focus had been on their stealth maneuvers and the overall location and threat level of the Drifter Convoy.

"They've got to be playing some kind of game," Eowyn finally finished her thought. "I'm reading one Guardian *here*, at the front of the Convoy; and one *here*, at the tail end. And that's *it*."

"And only eight escorts," Henry concluded for her, looking closely at the data now. "That's a *fifth* of the warships I was expecting. What about the civilian numbers?"

"We've got enough information from *Shaka*'s scans to identify specific larger ships," his Ops officer pointed out. "I've mostly delegated that to Commander Bach's people, but the numbers are lining up."

He nodded slowly, then pinged his shared channel with *Paladin*'s Captain.

"Okafor, your people are seeing the same data mine are," he noted. "Are you seeing the same problem I am?"

"Where's their security force?" Ihejirika rumbled instantly. "So far, Commander Bach's team has identified over sixty individual ships and matched them to *Shaka*'s data. Every ship we've looked for appears to be there, except the warships."

"We know they had at least one detachment of a Guardian and

six escorts out to ambush us, but that doesn't explain them missing *nine capital ships*," Henry said grimly. "I'm with Commander Eowyn. They're playing games—but our approach and drones should let us see through whatever illusions they're working."

"We know they detached something when they passed through Nohtoin," Eowyn pointed out. "Maybe a larger chunk of their warships than we expected?"

"They'd never cut the defenses of the Convoy itself this much," Ihejirika said. "Something's *wrong*, Commodore."

"Closest approach?" Henry asked, careful to maintain his outward calm.

And his inward calm, for that matter. This was *strange*. It wasn't a threat—not an immediate one, anyway.

"Still two minutes," Eowyn replied. "Still no sign that we or the sensor drones have been detected. Clean and straight so far."

All of that made Henry *more* nervous. The hair on the back of his neck was standing up and every instinct of thirty years of military service was screaming *TRAP*.

Except he'd already done everything he could. If it was a trap, his ships would increase their acceleration twenty-fold and leave the Drifter Convoy behind at a significant percentage of the speed of light.

"There are no more contacts to resolve," Eowyn said quietly. "We have tentative IDs on all contacts. Confirming, six hundred and two contacts. Repeat, six zero two contacts. Eight warships, including two Guardians."

Range was under two million kilometers, and *now* it took conscious effort for Henry not to hold his breath.

"Minimum range in forty seconds."

More data was flowing in on each individual contact now, and Henry could see the work being done behind the scenes by both Eowyn's Operations team and *Paladin*'s Tactical department as new codes attached themselves to each contact.

Shaka had been in and amongst the Convoy and had more accurate data on most ships, but she'd also been attempting politeness. The level of even passive scans that Henry's ships were doing was detectable at reasonable range—they'd extended a series of antennae and receiver dishes they didn't normally have out.

If anyone was close enough to see them, they'd have known what they were doing. But sixteen hundred thousand kilometers wasn't that close, and there continued to be no sign they'd been detected.

"Minimum range in ten. Nine. Eight. Seven. Six. Five. Four. Three. Two. One."

Eowyn audibly exhaled.

"Minimum range. We are now at one million five hundred thousand and twenty-five thousand kilometers...and rising. We have passed the Convoy. All signs show that we were not detected."

"And the drones?" Henry asked.

"No activity to suggest that they have been detected. Once they're five light-seconds clear—in about ten minutes—we'll get a tightbeam download," she reported.

"We did it, ser."

"It can still get messy, Commander," Henry warned her. "But we appear to be clear. Once we have those downloads, I'll want your team and the Tactical team to start putting together a detailed analysis of the Convoy.

"We'll stick to them like a burr until Twelfth Fleet gets here, so there's no rush on that analysis. We'll want to make sure Admiral Rex has the clearest possible idea of what he's coming into."

"It...doesn't look like there's *anything* here, ser," Eowyn admitted. "I'm assuming their Guardians are somewhere else, but I can't think of where they'd have sent them."

"We'll watch for them," Henry assured her. "And if they come back, we'll let Admiral Rex know. Our job now is to keep a very careful eye on things—hopefully without being seen."

He could feel the tension relax on his bridge as they blazed past the ten-light-second mark. Once they were several light-minutes clear, they'd start the painstaking process of shedding their mind-boggling velocity.

"Huh, that's weird."

Chan probably hadn't even meant anyone else to hear their soft-spoken words. With the rest of the flag deck torn between beginning the analysis of the Drifter Convoy and watching the Convoy itself recede in the distance, however, the three words hung in the silence like falling rocks.

"Commander?" Henry asked.

"A communication relay drone on the outside of the Convoy just activated," Chan said quietly, concern clear in their voice. "For...one hundred twenty-six milliseconds. It looks like they sent a controlled-aperture transmission. Not quite a tightbeam but still limiting who received it."

"Any idea *who* got it?" Henry asked.

"Us," the coms officer admitted. "Unless I'm misreading this, the transmission zone lined up roughly with our thermal anomaly. I'm still resolving it, but it looks like an encrypted data pulse. It's not an encryption I recognize...but I can say one thing for sure."

"Other than that someone *did* see us?" Henry asked grimly.

"It's one of our encryptions, ser," Chan told him. "But they wouldn't have known to use it if they hadn't guessed we were out here."

CHAPTER FORTY-EIGHT

"It's my code," Sylvia said quietly after Chan briefed her.

Henry looked at her in surprise.

"Would you like to narrow that down a bit?" he asked dryly. He could think of about seven different reasons for the UPA ambassador to have given someone a secure encryption code while she'd been visiting the Convoy. Diplomatic ciphers, prearranged shared encryption protocols...recruited spies...

"That is my personal network encryption code that I was using to communicate with *Shaka* while I was aboard the Convoy," his partner said grimly. "I did *not* give that to the Drifters. Thankfully, I wasn't using it for anything confidential at the time—it's clearly not as secure as I thought."

"They've had weeks to reverse-engineer it," Chan said grimly, looking back at where Sylvia stood next to Henry's chair on the flag deck. "Months, really. But from just the snippets of standard back-and-forth support coms...that's impressive."

"It's only a level-three encryption," Sylvia noted. "Standard day-to-day codes, rotated every week or so. I spent enough time aboard their ships that they'd have...a reasonable sample, but still."

"Someone is showing off and I don't like it," Henry replied.

"Or someone wants to make very sure that only I can read what they've sent," the ambassador said. "Unfortunately for them, I don't much care about what the Drifters want. I'm passing you the record of the code my network still has, Commander."

Even with that, it took a minute. The internal network implants would keep a record of key markers of all of its historical encryption codes—they had a *lot* of storage—but they wouldn't keep the full encryption protocol.

With access to the base protocol, *Paladin* could regenerate the full protocol from those key markers and decrypt the data pulse. But even for the quantum computers aboard a UPSF destroyer, generating an entire specific encryption protocol was a time-consuming process.

"Got it," Chan finally reported. "Looks like a video and some attached data packets. Everything is in a stand-alone process right now," they noted. "I should be able to sanitize and play the video easily enough."

"Maybe we should watch this in your office, Commodore," Sylvia suggested. "Someone went to a great deal of effort to get this to us—and did so, from what you've said, without betraying our presence.

"I'm curious what it's about."

"All right," he agreed. "Eowyn, let me know if we have *any* situation changes."

THERE WAS a practiced ritual to Henry and Sylvia having work meetings in his office by now. The mental instruction for his coffeemaker to start as they headed there was almost unconscious—though there wasn't enough time for the machine to finish making the two cups in the time it took them to reach the office from the flag deck it was attached to.

Henry leaned against the wall by the machine, studying Sylvia as she, in turn, studied the ship models along the wall. The shelf held models of everything from the SF-114 Tomcat starfighter he'd flown when he first graduated through the two battlecruisers he'd commanded.

"Are you going to add DesRon Twenty-Seven to the shelf?" she asked absently, gently touching the thirty-centimeter-long model of *Raven* that was the most recent ship.

"I'm not sure," he admitted. "I'm not sure *how*, I suppose."

"You could do three smaller models," she suggested. "Destroyers the size of the starfighters from the other side."

"Maybe," he said, pulling the two coffee cups from the cupboard. "Something to think about when we're next back in UPA space." He chuckled softly. "Deeper in than Zion. Not many model-makers in Zion."

Zion held Base Fallout, once the logistics support base for the entire war against the Kenmiri and now the home base for the Peacekeeper Initiative. The system's civilian population had been mass-relocated by the Kenmiri at the start of the war, and the survivors had headed deeper into UPA space after their rescue.

Base Fallout was the *only* thing in Zion now.

"Let's see this message," Sylvia said with a sigh as she took the coffee. "I don't know what this is or even who is sending it, Henry. It's concerning."

"*I'm* concerned that someone was able to send it when the rest of the Convoy didn't even act like they'd seen us," Henry admitted. He took his seat and gave a mental command. The video appeared as a hologram above his desk as Sylvia moved a chair around to sit beside him.

The image of a single Drifter hung in the air, frozen as he waited for Sylvia to be ready. Like every other Drifter he'd ever seen, the individual was wrapped in heavy robes that obscured their features.

They wore a Face Mask, a unique mask that identified them as an individual, of a plain silver background with blue spiraling lines.

"I know that mask, though I won't guarantee that it's the same Drifter under it," Sylvia told him. "They're a member of the Council of Ancients, the leaders of the Convoy."

"Right, gerontocracy," Henry said. It wasn't *entirely* accurate that the Council of Ancients was made up of the oldest members of the Convoy—but that had been the case once and still likely applied to a significant chunk of them.

"Not quite," she corrected, echoing his thoughts. "But you knew that. This one did a lot of the talking while I was there. I wonder what they want to say now."

"Let's find out."

Henry started the message playback and leaned back in his seat.

"As I am recording this message," the Drifter said in slow Kem, "several friends of mine have located a strange anomaly in this system that they believe represents a potential use of the Terrans' new gravity drive for stealth.

"We have no certainty that this message will be received, but our desperation at this point is without limits. While I believe the anomaly would pass without notice by most, I have arranged for it to be buried in our shared network.

"If this message is being viewed by its intended recipients, my risk has paid off." There was a vague impression of a shrug under the robes. "If not, I am only talking to myself.

"I am Blue-Spirals-On-Silver," they introduced themselves—and from Sylvia's mostly concealed surprise, Henry realized they had never introduced themselves to her. "I am the Fourth Speaker of the Council of Ancients of the Blue Stripe Green Stripe Orange Stripe Convoy.

"And I am praying to gods I have not worshipped since I was a child that this message has reached a UPSF commander in the Blue First Dawn System."

Blue-Spirals-On-Silver was silent for several seconds.

"From what Blue-Stripe-Third-Green tells me, Sylvia Todor-ovich is aboard the ships pursuing us, so this stolen encryption should serve. It serves *me* by concealing our effort from our shared enemy.

"But I should start at the beginning," they said finally. "You will want to know why we betrayed you, and it is all of one piece."

The masked face looked down for a few moments, then focused on the camera.

"When the Kenmiri retreated, my Convoy was in the Osiris Province," they told Henry and Sylvia. "In the territory the Kenmiri Remnant still claim."

The twenty Kenmiri provinces had been named for their ancient gods. When humanity had managed to acquire translations, they discovered that the section of space they'd named for the Egyptian sun god Ra because of an old TV show was named for an old *Kenmiri* sun god.

The naming schema had stuck after that, with the UPA picking corresponding Egyptian gods for each of the Kenmiri province names.

Osiris was one of the eight sectors the Kenmiri hadn't abandoned, the core of four thousand suns they had retreated to to concentrate their numbers. It was the next sector "inward" from Ra.

"We believed, for a time, that things would go on as always for us," Blue-Spirals-On-Silver said. "And then the subspace coms failed. We now know the Kenmiri made this happen, but who were we to realize the carrier was artificial? All of our technology was theirs once.

"But it was revealed that there was more than one plan based around the shutdown of the subspace network," the Drifter said grimly. "Within days of our loss of communications with the other Convoys, we were ambushed.

"The Convoys always survived by being more trouble to destroy than we were worth," Blue-Spirals-On-Silver noted. "After the Retreat, the metrics had changed. We were surrounded by dread-noughts and informed that we had a simple choice: my Convoy would act as spies for the Kenmiri in the Abandoned Sectors...or we would be destroyed.

"All that we do—all that we have ever done—is to preserve our Convoy."

Those words hung in the air in Henry's office as he looked at Sylvia. This was far beyond his worst fears. The entire Drifter Convoy was a Kenmiri asset?

"We agreed." The Drifter's tone was heavy, even their mask and a second language failing to conceal their weariness and grief. "We were forced to give up many of our weapons. Our escorts were replaced with Kenmiri-crewed ships. Bombs and agents were planted in key vessels throughout the Convoy.

"We had no choice but to continue to comply, even once we had left their space. And they had some kind of communication with the Remnant still," Blue-Spirals-On-Silver explained. "We delivered listening posts, Warrior contingents, stealth ships... We have traversed much of this sector now and left a trail of Kenmiri infiltrators behind us.

"But that was not enough...and when Sylvia Todorovich approached us, they altered the deal."

Henry had suspected as much. Now he needed to know how badly things had gone. If the Drifters were a Kenmiri asset, Twelfth Fleet's deployment was more critical than he'd ever feared.

"We betrayed your peace summit and attempted to keep you at war. There were enough of us that could argue a value to us that we convinced ourselves it was for the best...until the plan failed, and thousands of our siblings had died for a Kenmiri plot.

"And then, as we planned to run as far and as fast as we could, far beyond the reach of the United Planets Alliance, the Kenmiri altered the deal *again*. We were to delay, to travel slowly, to allow ourselves to be *bait*. Our warships were to strike at targets they gave us, aggravating wars across the sector and clearing the way for a trap that would consume an entire UPSF fleet.

"We refused."

Henry blinked in surprise and glanced over at Sylvia. She looked equally thrown, but her focus remained on the video.

"Our Kenmiri commander destroyed four of our Guardians with the press of a button," Blue-Spirals-On-Silver told them. "He threatened to destroy *garden ships* next. We had no choice...and the traps were laid. Our Guardians dispersed across the stars around us, to eliminate scouts and weaken your fleet before it reached us."

That...made a disturbing amount of sense, Henry realized. The question, though, was *Where is the trap?* There were no warships there that could threaten Twelfth Fleet. Even if there were still five more Guardians in the star systems around Blue First Dawn, that wasn't enough to stop three full carrier groups.

"The escorts that are guarding our Convoy today are all Kenmiri," the Drifter told them. "They are more advanced than you think, with drives and shields that are more powerful than you have seen before.

"But they lack the resonance weapons. Those were a *Drifter* weapon and one we concealed from the Kenmiri to protect the other Convoys. The Kenmiri have never seen them deployed and do not know they exist. That will give you a thin edge for what must be done."

"And now the kicker," Sylvia murmured. "They've told us the sob story. Now the request."

"The Kenmiri did not trust us with their new communicator," Blue-Spirals-On-Silver said. "It is apparently larger and cannot be mounted on their escorts or their new raiders. Only their dreadnoughts are large enough to carry the new subspace communicator."

"Oh, fuck them all," Henry whispered. The dreadnoughts in the hands of the Vesheron factions were universally smaller and older ships. A fully updated, modern Kenmiri dreadnought...

"They believe they have a countermeasure to your starfighters at last," the Drifter warned. "I do not know what it is; they did not share it with my people. But they believed that two of their new dreadnoughts, combined with our Guardians and the escorts they'd concealed amongst my people, would suffice to overcome the fleet you sent after us.

"They could not easily join us in Eerdish space; it would have been too obvious. But they made their precautions. One of the Guardians you see in the Convoy is an older dreadnought, refitted with their subspace coms and with several of our modules attached to disguise it.

"The other two and their escorts were never more than a skip away—and now, they orbit Blue First Dawn's counterpart. From there, they will ambush any attack on the Convoy and destroy it."

"Can they?" Sylvia whispered, the message automatically pausing.

"It depends on how upgraded those new dreadnoughts are and what their anti-fighter system is," Henry admitted. "Rex's people would be careful when launching strikes into the Convoy, focusing on precision over firepower.

"If we missed two dreadnoughts...there would be a vulnerability. Maybe enough of one." Henry cursed under his breath as he looked at the frozen image of the Drifter leader.

"Let's see what else the Drifters have to say," he told her. "I *think* this information might be enough... Maybe."

He unpaused the message.

"I want this nightmare to end," Blue-Spirals-On-Silver said calmly. "I have been working with agents throughout the Convoy, and we have a plan. The Kenmiri have underestimated us, as everyone always has.

"I...believe we can free ourselves. We have a plan for the dreadnought and escorts that are among us, and we have plans for the bombs and garrisons they have emplaced.

"It will not be without bloodshed, but we *can* defeat the Kenmiri among us," the Drifter said firmly. "But we *cannot* defeat two modern dreadnoughts and their escorts. I have attached their most recent coordinates and every scrap of data we have assembled on their ships.

"If you can destroy those dreadnoughts, we are prepared to make appropriate reparations for our crimes against your people...but you must act quickly. I suspect—I fear—that they have plans for your fleet that you may not be able to overcome.

"I pray to the gods of my childhood that this message has been received. I...pray to them for your success—and for the salvation of my people.

"Step by step, with each seeming necessary and logical, I have broken my oaths and betrayed my Convoy. With this message, I hope to begin to set things right."

CHAPTER FORTY-NINE

ONCE AGAIN, A HOLOGRAPHIC IMAGE HUNG IN THE MIDDLE OF A virtual conference of Henry's officers. The ship's lines were familiar to every one of them, Henry knew. There were very few people in the Peacekeeper Initiative who hadn't served in the War—most of the post-War recruits didn't feel quite the same need to make things right —and the Kenmiri dreadnoughts had been the backbone of the alien fleet.

The *scale* of this particular dreadnought was something else again.

"Fourteen hundred meters from end to end," Eowyn listed. "Based off usual ratios and methodologies, her armor will be approximately twenty meters of raw asteroid rock, backed by another five meters of advanced alloys and ceramics.

"Mass, according to the Drifters' data, is approximately sixteen million tons. They've confirmed her base armament of fifteen super-heavy plasma-cannon turrets."

Those flashed bright red on the exterior of the dreadnought's immense hull. Forged out of a handy asteroid and still armored with the bulk of that rock, no dreadnought was *quite* the same shape as any other.

"Assuming standard ratios, that would give *each* dreadnought forty-five heavy lasers and seventy-five missile launchers," the Operations officer continued. "According to the Drifters, their engines have been heavily upgraded, permitting one-point-five KPS-squared of fully compensated thrust.

"Shields have similarly been upgraded, including an underlayer similar to the Guardian we encountered at Ra-Two-Sixty-One. We do not know what their new anti-fighter weapon system is," she concluded, "but their plan and deployment strength strongly suggest they think it will counteract multiple carriers' worth of our best."

The conference was silent until Henry leaned forward.

"There is a standard eight-megaton dreadnought accompanied by six escorts guarding the Drifter Convoy itself," he told them. "Only one of the eight warships we saw at the Convoy belongs to the Drifters."

"According to our intel *from* the Drifters," Ihejirika pointed out. "This could all be a deception."

"Yes," Henry agreed. "Eowyn?"

"We have confirmed the presence of the Kenmiri superdreadnoughts at Blue First Dawn Beta," the young woman said grimly. "We believe they have another six escorts with them—and I suspect even the smaller ships and the older dreadnought have been refitted with the new engines."

"The Drifters may be lying to us," Henry said. He shrugged. "We can't really guess one way or another, but the story Blue-Spirals-On-Silver spins fits the known facts. And the superdreadnoughts they warned us about exist.

"I do not wish to underestimate or overestimate our enemy," he continued. "But if the Kenmiri believe that two of these superdreadnoughts can challenge a major UPSF deployment, I am uninclined to let Twelfth Fleet walk into the trap unwarned."

"Drones with all of this information have already been sent to La-

Tar," Chan said. "It will be weeks before Twelfth Fleet arrives. There will be plenty of time for us to assess the threat of these new ships before Admiral Rex needs to deal with them."

"There is one more problem," Sylvia said. Every one of Henry's officers turned their attention to her.

"According to Blue-Spirals-On-Silver's message, they are expecting to rendezvous with the superdreadnoughts after they refuel the fleet. While Admiral Rex will still likely have overwhelming firepower, he will need to be far more careful with the *application* of that firepower if the Kenmiri forces are intermingled with civilian Drifter ships.

"I would hope he would hesitate to cause massive collateral damage if the Drifters were *actually* our enemy—but now that we suspect that they have been trapped and forced into this, permitting them to be used as living shields both risks atrocity on our part...and limits the UPSF's ability to properly engage the superdreadnoughts.

"What would the usual solution to that be, Commodore Wong?"

Henry concealed a wince as she turned to him.

"Close-range fighter strikes," he said levelly. "Especially given the Lancers' increased defensive shields and maneuverability, sending them *into* the Drifter Convoy to launch their missiles at close range, where there can be no errors."

"And if the Kenmiri truly have some kind of anti-fighter superweapon..." Teunissen trailed off. "That's exactly what they want."

The conference was silent for a second as everyone stared at the hologram of the superdreadnought.

"So, what's the plan, ser?" Ihejirika finally asked. "I'm guessing you have one."

"I do," Henry agreed. "The Drifters believe that they can secure the Convoy against the escorts, bombs and garrisons the Kenmiri have emplaced. Of course, doing so while there is a pair of Kenmiri superdreadnoughts mere hours away is suicide.

"So, we remove the superdreadnoughts."

"Ser, DesRon Twenty-Seven is currently two *destroyers*,"

Teunissen argued, slowly trailing off as she realized both Ihejirika and Eowyn were looking at Henry and still waiting for the rest of the plan.

"You're insane," she finally said.

"As Blue-Spirals-On-Silver said, *desperation without limits*," Henry said grimly. "I have to fear that the Kenmiri commander has a solid idea of what we're likely to send against him. That means that they truly believe that three dreadnoughts and twelve escorts—maybe with a gunship or two among the escorts—are enough to face down Twelfth Fleet.

"No Kenmiri Warrior would rely on the Drifter Guardians and escorts to even up the balance. They'll use them, but only in the way they always used slave janissaries. As cannon fodder."

He shook his head.

"No, their plan is based on those two superdreadnoughts outweighing three fleet carriers and six battlecruisers. I don't see it, but we don't know what upgrades they've applied beyond the size," he reminded his team.

"But right now, they don't know we're here. We know *exactly* where they are—and they've conveniently positioned themselves next to the second-largest object in the entire star system."

He had their undivided attention. Rank and authority commanded their obedience, so all of them would listen—but that wouldn't be enough for this. For this to work, everyone from his Captains down to his most junior gunnery officers had to *believe* it could work.

"Thanks to the Drifters, we know their every weakness and they have handed us *every* advantage," he said quietly. "We may have ended the War in the worst way possible, but we fought it for good reasons and for a good cause.

"Six million people in this system are now slaves of the Kenmiri once more. If we strike hard, if we do this *right*, we can free them. Render Twelfth Fleet's presence entirely unnecessary—and send a message to the Kenmiri Remnant that will echo across the galaxy.

"We can do this," he finished fiercely. "Ihejirika, Teunissen? Are you with me?"

"Never haven't been, ser," Okafor Ihejirika said instantly. "*Paladin* awaits your command."

Everyone looked at Nina Teunissen and she snorted.

"It's not like I'm not going to follow your orders, whatever they are, ser," she pointed out.

"This is going to take more than obedience to orders, Captain," Henry told her. "It's going to take the kind of mad courage that won the Red Wings Campaign. The kind of do-or-die that the United Planets Space Force is *known* for. So...are you with me?"

This time, she laughed and shook her head.

"Who am I kidding?" she asked. "Aye, ser. To the depths of hell and out the other side. Damnation to slavers and kings, after all."

"Damnatio est praefectis," Sylvia murmured, the Latin sounding surprisingly appropriate and terrifying at that moment.

"What do we do?" Ihejirika asked.

"First...how many penetrator-warhead busses do we have and can we fabricate in the next few hours?"

CHAPTER FIFTY

For the second time in less than twenty-four hours, Henry's ships blasted past ten thousand kilometers per second and cut their acceleration. This time, they were hurtling toward Blue First Dawn Beta and the Kenmiri fleet waiting for them.

That felt strangely right in a way that many of Henry's battles of the last few years hadn't. The Kenmiri had been the enemy for most of his adult life, and while he regretted what he'd done to them as a species, he was unsurprised to see them back.

"Range is one light-minute," Eowyn reported calmly. "We are closing at ten thousand kilometers per second. Current acceleration... point-zero-two KPS-squared."

Enough to keep the gravity drive up and smear their thermal signature across thousands of kilometers of space.

"The Kenmiri are smart," Henry murmured. "They'll see us coming sooner rather than later."

"Hopefully not soon enough, right?" his Ops officer asked.

He smiled predatorily.

"They're already too late, I suspect," he told her. "Time to weapons range?"

"Our base velocity puts missile range at over three and a half million kilometers, ser," she noted. "Twenty-four minutes."

"And laser range?" he asked.

"Five minutes after that, we'll hit two light-seconds," Eowyn told him.

"And we'll clear through laser range in two minutes," Henry calculated aloud. "And once we're past them, nobody's missiles are hitting *anybody*."

Unless the Kenmiri had dramatically upgraded their missile launchers, they gave their missiles the same initial thousand kilometers per second as his did. Against a base velocity of ten thousand KPS, the missile didn't have the delta-v to play catch-up.

He leaned back in his chair and laced his fingers together, studying both the big tactical display on the screens around him and the additional layers fed into it by his internal network. Battle stations meant there were no true holograms visible anywhere on the flag deck—the tech was still too fragile for the UPSF's designers to include as part of the combat systems—but his network implants could duplicate the effect.

"Ihejirika, Teunissen," he greeted his Captains. "We're well past the time to tell me if you have a *problem*, but now is the time for concerns or suggestions."

"There's a lot of damn metal over there, Commodore," Ihejirika said grimly. "Two superdreadnoughts and we got the escort number wrong. I make it eight escorts and four gunships.

"This is going to hurt."

"Them," Henry replied. "Ignore the escorts and gunships. We tank their fire on the grav-shields and we focus our lasers on Target Bravo."

"We can do this," Teunissen said—but there was a shakiness to her voice. *Maharatha*'s Captain was senior to Ihejirika—*Paladin* was Henry's flag captain's first command—but Henry knew Ihejirika had seen more action.

There was a reason he'd picked the brand-new Lieutenant Colonel as his flag captain, after all.

"Yes, we can," Henry told her.

"And the Drifters?" Ihejirika asked.

"No way to tell if they got our message," Henry admitted. "But if they *did*, they'll be kicking off in about thirty minutes."

They were almost four light-minutes from the Drifter Convoy. The Kenmiri detachments would probably have instantaneous communications—but if it worked the same way as the listening-post system, Henry would *know* when the superdreadnoughts told the Convoy escorts they were in trouble.

Part of him hoped that the Warrior in command of the ships in front of him would underestimate him. That they'd see two destroyers and assume there was no *real* danger.

But the Kenmiri were *smart* and the Warriors were good at what they did. The Kenmiri commander would almost certainly make the same assumption versus Henry's two destroyers that *he'd* made versus their two superdreadnoughts: that the operation wouldn't have been launched without a plan for success.

"Missile range in ten minutes," Eowyn reported. "Range is nine-point-seven million kilometers. Kenmiri force has not yet reacted to our approach, and no active scans have been detected."

Henry could live with the Kenmiri seeing his ships earlier than he wanted. Active scans, though, would be a pain in the ass.

"Now we wait," he told his Captains and flag-deck staff. "We wait and we see if the Kenmiri are half as clever as I think they are."

"MISSILE RANGE."

The two calm words hung in the silence of the flag deck. Even Henry was trying not to hold his breath as he checked a countdown.

"Thirty seconds to Point Weber," Eowyn continued a moment later. "Checks are commencing."

"Do we open fire?" Ihejirika asked.

"Negative," Henry ordered. "They'd see it now. We wait until we're seen—or we hit Weber. Dial in Target Bravo as closely as you can without active sensors and prepare to go to full thrust."

Fifteen seconds. Ten. Five.

"Weber. Salvo one activating," Eowyn barked. "Salvo two activating. Salvo three activating."

The chant echoed through the flag deck as salvo after salvo of preplaced missiles lit off their drives. They'd been fired ahead of Henry's ships, their launcher velocity adjusted to match his planned ten-thousand-kilometers-a-second approach.

Now twenty full salvos from his two ships, *seven hundred* missiles, came to life and hurtled toward Target Alpha at their maximum ten KPS^2 acceleration—and their activation sequences had been carefully programmed.

Those seven hundred missiles didn't come at the superdreadnought as twenty separated salvos. They came in a single coordinated time-on-target salvo, screaming in almost two million kilometers ahead of Henry's two ships.

"Enemy defenses active," Eowyn reported. "Damn, that was fast."

"They were already up," Henry replied. "Kenmiri don't shut them down. They're heavily armed professional paranoids. Impact?"

"Sixty seconds and counting," she snapped. "Enemy defensive lasers are firing. I have active sensor sweeps—they're looking for us."

"Ihejirika, Teunissen. Now, please."

Destroyer Squadron Twenty-Seven came to life in the wake of their missiles.

Gravity shields went to full power, twelve-thousand-gravity defensive shears snapping into existence and tearing the incoming sensor data to pieces for a moment before the computers compensated. Gravity maneuvering systems went from a trickle of minimum power to full strength. Active scanners flickered to life as well, responding to the Kenmiri radar and lidar with scanning beams of their own.

"All laser capacitors report full on both ships," Eowyn told Henry. "First salvos on Target Bravo are away. Defensive network is online—enemy escorts are pushing forward to cover Target Alpha from the Weber salvo."

"It won't be enough," Henry said flatly.

He was right. He *had* to be right. He'd built the entire plan around the fact that his enemy wasn't expecting an attack and didn't know what warning signs to look for to find GMS ships. That had let him set up a single salvo with a third of his squadron's missiles.

"We're losing missiles fast. We're coming in fast but their defensive gunners are *good*."

"They're *Kenmiri*," Henry snapped. "Leave Weber to the onboard AIs. Run the defensive algorithms, Eowyn. We're coming into the teeth of *way* too many missiles."

The Kenmiri had nailed down DesRon Twenty-Seven's location as the UPSF missiles drove home—and now three hundred missiles blazed into space to return the favor.

It was the last salvo Target Alpha would ever launch. The systems had been online and the Kenmiri gunnery teams were good, but they hadn't been expecting an attack, and missiles hurtling in at over twelve thousand KPS were a challenge at the best of times.

Three hundred of Henry's missiles reached Target Alpha and vanished from three-dimensional space. He'd put every single penetrator missile his squadron had on that strike—and even a superdreadnought wasn't built to handle that.

"Target Alpha is... Holy shit," Eowyn whispered. "Target Alpha is *gone*."

Dozens of five-hundred-megaton warheads detonated between the capital ship's two layers of shields—but dozens more detonated *inside* her armor. When the explosions cleared, a sixteen-million-ton superdreadnought had been completely vaporized.

"We have incoming plasma fire!"

Henry wasn't sure which one of Eowyn's team had barked the alert. In almost the same moment, a dozen red, flashing warning lights appeared on his screen.

"No blowthrough," Ihejirika snapped. "But that came *way* too clo—"

The missiles were right on the plasma blasts' heels, detonating in their own shaped-charge plasma blasts that washed over the gravity shield like a breaking tsunami.

Paladin spasmed around Henry and more warning lights flashed up on his screen.

"Blowthrough," the destroyer's captain said, almost unnecessarily. "Lasers are still up and it's our turn now."

The dreadnought had *big* plasma guns, both longer-ranged and more powerful than Henry was used to. They'd hit at almost seven hundred thousand kilometers—but both of his ships had survived.

There were warning signs scattered across both his ships' schematics in his displays. Target Alpha's death hadn't been without consequences, but both of his destroyers were still entirely in the fight —and their lasers stabbed across the void toward Target Bravo.

"Target is evading. Target is returning fire."

For every beam Henry's command flung at the Kenmiri, the superdreadnought alone flung ten back. The escorts added another twenty, but the gravity shields twisted the photons and flung them away.

"Superdreadnought is lighter on beams than projected," Eowyn said grimly. "Forty versus forty-five expected. Just as many turrets, though."

Those turrets were on full rapid fire now, spitting near-cee blasts of plasma at Henry's ships. For the first time since taking command of the *Cataphracts*, Henry truly appreciated how powerful the new ships' shields were.

He'd commanded *Panther* at the end of the war, a *Jaguar*-class battlecruiser a generation behind *Raven*. Designed to fight a Kenmiri dreadnought and win without significant damage, *Panther* would still

have been obliterated in the first salvos from these superdreadnoughts.

But the *Cataphract*s had more powerful shields than even *Raven*,
shields the wartime battlecruisers would have killed for, and those
shields shrugged aside the superdreadnought's massive beams and
plasma cannons as the two destroyers hurtled into the heart of the
enemy formation.

"We're through their shields!" Ihejirika snapped from the bridge
as *Paladin*'s paired lasers were finally carried to a range where even
the superdreadnought's mighty energy screens failed. Iron and
ceramics boiled away as the beams hammered into the ship's hull,
cutting massive gouges through her.

Then the shields were back up—at *that* point, failing elsewhere as
Maharatha's beams repeated the feat.

"We're too close," Teunissen barked over the channel. "The lasers
are getting closer and—"

Henry didn't need to check his scans. He *knew* that sudden
silence. At the ranges they were in now, the gravity shield couldn't
stand up to direct laser fire for long—and they were being hammered
with missiles every few seconds.

Their own missiles were too few—and *Maharatha* was gone. Four
hundred of his people were gone with her, but he couldn't grieve.

Not yet.

"We're clear, we're clear!" Ihejirika barked. "We're past, their
missiles can't catch up."

"Keep the lasers on her," Henry ordered. "Sixty seconds, people.
We have to make it *sixty more seconds*."

Okafor Ihejirika's command twisted in the dim light of Blue First
Dawn's largest planet like a worm on a hook. Lasers and plasma scattered in the void around her, as many shots missing as being tossed
aside by the shield—but her own beams stayed on the superdreadnought, burning through once again as they fled.

"Escorts and gunships are accelerating in pursuit," Eowyn
reported. "Estimate one-point-*seven* KPS-squared."

"Not enough," Henry murmured. "Did we... Did we do it, Okafor?"

Silence answered him. The range ticked over two light-seconds and *Paladin*'s beams vanished. The Kenmiri weapons still pocked the space around her, but there was a dull silence aboard the destroyer as her own weapons calmed.

"Scans are focused on the superdreadnought," Ihejirika confirmed quietly. "Escorts are in hot pursuit of us; they're gaining a lot of speed but they're not closing the range. Do we let them?"

"Hang out a trail, Captain," Henry ordered. "The later they realize what we've done, the less they can do. But I need to know.

"Did it work?"

"Scans complete," the destroyer Captain said. "Target Bravo's engines are completely disabled. Her vector is toward Blue First Dawn Beta.

"Tactical is estimating thirty-five minutes to crush depth."

Henry smiled coldly and looked at the escorts chasing him.

"Unless your engineers are even better than I think they are, you should not be chasing me," he told their icons.

CHAPTER FIFTY-ONE

ENERGY SCREENS, UNLIKE GRAVITY SHIELDS, TRANSFERRED A portion of the momentum of impacts to the protected bubble. The momentum was transferred across the *entire* bubble, so it was rarely registered on the inside—but every missile that had detonated seemingly uselessly against Target Bravo's shields had pushed the superdreadnought ever so slightly toward the planet beneath her.

And the lasers had done the same—and been targeted on the superdreadnought's engines with a precision only enabled by the Drifter's near-perfect data on these *exact* ships.

Now Target Bravo fell. It wasn't a fast process at first, but it accelerated slowly. Ten minutes after *Paladin* left laser range, the superdreadnought touched the top of Blue First Dawn Beta's atmosphere—and they *finally* called the escorts back.

"It's too late," Eowyn said grimly. "Ten minutes just to shed their velocity. Another twenty to get back and match *v* with Target Bravo. They're only going to get there in time to watch her die."

"No," Henry countered. "They're going to get there in time to pick up the escape pods and evac shuttles. And I'm glad to see it, honestly."

He couldn't see Target Bravo directly anymore. *Paladin* had put the gas giant between herself and the superdreadnought, shielding herself from any clever ideas the Kenmiri might have at the last minute. They were watching through a sensor drone on the other side of the planet, which put everything several minutes out of date.

Escape pods and shuttles were starting to flee the superdreadnought now. Even combined, the small craft wouldn't have had enough thrust to move the immense mass of their mothership, but they could get the crew clear.

"Glad, ser?" Eowyn asked.

"I hate the Kenmiri," Henry admitted aloud. He didn't even like to hear himself say it, but it was true. "I hate everything they've done, everything they stand for, everything they created. But I also destroyed any future their race had.

"The Kenmiri who died today cannot be replaced, Commander Eowyn." He looked at the scans of the doomed superdreadnought, surprised at the emotions he was feeling. "I will fight them without hesitation. I will stand against all of their works and any attempt to restore their power.

"But I will not hasten their demise any more than I must. We are already well revenged. I *hope* those captains have the moral courage to retreat once they've picked up the evacuees."

He shook his head.

"They could still win," he admitted. "Or, at the very least, destroy *Paladin*. But a lot of the people they're pulling from the wreck of that superdreadnought would die along the way. If they want *Paladin*, they'll bleed for her."

"Yes, ser."

Henry turned his attention to other situations.

"Chan, do we have any updates from the Drifter Convoy?" he asked.

"Nothing yet, ser. On the other hand, Target Bravo pulsed a subspace message right after Target Alpha was destroyed," the coms officer told him. "And they never got a response. I think our masked friends may have done all right."

"They better have."

Henry considered the situation for a few moments.

"Captain Ihejirika, set your course for the Blue Stripe Green Stripe Orange Stripe Convoy," he ordered. "We'll keep an eye on our Kenmiri friends, but it's time to start wrapping this up."

THE SUPERDREADNOUGHT CONTINUED its slow fall to its doom as *Paladin*'s course curved toward the Drifter Convoy. At fifteen minutes after it hit the gas giant's atmosphere, the pace of evacuation ships leaving suddenly spiked.

Even from a distance, Henry could see as various systems began to flick out across the ship. Her captain had made the difficult choice to write the superdreadnought off as a lost cause to save the crew—a decision that probably had slightly different weights when your species was dying.

For the last few minutes before it hit crush depth, the stream of small craft slowly declined until nothing left the ship for a full minute. By that point, the sensor drone could barely even make out the dreadnought. It was over a thousand kilometers deep inside the gas giant and sinking lower by the second.

And then, moments before Henry's people calculated it would reach crush depth, a massive explosion lit up the surface of the gas giant.

"What do we have on that?" he asked.

"Multiple fusion charges, estimated total yield at least a hundred gigatons," Eowyn said. "Either suicide charges or they overloaded their fusion cores—or *both*. Making damn sure no one could salvage anything from the wreck."

The escorts and gunships were still making their way back to orbit of Blue First Dawn Beta, but the escape pods and shuttles were clustering together. It looked like there were *probably* enough small craft to carry the warship's entire crew.

"Let's watch what they do carefully," Henry murmured. "What's our ETA to the Convoy?"

"Still an hour to bring our velocity to zero, then five to zero-zero with the Drifters," Eowyn reported. "Commander Bach is maneuvering some of the sensor probes around to get us a better look at them and see what's going on there."

Six hours. Henry nodded to his Ops officer and leaned back in his chair again. Nothing left for the Commodore to do. He only had one ship left. Most people would say trading a destroyer for two *superdreadnoughts* was good work, but it still left him with limited resources for what came next.

Nina Teunissen hadn't deserved to die like that, but who did? Going back over the recording of the action, Henry caught the exact moment of *Maharatha*'s destruction.

With fifteen superheavy plasma cannon from the superdreadnought and four heavy plasma cannon from the gunships, plus the hundreds of missiles that had hurled themselves against DesRon Twenty-Seven's shields, he was lucky to have *only* lost one ship.

It had been one of the superdreadnought's guns, he judged. The blast had been on track to *miss*, but the same gravity shear that protected the ship had torn the plasma ball into pieces—and changed the course enough that three of those pieces had hammered into *Maharatha* like the flaming arrows of an angry sun god.

"Kenmiri escorts have made rendezvous with the evacuation ships," Eowyn reported. "Gunships have assumed a defensive formation. Hrm. They're certainly not expecting *help* from the Convoy."

"That's a good sign," Henry agreed. "Do we have those eyes on the Convoy yet?"

"Just coming in now," Ihejirika told him. "Feeding to your display."

For a moment, the Blue Stripe Green Stripe Orange Stripe Convoy looked unchanged from when they'd made their high-speed scouting run. Then Henry began to pick out the subtle and not-so-subtle changes.

The factory ships had carried out a coordinated movement that had positioned their raw-material hoppers around the garden ships. Other ships were moving in to fill gaps in the sphere as Henry watched, the Convoy using their own hulls to protect the factory and garden ships that allowed them to survive.

The factory ships would be hard to replace—but without the garden ships, the Convoy could easily starve before they found a food source. Five million people were *not* easy to feed.

"I'm picking up no warships in the Convoy," Eowyn said quietly. "Both Guardians are gone. All of the escorts are gone."

"Most of the passenger ships will have some limited defensive and offensive firepower," Henry told her. "Look for targeting radar if we can."

"It'll take a moment. Let me check."

She turned her focus back to her screens for a few moments.

"You're right," she confirmed. "It looks like the outer shell has active targeting radar sweeping the space around them. I'm guessing missile launchers and lasers, but those are very much last-ditch defenses, ser."

"And the Kenmiri probably underestimated them," Henry said. "I would assume that's what killed the dreadnought."

Those beams might not be as powerful as a dreadnought's or as well aimed or have as reliable a power-supply...but there were *hundreds* of them scattered through the Convoy. Only fear and a carefully calibrated amount of violence had kept the Convoy in line.

That was the Kenmiri way. And here, like in so many other places in the past, it had finally failed.

CHAPTER FIFTY-TWO

THE DEFENSIVE SHELL WAS STILL INTACT WHEN *PALADIN* CAME to a relative halt exactly nine hundred thousand kilometers from the Convoy. Scans were telling Henry how many missile launchers the Drifters had—and while it was significant, there were a *lot* more lasers in the Convoy.

If those missile launchers were all loaded with resonance warheads, they could make a serious mess of his ship. On the other hand, the gravity shield versus lasers was a probability game—and having a thousand lasers to throw at it was one way to play that game.

There'd only been intermittent communication as they'd approached. Enough for Henry to know that the situation was a chaotic mess—but he now knew something *else*. Something the Drifters might not know yet.

The Kenmiri were leaving. The escorts and gunships had to be stuffed to the bulkheads with the crew they'd rescued from the doomed superdreadnought, and whoever was in command had chosen to preserve those lives over pushing for a meaningless victory.

They were still a few hours from the skip line, but they were far enough along their vector that Henry had no worries about them coming back.

"Are we on?" he asked Chan.

"Feed is live when you want it, ser. Broad-beam to the entire Convoy," they confirmed.

He nodded his thanks to them and glanced over at Sylvia. His diplomatic attaché had stayed off the bridge during the battle, but now they were on the edge of her bailiwick.

"This one is still mine, Ambassador," he told her. "There will be time for diplomacy later, but right now...this is still a military situation."

"I've got your back," she confirmed. "I know what you're thinking—and I think you're right."

He raised an eyebrow at her. If she'd guessed what he was thinking, he hoped she was ahead of the Drifters.

With a soft exhalation, he masked his face, stilling his muscles and eyes as he focused on the recorder in front of him. A mental command activated the camera and he simply glared at it for several seconds.

"Blue Stripe Green Stripe Orange Stripe Convoy, this is Commodore Henry Wong of the United Planets Space Force," he said in Kem. "We have defeated the Kenmiri forces in this system.

"We are here, however, because of the actions of warships under the authority of *this* Convoy," he told them. "I must speak with the Council of Ancients or with Fourth Speaker Blue-Spirals-On-Silver.

"We will maintain our position for now while you find someone able to negotiate with me, but I warn you: my patience is not infinite, and I already destroyed two superdreadnoughts today.

"I am waiting for your response."

Another command from his internal network stopped the recording and transmitted the message.

"How long do you think?" Sylvia asked.

"Not very long," he admitted. "I don't know how seriously they're going to take my threats—they have a lot of ships and a lot of weapons over there, but *Paladin* will shortly be the only warship left in the system."

The flag deck was quiet. Eowyn's Operations team was coordinating with Commander Bach's Tactical team to analyze the ships in front of them. Every few moments, another ship in the Convoy flashed as the analysts updated the information on it.

There was nothing left with any kind of heavy armament. Most of the ships had a single offensive laser, a small suite of antimissile systems and two missile launchers.

The aggregate was still impressive—and even the civilian launchers might have the resonance warheads that had wrecked *Cataphract*.

Still, Henry suspected that coordination would be badly lacking in anything resembling a real fight—and the current chaotic mess of the Convoy wouldn't help. It made for a hell of a sucker punch and it was intimidating, but there was a reason the Drifter Convoys usually had real warships in company.

"Ser, we have an incoming com request," Chan reported. "It appears to be coming from the center of the Convoy. I'd guess one of the garden ships, but there are enough other ships in the way to make identification difficult."

"Understood," Henry told them. "Connect it to the main screen. Show them a feed of myself and Ambassador Todorovich."

His internal network warned him when the cameras on him and Sylvia came online. He leveled his best working glare on the familiar masked individual on the screen.

It was *not* Blue-Spirals-On-Silver. The Face Mask on the screen had a diagonal blue stripe over a white base, with its bottom third painted green. Ambassador Blue-Stripe-Third-Green stood in front of one of the forested glades the Drifters used for important ceremonies and private meetings aboard the garden ships.

"Commodore Henry Wong," Blue-Stripe-Third-Green greeted him. "I will not pretend I am pleased to see you again—but I *am*, perhaps, grateful." They then nodded to Sylvia. "Ambassador Todor-ovich as well. It seems you have completed your mission."

"My mission was to find your Convoy," Henry said bluntly. "I completed *that* mission several days ago, and the power of the United Planets Alliance is already in motion. Blue-Spirals-On-Silver, however, managed to suggest that the situation was more complicated than we perceived."

"It was and is," Blue-Stripe-Third-Green confirmed. "We successfully neutralized the Kenmiri presence in the Convoy, but not without a price." They paused. "You will have already detected that *Signs of Providence* is no more. Protector-Commander Third-White-Fifth-Gold perished with her.

"Our commandos have secured most of the critical systems of most of our ships," they said carefully. "Careful preparation allowed us to disable *almost* all of the bombs."

"Almost," Henry prodded.

"The garden ship *Alignment of Dreams* is also no more," Blue-Stripe-Third-Green said quietly. "Blue-Spirals-On-Silver was aboard her, leading a desperate attempt to reach a bomb we learned about too late. One hundred twenty-six thousand of my people are now dead—and so is a third of the Council of Ancients."

"A UPSF destroyer died here today," Henry replied. "I mourn your dead with you, Ambassador, but we have losses of our own—and I remind you that Blue Stripe Green Stripe Orange Stripe are no longer my allies."

"I understand," Blue-Stripe-Third-Green said heavily. "We are prepared to negotiate, Commodore. We understand that we have gravely betrayed the trust of those who should have been our friends, but we felt we had no choice—and the deaths today are a bitter reminder of the threat that hung over us when we made no choices."

"The past is what the past is," Henry told the Drifter. "You speak for your people, Blue-Stripe-Third-Green. I speak for mine. For those who have died. For those who have been betrayed.

"You brought these stars to the edge of war for your own fear and gain," he concluded. "Regardless of your reasons, if we are to have peace...I have no choice but to ask for the formal surrender of the Blue Stripe Green Stripe Orange Stripe Convoy."

Sylvia's calm certainty next to him didn't even flicker. She clearly *had* guessed what he intended.

From the dead silence of the rest of the flag deck, most of Henry's staff *hadn't*.

With the Face Mask guarding their emotions and thoughts, he couldn't tell if Blue-Stripe-Third-Green had, but the Drifter was silent for a long time.

"You understand, Commodore, that I am bound by sacred oaths and sacred charges?" they asked.

"You have my word, upon the honor of my dead, that your people will come to no harm so long as they cooperate," Henry told the Drifter. "And as our prisoners, we will defend you as our own."

He expected Blue-Stripe-Third-Green to stall—to ask for time to meet with the rest of the Council of Ancients. Henry didn't even think that the former Ambassador had the *authority* to surrender the entire Convoy.

"Worlds turn and stars burn and what is becomes what was," Blue-Stripe-Third-Green intoned. The words meant something, Henry suspected, but he didn't know them.

"I trust your honor, Henry Wong. And so, my Convoy must trust your honor. You have our surrender."

CHAPTER FIFTY-THREE

THE EERDISH SYSTEM WAS SWARMING WITH STARSHIPS. SYLVIA Todorovich stood on *Paladin*'s observation deck—a rather cramped space aboard the destroyer—and watched as Twelfth Fleet moved into their assigned positions.

Theoretically, the carriers, battlecruisers and destroyers were Blue Stripe Green Stripe Orange Stripe's jailers, but the sphere of warships taking shape around the Drifter ships looked more like guard dogs.

The Drifters weren't going to be permitted to *leave*—the three Terran carriers had replaced two Eerdish carriers making the same point—but they also weren't going to be permitted to come to harm.

The garden ships were directly "above" Sylvia, in the middle of the view from the observation deck as *Paladin* maintained a watchful position over the most vulnerable of the Drifters' vessels. The loss of one of the big agricultural ships was a blow that the Convoy would take years to recover from, though the Eerdish had so far been happy to feed the Drifters as needed.

A smile quirked across her lips, an emotion she would have let few people other than Henry Wong or Felix Leitz see. Part of the reason the Eerdish had been so happy to cooperate had been that *everything* was being paid for "on account," so to speak, by the UPA.

She knew what the payment for that debt was going to be. One of Admiral Rex's carriers would shortly have a new mission, sortieing alongside several of the Eerdish and Enteni carriers to make a very specific point to the Kozun.

Hopefully, that point would be made without bloodshed—but Sylvia had made that decision for the UPA. The E-Two Alliance were now friends of Terra. So were the Kozun. Like the Roman Empire of long ago, the UPA would prevent their *friends* from fighting each other.

One way...or another.

The Kozun would be better off this way, though she suspected it would take Mal Dakis a while to realize it.

A soft ping in her internal network told her Leitz was reaching out to her.

"What is it, Felix?" she asked.

"It's almost time, Ambassador," his mental voice said. "Admiral Rex is on his way to *Light of Eternity* already, as is the Sovereign of Sovereign's representative."

She nodded in silence. It was time to turn verbal agreements and promises made by plenipotentiaries into actual treaties. Part of what was being signed was a peace treaty with the Drifters—a gentler one than she'd expected to write after the Lon System.

"Ambassador?" Leitz repeated.

"I'm on my way," she told him. "We've got work to do."

LIGHT OF ETERNITY wasn't the garden ship Sylvia had visited when she'd come to the BGO Convoy before, but it had many of the same fixtures and patterns. Everything, including the "decorative" trees, produced edible fruit and breathable air.

Most people looked at the garden ships and saw food, Sylvia

knew, but she suspected their natural CO_2–O_2 conversion was also hugely valuable to the Convoy. The tree-lined thoroughfares of the garden ship served many purposes.

They led to a very similar stone amphitheater to the one where she'd met the Council of Ancients aboard that other garden ship. There were fewer Ancients present today than there had been then. Instead of the full Council, only the four Speakers were gathered.

Normally it would be five, but Blue-Spirals-On-Silver's replacement hadn't been selected yet. Blue-Stripe-Third-Green, it turned out, had been the Fifth Speaker. The number was merely seniority, however, and all of them were the coequal "guides" of the Council that ruled the Convoy.

Standing at the center of the amphitheater, waiting, and welcoming each delegation, was a figure Sylvia *hadn't* met before. The shrouded First Speaker hadn't been among the Council of Ancients she'd met and negotiated with, which she found odd.

Studying the First Speaker now, she was intrigued. Their mask was a single golden diagonal stripe across a blue background, a pattern she hadn't seen before. They were shorter than most of the people around them, their robes covering what looked like the hunched posture of extreme age.

Even through the all-enshrouding robes, it seemed that the First Speaker was *old*.

"Greetings Ambassador Todorovich, Commodore Wong," the First Speaker said as they approached. "This meeting is certainly more positive than I once feared, when I was told the Destroyer himself was pursuing us."

"What happened to the Kenmorad was the action of many, in response to crimes woven across centuries of horror," Henry said quietly from Sylvia's side. "I would not repeat it if I had a choice."

"Wise words, Commodore," the Drifter said. "We are all shaped by what was. I hope that shaping is gentler for you in future than it was in the past."

Sylvia traded nods with the Drifter leader and led Henry to their seats.

The real work of all of this was already done. She had a lot of documents to sign for the United Planets Alliance, but she knew what they all said. She'd helped write most of them—she certainly wasn't going to have time to read them there!

A MIX of Eerdish food and garden ship–grown food covered buffet tables that wouldn't have looked out of place in any star system Sylvia had ever visited. Neatly lettered labels in Kem warned about ingredients that could be allergens—or even toxins!—for assorted species that were present.

The Eerdish might look human most of the time, but their equivalent to alcohol would render a human hallucinatory with a single sip —and unconscious after a single shot.

"Ambassador."

Sylvia looked away from the buffet tables to find the First Speaker hunched over just behind her. A GroundDiv security trooper—not *quite* her bodyguard but certainly never out of sight— hovered nearby.

"First Speaker. I appreciate your Convoy agreeing to host this gathering," she told them.

"We are aware of our position here, Ambassador Todorovich," Gold-Stripe-On-Blue told her. "Your people have chosen wisdom and mercy, recognizing the threats and violence applied to us, but we remain the supplicant here."

"Less so, I imagine, once you have gathered what remains of your warships."

Henry had bluntly forbidden the Drifters from calling for their ships as they'd trekked to Eerdish. Only now that Twelfth Fleet gave the UPA the unquestioned military dominance would the Drifters be permitted to call for the warships the Kenmiri had made them scatter.

"We fear the Kenmiri more than ever now," Gold-Stripe-On-Blue said. "We will remain in the Ra Sector, under the watchful eyes of once-and-future friends, for a while yet. Our remaining ships will be no threat to anyone."

"I hope not," she murmured.

"But...that is not why I came to you," they said, their voice suddenly equally quiet. "If you could call Commodore Wong over? I have someone the two of you must meet."

"*Must?*" Sylvia echoed—but she was sending Henry a silent network message as she challenged the Drifter.

"For the good of all of us, I think," Gold-Stripe-On-Blue said unperturbably. They still jerked in surprise as Henry materialized out of the crowd.

"You called, Ambassador?" he said levelly.

"*Humans,*" the Drifter hissed before they could restrain themselves.

None of the aliens humanity had contacted were comfortable with the level of neural implantation humans took for granted. It had led to some *interesting* misunderstandings during the war, Sylvia knew, including some of the Vesheron thinking Terrans had a hive mind.

Of course, if all of *her* people's computers had been designed by Kenmiri Artisans, she'd have hesitated to put one in her head, too, she supposed.

"The First Speaker wishes to introduce us to someone," Sylvia told her partner. "What is going on?"

"I cannot explain here," the Speaker said. "Follow, please. You have my word there is no danger."

Sylvia took a moment to make sure Henry was armed. His energy pistol was more decorative than anything else, but it was still an extraordinarily dangerous weapon.

"*We'll be fine,*" he sent via their internal networks. "*I'll keep a link with GroundDiv.*"

"Very well," she told Gold-Stripe-On-Blue. "Lead the way."

CHAPTER FIFTY-FOUR

THEY WERE LED OUT OF THE PARTY AND INTO AN ELEVATOR concealed by a stand of berry bushes. Sylvia traded a concerned gaze with Henry, but he nodded calmly to her. Their security detail knew where they were and was tracking them.

"I apologize for the shadows," Gold-Stripe-On-Blue told them, leading the pair of Terrans into a brightly lit hallway underneath the garden. The roof was transparent, showing the dirt and roots above them.

"There are secrets the Drifters cannot share," the Drifter continued. "But in this case, the decision was not mine. I cannot force protection on one who does not wish it."

Now Sylvia was confused. Not concerned, not really, but confused. Still, she and Henry followed the First Speaker to a nondescript door in the maintenance hallway. It slid open at Gold-Stripe-On-Blue's touch, and he gestured for them to precede him.

"I will wait here," he told them. "To reduce...threat."

"*Trap?*" she sent Henry.

"*No,*" he replied. "*Not sure what this is...but it's not a trap.*"

She stepped past the Drifter leader into a small room. It looked like it normally served as an office for someone responsible for these maintenance halls, but the shelves were bare and the desk had been shoved against the wall.

There was a single Drifter in the space, looking at the blank back wall when they entered. The being waited in silence until the door closed, then turned to face them.

Their Face Mask was a red diagonal cross on a black background, with the left-hand segment colored green.

"My Drifter name is Red-Cross-Fourth-Green," the stranger introduced themselves. Something about their Kem was odd. The smooth accent wasn't familiar to Sylvia, and she thought she'd heard *every* possible Kem accent. "I know who you both are, Ambassador Sylvia Todorovich, Commodore Henry Wong. I only recently arrived in this system, but you and I *must* speak."

"There have been no new Drifter ships since we arrived," Henry countered. "How did you only *just* arrive?"

"You are not yet as capable of penetrating the new stealth fields as you think you are," Red-Cross-Fourth-Green said calmly. "My vessel is small and low-energy. A warship could never have sneaked through your blockade, but my courier did."

"I am starting to feel that I should be arresting you, not speaking with you," Henry snapped.

"Peace, Henry," Sylvia said softly. She was studying the Drifter, and the pieces were starting to come together. "Who *are* you, Red-Cross-Fourth-Green?" she demanded.

The hooded and masked head bowed in a swift nod—and then the Drifter did something no Drifter had ever done in front of her.

They took off their mask. They drew their hood back as they lay the metal-and-fabric device aside, revealing the sharp mandibles, quivering antennae, and dark red carapace of a Kenmiri Artisan.

"I *am* Red-Cross-Fourth-Green," the Kenmiri told them.

Sylvia was surprised to realize that Henry hadn't even gone for his gun. He was watching the Kenmiri like a coiled spring, but he had not yet leapt to action.

"That is what your Vesheron always misunderstood about the Drifters," Red-Cross-Fourth-Green told them. "We *began* as a safety valve for the Kenmiri. Not everyone fit into the neat caste and gender roles that our society demanded."

They spread their arms wide.

"So, here we are," they noted. "Do not feel false hope, Commodore," they warned Henry. "There are no Kenmorad among the Drifters this generation. We checked."

"Why are you here?" Sylvia's partner ground out.

"I have passed in and out of the Drifter Convoys for thirty-two years," the Kenmiri told them. "There have always been some of us who can pass in both societies—interfaces, so to speak. When the Empire retreated, I hoped that it was a sign of a wiser era for my people—even if it was the era of our end—and so, when the Council of Artisans called me home, I went."

"You speak for the Empire?" Sylvia asked.

"No one speaks for the Empire," Red-Cross-Fourth-Green snapped. "The Empire is *dead*. Only the Councils remain, and they are divided. The Council of Artisans is hardly innocent of the Kenmiri's crimes, but they are focused, for now, on survival."

"And the Council of Warriors?" Henry said, his tone sharp.

"They are broken," the Kenmiri told them. "Some—most, I think —cleave to the dream of surviving and have pledged to the Council of Artisans. They understand that the caste bred to the wars of today cannot see a path to the future.

"The others..."

There was a long silence, and the Kenmiri exhaled a long breath that rattled through their mandibles and antennae.

"A faction of our Warriors has decided that if we are to die, we shall not die alone," Red-Cross-Fourth-Green told them. "The Council has decided to...ignore them."

"And you?" Sylvia asked.

"I am a Drifter," the Kenmiri told them. "This is, I think, the last time I will remove my mask before another. My time as an interface is done, but for the sake of all of our peoples, this was a task that I must complete.

"My kin plan violence on a scale unseen—and they have set their eyes on the Ra Sector. You have seen the beginning of their operation. I will tell you all I know."

"And in exchange?" Sylvia said.

"You will stop them."

JOIN THE MAILING LIST

Love Glynn Stewart's books? Join the mailing list at

GLYNNSTEWART.COM/MAILING-LIST/

to know as soon as new books are released, special announcements, and a chance to win free paperbacks.

ABOUT THE AUTHOR

Glynn Stewart is the author of *Starship's Mage*, a bestselling science fiction and fantasy series where faster-than-light travel is possible–but only because of magic. His other works include science fiction series *Duchy of Terra*, *Castle Federation* and *Exile*, as well as the urban fantasy series *ONSET* and *Changeling Blood*.

Writing managed to liberate Glynn from a bleak future as an accountant. With his personality and hope for a high-tech future intact, he lives in Southern Ontario with his partner, their cats, and an unstoppable writing habit.

VISIT GLYNNSTEWART.COM FOR NEW RELEASE UPDATES

CREDITS

The following people were involved in making this book:
Copyeditor: Richard Shealy
Proofreader: M Parker Editing
Cover art: Sam Leung
Typo Hunter Team
Faolan's Pen Publishing team: Jack, Kate, and Robin.

 facebook.com/glynnstewartauthor

OTHER BOOKS
BY GLYNN STEWART

For release announcements join the
mailing list or visit **GlynnStewart.com**

STARSHIP'S MAGE
Starship's Mage
Hand of Mars
Voice of Mars
Alien Arcana
Judgment of Mars
UnArcana Stars
Sword of Mars
Mountain of Mars
The Service of Mars
A Darker Magic
Mage-Commander
Beyond the Eyes of Mars
Nemesis of Mars (*upcoming*)

Starship's Mage: Red Falcon
Interstellar Mage
Mage-Provocateur
Agents of Mars

Pulsar Race: A Starship's Mage Universe Novella

DUCHY OF TERRA
The Terran Privateer
Duchess of Terra
Terra and Imperium
Darkness Beyond
Shield of Terra
Imperium Defiant
Relics of Eternity
Shadows of the Fall
Eyes of Tomorrow

Printed in Great Britain
by Amazon

52409398R00209